ALL PASSION SPENT
THE RETURN OF THE SOLDIER
TWO DAYS IN ARAGON

ALL PASSION SPENT
Vita Sackville-West

THE RETURN OF THE SOLDIER
Rebecca West

TWO DAYS IN ARAGON
M. J. Farrell

GUILD PUBLISHING LONDON

This omnibus edition published 1987 by
Guild Publishing
by arrangement with Virago Press

First reprint 1987

Printed in Great Britain by Richard Clay Ltd,
Bungay, Suffolk

CONTENTS

ALL PASSION SPENT

Vita Sackville West

VICTORIA MARY SACKVILLE-WEST

(1892-1962) was born at Knole in Sevenoaks, Kent. Her parents were first cousins, her father being the third Baron Sackville and her mother the illegitimate daughter of Lionel Sackville-West and the Spanish dancer Pepita. Knole was to be an abiding passion throughout her life, the inspiration of much of her writing, and the source of great sorrow when, as a woman, she was unable to inherit it on her father's death. Vita was educated at home, except for three years spent at a school in London where she came to know Violet Keppel (later Trefusis) with whom, from 1918-21, she was to have a passionate affair.

In 1910 Vita met Harold Nicolson, the young diplomat whom she married three years later. In 1915 they bought a cottage two miles from Knole where they planned their first garden; three years later Vita Sackville-West's first novel, *Heritage*, was published. A distinguished novelist, poet, short-story writer, biographer, travel writer, critic, historian and gardener, her novels include *The Edwardians* (1930), *All Passion Spent* (1931) and *Seducers in Ecuador* (1942); of her poetry, *The Land* (1926) was awarded the Hawthornden Prize and *The Garden* (1946) won the Heinemann Prize.

During the 1920s her close and influential friendship with Virginia Woolf was at its height, culminating in the publication of Virginia Woolf's novel *Orlando* (1928), a celebration of her friend. In 1930 Harold and Vita bought Sissinghurst Castle in Kent, where they created their famous garden. A Fellow of the Royal Society of Literature and a JP for Kent, Vita Sackville-West was made a Companion of Honour in 1948. She died at Sissinghurst, after an operation for cancer, at the age of seventy.

Virago publishes *The Edwardians, All Passion Spent, Family History* (1932) and *No Signposts in the Sea* (1961). *Seducers in Ecuador* & *The Heir* (1922) is forthcoming.

INTRODUCTION

Vita Sackville-West began writing *All Passion Spent* in the spring of 1930. Her title could hardly be less applicable to her own situation at the time: at thirty-eight, she was at the height of her energies. She had just bought the romantic ruins of Sissinghurst Castle, though she and her husband Harold Nicolson were not to live there full-time for another couple of years; and she had just finished correcting the proofs of *The Edwardians*, which turned out to be a great popular success. In the year that she worked on her new novel she was spending all her spare time at Sissinghurst, clearing the rubble and rubbish of decades from what was to be the famous garden, and supervising the builders. She also wrote a long poem, 'Sissinghurst', which expressed the deep significance to her of this new commitment. Always a person for whom places were at least as important as people, and with this new passion for Sissinghurst dominating her daily life, it is not surprising that a house plays such a large part in *All Passion Spent*.

The novel was published by the Woolfs' Hogarth Press in May 1931. On 11 June, Virginia Woolf wrote to her that sales were '*very* good . . . Lord! What fun!' Vita had been worried about the book when she saw it in proof—'it is quite, quite meaningless'—but became reconciled to it after publication as she never was to *The Edwardians*. She received a great many letters about *All Passion Spent*, mainly from women who recognised their own situation in Lady Slane's, and this pleased her. Leonard Woolf, her publisher, said that this was her best novel, and she herself felt that it was 'a better book' than the more flamboyant *Edwardians*, compared with which it seems drawn in pastels.

This effect of anaemic, whimsical delicacy is misleading. Vita Sackville-West built into *All Passion Spent* much of her lifelong anger about the way society distorts and inhibits the individual, particularly if that individual is a woman. This unlikely alliance of manner and matter is the most curious thing about the novel and, artistically, its achievement.

She dedicated to 'Benedict and Nigel who are young this story of people who are old'. (Her sons were sixteen and thirteen at the time.) The dramatis personae of *All Passion Spent* are very old indeed. The Earl of Slane, after a distinguished career in public life, has just died aged ninety-four; his six children, none of them under sixty, are 'large and black and elderly, with grandchildren of their own'. When the story opens, these 'old black ravens' are discussing the future of their 88-year-old mother, Lady Slane. They do not foresee any difficulties with her; she has been the perfect wife: 'all her life long, gracious and gentle, she had been wholly submissive—an appendage.' They see her staying quietly with each of them in turn—like a Queen Lear, as one might say.

But this novel reverses the usual order of things. It is the children who are staid and narrow-minded, and their gentle aged mother who turns out to be revolutionary. She will live her own life, for the first time, according to her own inclinations and her own creeds, alone with her old French maid Genoux (the name of Vita Sackville-West's French maid in real life) in a small house in Hampstead she fell in love with thirty years before. She doesn't want her children to visit her, and she certainly does not want to see her grandchildren.

10

She finds the house empty, waiting for her; and here the author dwells lovingly on its spirit and character, 'an entity with a life of its own'. We know it is Georgian, red brick, and one of a row: from all the circumstantial evidence, I always imagine it to be in Church Row. Vita Sackville-West and Virginia Woolf, their romantic attachment no longer so urgent (for Vita at any rate) in its demands, sustained their friendship by means of excursions together. They went several times to Hampstead by Underground, as does Lady Slane; they walked on the Heath, like Lady Slane and Mr FitzGeorge; they visited Keats' house, described here as 'that little white box of strain and tragedy marooned among the dark green laurels'. And all the time they talked. There is a strong connection between the ideas of *All Passion Spent* and those of Virginia Woolf's two non-fiction books about women, *A Room of One's Own* (1929) and *Three Guineas*. Vita went with Virginia Woolf to Cambridge to hear her give the lectures that were the basis for the first book, and the second was conceived at the time of *All Passion Spent* though not published until 1938.

Lady Slane, from the triple vantage point of widowhood, old age, and tranquil Hampstead, surveys her marriage. Her indictment of the married state is softened by this indirect approach and by her gentle personality. She recalls her role as loving 'appendage'; she has been 'a lonely woman, at variance with the creeds to which she apparently conformed'—these passages echoing the descriptions of women submerging their own values 'in deference to the opinion of others' in *A Room of One's Own*.

There are on a first reading two unsatisfactory elements in the depiction of Lady Slane. Clearly a woman of sensibility and experience—an exvicereine—and on very familiar terms with the works of Shakespeare, she is nevertheless repeatedly called 'not clever'. So not-clever is she that she could not follow her husband's career, or 'know what people meant when they

11

referred to the Irish Question or the Women's Movement, or to Free Trade and Protection'. She cannot understand the stock market; she cannot even make out a cheque properly. Why does she have to be so incapable?

What Vita Sackville-West was trying to do was to represent pure femininity. This she saw in terms of sheer impracticality, 'laces and softnesses', in opposition to the 'masculine' world of business, politics and visible achievement. Lady Slane realises that masculinity has been the 'keynote' of her husband's character: he craved a life of action, while she craved a life of contemplation. 'They were indeed two halves of one dissevered world.'

Virginia Woolf wrote in *A Room of One's Own* that a great mind was 'androgynous'. Vita herself was a masculine woman, and her husband a man with a strong feminine streak. Lady Slane's undiluted femininity, in Vita's eyes, is a disability as well as a grace. These themes, explored by both Vita and Virginia Woolf, were also discussed at much the same time, and with much the same conclusions, in Rebecca West's novel *Harriet Hume* (1928). The concensus on the masculine-feminine question in these three very different writers is striking, and a close reading of *Harriet Hume* and *All Passion Spent* reveals quite significant similarities.

The second apparently unsatisfactory element is that although the central frustration of Lady Slane's life is that marriage prevented her from following her vocation to be a painter, it seems clear that this ambition was never more than a dream: she never once set brush to canvas, so far as we know. This makes her frustration and sacrifice seem phoney, a vain whim. But Vita Sackville-West is making a point here as well. Talent, she writes later in the book, is beside the point. 'Achievement was good, but the spirit was better. To reckon by achievement was to make a concession to the prevailing system of the world.' Virginia Woolf developed this in *Three Guineas* when she argued

12

that the 'masculine' system of competition, rewards and hier-
archies led to the aggressiveness that made men start wars.

Lady Slane's three friends reinforce this philosophy. Mr
Bucktrout, Mr Gosheron and Mr FitzGeorge are all 'fond fan-
tastics', lovers of beauty, artists 'in appreciation', eccentric in
their disregard for success-values. The world is horrible, says Mr
Bucktrout, because it is based on competitive struggle, which
produces what men call 'civilisation', but which is not civilisation at all. *Three Guineas* makes the same point.

The conventional supremacy of masculine values had forced
Lady Slane on marriage to forego her separate existence—while
her husband continued 'to enjoy his free, varied, and masculine
life . . . It would not do, in such a world of assumptions, to
assume that she had equal rights with Henry.' To judge from all
this, *All Passion Spent* would seem an unequivocally femininist
novel.

Vita Sackville-West fought hard against the conventions that
made a wife an 'appendage'. Unlike Lady Slane, she declined to
be the 'diplomatic wife', and indeed persuaded her husband to
give up his career in diplomacy; apart from brief visits, she stayed
at home when he was *en poste* abroad. Her work came first. She
declined to be the 'politician's wife' when later he sat for Parliament. She used her own name; she was dismissive about the
domestic virtues; she did not think the pleasure of having children compensated for the resulting lack of personal freedom. She
railed against the bureaucracy that labelled her 'Mrs Harold
Nicolson' or 'housewife'; whenever she was defined as the wife
of her husband, she complained loudly. And yet she invariably
prefaced her complaints with the words 'You know I am no
feminist, but . . .'

It was not a question of women's rights, in her view, but of
human rights. (In *Three Guineas* Virginia Woolf too condemned
the word 'feminist' as 'a vicious and corrupt word that has done

13

much harm in its day'.) In *All Passion Spent* Vita Sackville-West redefines feminism negatively, to describe 'the freemasonry among women, which was always prying and personal and somehow a trifle obscene'. This claustrophobic female conspiracy was at its most potent before the wedding, in weeks 'dedicated wholly to the rites of a mysterious feminism' designed to deliver the bride over so that she might minister to a man. Seen in this light feminism, as separatism, is the deadest of dead ends.

Even though Lady Slane as a young woman felt defrauded of her chosen life by marriage, she did not blame her husband and, as the author writes in a key passage, 'she was no feminist'—using the word here in its more usual sense:

> She was too wise a woman to indulge in such luxuries as an imagined martyrdom. The rift between herself and life was not the rift between man and woman, but the rift between the worker and the dreamer. That she was a woman, and Henry a man, was really a matter of chance. She would go no further than to acknowledge that the fact of her being a woman made the situation a degree more difficult.

'Feminine' values are not confined to women: Lady Slane's semi-comic fellow-dreamers—Mr Bucktrout, Mr Gosheron and Mr FitzGeorge—are, after all, men; and the maid Genoux, Lady Slane's only female intimate, is a 'worker' to her worn finger-ends.

It would be wrong to go away with the idea that the influence of Virginia Woolf's thinking, still less of Rebecca West's, was decisive in *All Passion Spent*. In her evocation of Lady Slane's past, Vita Sackville-West drew on her own experience; she was an excellent travel writer, as her *Passenger to Tehran* and *Twelve Days* attest, and the most vivid writing in this novel is about strange foreign scenes—such as the cloud of white and yellow

14

butterflies that accompanied the Slanes on a desert road in Persia, exploited as an image for Lady Slane's 'irreverent, irrelevant thoughts'.

Years before she ever met Virginia Woolf, she had forcefully expressed—in her letters, fictions, and an unpublished play, 'Marriage'—her feelings about the way society repressed women's individuality. There are themes in *All Passion Spent* that are Vita's alone. The young girl's fantasy of escape from conventional girlhood to freedom in the guise of a young man were the young Vita's. Lady Slane's ideal of 'detachment' had been Vita's ever since her disastrous imbroglio with Violet Trefusis—even though, swinging between the extremes of passionate attachment and equally passionate reclusiveness, she never achieved it.

The question of compromise also exercised Vita. Mr Bucktrout says: 'Most people fall into the error of making their whole lives a fuzz, pleasing nobody, least of all themselves. Compromise is the very breath of negation.' Her characters, at the end of their lives, did not compromise; but she herself had to. In 1928 she wrote to her husband that she was 'not a good person for you to be married to'; life for both of them, she said, 'resolves itself into a compromise which is truly only satisfactory to neither'. She made the compromise because of love. 'But I love you, I can never cure myself of loving you, so what is to be done?' In *All Passion Spent*, into which she poured so many of her own ambivalent feelings, Lady Slane's love for her husband is 'a straight black line drawn right through her life. It had hurt her, it had damaged her, but she had been unable to curve away from it.'

Lady Slane's jewels, and her unexpected inheritance, also had a special significance for Vita Sackville-West, whose own lavish jewels—emeralds, diamonds, pearls—became hateful to her amid the general poverty of the Depression. The wealth that made the creation of Sissinghurst possible came from a vast legacy to her mother from her admirer Sir John Murray Scott—a legacy that her mother had not only welcomed avidly but fought in the courts to retain. Vita Sackville-West distrusted her mother's values profoundly but was unable to relinquish the money and valuables that made her own chosen life possible. Lady Slane, in her simplicity, did what Vita in her soul thought should be done. She was 'true to herself'—and for Vita, who was a complex person drawn to the great simplicities, the guiding motto for life was 'To thine own self be true.'

Lady Slane has the emotional energy, at the end, for only one last 'strange and lovely thing', which gives the book its optimistic and inspirational finale. For serene Lady Slane, 'Those days were gone when feeling burst its bounds and poured hot from the foundry, when the heart seemed likely to split with complex and contradictory desires'. Not so, for Vita Sackville-West. As she drew near the end of writing the book, she was overcome by irrational depression. She wrote to Virginia Woolf: 'If I, who am the most fortunate of women can ask What is life for? how can other people live at all?' A few days after completing the manuscript, she plunged into a new love affair and felt alive again. For she was still in the excitable 'middle years' that now meant nothing to her Lady Slane. What is more, to the end of her life Vita Sackville-West was to be to some extent 'split with complex and contradictory desires'. *All Passion Spent*, the theme and title of her best novel, was not to be her own epitaph.

Victoria Glendinning, Graveley, 1982

Part One

Henry Lyulph Holland, first Earl of Slane, had existed for so long that the public had begun to regard him as immortal. The public, as a whole, finds reassurance in longevity, and, after the necessary interlude of reaction, is disposed to recognise extreme old age as a sign of excellence. The long-liver has triumphed over at least one of man's initial handicaps: the brevity of life. To filch twenty years from eternal annihilation is to impose one's superiority on an allotted programme. So small is the scale upon which we arranged our values. It was thus with a start of real incredulity that City men, opening their papers in the train on a warm May morning, read that Lord Slane, at the age of ninety-four, had passed away suddenly after dinner on the previous evening. 'Heart failure,' they said sagaciously, though they were actually quoting from the papers; and then added with a sigh, 'Well, another old landmark gone.' That was the dominant feeling: another old landmark gone, another reminder of insecurity. All the events and progressions of Henry Holland's life were gathered up and recorded in a final burst of publicity by the papers; they were gathered together into a handful as hard as a cricket-ball, and flung in the faces of the public, from the days of his 'brilliant university career,' through the days when Mr. Holland, at an astonishingly early age, had occupied a seat in the Cabinet, to this very last day when as Earl of Slane, K.G.,

17

G.C.B., G.C.S.I., G.C.I.E., etc. etc.—his diminishing honours trailing away behind him like the tail of a comet—he had drooped in his chair after dinner, and the accumulation of ninety years had receded abruptly into history. Time seemed to have made a little jump forward, now that the figure of old Slane was no longer there with out-stretched arms to dam it back. For some fifteen years he had taken no very active part in public life, but he had been *there*, and on occasion the irrefutable suavity, common sense, and mockery of his eloquence in Parliament had disturbed, though it could not actually arrest, his more extreme colleagues upon the brink of folly. Such pronouncements had been rare, for Henry Holland had always been a man to appreciate the value of economy, but by their very rarity they produced a wholesome sense of uneasiness, since men knew them to be backed up by a legend of experience: if the old man, the octogenarian, the nonagenarian, could bestir himself to the extent of stalking down to Westminster and unburdening himself, in his incomparable way, of opinions carefully, soberly, but cynically gestated, then the Press and the public were compelled into attention. Nobody had ever seriously attacked Lord Slane. Nobody had ever accused Lord Slane of being a back-number. His humour, his charm, his languor, and his good sense, had rendered him sacrosanct to all generations and to all parties; of him alone among statesmen and politicians, perhaps, could that be said. Perhaps, because he seemed to have touched life on every side, and yet never seemed to have touched life, the common life, at all, by virtue of his proverbial detachment, he had never drawn upon himself the execration and mistrust commonly accorded to the mere expert. Hedonist, humanist, sportsman, philosopher, scholar, charmer, wit; one of those rare Englishmen whose fortune it is to be born equipped with a truly adult mind. His colleagues and his subordinates had been alternately delighted and infuriated by his assumed reluctance to deal with

18

any practical question. It was difficult to get a yes or a no out of
the man. The more important a question was, the more flipp-
antly he dealt with it. '*Yes*,' he would write at the bottom of a
memorandum setting forth the advantages of two opposite lines
of policy; and his myrmidons passed their hands over their
brows, distraught. He was destroyed as a statesman, they said,
because he always saw both sides of the case; but even as they
said it with exasperation, they did not mean it, for they knew
that on occasion, when finally pushed into a corner, he would be
more incisive, more deadly, than any man seated four-square and
full of importance at a governmental desk. He could cast his eye
over a report, and pick out its heart and its weakness before
another man had had time to read it through. In his exquisitely
courteous way, he would annihilate alike the optimism and the
myopia of his correspondent. Courteous always, and civilised,
he left his competitors dead.

His personal idiosyncrasies, too, were dear to the public as to
the caricaturists; his black satin stock, his eyeglass swung on
an extravagantly wide ribbon, the coral buttons to his evening
waistcoat, the private hansom he maintained long after motors
had come into fashion—by all this was he buttressed through the
confused justice and injustice of legend; and when, at the age of
eighty-five, he finally succeeded in winning the Derby, no man
ever received a greater ovation. His wife alone suspected how
closely those idiosyncrasies were associated with a settled policy.
The least cynical of people by nature, she had learned to lay a
veneer of cynicism over herself after seventy years' association
with Henry Holland. 'Dear old man,' said the City men in the
train; 'well, he's gone.'

He was gone indeed, very finally and irretrievably gone. So
thought his widow, looking down at him as he lay on his bed in
Elm Park Gardens. The blinds were not lowered, for he had
always stipulated that when he came to die the house should not

19

be darkened, and even after his death nobody would have dreamed of disobeying his orders. He lay there in the full sunlight, sparing the stone-mason the trouble of carving his effigy. His favourite great-grandchild, to whom everything was permitted, had often twitted him, saying that he would make a handsome corpse; and now that the joke had become a reality, the reality gained in impressiveness for having been anticipated by a joke. His was the type of face which, even in life, one associates prophetically with the high dignity of death. The bony architecture of nose, chin, and temples, stood out in greater relief for the slight sinking of the flesh; the lips took a firmer line, and a lifetime of wisdom lay sealed behind them. Moreover, and most importantly, Lord Slane looked as *soigné* in death as he had looked in life. 'Here,' you would say, even though the bedclothes covered him, 'is a dandy.'

Yet, for all its dignity, death brought a revelation. The face which had been so noble in life lost a trifle of its nobility in death; the lips which had been too humorous to be unpleasantly sardonic now betrayed their thinness; the carefully concealed ambition now revealed itself fully in the proud curve of the nostril. The hardness which had disguised itself under the charming manner now remained alone, robbed of the protection of a smile. He was beautiful, but he was less agreeable. Alone in the room his widow contemplated him, filled with thoughts that would greatly have surprised her children, could they but have read her mind.

Her children, however, were not there to observe her. They were collected in the drawing-room, all six of them; two wives and a husband bringing the number up to nine. A sufficiently formidable family gathering—old, black ravens, thought Edith, the youngest, who was always flustered and always trying to confine things into the shape of a phrase, like pouring water into a ewer, but great gouts of meaning and implication invariably ran over and slopped about and were lost. To attempt to recapture them after they had spilt was as hopeless as trying to hold the water in your hand. Perhaps, if one had a note-book and pencil always ready—but then the thought would be lost while one was looking for the right word; and, moreover, it would be difficult to use a note-book without everybody seeing. Shorthand?—but one must not let one's thoughts run on like this; one must discipline one's mind, keeping one's attention on the present matter, as other people seemed to do without any difficulty; though, to be sure, if one had not learnt that lesson by the time one was sixty, one was never likely to learn it. A formidable family gathering, thought Edith, coming back: Herbert, Carrie, Charles, William, and Kay; Mabel, Lavinia; Roland. They went in groups: the Hollands themselves, the sisters-in-law, the brother-in-law; then they sorted themselves differently: Herbert and Mabel, Carrie and Roland; Charles; William and Lavinia; and then Kay all by himself. It was not often that they all met together, none missing—curious, Edith thought, that Death should be the convener, as though all the living rushed instantly together for protection and mutual support. Dear me, how old we all are. Herbert must be sixty-eight, and I'm sixty; and Father was over ninety, and Mother is eighty-eight. Edith, who had begun making a sum of their total ages, surprised them all very much by asking, 'How old are you, Lavinia?' Thus taken aback, they rebuked Edith by their stare; but that was Edith all over, she never listened to what was being said, and then suddenly came out with some irrelevant remark. Edith could have told them that all her life she had been trying to say what she meant, and had never yet succeeded. Only too often, she said something precisely the opposite of what she wanted to say. Her terror was that she should one day use an indecent word by mistake. 'Isn't it splendid that Father is dead,' she might say, instead of, 'Isn't it terrible'; and there were other possibilities,

21

even more appalling, by which one might use a really dreadful word, the sort of word that butcher-boys scrawled in pencil on the white-washed walls of the basement passage, and about which one had to speak, most evasively, to the cook. An unpleasant task; the sort of task that fell to Edith in Elm Park Gardens and to a thousand Ediths all over London. But of these preoccupations her family knew nothing.

They were gratified now to see that she blushed, and that her hands went up nervously to fiddle with the grey strands of her hair; the gesture implied that she had not spoken. Having reduced her to this confusion, they returned to their conversation, suitably hushed and mournful. Even the voices of Herbert and Carrie, habitually insistant, were lowered. Their father lay upstairs, and their mother was with him.

'Mother is wonderful.'

Over and over, thought Edith, they had reiterated that phrase. Surprise was in their accents, as though they had expected their mother to rant, rave, scream, give herself up for lost. Edith knew very well that her brothers and sister privately entertained a theory that their mother was rather a simpleton. From time to time she let fall remarks that could not be reconciled with ordinary sense; she had no grasp on the world as it was; she was apt to say impetuous things which, although uttered in English, made no more sense than had they been uttered in an outer-planetary language. Mother was a changeling, they had often said politely, in the bitter-sweet accents reserved for a family joke; but now in this emergency they found a new phrase: Mother is wonderful. It was the thing they were expected to say, so they said it, several times over, like a refrain coming periodically into their conversation and sweeping it upwards on to a higher level. Then it drooped again; became practical. Mother was wonderful, but what was to be done with Mother? Evidently, she could not go on being wonderful for the rest of her life. Somewhere, somehow, she must be allowed to break down, and then, after that was over, must be stowed away; housed, taken care of. Outside, in the streets, the posters might flare: DEATH OF LORD SLANE. The journalists might run up and down Fleet Street assembling their copy; they might pounce on the pigeon-holes—that macabre columbarium—where the obituary notices were stored in readiness; they might raid each other's information: 'I say, is it true that old Slane always carried his cash in coppers? wore crêpe soles? dipped his bread in his coffee?' Anything to make a good paragraph. Telegraph-boys might ring the bell, propping their red bicycles against the kerb, delivering their brown messages of condolence, from all over the world, from all parts of the Empire, especially where Lord Slane had served his term of government. Florists might deliver their wreaths—already the narrow hall was full of them—'indecently soon,' said Herbert, peering jealously nevertheless at the attached cards through his monocle. Old friends might call—'Herbert—so dreadfully sudden—of course, I didn't expect to see your dear Mother—' But obviously they had expected it, had expected to be the sole exception, and Herbert must turn them away, rather enjoying it: 'Mother, you understand, is naturally rather overcome; wonderful, I must say; but just at present, you'll understand, I'm sure, is seeing nobody but Us'; and so with many pressings of Herbert's hand they took their departure, having got no further than the hall or the doorstep. Reporters might loiter on the pavement, dangling cameras like black concertinas. All this might go on outside the house, but inside it, upstairs, Mother was with Father and the problem of her future lay heavy upon her sons and daughters.

Of course, she would not question the wisdom of any arrangements they might choose to make. Mother had no will of her own; all her life long, gracious and gentle, she had been wholly submissive—an appendage. It was assumed that she had

23

not enough brain to be self-assertive. 'Thank goodness,' Herbert sometimes remarked, 'Mother is not one of those clever women.' That she might have ideas which she kept to herself never entered into their estimate. They anticipated no trouble with their mother. That she might turn round and play a trick on them—several tricks—after years of being merely a fluttering lovable presence amongst them, never entered into their calculations either. She was not a clever woman. She would be grateful to them for arranging her few remaining years.

They stood in the drawing-room in a group, uncomfortably shifting from one foot to the other, but it never occurred to them to sit down. They would have thought it disrespectful. For all their good solid sense, death, even an expected death, disconcerted them just a little. Around them hung that uneasy, unsettled air which attends those about to set out on a journey or those whose lives have been seriously disturbed. Edith would have liked to sit down, but dared not. How large they all were, she thought; large and black and elderly, with grandchildren of their own. How lucky, she thought, that we all wear so much black habitually, for we certainly could not have got our mourning yet, and how terrible it would have been for Carrie to arrive in a pink shirt. As it was, they were all black as crows, and Carrie's black gloves lay on the writing-table with her boa and her bag. The ladies of the Holland family still wore boas, high collars, and long skirts which they had to hold up when they crossed the road; any concession to fashion was, they felt, unbecoming to their age. Edith admired her sister Carrie. She did not love her, and she was frightened of her, but she admired and envied her tremendously. Carrie had inherited her father's eagle nose and commanding presence; she was tall, pale, and distinguished. Herbert, Charles, and William were tall and distinguished also; only Kay and Edith were dumpy. Edith's thoughts were straying again: we might belong to a different

24

family, she thought, Kay and I. Kay in fact was a chubby little old gentleman, with bright blue eyes and a neat white beard; there, again, he differed from his brothers who were clean-shaven. What a queer thing appearance was, and how unfair. It dictated the terms of people's estimate throughout one's whole life. If one looked insignificant, one was set down as insignificant; yet, one probably didn't look insignificant unless one deserved it. But Kay seemed quite happy; he didn't worry about significance, or about anything else; his bachelor rooms, and his collection of compasses and astrolabes seemed to satisfy him quite as well as public esteem, or a wife and a more personal life. For he was the greatest living authority upon globes, compasses, astrolabes, and all kindred instruments; lucky Kay, thought Edith, to have concentrated so contentedly upon one little department. (Curious symbols to have chosen, though, for one who had never loved the sea or climbed a mountain; to him, they were collector's pieces, ranged and ticketed, but to Edith, the romantic, a vast dark world rose beyond their small brass and mahogany, their intricacy of pivots and gimbals, discs and circles, the guinea-gold brass and the nut-brown wood, the signs of the Zodiac and the dolphins spouting up the ocean; a vast dark world where nothing was charted on the maps but regions of danger and uncertainty, and ragged men chewed bullets to allay their thirst.) 'Then there is the question of income,' William was saying.

How characteristic of William to mix up Mother's future with questions of income; for to William and Lavinia parsimony was in itself a career. An apple bruised by falling prematurely from the tree must immediately be turned into a dumpling lest it be wasted. Waste was the bugbear of William's and Lavinia's life. The very newspaper must be rolled into spills to save the matches. They had a passion for getting something for nothing. Every blackberry in the hedgerow was an agony to Lavinia until

25

she had bottled it. Living, as they did, at Godalming with two acres of ground, they spent painful-happy evenings in calculation as to whether a pig could be made to pay on the household scraps, and whether a dozen hens could out-balance their corn in eggs. Well, thought Edith, they must pass the time very absorbingly with such a constant preoccupation; but how miserable it must make them to think of all the sacks of gold squandered by them since their marriage. Let me see, thought Edith, William is the fourth, so he must be sixty-four; he must have been married for thirty years, so if they have spent fifteen hundred a year—what with the children's education and all—that makes forty-five thousand pounds; sacks and sacks of treasure, such as the divers are always looking for at Tobermory. But Herbert was saying something. Herbert was always full of information; and the surprising thing was, for such a stupid man, it was usually correct.

'I can tell you all about that.' He put two fingers inside his collar, adjusted it, jerking his chin upward, cleared his throat, and gave a preliminary glare at his relations. 'I can tell you all about that. I discussed it with Father—he took me, I may say, into his confidence. Ahem! Father, as you know, was not a rich man, and most of his income dies with him. Mother will be left with a net income of five hundred a year.'

They digested this fact. William and Lavinia exchanged glances, and it could be seen that their minds were involved in rapid and experienced calculations. Edith, who passed privately among her relations for a half-wit, could on occasions be surprisingly shrewd—she had a habit of seeing through people's words right down into their motives, and of stating her deductions with a frankness that was disconcerting rather than discreet. She knew now quite well what William was about to say, though for once she held her tongue. But she chuckled to herself as she heard him say it.

26

'I suppose Father didn't happen to mention the jewels in the course of his confidences, did he, Herbert?'

'He did. The jewels, as you know, form not the least valuable part of his estate. They were his private property, and he has seen fit to leave them unconditionally to Mother.'

That's a smack for Herbert and Mabel, thought Edith. I suppose they expected Father to leave the jewels, like heirlooms, to his eldest son. A glance at Mabel's face showed her, however, that the announcement came as no surprise. Evidently Herbert had already repeated his father's confidences to his wife—and Mabel had been lucky, thought Edith, if Herbert had betrayed no irritation against her for thus failing to turn him into a successful legatee.

'In that case,' said William decisviely—for although he and Lavinia had hoped for a portion of the jewels, it was pleasing to think that Herbert and Mabel also had been disappointed—'in that case Mother will certainly wish to sell them. And quite right too. Why should she keep a lot of useless jewellery lying in the bank? In my opinion the jewels should fetch from five to seven thousand pounds, properly handled.'

'But more important than the question of jewels or income,' Herbert proceeded, 'is the question of where Mother is to live. She cannot be left alone. In any case, she could not afford to keep on this house. It must be sold. Where, then, is she to go?' Another glare. 'Clearly, it is our duty to look after her. She must make her home among us.' It was like a set speech.

All these old people, thought Edith, disposing of a still older person! Still, it seemed inevitable. Mother would parcel out her year: three months with Herbert and Mabel, three with Carrie and Roland, three with Charles, three with William and Lavinia—then where did she herself and Kay come in? Rising once more to the surface of her reflections, she launched one of her sudden and ill-chosen remarks, 'But surely I ought to bear

27

the brunt—I've always lived at home—I'm unmarried.'

'Brunt?' said Carrie, turning on her. Edith was instantly annihilated. 'Brunt? My dear Edith! Who spoke of brunt? I'm sure we shall all regard it as a joy—a privilege—to do our part in looking after Mother in these last sad years of her life—for sad they must be, deprived of the one thing she lived for. Brunt, I think, is scarcely the word, Edith.'

Edith subserviently agreed: it wasn't. Spoken like that, repeated several times over, without the support of its usual little phrase, it acquired a strange and uncouth semblance, like spick without span, hoity without toity, turvy without topsy. It became a rude and Saxon word, like woad, or witenagemot; brunt, blunt; a blunt word. And what did it mean, to bear the brunt? What was a brunt, anyhow? No, brunt was not the word. 'Well,' said Edith, 'I think I ought to live with Mother.'

She saw relief spread itself over Kay's face; he had been thinking, that was evident, of his snug little rooms and his collection. Herbert's voice had been as a trumpet threatening the walls of his Jericho. The others, also, considered Edith and the possibility she offered them. The unmarried daughter; she was the obvious solution. But the Hollands were not people to evade a duty, and the more irksome the duty, the less likely were they to evade it. Joy was a matter they seldom considered, but duty was ever present with them, seriously always and sometimes grimly. Their father's energy had passed on to them, turning a trifle sour on the way. Carrie spoke up for her relations. Carrie was good; but, like so many good people, she always managed to set everybody by the ears.

'There is certainly something in what Edith says. She has always lived at home, and the change would not be very great for her. I know, of course, that she has often wished for independence and a home of her own; dear Edith,' she said, with a digressive smile; 'but quite rightly, as I think,' she continued, 'she refused to leave Father and Mother so long as she could be of use to them. I feel now, however, that we ought all to take our share. We must not take advantage of Edith's unselfishness, or of Mother's. I am sure I speak for you too, Herbert, and for you, William. It would be greatly to Mother's benefit if, instead of embarking on a new house, she could make her home amongst us all in turn.'

'Quite so,' said Herbert approving, and again adjusting his collar; 'quite so, quite so.'

William and Lavinia again exchanged glances.

'Of course,' William began, 'in spite of our limited income Lavinia and I would always be happy to welcome Mother. At the same time I think some financial arrangement should be come to. So much more satisfactory for Mother. She would then feel no embarrassment. Two pounds a week, perhaps, or thirty-five shillings . . .'

'I entirely agree with William,' said Charles unexpectedly; 'speaking for myself, a general's pension is so absurdly inadequate that I should find an additional guest a serious drain on my resources. As you know, I live very modestly in a small flat. I have no spare bedroom. Of course, I have hopes that the question of pensions may some day be adjusted. I have written a long memorandum to the War Office about it, also a letter to *The Times*, which no doubt they are holding in reserve until a suitable occasion, as they have not yet printed it, though, I confess, I see very little hope of reform under this present miserable Government.' Charles snorted. He felt that that was rather a good speech, and looked round at his family for approval. He was not General Sir Charles Holland for nothing.

'Isn't it rather delicate . . .' began the new Lady Slane.

'Be quiet, Mabel,' said Herbert. He was seldom known to address any other phrase to his wife, nor did Mabel often succeed in getting beyond her four or five opening words. 'This is

29

entirely a family matter, please. In any case, it cannot be discussed in any detail until after—h'm—poor Father's funeral. I do not quite know how this unpleasant subject has arisen. (That's one for William, thought Edith.) In the meantime Mother must, of course, be our first consideration. Anything which can be done to spare her feelings. . . . After all, we must remember that her life is shattered. You know that she lived only for Father. And we should be very seriously and rightly blamed if we were to abandon her now to her loneliness.'

Ah, that's it, thought Edith: what will people say? So they mean to combine people's good opinion with getting a little of poor Mother's money. Wrangle, wrangle, she thought—for she had had some previous taste of family discussions; they'll wrangle for weeks over Mother like dogs quarrelling over an old, a very old, bone. Only Kay will try to keep out of it. William and Lavinia will be the worst; they'll want to get Mother as a paying guest, and then look down their noses while their friends praise them. And Carrie will wear an air of high martyrdom. This is the sort of thing, she thought, which happens when people die. Then she discovered that underneath this current of thought was running another current, concerned with whether she would now be able to live independently; she saw the little flat which would be her own; the cheerful sitting-room; the one servant, and the latchkey; the evenings over the fire with a book. No more answering letters for Father; no more accompanying Mother when she went to open hospital wards; no more adding up the house-books; no more taking Father for a walk in the Park. And at last she would be able to have a canary. How could she help hoping that Herbert, Carrie, Charles, and William would divide Mother between them? Shocked though she was by their blatancy, she acknowledged inwardly that she was no better than the rest of her family.

*   *   *

Edith was frightened of being left in this strange house, alone
with her living mother and her dead father. She could not own
to her fear, but she did everything in her power to delay the
departure of her brothers and sister. Even Carrie and Herbert,
whom she rather disliked, and Charles and William, whom she
rather despised, became desirable to her as presences and
companions. She invented pretexts to keep them back, dreading
the moment when the front door would shut finally behind
them. Even Kay would have been better than nothing. But Kay
slipped from her before the others. She fluttered after him on to
the landing; he turned to see who was following him; turned,
with his neat little white beard and his comfortable little
paunch, crossed by a watch-chain. 'You're going, Kay?' He
was annoyed, because he imagined a reproof in Edith's tone,
where, really, he should have detected only an appeal. He was
annoyed, because he already had a sense of guilt in his intention
of keeping an engagement; ought he, rather, to have remained
to dinner at Elm Park Gardens? Then he had consoled his conscience by reflecting that the servants must not be given any
extra trouble. So, when Edith ran after him, he turned, looking
as patiently annoyed as it was possible for him to look. 'You're
going, Kay?'

Kay was going. He must get some dinner. He could come
back later, if Edith thought it desirable. He added this, being
cowardly though self-indulgent, and anxious to avoid unplea-
santness at any cost. Fortunately for him, Edith was cowardly
too, and immediately retracted any reproof or appeal her pursuit
might have been intended to convey. 'Oh no, Kay, of course
not; why should you come back? I'll look after Mother. You'll
be coming in to-morrow morning?'

Yes, said Kay, relieved; he'd come in to-morrow morning.
Early. They kissed. They had not kissed for many years; but that
was one of the strange effects of death; elderly brothers and

31

sisters pecked at one another's cheeks. Their noses, from lack of custom, got in the way. Both of them looked up the dark well of the staircase, after they had kissed, towards the floor where their father lay, and then in sudden embarrassment Kay scuttled off down the stairs. He felt a relief as he shut himself out into the street. A May evening; normal London; taxis passing in the King's Road; and FitzGeorge waiting for him at the club. He must not keep Fitz waiting. He would not go by bus. He would take a taxi.

FitzGeorge was his oldest, indeed his only, friend. Over twenty years of difference in age separated them, but after threescore such discrepancies begin to close up. The two old gentlemen had many tastes in common. They were both ardent collectors, the only difference between them being a difference of wealth. FitzGeorge was enormously rich; a millionaire. Kay Holland was poor—all the Hollands were comparatively poor, although their father had been Viceroy of India. FitzGeorge could buy anything he liked, but such was his eccentricity that he lived like a pauper in two rooms at the top of a house in Bernard Street, and took pleasure in a work of art only if it had been his own discovery and a bargain. Since he possessed an extraordinary instinct for discoveries and bargains—finding unsuspected Donatellos in the basement of large furniture shops in the Tottenham Court Road—he had amassed at small cost (to his own delight and to Kay Holland's envious but exasperated admiration) a miscellaneous collection coveted by the British and the South Kensington Museums alike. Nobody knew what he would do with his things. He was just as likely to bequeath them all to Kay Holland as to make a bonfire of them in Russell Square. Obvious heirs he had none, any more than he had obvious progenitors. Meanwhile he kept his treasures closely round him; the few people privileged to visit him in his two rooms came away with a tale of Ming figures rolled up in a pair

32

of socks, Leonardo drawings stacked in the bath, Elamite pottery ranged upon the chairs. Certainly, during the visit one had to remain standing, for there was no free chair to sit on; and jade bowls must be cleared away before Mr. FitzGeorge could grudgingly offer one a cup of the cheapest tea, boiling the kettle himself on a gas-ring. The only visitors to receive a second invitation were those who had declined the tea.

Nearly everybody knew him by sight. When people saw his square hat and old-fashioned frock-coat going into Christie's they said, 'There's old Fitz.' Winter or summer, his costume never varied; square hat, frock-coat, and usually a parcel carried under his arm. What the parcel contained was never divulged; it might be a Dresden cup, or a kipper for Mr. FitzGeorge's supper. Londoners felt affectionately towards him, as one of their genuine eccentrics, but no one, not even Kay Holland, would have dreamed of calling him Fitz to his face, however glibly they might say 'There's old Fitz' when they saw him pass. It was said that the happiest event of his life was the death of Lord Clanricarde; on that day, old Fitz had walked down St. James's Street with a flower in his buttonhole, and all the other gentlemen sitting in club windows had known perfectly well why.

Although Mr. FitzGeorge and Kay Holland had been friends for some thirty years, no personal intimacy existed between them. When they sat at dinner together—a familiar spectacle in Boodle's or the Thatched House Club, each paying his share, and drinking barley-water—they discussed prices and catalogues as inexhaustibly as lovers discuss their emotions, but beyond this they nothing of each other whatsoever. Mr. FitzGeorge knew, of course, that Kay was old Slane's son, but Kay knew no more of Mr. FitzGeorge's parentage than anybody else. Quite possibly Mr. FitzGeorge himself knew nothing of it either; so people said, basing their suspicions on the suggestive prefix to

33

his name. Certainly Kay had never asked him; had never even hinted at any curiosity on the subject. Their relationship was beautifully detached. This explains why Mr. FitzGeorge awaited Kay's arrival in some perturbation, uncomfortably aware that he ought to make some allusion to the Hollands' bereavement, but shrinking from this infringement of their tacit understanding. He felt vexed with Kay; it was inconsiderate of him to have lost his father, inconsiderate of him not to have cancelled their appointment; yet Mr. FitzGeorge knew quite well that a cancelled appointment was a crime he never forgave. Very cross, he watched for Kay's approach, drumming on the window at Boodle's. He must say something, he supposed; better to do it at once, and get it over. Surely Kay was not going to be late? He had never yet been late for an appointment, in thirty years; never been late, and never failed to turn up. Mr. FitzGeorge drew an enormous silver turnip, price five shillings, from his pocket and looked at the time. Seventeen minutes past eight. He compared it with the clock on St. James's Palace. Kay was late; two whole minutes.—But there he was, getting out of a taxi.

'Evening,' said Kay, coming into the room.

'Evening,' said Mr. FitzGeorge. 'You're late.'

'Dear me, so I am,' said Kay. 'Let us go in to dinner at once, shall we?'

During dinner they talked about a pair of Sèvres bowls which Mr. FitzGeorge alleged that he had discovered in the Fulham Road. Kay, who had seen them too, was of the opinion that they were fakes, and this divergence led to one of those discussions which both old gentlemen so thoroughly enjoyed. But this evening, Mr. FitzGeorge's pleasure was spoilt; he had not said what he intended to say, and every moment made the saying of it more awkward and more impossible. His irritation against Kay was increased. It was the first unsuccessful meal that

34

they had ever had together, and the disappointment made
Mr. FitzGeorge reflect that all friendship was a mistake; he
regretted crossly that he had ever allowed himself to become
involved with Kay; other people had always been kept at arm's
length, a most commendable system; it was a mistake, a great
mistake, to admit exceptions. He scowled across the table at
Kay, drinking his barley-water and carefully wiping his neat
little beard, unaware of the hostility he was arousing.

'Coffee?' said Mr. FitzGeorge.

'I think so—yes, coffee.'

Poor old chap, he looks tired, thought Mr. FitzGeorge suddenly; not quite so spruce as usual; he's drooping a little; he's
been making an effort to talk. 'Have a brandy?' he said.

Kay looked up, surprised. They never had brandy.

'No, thanks.'

'Yes. Waiter, give Mr. Holland a brandy. Put it down on my
bill.'

'I really . . .' began Kay.

'Nonsense. Waiter, the best brandy—the eighteen forty.
When all's said and done, Holland, I saw you in your cradle.
The eighteen forty brandy was only thirty years old or so then.
So don't make a fuss.'

Kay made no fuss, startled as he was by this sudden revelation
that old Fitz had seen him in his cradle. His mind flung itself
back wildly into time and space. Time: 1874; space: India. So
old Fitz must have been in India in 1874. 'You never told me
that you had been in Calcutta then,' said Kay, sipping his
brandy over his little Vandyck beard. 'Didn't I?' said old Fitz
negligently, as though it were of no importance; 'well, I was.
My guardians didn't approve of universities, and sent me round
the world instead. (Strange revelations! so old Fitz, in his adolescence, had been controlled by guardians?) Your parents were
very kind to me,' Mr. FitzGeorge proceeded; 'naturally, your

father as Viceroy hadn't much leisure, but your mother, I remember, was most gracious; most charming. She was young then; young, and very lovely. I remember thinking that she was the most lovely thing I had seen in India.—But you're wrong about those bowls all the same, Holland. You know nothing whatever about china—never did, never will. It's too fine a taste for you. You ought to confine yourself to junk like your astrolabes. That's all you're fit for. Setting yourself up as a judge of china, indeed! And against me, who have forgotten more about china than you ever learnt.'

Kay was well accustomed to such abuse; he liked being bullied by old Fitz; it gave him a little tremor of delight. He sat listening while old Fitz told him that he did not deserve the name of connoisseur, and would have done much better to go in for collecting stamps. He knew that Fitz did not mean a word of it, but enjoyed pecking at him like an old, pecking, courting pigeon, while Kay averted his head and dodged the blows, laughing a little meanwhile, ever so slightly arch, and looking down at the table-cloth, fingering the knives and forks. Their relations had miraculously got back to the normal, and so greatly did Mr. FitzGeorge's spirits rise at this re-establishment that he said presently he was dashed if he wouldn't have a brandy too. He had forgotten all about that difficult allusion he intended to make, or thought he had forgotten, but perhaps it had really been in his mind all the time, for when they came out of the club together, and stood on the steps preparing to part, while Kay pulled on his chamois-leather gloves—Mr. FitzGeorge had never owned a pair of gloves in his life, but Kay Holland was never seen without his hands gloved in butter-yellow—to his own surprise he heard himself growl out, 'Sorry to hear about your father, Holland.'

There, it was said, and St. James's Street had not opened to swallow him up. It was said; it had been quite easy, really. But

36

what on earth was prompting him to go further to make the most incredible, unnecessary proposal?—'Perhaps some day you'll take me to call on Lady Slane.' Now what had possessed him to say that? Kay looked taken aback; and no wonder. 'Oh, yes—yes, certainly—if you'd care to come,' he said hurriedly. 'Well, good-night—good-night,' and he hurried away, while old Fitz stood staring after him, wondering whether he had made it impossible for himself ever to see Kay Holland again.

The house was strange—thus Edith pursued her thoughts—there was such a contrast between what went on inside and what went on outside. Outside it was all blare and glare and publicity, what with the posters, and the reporters still hanging about the area railings, and the talk of Westminster Abbey, and speeches in both Houses of Parliament. Inside it was all hushed and private, like a conspiracy; the servants whispered, people went soundlessly up and down stairs; and whenever Lady Slane came into the room everybody stopped talking, and stood up, and somebody was sure to go forward and lead her gently to a chair. They treated her rather as though she had had an accident, or had gone temporarily off her head. Yet Edith was sure her mother did not want to be led to chairs, or to be kissed so reverently and mutely, or to be asked if she was sure she wouldn't rather have dinner in her room. The only person to treat her in a normal way was Genoux, her old French maid, who was nearly as old as Lady Slane herself, and had been with her for the whole of her married life. Genoux moved about the house as noisily as ever, talking to herself as her custom was, muttering to herself about her next business in her extraordinary jumble of French and English; she still burst unceremoniously into the drawing-room in pursuit of her mistress, whoever might be there, and horrified the assembled family by asking, 'Pardon, miladi, est-ce que ça vaut la peine d'envoyer les shirts de

37

milord à la wash?' They all looked at Lady Slane as though they expected her to fall instantly to pieces, like a vase after a blow, but she replied in her usual quiet voice that yes, his lordship's shirts must certainly be sent to the wash; and then, turning to Herbert, said, 'I don't know what you would like me to do with your father's things, Herbert; it seems a pity to give them all to the butler, and anyway they wouldn't fit.'

Her mother and Genoux, Edith thought, alone refused to adapt themselves to the strangeness of the house. She could read disapproval in the eyes of Herbert, Carrie, Charles, and William; but naturally no disapproval could be openly expressed. They could only insist, implicitly, that their own convention must be adopted: Mother's life was shattered, Mother was bearing up wonderfully, Mother must be sheltered within the privacy of her disaster, while the necessary business was conducted, the necessary contact with the outside world maintained, by her capable sons and her capable daughter. Edith, poor thing, wasn't much use. Everybody knew that Edith always said the wrong thing at the wrong moment, and left undone everything that she was supposed to do, giving as her excuse that she had been 'too busy'; nor was Kay of much use either, but then he scarcely counted as a member of the family at all. Herbert, Carrie, William, and Charles stood between their mother and the outside world. From time to time, indeed, some special rumour was allowed to creep past their barrier: the King and Queen had sent a most affectionate message—Herbert could scarcely be expected to keep that piece of news to himself. Huddersfield, Lord Slane's native town, desired the approval of the family for a memorial service. The King would be represented at the funeral by the Duke of Gloucester. The ladies of the Royal School of Embroidery had worked—in a great hurry—a pall. The Prime Minister would carry one corner of it; the Leader of the Opposition another. The French Government were sending a representative; and it was said that the Duke of Brabant might attend on behalf of the Belgian. These bits of information were imparted to his mother by Herbert in driblets and with caution; he was feeling his way to see how she would receive them. She received them with complete indifference. 'Very nice of them, to be sure,' she said; and once she said, 'So glad, dear, if you're pleased.' Herbert both relished and resented this remark. Any tribute paid to his father was paid to himself, in a way, as head of the family; yet his mother's place, right-fully, was in the centre of the picture; these three or four days between death and burial were, rightfully, her own. Herbert prided himself on his sense of fitnes. Plenty of time, afterwards, to assert himself as Lord Slane. Generation must tread upon the heels of generation—that was a law of nature; yet, so long as his father's physical presence remained in the house, his mother had the right to authority. By her indifference, she was abdicating her position unnecessarily, unbecomingly, soon. She ought, posthumously, for these three or four days, to rally supremely in honour of her husband's memory; any abrogation of her right was unseemly. So it ran in Herbert's code. But perhaps, chat-tered the imp in Edith, perhaps she was so thoroughly drained by Father in his lifetime that she can't now be bothered with his memory?

Certainly the house was strange, with a particular strangeness that had never invaded it before and could never invade it again. Father could not die twice. By his dying he had created this particular situation—a situation which, surely, he had never foreseen; the sort of situation which nobody would foresee until it came actually into being. Nobody could have foreseen that Father, so dominant always, so paramount, would by the mere act of dying turn Mother into the most prominent figure. Her prominence might last only for three or four days; but during that brief spell it must be absolute. Everybody must defer. She, and she alone, must decide whether the doors of Westminster Abbey should or should not revolve upon their hinges; a nation must wait upon her decision, a Dean and Chapter truckle to her wishes. Very gently, and cautiously, she must be consulted on every point, and her views ascertained. It was very strange that somebody so self-eclipsing should suddenly have turned into somebody so important. It was like playing a game; it reminded Edith of the days when Father in one of his gay moods would come into the drawing-room after tea to find Mother with all the children around her, reading to them perhaps out of a story-book, and would clap the book shut and say that now they would all play follow-my-leader all through the house, but that Mother must lead. So they had gone, capering through silent chanceries and over the parquet floors of ballrooms, where the chandeliers hung in their holland bags, performing all kinds of absurd antics on the way—for Mother had an inexhaustible invention—and Father would follow last, bringing up the tail, but always playing the clown and getting all his imitations wrong, whereat the children would shriek with delight, pretending to put him right, and Mother would turn round with Kay clinging on to her skirts, to say with assumed severity, 'Really, Henry!' Many an Embassy and Government House had rung to their evening laughter. But once, Edith remembered, Mother (who was young then) had tumbled some papers in the archivist's room out of a file, and, as the children had scrambled joyfully to make the disorder worse, Father had darkened suddenly, he had conveyed displeasure in a grown-up way; his gaiety and Mother's had collapsed together like a rose falling to pieces; and the return to the drawing-room had been made in a sort of scolded silence, as though Jove stooping from Olympus had detected a mortal taking liberties in his pretended absence with his high concerns.

But now Mother might play follow-my-leader as she would;

for three or four days Mother might play follow-my-leader, leading the dignitaries of Europe and of Empire some dance up to Golder's Green or Huddersfield as the fancy took her, instead of resigning herself to Westminster Abbey or Brompton Cemetery as was expected; but the disappointment—to the imp in Edith's mind—lay in Mother's refusal to take any lead at all. She simply agreed to everything that Herbert suggested. Just as well might Herbert, at the age of seven, playing follow-my-leader, have prompted her, 'Now let's romp through the kitchens;' her acquiescence to-day, when she was eighty-eight and Herbert sixty-eight, shocked Edith as something unfitting. It shocked Herbert too—though, true son of his father, he was flattered by womanly dependence. Only for these three or four days—since he was playing a game, subcribing to a convention—did he demand of his mother that she should hold opinions of her own. Yet at the same time, such was his masculine contrariness, he would have resented any decision running counter to his own ideas.

Herbert, then, became gentler and gentler as he saw his own ideas adopted and yet could persuade himself that they had originated with his mother and not with him. He came down from his mother's room to his brothers and sisters, again—continuously, as it seemed to Edith—assembled in the drawing-room. Mother wanted the Abbey; therefore the Abbey it must be. After all, Mother was doubtless right. All England's greatest sons were buried in the Abbey. He himself would have preferred the parish church at Huddersfield, he said, though Edith shrewdly estimated the honesty of this remark, and in speaking for himself he thought he might speak for them all; but Mother's wishes must be considered. They must bow to the publicity of the Abbey. After all, it was an honour—a great honour—the crowning honour of their father's life. Carrie, William, and Charles inclined their heads in silence at this solemn thought.

41

Edith, on the other hand, thought how much amused her father would have been, and at the same time how much gratified, though professing scornfulness, could he have watched himself being buried in the Abbey.

The pall worked by the ladies of the Royal School of Embroidery was undoubtedly very sumptuous. Heraldic emblems were embossed on violet plush. The Prime Minister duly carried his corner, becomingly serious, and so satisfactorily in character that no one seeing him could have hesitated to say, 'There goes a Prime, or at any rate a Cabinet, Minister of England.' The Leader of the Opposition kept step with the Prime Minister; for an hour they had buried their differences, which, indeed, were part of a game too, since under the tuition of a common responsibility they had both absorbed much the same lessons, though their adherents forbade them to repeat them in the same language. The two young princes, ushered hurriedly though respectfully to their seats, wondered, perhaps, why fate had isolated them from other young men, by condemning them to cut tapes across new arterial roads or to honour statesmen by attending their funerals. More probably, they took it all as part of the day's work.

But where, meanwhile, Edith wondered, was reality?

After the funeral was over, everything at Elm Park Gardens subtly changed. Consideration towards Lady Slane was still observed, but a note of impatience crept in, a note of domination, held rather insistently by Herbert and Carrie. Herbert had become, quite definitely, the head of the family, and Carrie his support. They were prepared to take a firm though kind line with their mother. She could still be led to a chair, and, once lowered into it, could still be patted on the shoulder with a kindly protective gesture, but she must be made to understand that the affairs of the world were waiting, and that this pause of

42

concession to death could not go on for ever. Like the papers in Lord Slane's desk, Lady Slane must be cleared up; then Herbert and Carrie could get back to their business. Nothing not put actually into words could have been conveyed more plainly.

Very quiet, very distinguished, very old, very frail, Lady Slane sat looking at her sons and daughters. Her children, who were accustomed to her, took her appearance for granted, but strangers exclaimed in amazement that she could not be over seventy. She was a beautiful old woman. Tall, slender, and pale, she had never lost her grace or her carriage. Clothes upon her ceased to be clothes and became draperies; she had the secret of line. A fluid loveliness ran over all her limbs. Her eyes were grey and deeply set; her nose was short and straight; her tranquil hands the hands of a Vandyck; over her white hair fell a veil of black lace, highly becoming. Her gowns for years past had always been soft, indefinite, and of unrelieved black. Looking at her, one could believe that it was easy for a woman to be beautiful and gracious, as all works of genius persuade us that they were effortless of achievement. It was more difficult to believe in the activity that Lady Slane had learned to pack into her life. Duty, charity, children, social obligations, public appearances—with these had her days been filled; and whenever her name was mentioned, the corollary came quick and slick, 'Such a wonderful help to her husband in his career!' Oh yes, thought Edith, Mother is lovely; Mother, as Herbert says, is wonderful. But Herbert is clearing his throat. What's coming now?

'Mother, dear . . .' A form of address semi-childish, semi-conventional; Herbert putting his fingers into his collar. Yet she had once sat on the floor beside him, and shown him how to spin his top.

'Mother, dear. We have been discussing . . . we have, I mean, felt naturally troubled about your future. We know how

43

devoted you were to Father, and we realise the blank that his loss must leave in your life. We have been wondering— and that is why we have asked you to meet us all here in the drawing-room before we separate again to our different homes—we have been wondering where and how you will choose to live?'

'But you have decided it already for me, Herbert, haven't you?' said Lady Slane with the utmost sweetness.

Herbert put his fingers into his collar and peeked and preened until Edith feared that he would choke.

'Well! decided it for you, Mother, dear! decided is scarcely the word. It is true that we have sketched out a little scheme, which we could submit for your approval. We have taken your tastes into consideration, and we have realised that you would not like to be parted from so many interests and occupations. At the same time . . .'

'One moment, Herbert,' said Lady Slane; 'what was that you said about interests and occupations?'

'Surely, Mother, dear,' said Carrie reproachfully, 'Herbert means all your committees, the Battersea Club for Poor Women, the Foundlings' Ward, the Unfortunate Sisters' Organisation, the . . .'

'Oh yes,' said Lady Slane; 'my interests and occupations. Quite. Go on, Herbert.'

'All these things,' said Carrie, 'would collapse without you. We realise that. You founded many of them. You have been the life of others. Naturally, you won't want to abandon them now.'

'Besides, dear Lady Slane,' said Lavinia—she had never unbent sufficiently to address her mother-in-law by any other name—'we realise how bored you would be with nothing to do. You so active, so energetic! Oh no, we couldn't visualise you anywhere but in London.'

Still Lady Slane said nothing. She looked from one to the

44

other with an expression that, in one so gentle, was surprisingly ironical.

'At the same time,' Herbert proceeded, reverting to his original speech whose interruption he had endured, patient though not pleased, 'your income will scarcely suffice for the expenses of a house such as you are entitled to expect. We propose, therefore . . .' and he outlined the scheme which we have already heard discussed, and may consequently spare ourselves the trouble of listening to again.

Lady Slane, however, listened. She had spent a great deal of her life listening, without making much comment, and now she listened to her eldest son without making any comment at all. He, for his part, was unperturbed by her silence. He knew that all her life she had been accustomed to have her comings and goings and stayings arranged for her, whether she was told to board a steamer for Capetown, Bombay, or Sydney; to transport her wardrobe and nursery to Downing Street; or to accompany her husband for the week-end to Windsor. On all these occasions she had obeyed her directions with efficiency and without surprise. Becomingly and suitably dressed, she had been ready at any moment to stand on quay or platform, waiting until fetched beside a pile of luggage. Herbert saw no reason now to doubt that his mother would dole out her time according to schedule in the spare bedrooms of her sons and daughters.

When he had finished, she said: 'That's very thoughtful of you, Herbert. It would be very kind of you to put this house in the agents' hands to-morrow.'

'Capital!' said Herbert; 'I'm so glad you agree. But you need not feel hurried. No doubt some little time must elapse before the house is sold. Mabel and I will expect you at your convenience.' And he stooped and patter her hand.

'Oh, but wait,' said Lady Slane, raising it. It was the first gesture she had made. 'You go too fast, Herbert. I don't agree.'

They all looked at her in consternation.

'You don't agree, Mother?'

'No,' said Lady Slane, smiling. 'I am not going to live with you, Herbert; nor with you, Carrie; nor with you, William; nor with you, Charles, kind though you all are. I am going to live by myself.'

'By yourself, Mother? It's impossible—and anyway, where would you live?'

'At Hampstead,' replied Lady Slane, nodding her head quietly, as though in response to an inner thought.

'At Hampstead?—but will you find a house that will suit you; convenient, and not too dear?—Really,' said Carrie, 'here we are discussing Mother's house as though everything were settled. It is absurd. I don't know what has come over us.'

'There is a house,' said Lady Slane, again nodding her head; 'I have seen it.'

'But, Mother, you haven't been to Hampstead.' This was intolerable. Carrie had known all her mother's movements day by day for the past fifteen years at least, and she revolted against the suggestion that her mother had visited Hampstead without her knowledge. Such a hint of independence was an outrage, almost a manifesto. There had always been so close and continuous a connection between Lady Slane and her eldest daughter; the plans for the day would always be arranged between them; Genoux would be sent round with a note in the morning; or they would telephone, at great length; or Carrie would come round to Elm Park Gardens after breakfast, tall, practical, rustling, self-important, equipped for the day with her gloves, her hat, and her boa, a shopping list slipped into her bag, and the agenda papers for the afternoon's committee, and the two elderly ladies would talk over the day's doings while Lady Slane went on with her knitting, and then they would go out together at about half-past eleven, two tall figures in black, familiar to the

46

other old ladies of the neighbourhood; or if their business, for once, did not lie in the same direction, Carrie would at least drop into Elm Park Gardens for tea, and would learn exactly how her mother had spent her day. It was surely impossible that Lady Slane should have concealed an expedition to Hampstead.

'Thirty years ago,' said Lady Slane. 'I saw the house then.' She took a skein of wool from her work-basket and held it out to Kay. 'Hold it for me, please, Kay,' and after first carefully breaking the little loops she began to wind. She was the very incarnation of placidity. 'I am sure the house is still there,' she said, carefully winding, and Kay with the experience of long habit stood before her, moving his hands rhythmically up and down, so that the wool might slip off his fingers without catching. 'I am sure the house is still there,' she said, and her tone was a mixture between dreaminess and confidence, as though she had some secret understanding with the house, and it were waiting for her, patient, after thirty years; 'it was a convenient little house,' she added prosaically, 'not too small and not too large—Genoux could manage it single-handed I think, with perhaps a daily char to do the rough work—and there was a nice garden, with peaches against the wall, looking south. It was to be let when I saw it, but of course your father would not have liked that. I remember the name of the agent.'

'And what,' snapped Carrie, 'was the name of the agent?'

'It was a funny name,' said Lady Slane, 'perhaps that's why I remember it. Bucktrout. Gervase Bucktrout. It seemed to go so well with the house.'

'Oh,' said Mabel, clasping her hands, 'I think it sounds too delicious—peaches, and Bucktrout. . . .'

'Be quiet, Mabel,' said Herbert. 'Of course, my dear Mother, if you are set on this—ah—eccentric scheme, there is no more to be said about it. You are entirely your own mistress, after all. But will it not look a little odd in the eyes of the world, when

47

you have so many devoted children, that you should elect to live alone in retirement at Hampstead? Far be it from me to wish to press you, of course.'

'I don't think so, Herbert,' said Lady Slane, and having come to the end of her winding, she said 'Thank you, Kay,' and making a loop on a long knitting needle she started on a fresh piece of knitting. 'Lots of old ladies live in retirement at Hampstead. Besides, I have considered the eyes of the world for so long that I think it is time I had a little holiday from them. If one is not to please oneself in old age, when is one to please oneself? There is so little time left!'

'Well,' said Carrie, making the best of a bad job, 'at least we shall see to it that you are never lonely. There are so many of us that we can easily arrange for you to have at least one visitor a day. Though, to be sure, Hampstead is a long way off, and it is not always easy to fit in the arrangements about the motor,' she added, looking meaningly at her small husband, who quailed. 'But there are always the great-grandchildren,' she said, brightening; 'you'd like to have them coming in and out, keeping you in touch; I know you wouldn't be happy without that.'

'On the contrary,' said Lady Slane, 'that is another thing about which I have made up my mind. You see, Carrie, I am going to become completely self-indulgent. I am going to wallow in old age. No grandchildren. They are too young. Not one of them has reached forty-five. No great-grandchildren either; that would be worse. I want no strenuous young people, who are not content with doing a thing, but must needs know why they do it. And I don't want them bringing their children to see me, for it would only remind me of the terrible effort the poor creatures will have to make before they reach the end of their lives in safety. I prefer to forget about them. I want no one about me except those who are nearer to their death than to their birth.'

48

Herbert, Carrie, Charles, and William decided that their mother must be mad. They took a step forward, and from having always thought her simple, decided that old age had definitely affected her brain. Her madness, however, was taking a harmless and even a convenient form. William might be thinking rather regretfully of the lost subsidy to his house-books, Carrie and Herbert might remain still a little dubious about the eyes of the world, but, on the whole, it was a relief to find their mother settling her own affairs. Kay gazed inquiringly at his mother. He had taken her so much for granted; they had all taken her so much for granted—her gentleness, her unselfishness, her impersonal activities—and now, for the first time in his life, it was becoming apparent to Kay that people could still hold surprises up their sleeves, however long one had known them. Edith alone frolicked in her mind. She thought her mother not mad, but most conspicuously sane. She was delighted to see Carrie and Herbert routed, by their mother quietly disentangling herself from their toils. Softly she clapped her hands together, and whispered 'Go on, Mother! go on!' Only a remnant of prudence prevented her from saying it out loud. She revelled in her mother's new-found eloquence—not the least of the surprises of that surprising morning, for Lady Slane habitually was reserved in speech, withholding her opinion, concealing even the expression on her face as she bent her head over her knitting or embroidery, when her occasional 'Yes, dear?' gave but little indication of what she was really thinking. It now dawned upon Edith that her mother might have lived a full private life, all these years, behind the shelter of her affectionate watchfulness. How much had she observed? noted? criticised? stored up? She was speaking again, rummaging meanwhile in her work-bag.

'I have taken the jewels out of the bank, Herbert. You and Mabel had better have them. I wanted to give them to Mabel years ago, but your father objected. However, here are some of them,' and as she spoke she turned the bag over and shook the contents out on to her lap, a careless assortment of leather cases, tissue paper, some loose stones, and skeins of wool. With her fine hands she began picking them over. 'Ring the bell for Genoux, Edith,' she said, glancing up. 'I never cared about jewels, you know,' she said, speaking to herself rather than to her family at large, 'and it seemed such a pity—such a waste— that so many should have come my way. Your father used to say that I must be able to deck myself out on Occasions. When we were in India, he used to buy back a lot of things at the Tash-i-Khane auctions. He had a theory that it pleased the princes to see me wearing their gifts, even though they knew perfectly well that we had bought them back. I dare say he was right. But it always seemed rather silly to me—such a farce. I had a big topaz once, a big bronze topaz, unset, cut into dozens of facets; I wonder if you children remember it? I used to make you look at the fire through it. It made hundreds of little flames; some went the right way up, and others upside down. When you came down after tea we used to sit in front of the fire looking through it, like Nero at the burning of Rome. Only it was brown fire, not green. I don't suppose you remember. That was sixty years ago. I lost it, of course; one always does lose the things one values most. I never lost any of the other things; perhaps because Genoux always had charge of them—and she used to invent the most extraordinary places to hide them in—she mistrusted safes, so she used to drop my diamonds into the cold water jug—no robber would think of looking for them there, she said. I often thought that if Genoux died suddenly I shouldn't know where to look for the jewels myself—but the topaz I used to carry in my pocket.' Here Lady Slane's dreamy reminiscences were cut short as Genoux came in, rustling like a snake in dry leaves, creaking like a saddle, for until May was out, Genoux would not

50

abandon the layers of brown paper that reinforced her corsets and her combinations against the English climate. 'Miladi a sonné?'

Yes, thought Edith, there's nobody here for Genoux but Mother; only Mother can have rung the bell; only Mother can have an order to give, though we are all assembled: Herbert peeking over his collar, Carrie drawing herself up, outraged, Charles twisting his moustaches like somebody sharpening a pencil—though who cares for Charles? not even the War Office, and Charles knows it. They all know that nobody cares for them; that's why they talk so loud. Mother has never talked at all—until to-day; yet Genoux comes in as though Mother were the only person in the room, in the house, fit to give an order. Genoux knows where respect is due. Genoux takes no account of insistent voices. 'Miladi a sonné?'

'Genoux, vous avez les bijoux?'

'Mais bien sûr, miladi, que j'ai les bijoux. J'appelle ça le trésor. Miladi veut que j'aille chercher le trésor?'

'Please, Genoux,' said Lady Slane, determined, though Genoux sent a glance round the family circle as though Herbert, Carrie, Charles, William, Lavinia, and even the snubbed and innocuous Mabel were the very robbers against whose coming she had dropped the diamonds nightly into the jug of cold water. Indian verandahs and South African stoeps had, in the past, whispered in Genoux' imagination with the stealthy footsteps of robbers bent upon the viceregal jewels—'ces sales nègres;'—but now a more immediate, because a more legitimate and English, danger menaced these jealously guarded possessions. Miladi, so gentle, so vague, so detached, could never be trusted to look after herself or her belongings. Genoux was by nature a watchdog. 'Miladi se souviendra au moins que les bagues lui ont été très spécialement données par ce pauvre milord?'

51

Lady Slane looked down at her hands. They were, as the saying goes, loaded with rings. That saying means, in so far as any saying means anything at all—and every saying, every *cliché*, once meant something tightly related to some human experience—that the gems concerned were too weighty for the hands that bore them. Her hands were indeed loaded with rings. They had been thus loaded by Lord Slane—tokens of affection, certainly, but no less tokens of the embellishments proper to the hands of Lord Slane's wife. The great half-hoop of diamonds twisted round easily upon her finger. (Lord Slane had been wont to observe that his wife's hands were as soft as doves; which was true in a way, since they melted into nothing as one clasped them; and in another way was quite untrue, since to the outward eye they were fine, sculptural, and characteristic; but Lord Slane might be trusted to seize upon the more feminine aspect, and to ignore the subtler, less convenient, suggestion.) Lady Slane, then, looked down at her hands as though Genoux had for the first time drawn attention to them. For one's hands are the parts of one's body that one suddenly sees with the maximum of detachment; they are suddenly far off; and one observes their marvellous articulations, and miraculous response to the transmission of instantaneous messages, as though they belonged to another person, or to another piece of machinery; one observes even the oval of their nails, the pores of their skin, the wrinkles of their phalanges and knuckles, their smoothness or rugosities, with an estimating and interested eye; they have been one's servants, and yet one has not investigated their personality; a personality which, cheiromancy assures us, is so much bound up with our own. One sees them also, as the case may be, loaded with rings or rough with work. So did Lady Slane look down upon her hands. They had been with her all her life, those hands. They had grown with her from the chubby hands of a child to the ivory-smooth hands of an old

52

woman. She twisted the half-hoop of diamonds, and the half-hoop of rubies, loosely and reminiscently. She had worn them for so long that they had become a part of her. 'No, Genoux,' she said, 'soyez sans crainte; I know the rings are mine.'

But the other things were not hers in the same way; and indeed she did not want them. Genoux produced them one after the other, and handed them over to Herbert, counting as a peasant might count out a clutch of eggs to the buyer. Herbert, for his part, received them and passed them on to Mabel much as a bricklayer passing on bricks to his mate. He had a sense of value, but none of beauty. Lady Slane sat by, watching. She had a sense of beauty, though none of value. The cost of these things, their marketable price, meant nothing to her. Their beauty meant much, though she felt no proprietary interest; and their associations meant much, representing as they did the whole background of her life in its most fantastic aspect. Those sceptres of jade, brought by the emissaries of the Tibetan Lama! how well she remembered the ceremony of their presentation, when the yellow-coated emissaries, squatting, had drawn howls of music from bones the length of a mammoth's thigh. And she remembered checking her amusement, even while she sat conformably beside the Viceroy in his Durbar Hall, checking it with the thought that it was on a par with the narrow English amusement at the unfamiliar collection of consonants in a Polish name. What, save their unfamiliarity, caused her to smile at the wails drawn from a Tibetan thigh-bone? Kubelik might equally cause a Tibetan lama to smile. Then the Indian princes had come with their gifts that now Genoux delivered over to Herbert, the heir, in Elm Park Gardens. The Indian princes had known very well that their gifts would be pooled in the Tash-i-Khane, to be bought back according to the Viceroy's purse and discretion. Knobbly pearls, and uncut emeralds, heavily flawed, passed now between

Genoux's resentful hands and Herbert's, decently avid. Red velvet cases opened to display bracelets and necklaces; 'tout est bien en ordre,' said Genoux, snapping the cases shut. A small table was quite covered with cases by the time they had finished. 'My dear Mabel,' said Lady Slane, 'I had better lend you a portmanteau.'

Loot. The eyes of William and Lavinia glittered. Lady Slane remained oblivious of their covetous glances, and of their resentment at this one-sided distribution. Not so much as a brooch for Lavinia! It had simply never occurred to Lady Slane that she ought to divide the things; that was obvious. Lavinia and Carrie watched in silent rage. Such simplicity amounted to imbecility. But Herbert was well aware, and—so amiable are our secret feelings—rejoiced. He enjoyed their discomfiture, and further to increase it addressed Mabel quite affectionately for once: 'Put on the pearls, my dear; I am sure they will be most becoming.' Becoming they were not, to Mabel's faded little face, for Mabel who had once been pretty had now faded, according to the penalty of fair people, so that her skin appeared to be darker than her hair, and her hair without lustre, the colour of dust. The pearls, which had once dripped their sheen among the laces and softnesses of Lady Slane, now hung in a dispirited way round Mabel's scraggy neck. 'Very nice, dear Mabel,' said Lavinia, putting up her lorgnon; 'but how odd it is, isn't it, that these Oriental presents should always be of such poor quality? Those pearls are quite yellow, really, now that I come to look at them—more like old piano keys. I never noticed that before, when your mother wore them.'

'About the house, Mother,' began Carrie. 'Would tomorrow suit you to see it? I think I have a free afternoon,' and she began to consult a small diary taken from her bag.

'Thank you, Carrie,' said Lady Slane, setting the crown upon the surprises she had already given them, 'but I have made an appointment to see the house to-morrow. And, although it is very nice of you to offer, I think I will go there alone.'

It was something of an adventure for Lady Slane to go alone to Hampstead, and she felt happier after safely changing trains at Charing Cross. An existence once limited only by the boundaries of Empire had shrunk since the era of Elm Park Gardens began. Or perhaps she was one of those people on whom a continuous acquaintance with strange countries makes little impression— they remain themselves to the end; or perhaps she was really getting old. At the age of eighty-eight one might be permitted to say it. This consciousness, this sensation, of age was curious and interesting. The mind was as alert as ever, perhaps more alert, sharpened by the sense of imminent final interruption, spurred by the necessity of making the most of remaining time; only the body was a little shaky, not very certain of its reliability, not quite certain even of its sense of direction, afraid of stumbling over a step, of spilling a cup of tea; nervous; aware that it must not be jostled, or hurried, for fear of betraying its frail inadequacy. Younger people did not always seem to notice or to make allowance; and when they did notice they were apt to display a slight irritability, dawdling rather too markedly in order to keep pace with the hesitant footsteps. For that reason Lady Slane had never much enjoyed her walks with Carrie to the corner where they caught the bus. Yet, going up to Hampstead alone, she did not feel old; she felt younger than she had felt for years, and the proof of it was that she accepted eagerly this start of a new lap in life, even though it be the last. Nor did she look her age, as she sat, swaying slightly with the rocking of the Underground train, very upright, clasping her umbrella and her bag, her ticket carefully pushed into the opening of her glove. It did not occur to her to wonder what her travelling companions would think, could they know that two days previously she had buried her husband in Westminster Abbey. She was more immediately concerned with the extraordinary sensation of being independent of Carrie.

(Leicester Square.)

How Henry's death had brought about this sudden emancipation she could not conceive. It was just another instance of what she had vaguely noted all her life: how certain events brought apparently irrelevant results in their train. She had once asked Henry whether the same phenomenon were observable in the realm of politics, but although he had accorded her (as always, and to everyone) the gravest courtesy of his attention, he had obviously failed to understand what she meant. Yet Henry rarely failed to pick up the meaning of what people said. On the contrary, he would let them talk, keeping his keen humorous eyes upon them all the while, and then he would pick out the central point of their meaning, however clumsily they had indicated it, and, catching it up between his hands, would toss it about as a juggler with golden balls, until from a poor poverty-stricken thing it became a spray, a fountain, full of glitter and significance under the play of his incomparable intelligence—for this was the remarkable, the attractive thing about Henry, the thing which made people call him the most charming man in the world: that he gave the best of his intelligence to everybody on the slightest demand, whether a Cabinet Minister at the council table, or an intimidated young woman sitting next to him at dinner. He was never dismissive, perfunctory, or contemptuous. He seized upon any subject, however trivial; and the further removed from his own work or interests the better. He would discuss balldresses with a débutante, polo ponies with a subaltern, or Beethoven with either. Thus he deluded legions of people into believing that they had really secured his interest.

(Tottenham Court Road.)

But, when his wife asked him that question about events and irrelevant results, he was not disposed to take the matter up, and

56

had played instead with the rings on her fingers. She could see the rings now, making bumps under her black gloves. She sighed. Often she had pressed a tentative switch, and Henry's mind had failed to light up. She had accepted this at last, taking refuge in the thought that she was probably the only person in the world with whom he need not make an effort. It was perhaps an arid compliment, but a sincere one. She regretted it now: there were so many things she would have liked to discuss with Henry; impersonal things, nothing troublesome. She had had that unique opportunity, that potential privilege, for nearly seventy years, and now it was gone, flattened under the slabs of Westminster Abbey.

(Goodge Street.)

He would have been amused by her emancipation from Carrie. He had never liked Carrie; she doubted whether he had ever much liked any of his children. He never criticised anybody—that was one of his characteristics—but Lady Slane knew him well enough (although in a sense she did not know him at all) to know when he approved of a person and when he did not. His commendations were always measured; but, conversely, when withheld, their absence meant a great deal. She could not recollect one word of approval for Carrie, unless 'Damned efficient woman, my daughter,' could be counted as approval. The expression in his eye whenever he looked at Herbert had been unmistakable; nor had Charles ever succeeded in obtaining much sympathy from his father in his many grievances. (Euston.) Lord Slane had been apt to consider his son, the General, with an air of as-much-as-to-say, 'Now shall I bestir myself and give this rhetorical and peevish man my exact opinion of government offices, about which, after all, I know a great deal more than he does, or shall I not?' So far as Lady Slane knew he never had. He had preferred to endure in silence. William he quite markedly avoided, though Lady Slane, with dishonest loyalty for her own son, had always tried to attribute this avoidance to a dislike of Lavinia. 'My dear,' Henry had once said,

57

under pressure of exhortation, 'I find it difficult to accommodate myself to the society of minds balanced like a ledger,' and Lady Slane had sighed, and had said yes, it must be admitted that Lavinia had done poor William's nature a certain amount of harm. At which Lord Slane had replied, 'Harm? they are two peas in a pod,' which, for him, was a tart rejoinder.

(Camden Town.)

For Edith he had had a somewhat selfish affection. She had remained at home; she had been obliging; she had taken him for walks; she had answered some of his letters. True, she had often muddled them; had sent them off unsigned, or, if signed, without an address, in which case they had been returned through the Dead Letter Office to 'Slane, Elm Park Gardens,' a contretemps which always caused Lord Slane more amusement than annoyance. Never had Lord Slane had occasion to call his daughter Edith a damned efficient woman. Lady Slane had sometimes been tempted to think that he liked Edith more for the opportunities she afforded him of teasing her than for the reliance he placed upon her well-intentioned service.

(Chalk Farm.)

Kay. But before Lady Slane could consider what Lord Slane had made of that curious problem Kay, before she could pull up yet another fish of memory on a long line, she recollected a restriction she had placed upon herself, namely, not to let her memory wander until the days of complete leisure should be come; not to luxuriate until she could luxuriate fully and freely. Her feast must not be spoiled by snippets of anticipation. The train itself came to her assistance, for, after jerking over points, it ran into yet another white-tiled station, where a line of red tiles framed the name: Hampstead. Lady Slane rose unsteadily to her feet, reaching out her hand for a helpful bar; it was on these occasions and these alone, when she must compete with the rush of mechanical life, that she betrayed herself for an old lady. She became then a little

58

tremulous, a little afraid. It became apparent that in her frailty she dreaded being bustled. Yet, in her anxiety not to inconvenience others, she always took conductors at their word and hurried obediently when they shouted, 'Hurry along, please'; as, again, in her anxiety not to push herself forward, she always allowed others to board the train or the bus while she herself hung courteously back. Many a train and bus she had missed by this method, often to the exasperation of Carrie, who had invariably secured her own place, and was borne away, seeing her mother left standing on platform or pavement.

It was a wonder, arrived at Hampstead, that Lady Slane descended from the train in time, successfully clasping her umbrella, her bag, and her ticket inside her glove, but descend she did, and found herself standing in the warm summer air with the roofs of London beneath her. The passers-by ignored her, standing there, so well accustomed were they to the sight of old ladies in Hampstead. Setting out to walk, she wondered if she remembered the way; but Hampstead seemed scarcely a part of London, so sleepy and village-like, with its warm red-brick houses and vistas of trees and distance that reminded her pleasantly of Constable's paintings. She walked slowly but happily, and without anxiety, as in a friendly retreat, no longer thinking of Henry's opinion of his children, or indeed of anything but the necessity of finding the house, *her* house, which thirty years ago had been one of just such a red-brick row, with its garden behind it. It was curious to think that she would see it again, so imminently. Thirty years. Ten years longer than the span needed for a baby to grow up into full consciousness. Who could tell what might have happened to the house during that span? whether it had seen turmoil, desolation, or merely placidity?

The house had indeed been waiting several years for someone to come and inhabit it. It had been let once only since Lady Slane first saw it, thirty years ago, to a quiet old couple with no more history than the ordinary history of human beings—eventful enough, God knows, in their own eyes, but so usual as to merge unrecorded into the general sea of lives—a quiet old couple, their peripetias left behind them; they had come there to fade slowly, to drift gently out of existence, and so they had faded, so they had drifted; they had, in fact, both drawn their last breath in the bedroom facing south, above the peaches—so the caretaker told Lady Slane, by way of encouragement, snapping up the blinds and letting in the sun, in an off-hand way, talking meanwhile, and wiping a cobweb off the window-sill with a sweep of her lifted apron, and looking back at Lady Slane as much as to say, 'There, now, you can see what it's like—not much to look at—just a house to let—make up your mind quickly, for good-ness' sake, and let me get back to my tea.' But Lady Slane, standing in the deserted room, said quietly that she had an appointment with Mr. Bucktrout.

The caretaker might go, she said; there was no need for her to wait; and some note of viceregal authority must have lingered in her voice, for the caretaker's antagonism changed to a sort of bedraggled obsequiousness. All the same, she said, she must lock up. There were the keys. Day in, day out, she had unlocked the house, flicked it over with a hasty duster, and locked it up again, to return to its silence and the occasional fall of plaster from the walls. During the night the plaster had fallen, and must be swept up in the morning. It was terrible the state an unoccupied house got into. The very ivy came creeping in between the windows; Lady Slane looked at it, a pale young frond waving listlessly in the sunshine. Bits of straw blew about on the floor. An enor-mous spider scuttled quickly, ran up the wall, and vanished into a crevice. Yes, said Lady Slane, the caretaker might go, and no doubt Mr. Bucktrout would be so kind as to lock up.

The caretaker shrugged. After all, there was nothing in the

house for Lady Slane to steal, and she wanted her tea. Receiving a tip of half-a-crown, she went. Lady Slane was left alone in the house; she heard the front door slam as the caretaker went away. How wrongly caretakers were named: they took so little care. A perfunctory banging about with black water in a galvanised pail, a dirty clout smeared over the floor, and they thought their work was done. Small blame to them, perhaps, receiving a few shillings a week and expected to make their knuckles even more unsightly in the care of a house which, to them, was at best a job and at worst a nuisance. One could not demand of them that they should give the care which comes from the heart. Very few months of such toil would blunt one's zeal, and caretakers had a lifetime of it. Nor could one expect them to feel how strange a thing a house was, especially an empty house; not merely a systematic piling-up of brick on brick, regulated in the building by plumb-line and spirit-level, pierced at intervals by doors and casements, but an entity with a life of its own, as though some unifying breath were blown into the air confined within this square brick box, there to remain until the prisoning walls should fall away, exposing it to a general publicity. It was a very private thing, a house; private with a privacy irrespective of bolts and bars. And if this superstition seemed irrational, one might reply that man himself was but a collection of atoms, even as a house was but a collection of bricks, yet man laid claim to a soul, to a spirit, to a power of recording and of perception, which had no more to do with his restless atoms than had the house with its stationary bricks. Such beliefs were beyond rational explanation; one could not expect a caretaker to take them into account.

Lady Slane experienced the curious sensation common to all who remain alone for the first time in an empty house which may become their home. She gazed out of the first-floor window, but her mind ran up and down the stairs and peeped into rooms, for already, at this her first visit, the geography had

61

impressed itself familiarly; that in itself was a sign that she and the house were in accord. It ran down even into the cellar, where she had not descended, but whose mossy steps she had seen; and she wondered idly whether fungi grew there—not the speckled orange sort but the bleached kind—unwholesome in a more unpleasant way. It seemed likely that fungi should be included among the invaders of the house, and this brought her back to the bare room in which she stood, with its impudent inhabitants blowing, waving, running, as they listed.

These things—the straw, the ivy frond, the spider—had had the house all to themselves for many days. They had paid no rent, yet they had made free with the floor, the window, and the walls, during a light and volatile existence. That was the kind of companionship that Lady Slane wanted; she had had enough of bustle, and of competition, and of one set of ambitions writhing to circumvent another. She wanted to merge with the things that drifted into an empty house, though unlike the spider she would weave no webs. She would be content to stir with the breeze and grow green in the light of the sun, and to drift down the passage of years, until death pushed her gently out and shut the door behind her. She wanted nothing but passivity while these outward things worked their will upon her. But, first of all, it was necessary to know whether she could have the house.

A slight sound downstairs—was it the opening of a door?—made her listen. Mr. Bucktrout? Her appointment with him was for half-past four, and the hour was already struck. She must see him, she supposed, though she hated business, and would have preferred to take possession of the house as the straw, the ivy, and the spider had taken possession, simply adding herself to their number. She sighed, foreseeing a lot of business before she could sit at peace in the garden; documents would have to be signed, orders given, curtains and carpets chosen, and various human beings set in motion, all provided with hammers, tin-tacks, needles, and thread, before she and her belongings could settle down after their last journey. Why could one not possess the ring of Aladdin? Simplify life as one might, one could not wholly escape its enormous complication.

The thought struck her that the Mr. Bucktrout whose name she had noted thirty years ago might well have been replaced by some efficient young son, and great was her relief when, peeping over the banisters, she saw, curiously foreshortened to her view, a safely old gentleman standing in the hall. She looked down on his bald patch; below that she saw his shoulders, no body to speak of, and then two patent-leather toes. He stood there hesitant; perhaps he did not know that his client had already arrived, perhaps he did not care. She thought it more probable that he did not care. He appeared to be in no hurry to find out. Lady Slane crept down a few steps, that she might get a better view of him. He wore a long linen coat like a house-painter's; he had a rosy and somewhat chubby face, and he held one finger pressed against his lips, as though archly and impishly preoccupied with some problem in his mind. What on earth is he going to do, she wondered, observing this strange little figure. Still pressing his finger, as though enjoining silence, he tiptoed across the hall to where a stain on the wall indicated that a barometer had once hung there; then rapidly tapped the wall like a woodpecker tapping a tree; shook his head; muttered 'Falling! falling!'; and, picking up the skirts of his coat, he executed two neat pirouettes which brought him back to the centre of the hall, his foot pointed nicely before him.

'Mr. Bucktrout?' said Lady Slane, descending.

Mr. Bucktrout gave a skip and changed the foot pointed before him. He paused to admire his instep. Then he looked up. 'Lady Slane?' he said, performing a bow full of elaborate courtesy.

'I came about the house,' said Lady Slane, quite at her ease

63

and drawn by an instant sympathy to this eccentric person.

Mr. Bucktrout dropped his skirts and stood on two feet like anybody else. 'Ah yes, the house,' he said; 'I had forgotten. One must be business-like, although the glass is falling. So you want to see the house, Lady Slane. It is a nice house—so nice that I wouldn't care to let it to everybody. It is my own house, you understand; I am the owner, as well as the agent. If I had been merely the agent, acting on the owner's behalf, I should have felt it my duty to let when I could. That is why it has remained empty for so long. I have had many applicants, but I liked none of them. But you shall see it.' He put a slight emphasis on the 'you'.

'I have seen it,' siad Lady Slane; 'the caretaker showed me over.'

'Of course. A horrid woman. So harsh, so sordid. Did you give her a tip?'

'Yes,' said Lady Slane, amused. 'I gave her half-a-crown.'

'Ah, that's a pity. Too late now, though. Well, you have seen the house. Have you seen it all? Bedrooms, three; bathroom, one; lavatories, two, one upstairs and one down; reception rooms, three; lounge hall; usual offices. Company's water; electric light. Half an acre of garden; ancient fruit-trees, including a mulberry. Fine cellar; do you care for mushrooms? you could grow mushrooms in the cellar. Ladies, I find, seldom care much for wine, so the cellar might as well be used for mushrooms. I have never yet met with a lady who troubled to lay down a pipe of port. And so, Lady Slane, having seen the house, what do you think of it?'

Lady Slane hesitated, as the fanciful idea crossed her mind of telling Mr. Bucktrout the exact thoughts which had occurred to her while she awaited him; she felt confident that he would receive them with complete gravity and without surprise. But, instead, she confined herself to saying with the approved caution and reticence of a potential tenant, 'I think it would probably suit me very well.'

'Ah, but the question is,' said Mr. Bucktrout, again putting his finger to his lips, 'will you suit *it?* I have a feeling that you might. And, in any case, you would not want it after the end of the world.'

'I expect my own end will come before that,' said Lady Slane, smiling.

'Not unless you are very old indeed,' said Mr. Bucktrout seriously. 'The end of the world is due in two years' time—I could convince you by a few simple mathematical calculations. Perhaps you are no mathematician. Few ladies are. But if the subject interests you I could come to tea with you one day when you are established and give you my demonstration.'

'So I am going to be established here, am I?' said Lady Slane.

'I think so—yes—I think so,' said Mr. Bucktrout, putting his head on one side and looking obliquely at her. 'It seems likely. Otherwise, why should you have remembered the house for thirty years—you said so in your letter—and why should I have turned away so many tenants? The two things seem to come together, do they not, to converge at a point, after describing separate arcs? I am a great believer in the geometrical designs of destiny. That is another thing I should like to demonstrate to you one day if I may come to tea. Of course, if I were only the agent I should never suggest coming to tea. It would not be meet. But, being also the owner, I feel that once we have finished all our business we may meet upon an equal footing.'

'Indeed, I hope you will come whenever you feel inclined, Mr. Bucktrout,' said Lady Slane.

'You are most gracious, Lady Slane. I have few friends, and I find that as one grows older one relies more and more on the society of one's contemporaries and shrinks from the society of the young. They are so tiring. So unsettling. I can scarcely, nowadays, endure the company of anybody under seventy. Young people compel one to look forward on a life full of effort. Old people permit one to look backward on a life whose effort is over and done with. That is reposeful. Repose, Lady Slane, is one of the most important things in life, yet how few people achieve it? How few people, indeed, desire it? The old have it imposed upon them. Either they are infirm, or weary. But half of them still sigh for the energy which once was theirs. Such a mistake.'

'That, at any rate, is a mistake of which I am not guilty,' said Lady Slane, betraying herself with relief to Mr Bucktrout.

'No? Then we are agreed upon at least one of the major subjects. It is terrible to be twenty, Lady Slane. It is as bad as being faced with riding over the Grand National course. One knows one will almost certainly fall into the Brook of Competition, and break one's leg over the Hedge of Disappointment, and stumble over the Wire of Intrigue, and quite certainly come to grief over the Obstacle of Love. When one is old, one can throw oneself down as a rider on the evening after the race, and think, Well, I shall never have to ride that course again.'

'But you forget, Mr. Bucktrout,' said Lady Slane, delving into her own memories, 'when one was young, one enjoyed living dangerously—one desired it—one wasn't appalled.'

'Yes,' said Mr. Bucktrout, 'that is true. When I was a young man I was a Hussar. My greatest pleasure was pig-sticking. I assure you, Lady Slane, that I touched the highest moment of life whenever I saw a fine pair of tusks coming at me. I have several pairs, mounted, in my house to-day, which I should be pleased to show you. But I had no ambition—no military ambition. I never had the slightest wish to command my regiment. So of course I resigned my commission, since when I have learnt that the pleasures of contemplation are greater than the pleasures of activity.'

66

The image of Mr. Bucktrout as a Hussar, thus evoked by his queerly stilted phrases, moved Lady Slane to an amusement which she was careful to conceal. She found it easy to believe that he had never cherished any military ambition. She found him entirely to her liking. Still, it was necessary to recall him to practical matters, she supposed, though heaven knows that this rambling conversation was for her a new and luxurious indulgence. 'But now, about the house, Mr. Bucktrout,' she began, much as Carrie had resumed the topic with herself after that flow of passing jewels; it was a relapse into the old viceregal manner that brought Mr. Bucktrout back from pig-sticking in the scrub to the subject of rents in Hampstead. 'I like the house,' said Lady Slane, 'and apparently,' she added with a smile that undid the viceregal manner, 'you approve of me as a tenant. But what about business? What about the rent?'

He gave her a startled look; evidently, he had been busy pig-sticking by himself in the interval; had returned to life as a Hussar, forgetting himself as owner and agent. He put his finger to his nose this time, quizzing Lady Slane, giving himself time to think. The subject seemed distasteful to him, though relics of a business training tugged at him, jerking some string in his mind; he lived, naturally, in a world where rents were not of much importance. So did Lady Slane; and thus a pair more ill-assorted, and yet better assorted, to discuss rents could scarcely be imagined. 'The rent . . . the rent . . .' said Mr. Bucktrout, as one who endeavours to establish connection with some word in a foreign language he once has known.

Then he brightened. 'Of course: the rent,' he said briskly. 'You want to take the house on a yearly tenancy?' he said, recovering his vocabulary after his excursion of fifty years back into his pig-sticking days as a Hussar. 'It would scarcely be worth your while,' he added, 'to take it on more than a yearly tenancy. You might vacate it at any moment, and your heirs would not wish to have it on their hands. I think that on that basis we might come to a satisfactory agreement. I like the idea of a tenant who will give me recovery of the house within a short period. Apart from my personal predilection for you, Lady Slane, abruptly sprung though that predilection may be, I relish the idea that this particular house should return at short intervals again into my keeping. From that point of view alone, you would suit me admirably as a tenant. There are other points of view, of course—as in this life there invariably are—but in the interests of business I must for the present ignore them. Those other points of view are purely sentimental—*ee gee*, that I should fancy you as the occupier of this particular house (speaking as the owner, not the agent), and that I may look forward to agreeable afternoons at tea-time when I may set before you, as a lady of understanding, my several little demonstrations. Those considerations must stand aside for the moment. We are here to discuss the question of rent.' He pointed a foot; recollected himself; took it back; and cocked at Lady Slane an eye full of satisfaction and triumph.

He puts it delicately, admirably, thought Lady Slane; it would scarcely be worth my while to take the house on more than a yearly tenancy, since at any moment I might vacate it by being carried out of it in my coffin. But what if he should pre-decease me? for although I am certainly an old woman, he is equally certainly an old man. Any delicacy of speech between people so near to death, is surely absurd? But people do not willingly speak in plain English of death, however fixedly its imminence may weigh on their hearts; so Lady Slane refrained from pointing out the possible fallacies of Mr. Bucktrout's argument, and merely said, 'A yearly tenancy would suit me very well. Still, that doesn't reply to my inquiry about the rent?'

Mr. Bucktrout was manifestly embarrassed at being thus chased into a corner. Although both owner and agent, he was

one of those who resent seeing their fantasies reduced to terms of
pounds and pence. Moreover, he had set his heart upon Lady
Slane as a tenant. He temporised. 'Well, Lady Slane, I counter
your inquiry. What rent would you be willing to pay?'

Delicacy again, thought Lady Slane. He doesn't say: 'What
rent could you afford to pay?' This fencing, this walking round
one another like two courting pigeons, was becoming ludicrous.
Henry would have struck down between them, cleaving the
situation with an axe of cold sense. Yet she liked the odd little
man, and was thankful, heartily thankful, that she had rejected
Carrie's company. Carrie, like her father, would drastically have
intervened, shattering thereby a relationship which had grown
up, creating itself, as swiftly and exquisitely as a little rigged ship
of blown glass, each strand hardening instantly as it left the tube
and met the air, yet remaining so brittle that a false note, jarring
on the ethereal ripples, could splinter it. Shrinking, Lady Slane
named a sum, too large; which Mr. Bucktrout immediately
halved, too small.

But between them they came to a settlement. Though it
might not be everybody's method of conducting business, it
suited them very well, and they parted very much pleased with
each other.

Carrie found her mother curiously reticent about the house.
Yes, she had seen it; yes, she had seen the agent; yes, she had
arranged to take it. On a yearly tenancy. Carrie exclaimed.
What if the agent got a better offer and turned her out? Lady
Slane smiled wisely. The agent, she said, wouldn't turn her out.
But, said Carrie, agents were such dreadfully grasping people—
quite naturally—they had to be grasping—what guarantee had
her mother that at the end of a year she might not be obliged to
look for another house? Lady Slane said that she anticipated no
such thing; Mr. Bucktrout was not that kind of person. Well,
but, said Carrie, exasperated, Mr. Bucktrout had his living to

make, hadn't he? Business wasn't based on philanthropy. And had her mother made any arrangements about repairs and decoration, she asked? whisking off on to another subject, since she gave up all hope of doing something about the lease; what about papering, and distempering, and leaks in the roof? Had her mother thought of that? Carrie, who had controlled all her mother's decision for years, really suffered a frenzy of mortification and anxiety, intensified by her inability to give free rein to her indignation, for she could not reasonably assume authority over an old lady of eighty-eight, if that old lady chose suddenly to imply that having reached the age of eighty-eight she was capable of managing her affairs for herself. Carrie was sure that she was capable of nothing of the sort; apart from her consternation at seeing herself deposed, she was genuinely concerned at seeing her mother heading straight and unrescuable into the most terrible muddle. Lady Slane meanwhile replied calmly that Mr. Bucktrout had promised to arrange with carpenters, painters, plumbers, and upholsterers on her behalf. It was kind of Carrie to worry, but quite unnecessary. She and Mr. Bucktrout would manage everything between them.

Carrie felt that it was useless even to mention the word Estimate. Her mother seemed to have gone right away from her, into a world ruled not by sense but by sentiment. A world in which one took other people's delicacy and nice feelings for granted. A world which, as Carrie knew very well, bore no relation to anything on this planet. It was all a part of the same thing as her mother's extraordinary indifference and obtuseness about the jewels. Who, in their senses, would have handed over five, perhaps seven, thousand pounds worth of jewels like that? Who, with any proper perception, would have failed to realise that Carrie and Lavinia ought to have at least a share? Not to mention Edith. They would not have grudged poor Edith a brooch. After all, Edith was Father's daughter. But her mother

70

had given everything away, as though it were so much useless lumber, just as she had now delivered herself and her purse gaily into the hands of an old shark called Bucktrout.

Carrie, however, found great consolation in talking the matter over at immense and repetitive length with her relations. Their solidarity was thereby increased. They all thoroughly enjoyed their gatherings over the tea-table—tea was their favourite, perhaps because the cheapest, meal—and nobody minded how often somebody else said the same thing, even framed in the same words. They listened each time with renewed approval, nodding their heads as though some new and illuminating discovery had just been made. Carrie and her relations found great reassurance in assertion and re-assertion. Say a thing often enough, and it becomes true; by hammering in sufficient stakes of similar pattern they erected a stockade between themselves and the wild dangers of life. The phrase 'Mother is wonderful,' so prevalent between the death and the funeral, was rapidly replaced by the phrase 'Dear Mother—so hopeless over anything practical.' But having said that—and having said it with commendable perseverance, in Queen's Gate where William and Lavinia lived, in Lower Sloane Street where Carrie and Roland lived, in the Cromwell Road where Charles had his flat, in Cadogan Square where Herbert and Mabel lived—having said that, they were brought up short against their inability to cope with that softly hopeless Mother. So amenable, so malleable always, she had routed them completely—she, and her house at Hampstead, and her Mr. Bucktrout. They had none of them seen Mr. Bucktrout; they had none of them been allowed to see him; even Carrie had been rejected, and her offer of lifts in the motor; but his invisibility added only fuel to the fire of their mistrust. He became 'This man who has Got Hold of Mother.' If Lady Slane had not already given all the pearls, the jade, the rubies, and the emeralds in that haphazard fashion to Herbert

71

and Mabel, they would have suspected her of handing them all over to Mr. Bucktrout at Mr. Bucktrout's suggestion. This Mr. Bucktrout, with his vagueness about the lease, with his helpfulness about carpenters, painters, plumbers, and upholsterers—what could he be but a shark? At the very best, his motive resolved itself for Carrie and her family into the ominous word Commission.

Meanwhile, Mr. Bucktrout had secured the services of Mr. Gosheron.

'You must understand,' he said to this estimable tradesman, 'that Lady Slane, despite her high position, is a lady of limited means. It is not always safe, Mr. Gosheron, to assume affluence in the aristocracy. Because a gentleman has been Viceroy of India and Prime Minister of England it does not mean that his relict is left well-off. Our public services, Mr. Gosheron, are conducted on very different principles. Therefore it becomes incumbent on you, Mr. Gosheron, to keep your estimate as low as is compatible with your own reasonable profit. As an agent, and also as an owner of property, I have some experience in such matters. And I assure you that I shall make it my business to check your estimates on Lady Slane's behalf as it were upon my own.'

Mr. Gosheron assured Mr. Bucktrout in return that he would never dream of taking advantage of her ladyship.

Genoux, from the first time that she saw him, took a fancy to Mr. Gosheron. 'Voilà un monsieur,' she said, 'qui connaît son travail. Il sait par exemple,' she added, 'quels weights il faut mettre dans les rideaux. Et il sait faire de la peinture pour que ça ne stick pas. J'aime,' she added, 'le bon travail—pas trop cher, mais pas de pacotille.' Genoux and Lady Slane, liberated from Carrie, spent very happy days with Mr. Bucktrout and Mr. Gosheron. Lady Slane liked everything about Mr. Gosheron, even to his appearance. He looked most respectable, and invariably wore an old bowler hat, green with

72

age, which he never removed even in the house, but which, in order to show some respect to Lady Slane, he would tilt forward by the back brim, and would then resettle into place. His hair, which had once been brown, but now was grey and stringy, invariably became disarranged by this tilting of the hat, so that after the tilting a strand stuck out at the back, fascinating Lady Slane, but unnoticed by its owner. He carried a pencil always behind his ear, a pencil so broad and of so soft a lead that it could serve for nothing except making a mark across a plank of wood, but which Lady Slane never saw used for any other purpose than scratching his head. In him she quickly recognised one of those craftsmen who find fault with all work not carried out under their own auspices. 'That's a poor sort of contraption,' Mr. Gosheron would mutter, examining the damper of the kitchen range. He contrived to imply always that, had the job been left to him, he would have managed it a great deal better. Nevertheless, he implied at the same time, a man of his experience could put it right; could improve, though not quite satisfactorily, on a thoroughly bad job. Silent as a rule, and subdued in the presence of Mr. Bucktrout, he occasionally indulged in an outburst of his own. Lady Slane was especially delighted when he indulged in outbursts, such as his outbursts against asbestos-roofed sectional bungalows. These outbursts were the more valuable for their rarity. 'I can't understand, my lady,' he said, 'how people can live without beauty.' Mr. Gosheron could see beauty in a deal board, if it were well-fitted, though naturally he preferred an oak one. 'And to think,' he said, 'that some people cover up the grain with paint!' Mr. Gosheron was not a young man; he was seventy if a day, but his traditions went back a hundred years or more. 'These lorries,' he said, 'shaking down the walls!' Henry Slane, always progressive, had seen beauty in lorries even as Mr. Gosheron saw it in a well-carpentered board; but Lady Slane, who for years had striven loyally to keep up

73

with the beauty of lorries, now found herself released back into a far more congenial set of values. She could dally for hours with Mr. Bucktrout and Mr. Gosheron, with Genoux following them about as a solid and stocky chorus. Planted squarely on her two feet, creaking within her brown paper linings, Genoux who had spent her life disapproving on principle of nearly everybody, regarded Mr. Bucktrout and Mr. Gosheron with an approval amounting almost to love. How different they were, how puzzlingly, pleasingly different, from the children of miladi!—for whom, nevertheless, Genoux nourished an awed respect. The two old gentlemen seemed so genuinely anxious that Lady Slane should have everything just as she liked it, yet should be spared all possible expense; when she made tentative suggestions, as to the inclusion of a glass shelf in the bathroom, or whatever it might be, they looked at each other with a glance of confederacy, almost a wink, and invariably said they thought that could be managed. That was the way Genoux liked to see miladi treated—as though she were something precious, and fragile, and unselfish, needing a protective insistence on the rights she would never claim for herself. No one had ever treated her quite like that before. Milord had loved her, of course, and had guarded her always from trouble (milord who always had such beautiful manners with everyone), but he himself was so dominating a personality that other people fell naturally into his shadow. Her children loved her too, or so Genoux supposed, for it was unthinkable to Genoux that a child should not love its mother, even after the age of sixty, but there had been times when Genoux could not at all approve of their manner towards their mother; Lady Charlotte, for instance, was really too tyrannical, arriving at Elm Park Gardens at all hours of the day, her very aspect enough to make a timid old lady tremble. Very often one could detect a veiled impatience behind her words. And they were all too energetic, in Genoux's opinion, except for Lady

74

Edith and Mr. Kay; they bustled their poor mother about, talking loudly and taking it for granted that her powers were equal with their own. Once, when Lady Slane was going out with Mr. William, she had proposed taking a taxi; but Mr. William had said no, they could quite well go in a bus, and Genoux, who was holding the front door open for them, had nearly produced her purse to offer Mr. William eighteen-pence. She wished now that she had indulged in that piece of irony. It was not reasonable to treat a lady of eighty-eight as though she were only sixty-five. Genoux, who herself was only two years younger than Lady Slane, waxed indignant whenever she put on Lady Slane's galoshes in the hall of Elm Park Gardens and handed her an umbrella to go out into the rain. It was not right, especially when one considered the state Lady Slane had been accustomed to, sitting up on an elephant with a mahout behind her holding a parasol over her head. Genoux had preferred Calcutta to Elm Park Gardens.

But at Hampstead, thanks to Mr. Bucktrout and Mr. Gosheron, the proper atmosphere had been at last achieved. It was modest; there were no aides-de-camp, no princes, but though modest it was warm, and affectionate, and respectful, and vigilant, and generous, just as it should be. Mr. Bucktrout expressed himself in a style which Genoux thought extremely distinguished. He was odd, certainly, but he was a gentleman— un vrai monsieur. He had strange and beautiful ideas; he was never in a hurry; he would break off in the middle of business to talk about Descartes or the satisfying quality of pattern. And when he said pattern, he did not mean the pattern on a wall-paper; he meant the pattern of life. Mr. Gosheron was never in a hurry either. Sometimes, by way of comment, he lifted his bowler hat at the back and scratched his head with his pencil. He spoke very little, and always in a low voice. He deplored the decay of craftsmanship in the modern world; refused to employ

75

trades-union men, and had assembled a troop of workmen most of whom he had trained himself, and who were consequently so old that Genoux was sometimes afraid they would fall off their ladders. The workmen, too, had entered into the conspiracy to please Lady Slane; they greeted her arrival always with beaming smiles, took off their caps, and hastened to move the paint-pots out of her way. Yet for all this leisurely manner pervading the house, the work seemed to proceed quite fast, and there was always some little surprise prepared for Lady Slane every time she came up to Hampstead.

Mr. Bucktrout even gave her little presents, though his delicacy restrained them to a nature so modest and inexpensive that she could accept them without embarrassment. Sometimes it was a plant for her garden, sometimes a vase of flowers set with a curious effect of brilliance on a window-sill in an empty room. He was compelled to set them on a window-sill, he explained, since there were as yet no tables or other furniture, but Lady Slane suspected that he really preferred the window-sill, where he could so dispose his gift that the rays of the sun would fall upon it at the very hour when he expected his tenant. She teased him sometimes by arriving half-an-hour late, but he was undefeated; and once a ring of wet three inches away betrayed him: seeing that she was late, he had gone upstairs again to shift his flowers along into the sun. Old age, thought Lady Slane, must surely content itself with very small pleasures, judging by the pleasure she experienced at this confirmation of her suspicions. Weary, enfeebled, ready to go, she still could amuse herself by playing a tiny game in miniature with Mr. Bucktrout and Mr. Gosheron, a sort of minuet stepped out to a fading music, artificial perhaps, yet symbolic of some reality she had never achieved with her own children. The artificiality lay in the manner, the reality in the heart which invented it. Courtesy ceased to be blankly artificial, when prompted by real esteem; it became, simply, one of the decent, veiling graces; a formula by which a profounder feeling might be conveyed.

They were too old, all three of them, to feel keenly; to compete and circumvent and score. They must fall back upon the old measure of the minuet, in which the gentleman's bow expressed all his appreciative gallantry towards women, and the lady's fan raised a breeze insufficient to flutter her hair. That was old age, when people knew everything so well that they could no longer afford to express it save in symbols. Those days were gone when feeling burst its bounds and poured hot from the foundry, when the heart seemed likely to split with complex and contradictory desires; now there was nothing left but a landscape in monochrome, the features identical but all the colours gone from them, and nothing but a gesture left in the place of speech.

Meanwhile Mr. Bucktrout brought his little offerings, and Lady Slane liked them best when they took the form of flowers. Mr. Bucktrout, as she began to discover him, revealed many little talents, among which a gift for arranging a bunch was not the least. He would make daring and surprising combinations of colour and form, till the result was more like a still-life painting than like a bunch of living flowers, yet informed with a life that no paint could rival. Set upon their window-sill, luminous in the sun, more luminous for the bare boards and plaster surrounding them, their texture appeared lit from within rather than from without. Nor did his inventiveness ever falter, for this week he would produce a bunch as garish as a gipsy, all blue and purple and orange, but next week a bunch discreet as a pastel, all rose and grey with a dash of yellow, and some feathery spray lightly touched with cream. Lady Slane, who might have been a painter, could appreciate his effects. Mr. Bucktrout was an artist, said Lady Slane; and even Genoux, who did not care for flowers in the house because they dropped their petals over

77

tables, and eventually had to be thrown away, making a damp
mess in the waste-paper basket, even Genoux commented one
day that 'Monsieur aurait dû se faire floriste.'

Little by little, seeing that his efforts were appreciated, his
offerings became more personal. The vase of flowers was supple-
mented by a bunch for Lady Slane to pin against her shoulder.
The first occasion having given rise to a difficulty, because,
searching under her laces and ruffles, anxious not to disappoint
the old gentleman, she could discover no pin, he thereafter
always provided a large black safety pin pushed securely through
the silver paper wrapped round the stalks, and Lady Slane dutifully used it, though she had been presciently careful to bring
one with her. Of such small, tacit, and mutual courtesies was
their relationship compact.

One day she asked him why he took so much trouble on her
behalf. Why had he made it his business to find Mr. Gosheron
for her, to supervise his estimates, to look into every detail of the
work? That, surely, was not customary in an agent, even in an
owner-agent? Mr. Bucktrout instantly became very serious. 'I
have been wondering, Lady Slane,' he said, 'whether you would
ask me that question. I am glad that you should have asked it,
for I am always in favour of letting the daylight into the thickets
of misunderstanding. You are right: it is not customary. Let us
say that I do it because I have very little else to do, and that so
long as you do not object, I am grateful to you for affording me
the occupation.'

'No,' said Lady Slane, shy but determined; 'that is not the
reason. Why do you take my interests in this way? You see,
Mr. Bucktrout, not only do you control Mr. Gosheron—who,
as a matter of fact, needs less controlling than any tradesman I
ever met—but from the first you have been anxious to spare me
as much as possible. I may not be very well versed in practical
matters,' she said with her charming smile, 'but I have seen

enough of the world to realise that business is not usually conducted on your system. Besides, my daughter Charlotte . . .
well, never mind about my daughter Charlotte. The fact
remains that I am puzzled, and also rather curious.'

'I should not like you to think me a simpleton, Lady Slane,'
said Mr. Bucktrout very gravely. He hesitated, as though
wondering whether he should take her into his confidence, then
went off with a rush on another little speech. 'I am not a
simpleton,' he said, 'nor am I a childish old man. I dislike
childishness and all such rubbish. I feel nothing but impatience
with the people who pretend that the world is other than it is.
The world, Lady Slane, is pitiably horrible. It is horrible because
it is based upon competitive struggle—and really one does not
know whether to call the basis of that struggle a convention or a
necessity. Is it some extraordinary delusion, or is it a law of life?
Is it perhaps an animal law from which civilisation may eventually free us? At present it seems to me, Lady Slane, that man
has founded all his calculations upon a mathematical system
fundamentally false. His sums work out right for his own pur-
poses, because he has crammed and constrained his planet into
accepting his premises. Judged by other laws, though the
answers would remain correct, the premises would appear
merely crazy; ingenious enough, but crazy. Perhaps some day a
true civilisation may supervene and write a big W. against all
our answers. But we have a long road to travel yet—a long road
to travel.' He shook his head, pointed his foot, and became sunk
in his musings.

'Then you think,' said Lady Slane, seeing that she must recall
him from his abstractions, 'that anyone who goes against this
extraordinary delusion is helping civilisation on?'

'I do, Lady Slane; most certainly I do. But in a world as at
present constituted, it is a luxury that only poets can afford, or
people advanced in age. I assure you that when I first went into

business, after I had resigned my commission, I was fierce. It is really the only word. Fierce. No one could get the better of me. And the more severe my conduct, the more respect I earned. Nothing earns respect so quickly as letting your fellows see that you are a match for them. Other methods may earn you respect in the long run, but for a short-cut there is nothing like setting a high valuation on yourself and forcing others to accept it. Modesty, moderation, consideration, nicety—no good; they don't pay. If you were to meet one of my earlier colleagues, Lady Slane, he would tell you that in my day I had been a regular Juggernaut.'

'And when did you give up these principles of ruthlessness, Mr. Bucktrout?' asked Lady Slane.

'You do not suspect me of boasting, Lady Slane, do you?' asked Mr. Bucktrout, eyeing her. 'I am telling you all this so that you should realise that *naïveté* is not my weakness. As I said, you must not be allowed to think me a simpleton.— When did I give up these principles? Well, I set a term upon them; I determined that at sixty-five business properly speaking should know me no more. On my sixty-fifth birthday—or, to put it more correctly, on my sixty-sixth—I woke a free man. For my practice had always been a discipline rather than an inclination.'

'But what about this house?' asked Lady Slane. 'You told me that for thirty years you had refused tenants if you didn't like them. Surely that was inclination, wasn't it? It could hardly be described as business?'

'Ah,' said Mr. Bucktrout, putting his finger to his nose, 'you are too shrewd, Lady Slane; you have too good a memory. But don't be too hard on me: this house was always my one little patch of folly. Or, should I say, my one little patch of sanity? I like to be exact in my expressions. I see, Lady Slane, that you are something of a tease. I mean no impertinence. If ladies did not tease, we should be in danger of taking ourselves too seriously. I always had a fancy, you see, that I should like to end my days in this house, so naturally I did not wish its atmosphere contaminated by any unsympathetic influence. You may have noticed—of course you have noticed—that its atmosphere is curiously ripened and detached. I have preserved that atmosphere with the greatest care, for although one cannot create an atmosphere, one can at least safeguard it against disturbance.'

'But if you want to live here yourself—very well, die here yourself,' said Lady Slane, seeing that he had raised a hand and was about to correct her, 'why have you let it to me?'

'Oh,' said Mr. Bucktrout easily and consolingly, 'your tenancy, Lady Slane, is not likely to interfere with my intentions.'

For courteous though he was, Mr. Bucktrout in this respect remained firmly unsentimental, making no bones about the fact that Lady Slane would require the house for a short period only. Whenever he discouraged her from unnecessary expenditure, he did so on the grounds that it was scarcely worth her while. When she mentioned central heating, he reminded her that she would spend but few winters, if any, in this her last abode. 'Though to be sure,' he added sympathetically, 'there is no reason why one should not be comfortable while one may.' Genoux, overhearing this remark, summoned her religion to the support of her indignation. 'Monsieur pense donc qu'il n'y a pas de radiateurs au paradis? Il se fait une idée bien mièvre d'un Bon Dieu peu up-to-date.' Still, Mr. Bucktrout persisted in his idea that oil lamps would suffice to warm the rooms. He worked out the amount of gallons of paraffin they would consume in one winter, and balanced them against the cost of a furnace and pipes to pierce the walls. 'But, Mr. Bucktrout,' said Lady Slane, now without malice, 'as owner and agent you ought to encourage me to put in central heating. Think how strongly it would appeal to your next tenant.' 'Lady Slane,'

81

replied Mr. Bucktrout, 'consideration of my text tenant remains in a separate compartment from consideration of my present tenant. That has always been my rule in life; and thanks to it I have always been able to keep my relationships distinct. I am a great believer in sharp outline. I dislike a fuzz. Most people fell into the error of making their whole life a fuzz, pleasing nobody, least of all themselves. Compromise is the very breath of negation. My principle has been, that it is better to please one person a great deal than to please a number of persons a little, no matter how much offence you give. I have given a great deal of offence in my life, but of not one offensive instance do I repent. I believe in taking the interest of the moment. Life is so transitory, Lady Slane, that one must grab it by the tail as it flies past. No good in thinking of yesterday or to-morrow. Yesterday is gone, and to-morrow problematical. Even to-day is precarious enough, God knows. Therefore I say unto you,' said Mr. Bucktrout, relapsing into Biblical language and pointing his foot as though to point his words, 'do not put in central heating, for you know not how long you may live to enjoy it. My next tenant is welcome to warm himself in hell. I am here to advise you; and my advice is, buy an oil-lamp—several oil-lamps. They will warm you and see you out, however often you may have to renew the wicks.' He changed his foot, and frisked his coat-tails in a little perorative flourish. Mr. Gosheron, rather embarrassed, tilted his hat.

This conviction of the transcience of her tenure arose, Lady Slane discovered, from two causes: Mr. Bucktrout's estimate of her own age, and his prophetic views as to the imminent end of the world. He discoursed gravely on this subject, undeterred by the presence of Genoux and Mr. Gosheron, who preferred to avoid such topics and wanted respectively to talk of linen-cupboards and distemper. Genoux's sheets must wait, and Mr. Gosheron's little discs of colour, miniature full-moons, called

Pompeian-red, Stone-grey, Olive-green, Shrimp-pink. Mr. Bucktrout's attention was too closely engaged with eternity for linen-cupboards and distemper to catch him in more than a perfunctory interest. He could bear with them for five minutes; not longer. After that he would stick his sarcasm into Mr. Gosheron, saying such things as that his yard-measure varied in length from room to room, according as it ran north and south, or east and west, and that Genoux's shelves could never be truly level, seeing that the whole universe was based upon a curve, all of which disconcerted Genoux and Mr. Gosheron, but made Genoux respect Mr. Bucktrout the more for his learning, and made Mr. Gosheron's hat tilt nearly on to the tip of his nose. Mr. Bucktrout, observing this confusion, enlarged with sadistic pleasure. He knew that he had an appreciative audience in Lady Slane, even while he kept his feet on the ground sufficiently for her protection. 'As you may know,' he said, standing in an unfinished room while painters suspended their brushes in order to listen, 'there are at least four theories presaging the end of the world. Flame, flood, frost, and collision. There are others, but they are so unscientific and so improbable as to be negligible. Then there are, of course, the prophetic numbers. In so far as I believe numbers to be a basic part of the eternal harmonies, I am a convinced Pythagorean. Numbers exist in the void; it is impossible to imagine the destruction of numbers, even though you imagine the destruction of the universe. I do not mean by this that I hold with such ingenuities as the great sacred number of the Babylonians, twelve million nine hundred and sixty thousand, as you remember, nor yet in such calculations as William Miller's, who, by a system of additions and deductions, decided that the world would end on March 21, 1843. No. I have worked out my own system, Lady Slane, and I can assure you that, though distressing, it is irrefutable. The great annihilation is close at hand.' Mr. Bucktrout was launched; he tiptoed across to the wall, and very carefully wrote up PΩMH with a bit of chalk. A painter came after him, and as carefully obliterated it with his brush.

'Mais en attendant, miladi,' said Genoux, 'mes draps?'

Lady Slane had never taken so much pleasure in anybody's company. She had never been so happy as with her two old gentleman. She had played her part among brilliant people, important people, she had accommodated herself to their conversation, and, during the years of her association with worldly affairs, she had learnt to put together the scattered bits of information which to her were so difficult to collate or even to remember; thus she was always reminded of the days of her girlhood, when vast gaps seemed to exist in her knowledge, and when she was at a loss to know what people meant when they referred to the Irish Question or the Woman's Movement, or to Free Trade and Protection, two especial stumbling blocks between which she could never distinguish instinctively, although she had had them explained to her a dozen times. She had always taken an enormous amount of trouble to disguise her ignorance from Henry. In the end she had learnt to succeed quite well, and he would disburden himself of his political perplexities without the slightest suspicion that his wife had long since lost the basis of his argument. She was secretly and bitterly ashamed of her insufficiency. But what was to be done about it? She could not, no, she simply could not, remember why Mr. Asquith disliked Mr. Lloyd George, or what exactly were the aims of Labour, that new and alarming Party. The most that she could do was to conceal her ignorance, while she scrambled round frenziedly in her brain for some recollected scrap of associated information which would enable her to make some adequate reply. During their years in Paris she had suffered especially, for the cleverness of French conversation (which she greatly

84

admired) always made her feel outwitted; and though she could
sit listening for hours in rapture to the spitting pyrotechnics of
epigram and summary, marvelling at the ability of other people
to compress into a phrase some aspect of life which, to her, from
its very importance, demanded a lifetime of reflection, yet her
quiescent pleasure was always spoilt by the dread that at a given
moment some guest in mistaken politeness would turn to her,
throwing her the ball she would be unable to catch, saying, 'Et
Madame l'Ambassadrice, qu'en pense-t-elle?' And though she
knew that inwardly she had understood what they were saying
far better than they had understood it themselves—for the
conversation of the French always seemed to turn upon the
subjects which interested her most deeply, and about which she
felt that she really knew something, could she but have
expressed it—she remained stupidly inarticulate, saying something non-committal or something that she did not in the least
mean, conscious meanwhile that Henry, sitting by, must be
suffering wretchedly from the poor figure his wife cut. Yet, in
private, he was apt to say, though rarely, that she was the most
intelligent woman he knew because, although often inarticulate, she never made a foolish remark.

That these agonies should remain private to herself was her
constant prayer; neither Henry nor the guests at her table must
ever find her out. There were other allied weaknesses of which
she was also ashamed, though in a slightly less degree: her
inability, for instance, to write out a cheque correctly, putting
the same amount in figures as in words, remembering to cross it,
remembering to sign her name; her inability to understand what
a debenture was, or the difference between ordinary and deferred
stock; and as for that extraordinary menagerie of bulls, bears,
stags, and contango, she might as well have found herself in a
circus of wild animals. She supposed dutifully that these things
were of major importance, since they were clearly the things

which kept the world on the move; she supposed that party politics and war and industry, and a high birth-rate (which she had learned to call manpower), and competition and secret diplomacy and suspicion, were all part of a necessary game, necessary since the cleverest people she knew made it their business, though to her, as a game, unintelligible; she supposed it must be so, though the feeling more frequently seized her of watching figures moving in the delusion of a terrible and ridiculous dream. The whole tragic system seemed to be based upon an extraordinary convention, as incomprehensible as the theory of money, which (so she had been told) bore no relation to the actual supply of gold. It was chance which had made men turn gold into their symbol, rather than stones; it was chance which had made men turn strife into their principle, rather than amity. That the planet might have got on better with stones and amity —a simple solution—had apparently never occurred to its inhabitants.

Her own children, do what she might, had grown up in the same traditions. Naturally. There they were, trying and striving, not content merely to *be*. Herbert, so sententious always, so ambitious in his stupid way; Carrie with her committees and her harsh managing voice, interfering with people who did not want to be interfered with, all for the love of interference, her mother felt sure; Charles with his perpetual grievances; William and Lavinia, always scraping and saving and paring, an occupation in itself. There was no true kindliness, no grace, no privacy in any of them. For Edith and Kay alone their mother could feel some sympathy: Edith, always in a muddle, trying to get things straight and only getting them more tangled, trying to stand back and take a look at life, the whole of it, an impossibility accepted by most people, but which really bothered Edith and made her unhappy (still, the uneasiness did her credit); Kay— well, of all her children, perhaps Kay, messing about among his compasses and astrolabes, was the one who strove and struggled least; the one who had, without knowing it, the strongest sense of his own entity, when he shut his door behind him and took out his duster to potter with it along the alignment of his shelves. Yes, Kay and Edith were nearest to her; that would be one of the secrets, one of the jokes, she would take away with her into the grave.

For the rest, she had been a lonely woman, always at variance with the creeds to which she apparently conformed. Every now and then she had known some delicious encounter with a spirit attuned to her own. There had been the young man who accompanied them to Fatihpur Sikhri; a young man whose name she had forgotten, or had never known; but into whose eyes she had looked for one moment, and then, disturbed, had dismissed by her very gesture of strolling off to rejoin the Viceroy and his group of sun-helmeted officials. Such encounters had been rare, and, thanks to the circumstances of her life, brief. (She retained, however, a conviction that many spirits were fundamentally attuned, but so thickly overlaid by the formulas of the world that the clear requisite note could no longer be struck.) With Mr. Bucktrout and Mr. Gosheron she found herself entirely at ease. She could tell Mr. Bucktrout without embarrassment that she was unable to distinguish rates from taxes. She could tell Mr. Gosheron that she was unable to distinguish between a volt and an ampère. Neither of them tried to explain. They gave up at once, and simply said, leave it to me. She left it, and knew that her trust would not be misplaced.

Strange, the relief and release that this companionship brought her! Was it due to the weariness of old age, or to the long-awaited return to childhood, when all decisions and responsibilities might again be left in the hands of others, and one might be free to dream in a world of whose sunshine and benignity one was convinced? And she thought, if only I were

87

young once more I would stand for all that was calm and contemplative, opposed to the active, the scheming, the striving, the false—yes! the false, she exclaimed, striking her fist into the palm of the other hand with unaccustomed energy; and then, trying to correct herself, she wondered whether this were not merely a negative creed, a negation of life; perhaps even a confession of insufficient vitality; and came to the conclusion that it was not so, for in contemplation (and also in the pursuit of the one chosen avocation which she had had to renounce) she could pierce to a happier life more truly than her children who reckoned things by their results and activities.

She remembered how, crossing the Persian desert with Henry, their cart had been escorted by flocks of butterflies, white and yellow, which danced on either side and overhead and all around them, now flying ahead in a concerted movement, now returning to accompany them, amused as it were to restrain their swift frivolity to a flitting round this lumbering conveyance, but still unable to suit their pace to such sobriety, so, to relieve their impatience, soaring up into the air or dipping between the very axles, coming out on the other side before the horses had had time to put down another hoof; making, all the while, little smuts of shadow on the sand, like little black anchors dropped, tethering them by invisible cables to earth, but dragged about with the same capricious swiftness, obliged to follow; and she remembered thinking, lulled by the monotonous progression that trailed after the sun from dawn to dusk, like a plough that should pursue the sun in one straight slow furrow round and round the world—she remembered thinking that this was something like her own life, following Henry Holland like the sun, but every now and then moving into a cloud of butterflies which were her own irreverent, irrelevant thoughts, darting and dancing, but altering the pace of the progression not by one tittle; never brushing the carriage with

88

their wings; flickering always, and evading; sometimes rushing on ahead, but returning again to tease and to show off, darting between the axles; having an independent and a lovely life; a flock of ragamuffins skimming above the surface of the desert and around the trundling waggon; but Henry, who was travelling on a tour of investigation, could only say, 'Terrible, the ophthalmia among these people—I must really do something about it,' and, knowing that he was right and would speak to the missionaries, she had withdrawn her attention from the butterflies and had transferred it to her duty, determining that when they reached Yezd or Shiraz, or wherever it might be, she also would take the missionaries' wives to task about the ophthalmia in the villages and would make arrangements for a further supply of boracic to be sent out from England.

But, perversely, the flittering of the butterflies had always remained more important.

Part Two

Her heart sat silent through the noise
And concourse of the street;
There was no hurry in her hands,
No hurry in her feet.

CHRISTINA ROSSETTI

Sitting there in the sun at Hampstead, in the late summer, under the south wall and the ripened peaches, doing nothing with her hands, she remembered the day she had become engaged to Henry. She had plenty of leisure now, day in, day out, to survey her life as a tract of country traversed, and at last become a landscape instead of separate fields or separate years and days, so that it became a unity and she could see the whole view, and could even pick out a particular field and wander round it again in spirit, though seeing it all the while as it were from a height, fallen into its proper place, with the exact pattern drawn round it by the hedge, and the next field into which the gap in the hedge would lead. So, she thought, could she at last put circles round her life. Slowly she crossed that day, as one crosses a field by a little path through the grasses, with the sorrel and the buttercups waving on either side; she crossed it again slowly, from breakfast to bed-time, and each hour, as one hand of the

clock passed over the other, regained for her its separate character: this was the hour, she thought, when I first came downstairs that day, swinging my hat by its ribbons; and this was the
hour when he persuaded me into the garden, and sat with me on
the seat beside the lake, and told me it was not true that with one
blow of its wing a swan could break the leg of a man. She had
listened to him, paying dutiful attention to the swan which had
actually drifted up to them by the bank, dipping its beak and
then curving to probe irritably into the snowy tuft of feathers
on its breast; but she was thinking less of the swan than of
the young whiskers on Henry's cheek, only her thoughts had
merged, so that she wondered whether Henry's brown curls
were as soft as the feathers on the breast of the swan, and all but
reached out an idle hand to feel them. Then he passed from the
swan, as though that had been but a gambit to cover his hesitation, and the next thing she knew was that he was speaking
earnestly, bending forward and even fingering a flounce of her
dress, as though anxious, although unaware of his anxiety, to
establish some kind of contact between himself and her; but for
her all true contact had been severed from the moment he began
to speak so earnestly, and she felt no longer even the slight tug of
desire to put out her hand and touch the curly whiskers on his
cheek. Those words which he must utter so earnestly, in order
that his tone might carry their full weight; those words which
he seemed to produce from some serious and secret place,
hauling them up from the bottom of the well of his personality;
those words which belonged to the region of weighty and adult
things—those words removed him from her more rapidly than
an eagle catching him up in its talons to the sky. He had gone.
He had left her. Even while she conscientiously gazed at him and
listened, she knew that he was already miles and miles away. He
had passed into the sphere where people marry, beget and bear
children, bring them up, give orders to servants, pay income-

tax, understand about dividends, speak mysteriously in the presence of the young, take decisions for themselves, eat what they like, and go to bed at the hour which pleases them. Mr. Holland was asking her to accompany him into that sphere. He was asking her to be his wife.

It was clearly impossible, to her mind, that she should accept. The idea was preposterous. She could not possibly follow Mr. Holland into that sphere; could follow him, perhaps, less than any man, for she knew him to be very brilliant, and marked out for that most remote and impressive of mysteries, a Career. She had heard her father say that young Holland would be Viceroy of India before they had heard the last of him. That would mean that she must be Vicereine, and at the thought she had turned upon him the glance of a startled fawn. Instantly interpreting that glance according to his desires, Mr. Holland had clasped her in his arms and had kissed her with ardour but with restraint upon the lips.

What was a poor girl to do? Before she well knew what was happening, there was her mother smiling through tears, her father putting his hand on Mr. Holland's shoulder, her sisters asking if they might all be bridesmaids, and Mr. Holland himself standing very upright, very proud, very silent, smiling a little, bowing, and looking at her with an expression that even her inexperience could define only as proprietary. In a trice, like that, she had been changed from the person she was into somebody completely different. Or had she not? She could not detect any metamorphosis as having taken place within herself to match the sudden crop of smiles on all those faces. She certainly felt the same as before. A sense of terror possessed her over the novelty of her opinion being sought on any matter, and she hastily restored the decision into the hands of others. By this method she felt that she might delay the moment when she must definitely and irrevocably become that other person.

93

She could go on, for a little, secretly continuing to be herself.

And what, precisely, had been herself, she wondered—an old woman looking back on the girl she once had been? This wondering was the softest, most wistful, of occupations; yet it was not melancholy; it was, rather, the last, supreme luxury; a luxury she had waited all her life to indulge. There was just time, in this reprieve before death, to indulge herself to the full. She had, after all, nothing else to do. For the first time in her life—no, for the first time since her marriage—she had nothing else to do. She could lie back against death and examine life. Meanwhile, the air was full of the sound of bees.

She saw herself as a young girl walking beside the lake. She walked slowly, swinging her hat; she walked meditatively, her eyes cast down, and as she walked she prodded the tip of her parasol into the spongy earth. She wore the flounced and feminine muslins of 1860. Her hair was ringleted, and one ringlet escaped and fell softly against her neck. A curly spaniel accompanied her, snuffling into the bushes. They had all the appearance of a girl and a dog in an engraving from some sentimental keepsake. Yes, that was she, Deborah Lee, not Deborah Holland, not Deborah Slane; the old woman closed her eyes, the better to hold the vision. The girl walking beside the lake was unaware, but the old woman beheld the whole of adolescence, as who should catch a petal in the act of unfolding; dewy, wavering, virginal, eager, blown by generous yet shy impulses, as timid as a leveret and as swift, as confiding as a doe peeping between the tree trunks, as light-foot as a dancer waiting in the wings, as soft and scented as a damask rose, as full of laughter as a fountain—yes, that was youth, hesitant as one upon an unknown threshold, yet ready to run her breast against a spear. The old woman looked closer; she saw the tender flesh, the fragile curves, the deep and glistening eyes, the untried mouth, the ringless hands; and, loving the girl that she had been, she

94

tried to catch some tone of her voice, but the girl remained silent, walking as though behind a wall of glass. She was alone. That meditative solitude seemed a part of her very essence. Whatever else might be in her head, it was certain that neither love, nor romance, nor any of the emotions usually ascribed to the young, were in it. If she dreamed, it was of no young Adam. And there again, thought Lady Slane, one should not wrong the young by circumscribing them with one sole set of notions, for youth is richer than that; youth is full of hopes reaching out, youth will burn the river and set all the belfries of the world ringing; there is not only love to be considered, there are also such things as fame and achievement and genius—which might be in one's heart, knocking against one's ribs, who knows? let us retire quickly to a turret, and see if the genius within one will not declare itself. But, dear me, thought Lady Slane, it was a poor lookout in eighteen-sixty for a girl to think of fame.

For Lady Slane was in the fortunate position of seeing into the heart of the girl who had been herself. She could mark not only the lingering step, the pause, the frowning brows, the prod of the parasol into the earth, the broken reflection quivering down into the waters of the lake; she could read also into the thoughts which accompanied this solitary ramble. She could make herself a party to their secrecy and their extravagance. For the thoughts which ran behind this delicate and maidenly exterior were of an extravagance to do credit even to a wild young man. They were thoughts of nothing less than escape and disguise; a changed name, a travestied sex, and freedom in some foreign city— schemes on a par with the schemes of a boy about to run away to sea. Those ringlets would drop beneath the scissors—and here a hand stole upward, as though prophetically to caress a shorn sleek head; that fichu would be replaced by a shirt—and here the fingers felt for the knot of a tie; those skirts would be kicked for ever aside—and here, very shyly this time, the hand dropped towards the opening of a trouser pocket. The image of the girl faded, and in its place stood a slender boy. He was a boy, but essentially he was a sexless creature, a mere symbol and emanation of youth, one who had forsworn for ever the delights and rights of sex to serve what seemed to his rioting imagination a nobler aim. Deborah, in short, at the age of seventeen, had determined to become a painter.

The sun, which had been warming her old bones and the peaches on the wall, crept westering behind a house so that she shivered slightly, and rising, dragged her chair forward on to the still sunlit grass. She would follow that bygone ambition from its dubious birth, through the months when it steadied and increased and coursed like blood through her, to the days when it languished and lost heart, for all her efforts to keep it alive. She saw it now for what it was: the only thing of value that had entered her life. Reality she had had in plenty, or what with other women passed for reality—but she could not go into those realities now, she must attach herself to that transcending reality for as long as she could hold it, it was so firm, it made her so happy even to remember how it had once sustained her; for she was not merely telling herself about it now, but feeling it again, right down in some deep place; it had the pervading nature of love while love is strong, unlike the cold recital of love in reminiscence. She burned again with the same ecstasy, the same exaltation. How fine it had been, to live in that state of rapture! how fine, how difficult, how supremely worth while! A nun in her novitiate was not more vigilant than she. Drawn tight as a firm wire, she had trembled then to a touch; she had been poised as a young god in the integrity of creation. Images clustered in her mind, but every image must be of a nature extravagantly lyrical. Nothing else would fit. A crimson cloak, a silver sword, were neither sumptuous enough nor pure enough to express the ardours of that temper. By God, she exclaimed, the young blood running again generously through her, that is a life worth living! The life of the artist, the creator, looking closely, feeling widely; detail and horizon included in the same sweep of the glance. And she remembered how the shadow on the wall was a greater delight to her than the thing itself, and how she had looked at a stormy sky, or at a tulip in the sun, and, narrowing her eyes, had forced those things into relation with everything that made a pattern in her mind.

So for months she had lived intensely, secretly, building herself in preparation, though she never laid brush to canvas, and only dreamed herself away into the far future. She could gauge the idleness of ordinary life by the sagging of her spirits whenever the flame momentarily burnt lower. Those glimpses of futility alarmed her beyond all reason. The flame had gone out, she thought in terror, every time it drooped; it would never revive; she must be left cold and unillumined. She could never learn that it would return, as the great garland of rhythm swept once more upwards and the light poured over her, warm as the reappearing sun, incandescent as a star, and on wings she rose again, steadying in their flight. It was thus a life of extremes that she lived, at one moment rapt, at another moment sunk in despondency. But of all this not one flicker mounted to the surface.

Some instinct, perhaps, warned her to impart her unsuitable secret to none, knowing very well that her parents, indulgent indeed, but limited, as was natural, would receive her declaration with a smile and a pat on the head, and an interchanged glance passing between themselves, saying as plainly as possible, 'That's our pretty bird! and the first personable young man who comes along will soon put these notions to rout.' Or, perhaps, it was merely the treasured privacy of the artist which kept her silent. She was as docile as could be. She would run errands in the house for her mother, strip the lavender into a great cloth,

97

make bags for it to lie between the sheets, write labels for the pots of jam, brush the pug, and fetch her cross-stitch after dinner without being bidden. Acquaintances envied her parents their eldest daughter. There were many who already had an eye on her as a wife for their son. But a thread of ambition was said to run through the modest and ordered household, a single thread, for Deborah's parents, arrived at middle age with their quiver-full of sons and daughters, preferred their easy rural domesticity to any worldly advantage, but for Deborah their aims were different: Deborah must be the wife of a good man, certainly, but if also the wife of a man to whose career she might be a help and an ornament—why, then, so much the better. Of this, naturally, nothing was said to Deborah. It would not do to turn the child's head.

Lady Slane rose again and drew her chair a little farther forward into the sun, for the shadow was beginning to creep, chilling her.

Her eldest brother had been away, she remembered; he was twenty-three; he had left home, as young men do; he had gone out into the world. She wondered sometimes what young men did, out in the world; she imagined them laughing and ruffling; going here and there, freely; striding home through the empty streets at dawn, or hailing a hansom and driving off to Richmond. They talked with strangers; they entered shops; they frequented the theatres. They had a club—several clubs. They were accosted by importunate women in the shadows, and could take their bodies for a night into their thoughtless embrace. Whatever they did, they did with a fine carelessness, a fine freedom, and when they came home they need give no account of their doings; moreover, there was an air of free-masonry among men, based upon their common liberty, very different from the freemasonry among women, which was always prying and personal and somehow a trifle obscene. But if the difference between her lot and her brother's occurred to Deborah, she said nothing of it. Beside the spaciousness of his opportunity and experience, she might justifiably feel a little cramped. If he, choosing to read for the Bar, were commended and applauded in his choice, why should she, choosing to be a painter, so shrink from announcing her decision that she was driven to secret and desperate plans for travesty and flight? There was surely a discrepancy somewhere. But everybody seemed agreed—so well agreed, that the matter was not even discussed: there was only one employment open to women.

The solidity of this agreement was brought home to Deborah from the moment that Mr. Holland led her to her mother from the lake. She had been a favourite child, but never had the rays of approval beaten down so warmly upon her. She was put in mind of those Italian pictures, showing heaven opened and the Eternal Father beaming down between golden rays like the sticks of a fan, so that one stretched out one's fingers to warm them at the glow of his benignity, as at the bars of a fire. So now with Deborah and her parents, not to mention the rest of her world, she was made to feel that in becoming engaged to Mr. Holland she had performed an act of exceeding though joyful virtue, had in fact done that which had always been expected of her; had fulfilled herself, besides giving enormous satisfaction to other people. She found herself suddenly surrounded by a host of assumptions. It was assumed that she trembled for joy in his presence, languished in his absence, existed solely (but humbly) for the furtherance of his ambitions, and thought him the most remarkable man alive, as she herself was the most favoured of women, a belief in which everybody was fondly prepared to indulge her. Such was the unanimity of these assumptions that she was almost persuaded into believing them true.

This was all very well, and for some days she allowed herself a little game of make-believe, imagining that she would be able to extricate herself without too much difficulty, for she was but eighteen, and it is pleasant to be praised, especially by those of whom one stands in affectionate awe; but presently she perceived that innumerable little strands like the thread of a spider were fastening themselves round her wrists and ankles, and that each one of them ran up to its other end in somebody's heart. There was her father's heart, and Mr. Holland's—whom she had learnt to call, but not very readily, Henry—and as for her mother's heart, that might have been a railway terminus, so many shining threads ran up into it out of sight—threads of pride and love and relief and maternal agitation and feminine welcome of fuss. Deborah stood there, bound and perplexed, and wondering what she should do next. Meanwhile, as she stood, feeling as silly as a May-queen with the streamers winding round her, she discerned upon the horizon people arriving with gifts, all converging upon her, as vassals bearing tribute: Henry with a ring—and the placing of it upon her finger was a real ceremony; her sisters with a dressing-bag they had clubbed together to buy; and then her mother with enough linen to rig a wind-jammer: table-cloths, dinner-napkins, towels (hand and bath), tea-cloths, kitchen rubbers, pantry cloths, dusters, and, of course, sheets, which when displayed proved to be double, and all embroidered with a monogram, not at first sight decipherable, but which on closer inspection Deborah disentangled into the letters D.H. After that, she was lost. She was lost into the foam and billows of silks, satins, poplins, and alpacas, while women knelt and crawled around her with their mouths full of pins, and she herself was made to stand, and turn, and bend her arm, and straighten it again, and was told to step out carefully, while the skirt made a ring on the floor, and was told that she must bear having her stays pulled a little tighter, for the lining had been cut a shade too small. It seemed to her then that she was always tired, and that people showed their love for her by making her more tired than she already was, by piling up her obligations and dancing round her until she knew not whether she stood still or spun round like a top; and time also seemed to have entered into the conspiracy, maliciously shortening the days, so that they rushed her along and were no more than a snowstorm of notes and tissue paper and of white roses that came every day from the florist by Henry's order. Yet all the time, as an undercurrent, the older women seemed to have a kind of secret among themselves, a reason for sage smiles and glances, a secret whereby something of Deborah's strength must be saved from this sweet turmoil and stored up for some greater demand that would be put upon her.

Indeed, these weeks before the wedding were dedicated wholly to the rites of a mysterious feminism. Never, Deborah thought, had she been surrounded by so many women. Matriarchy ruled. Men might have dwindled into insignificance on the planet. Even Henry himself did not count for much. (Yet he was there, terribly there, in the background; and thus, she thought, might a Theban mother have tired her daughter before sending her off to the Minotaur.) Women appeared from all quarters: aunts, cousins, friends, dressmakers, corsetières, milliners, and even a young French maid, whom Deborah was to have for her own, and who regarded her new mistress with wondering eyes, as one upon whom the gods had set their seal. In these rites Deborah—another assumption—was expected to play a most complicated part. She was expected to know what it was all about, and yet the core of the mystery was to remain hidden from her. She was to be the recipient of smiling congratulations, yet also she must be addressed as 'My little Deborah!' an exclamation from which she suspected that the adjective 'poor' was missing just by chance, and clipped in long embraces, almost valedictory in their benevolence. Oh, what a pother, she thought, women make about marriage! and yet who can blame

101

them, she added, when one recollects that marriage—and its consequences—is the only thing that women have to make a pother about in the whole of their lives? Though the excitement be vicarious, it will do just as well. Is it not for this function that they had been formed, dressed, bedizened, educated—if so one-sided an affair may be called education—safeguarded, kept in the dark, hinted at, segregated, repressed, all that at a given moment they may be delivered, or may deliver their daughters over, to Minister to a Man?

But how on earth she was going to minister to him, Deborah did not know. She knew only that she remained completely alien to all this fuss about the wonderful opportunity which was to be hers. She supposed that she was not in love with Henry, but, even had she been in love with him, she could see therein no reason for foregoing the whole of her own separate existence. Henry was in love with her, but no one proposed that he should forego his. On the contrary, it appeared that in acquiring her he was merely adding something extra to it. He would continue to lunch with his friends, travel down to his constituency, and spend his evenings at the House of Commons; he would continue to enjoy his free, varied, and masculine life, with no ring upon his finger or difference in his name to indicate the change in his estate; but whenever he felt inclined to come home she must be there, ready to lay down her book, her paper, or her letters; she must be prepared to listen to whatever he had to say; she must entertain his political acquaintances; and even if he beckoned her across the world she must follow. Well, she thought, that recalled Ruth and Boaz and was very pleasant for Henry. No doubt he would do his part by her, as he understood it. Sitting down by her, as her needle plucked in and out of her embroidery, he would gaze fondly at her bent head, and would say he was lucky to have such a pretty little wife to come back to. For all his grandeur as a Cabinet Minister, he would say it

102

like any middle-class or working-man husband. And she ought to look up, rewarded. For all his grandeur and desirability as Governor or Viceroy, he would disregard the blandishments of women ambitious for their husbands, beyond the necessary gallantries of social intercourse, and would be faithful to her, so that the green snake of jealousy would never slip across her path. He would advance in honours, and with a genuine pride would see a coronet appear on the head of the little black shadow which had doubled him for so many years. But where, in such a programme, was there room for a studio?

It would not do if Henry were to return one evening and be met by a locked door. It would not do if Henry, short of ink or blotting-paper, were to emerge irritably only to be told that Mrs. Holland was engaged with a model. It would not do if Henry were appointed governor to some distant colony, to tell him that the drawing-master unfortunately lived in London. It would not do, if Henry wanted another son, to tell him that she had just embarked on a special course of study. It would not do, in such a world of assumptions, to assume that she had equal rights with Henry. For such privileges marriage was not ordained.

But for certain privileges marriage had been ordained, and going to her bedroom Deborah took out her prayer-book and turned up the Marriage Service. It was ordained for the procreation of children—well, she knew that; one of her friends had told her, before she had time to stop her ears. It was ordained so that women might be loving and amiable, faithful and obedient to their husbands, holy and godly matrons in all quietness, sobriety, and peace. All this no doubt was, to a certain extent, parliamentary language. But still it bore a certain relation to fact. And still she asked, where, in this system, was there room for a studio?

Henry, always charming and courteous, and now very much

in love, smiled most indulgently when she finally brought herself to ask him if he would object to her painting after they were
married. Object! of course he would not object. He thought an
elegant accomplishment most becoming in a woman. 'I confess,' he said, 'that of all feminine accomplishments the piano is
my favourite, but since your talent lies in another direction, my
dearest, why then we'll make the best of it.' And he went on to
say how pleasant it would be for them both if she kept a record
of their travels, and mentioned something about water-colour
sketches in an album, which they could show their friends at
home. But when Deborah said that that was not quite what she
had in mind—she had thought of something more serious, she
said, though her heart was in her mouth as she said it—he had
smiled again, more fondly and indulgently than ever, and had
said there would be plenty of time to see about that, but for his
own part, he fancied that after marriage she would find plenty of
other occupations to help her pass the days.

Then, indeed, she felt trapped and wild. She knew very well
what he meant. She hated him for his Jovian detachment and
superiority, for his fond but nevertheless smug assumptions, for
his easy kindliness, and most of all for the impossibility of
blaming him. He was not to blame. He had only taken for
granted the things he was entitled to take for granted, thereby
ranging himself with the women and entering into the general
conspiracy to defraud her of her chosen life.

She was very childish, very tentative, very uncertain, very
unaware. But at least she did recognise that the conversation had
been momentous. She had her answer. She never referred to it
again.

Yet she was no feminist. She was too wise a woman to
indulge in such luxuries as an imagined martyrdom. The rift
between herself and life was not the rift between man and
woman, but the rift between the worker and the dreamer. That

she was a woman, and Henry a man, was really a matter of chance.
She would go no further than to acknowledge that the fact of her
being a woman made the situation a degree more difficult.

Lady Slane dragged her chair this time half-way down the little
garden. Genoux saw her from the windows and came out with a
rug, 'pour m'assurer que miladi ne prendra pas froid. Que dirait ce
pauvre milord, s'il pensait que miladi prenait froid? Lui, qui
toujours avait tant de soin de miladi!'

Yes, she had married Henry, and Henry had always been
extremely solicitous that she should not catch cold. He had taken
the greatest possible care of her; she might say with truth that she
had always led a sheltered life. (But was that what she had
wanted?) Whether in England, or in Africa, or in Australia, or in
India, Henry had always seen to it that she had the least possible
amount of trouble. Perhaps that was his way of compensating her
for the independence she had foregone for his sake. Perhaps
Henry—an odd thought!—had realised more than his convenience would ever allow him to admit. Perhaps he had consciously
or unconsciously tried to smother her longings under a pack of
rugs and cushions, like putting a broken heart to sleep on a feather
bed. She had always been surrounded by servants, secretaries, and
aides-de-camp, fulfilling the function of those little fenders
which prevent a ship from bumping too roughly against the quay.
Usually, indeed, they had exceeded their duties, from sheer devotion to Lady Slane, from a sheer wish to protect and spare her,
who was so gentle, so plucky, so self-effacing, and so feminine.
Her fragility aroused the chivalry of men, her modesty precluded
the antagonism of women, her spirit awoke the respect of both.
And as for Henry himself, though he liked to dally with pretty and
sycophantic women, bending over them in a way which often
gave Lady Slane a pang, he had never thought another woman in
the world worthy to compare.

Wrapped in the rug which in a sense had been put round her

knees by Henry, she wondered now how close had ever been the communion between them? The coldness with which she was now able to estimate their relationship frightened her a little, yet it took her back in some curious way to the days when she plotted to elude her parents and consecrate herself to an existence which, although conventionally reprehensible, should, essentially, be dedicated to the most severe and difficult integrity. *Then*, she had been face to face with life, and that had seemed a reason for a necessity for the clearest thinking; *now*, she was face to face with death, and that again seemed a reason for the truest possible estimate of values, without evasion. The middle period alone had been confused.

Confused. Other people would not think it confused. Other people would point to their marriage as a perfect marriage; to herself and Henry, severally, as the perfect wife and husband. They would say that neither had ever 'looked at' anybody else. They would envy them, as the partners in an honourable career and the founders of a satisfactory and promising dynasty. They would commiserate now with her in being left alone; but they would reflect that, after all, an old woman of eighty-eight who had had her life was not so much to be pitied, and might spend her remaining years in looking forward to the day when her husband—young once more, garlanded with flowers, and robed in some kind of night-gown—would stand waiting to greet her on the Other Side. They would say she had been happy.

But what was happiness? Had she been happy? That was a strange, clicking word to have coined—meaning something definite to the whole English-speaking race—a strange clicking word with its short vowel and its spitting double p's, and its pert tip-tilted y at the end, to express in two syllables a whole summary of life. Happy. But one was happy at one moment, unhappy two minutes later, and neither for any good reason; so what did it mean? It meant, if it meant anything at all, that

106

some uneasy desire wanted black to be black, and white, white; it meant that in the jungle of the terrors of life, the tiny creeping creatures sought reassurance in a formula. Certainly, there had been moments of which one could say: *Then*, I was happy; and with greater certainty: *Then*, I was unhappy—when little Robert had lain in his coffin, for instance, strewn with rose-petals by his sobbing Syrian nurse—but whole regions had intervened, which were just existence. Absurd to ask of those, had she been happy or unhappy? It seemed merely as though someone were asking a question about someone that was not herself, clothing the question in a word that bore no relation to the shifting, elusive, iridescent play of life; trying to do something impossible, in fact, like compressing the waters of a lake into a tight, hard ball. Life was that lake, thought Lady Slane, sitting under the warm south wall amid the smell of the peaches; a lake offering its even surface to many reflections, gilded by the sun, silvered by the moon, darkened by a cloud, roughened by a ripple; but level always, a plane, keeping its bounds, not to be rolled up into a tight, hard ball, small enough to be held in the hand, which was what people were trying to do when they asked if one's life had been happy or unhappy.

No, that was not the question to ask her—not the question to ask anybody. Things were not so simple as all that. Had they asked her whether she had loved her husband, she could have answered without hesitation: yes, she had loved him. There had been no moments when she could differentiate and say: *Then*, at such a moment, I loved him; and again, *Then*, at such another, I loved him not. The stress had been constant. Her love for him had been a straight black line drawn right through her life. It had hurt her, it had damaged her, it had diminished her, but she had been unable to curve away from it. All the parts of her that were not Henry Holland's had pulled in opposition, yet by this single giant of love they had all been pulled over, as the weaker

107

team in a tug-of-war. Her ambitions, her secret existence, all had given way. She had loved him so much, that even her resentment was subdued. She could not grudge him even the sacrifice he had imposed upon her. Yet she was not one of those women whose gladness in sacrifice is such that the sacrifice ceases to be a sacrifice. Her own youthful visions had been incompatible with such a love, and in giving them up she knew that she gave up something of incomparable value. That was what she had done for Henry Holland, and Henry Holland had never known it.

At last, she could see him and herself in retrospect; more precious than that, she could bear to examine him without disloyalty. She could bear to shed the frenzied loyalty of the past. Not that the anguish of her love had faded from her memory. She could still remember the days when she had prayed for the safety and happiness of Henry Holland, superstitiously, to a God in whom she had never wholly believed. Childish and ardent, the words of her prayer had grown, fitting themselves to her necessity. 'O Lord,' she had prayed nightly, 'take care of my beloved Henry, make him happy, keep him safe, O Lord, from all dangers, whether of illness or accident, preserve him for me who love him better than anything in heaven or earth.' Thus she had prayed; and as she prayed, every night, the words renewed their sharpness; whenever she whispered 'safe from all dangers, whether of illness or accident,' she had seen Henry knocked down by a dray, Henry breathing in pneumonia, as though either disaster were actually present; and when she whispered 'me who love him better than anything in heaven or earth,' she had undergone the nightly anxiety of wondering whether the inclusion of heaven were not blasphemous and might not offend a jealous God, for surely it was fringing on blasphemy to flaunt Henry as dearer to her than anything in earth or heaven—which involved God Himself, the very God she would propitiate—a

108

blasphemy which might strike deeper than her intended appeal? Yet she persisted in her prayer, for it was strictly up against the truth. Henry was dearer, far dearer, to her than anything else in heaven or earth. He had decoyed her even into holding him dearer than her own ambition. She could not say otherwise, to a God who (if He existed at all) would certainly know her heart whether she whispered it out in prayer or not. Therefore, she might as well give herself the nightly luxury of whispering the truth, heard of God, she hoped; unheard, she hoped, of Henry Holland. It was a comfort to her. After her prayer, she could sleep, having ensured safety for Henry for at least twenty-four hours, the limit she set upon the efficacy of her prayer. And Henry Holland, she remembered, had been a difficult and dangerous treasure to preserve, even with the support of secret intercession. His career had been so active, so detached from the sheltered life of her petitions! She, who would have chosen for him the methodical existence of a Dutch bulb-grower, a mynheer concerned with nothing more disturbing than the fertilisation of a new tulip, while the doves in their wicker cage cooed and spread their wings in the sun, she had seen him always in a processional life, threatened by bombs, riding on an elephant through Indian cities, shut away from her by ceremony or business; and when physical danger was temporarily suspended in some safe capital, London, Paris, or Washington—when, great servant of the State, he found employment at home or travelled abroad on some peaceful mission—then other demands were made upon her watchfulness: she must be swift to detect his need for reassurance when a momentary discouragement overcame him; when, mooning, he strayed up to her and drooped over her chair, saying nothing, but waiting (as she knew) for some soft protection to come from her and fold itself around him like a cloak, yet it must all be done without a word directly spoken; she must restore his belief that the

109

obstructiveness of his Government or the opposition of his rivals was due to their short-sightedness or envy, and to no deficiency within himself, yet must not allow him to know that she guessed at his mood of self-mistrust or the whole fabric of her comfort would be undone. And when she had accomplished this feat, this reconstruction of extreme delicacy and extreme solidity—when he left her, to go back strengthened to his business—then, with her hands lying limp, symbol of her exhaustion, and a sweet emptiness within her, as though her self had drained away to flow into the veins of another person—then, sinking, drowning, she wondered whether she had not secretly touched the heights of rapture.

Yet even this, the statement of her love and the recollection of its more subtle demands, failed to satisfy her in its broad simplification. The statement that she had loved, though indisputable, still admitted of infinite complexity. Who was the she, the 'I,' that had loved? And Henry, who and what was he? A physical presence, threatened by time and death, and therefore the dearer for that factual menace? Or was his physical presence merely the palpable projection, the symbol, of something which might justly be called himself? Hidden away under the symbol of their corporeality, both in him and in her, doubtless lurked something which was themselves. But that self was hard to get at; obscured by the too familiar trappings of voice, name, appearance, occupation, circumstance, even the fleeting perception of self became blunted or confused. And there were many selves. She could never be the same self with him as when she was alone; and even that solitary self which she pursued, shifted, changed, melted away as she approached it, she could never drive it into a dark corner, and there, like a robber in the night, hold it by the throat against the wall, the hard core of self chased into a blind alley or refuge. The very words which clothed her thoughts were but another falsification; no word could stand

110

alone, like a column of stone or the trunk of a tree, but must riot instantly into a tropical tangle of associations; the fact, it seemed, was as elusive and as luxuriant as the self. Only in a wordless trance did any true apprehension become possible, a wordless trance of sheer feeling, an extra-physical state, in which nothing but the tingling of the finger-tips recalled the existence of the body, and a series of images floated across the mind, un-named, unrelated to language. That state, she supposed, was the state in which she approached most closely to the self concealed within her, but it was a state having nothing to do with Henry. Was this why she had welcomed, as the next best thing, the love which by its very pain gave her the illusion of contact?

She was, after all, a woman. Thwarted as an artist, was it perhaps possible to find fulfilment in other ways? Was there, after all, some foundation for the prevalent belief that woman should minister to man? Had the generations been right, the personal struggle wrong? Was there something beautiful, something active, something creative even, in her apparent submission to Henry? Could she not balance herself upon the tight-rope of her relationship with him, as dangerously and precariously as in the act of creating a picture? Was it not possible to see the tones and half-tones of her life with him as she might have seen the blue and violet shadows of a landscape; and so set them in relation and ordain their values, that she thereby forced them into beauty? Was not this also an achievement of the sort peculiarly suited to women? of the sort, indeed, which women alone could compass; a privilege, a prerogative, not to be despised? All the woman in her answered, yes! All the artist in her countered, no!

And then again, were not women in their new Protestant spirit defrauding the world of some poor remnant of enchantment, some illusion, foolish perhaps, but lovely? This time the woman and artist in her alike answered, yes.

111

She remembered a young couple she had known—the man a secretary at the Paris Embassy; very young they were—receiving her visits, as their ambassadress, with suitable reverence. She knew that they loved her, but at the same time she always felt her visits to be an intrusion. She divined them to be so much in love that they must grudge any half-hour filched from their allowance of years together. And she, for her part, counted her visits to them as an agony, yet she was drawn towards them partly from affection, partly from a desire to martyrise herself by the sight of their union. 'Male and female created he them,' she said to herself always, coming away. Sometimes, coming away, she felt herself to be so falsely placed in relation to Henry that the burden of life became too heavy, and she wished she might die. It was no phrase: she really wished it. She was too honest not to suffer under the burden of such falsity. She longed at times for a relationship as simple, as natural, and as right as the relationship between those two very uninteresting but engaging young people. She envied Alec as he stood before the fire jingling the coins in his pocket and looking down on his wife curled into a corner of the sofa. She envied Madge her unquestioning acceptance of everything that Alec said or did. Yet in the midst of her envy something offended her: this intolerably masculine lordliness, this abject feminine submission.

Where, then, lay the truth? Henry by the compulsion of love had cheated her of her chosen life, yet had given her another life, an ample life, a life in touch with the greater world, if that took her fancy; or a life, alternatively, pressed close up against her own nursery. For a life of her own, he had substituted his life with its interests, or the lives of her children with their potentialities. He assumed that she might sink herself in either, if not in both, with equal joy. It had never occurred to him that she might prefer simply to be herself.

A part of her had acquiesced. She remembered acquiescing in

the assumption that she should project herself into the lives of her children, especially her sons, as though their entities were of far greater importance than her own, and she herself but the vehicle of their creation and the shelter of their vulnerable years. She remembered the birth of Kay. She had wanted to call him Kay, because just before his birth she had been reading Malory. Up till then, her sons had succeeded automatically to the family names—Herbert, Charles, Robert, William—but over the fifth son, for some reason, her wishes were consulted, and when she suggested Kay as a name Henry did not protest. He had been in a good humour and had said, 'Have it your own way.' She remembered that even in her weakness she had thought Henry generous. Looking down into the crumpled red face of her new baby—though crumpled red faces had become quite usual to her by then, at the sixth repetition—she had realised the responsibility of launching the little creature labelled by a name not of its own choosing, like launching a battleship, only instead of turrets and decks and guns she had to do with the miraculous tissue of flesh and brain. Was it fair to call a child Kay? A name, a label, exerted an unseen though continuous pressure. People were said to grow up in accordance with their names. But Kay, at any rate, had not grown up unduly romantic, though certainly he could not be said to resemble his brothers or elder sister.

Yet of all her children, Kay and Edith had alone inherited something of their mother—Kay with his astrolabes, Edith with her muddles. Carrie, characteristically, had given her least trouble; Carrie had managed her own way into the world. Herbert, as the eldest son, had arrived in pomp and with difficulty. William had been a mean, silent baby, with small eyes; greedy, too, as though determined to squeeze all the provision of her breast even as, to-day, he and Lavinia, his fitting mate, were determined to squeeze all their advantage from the local dairy.

113

Charles had arrived protesting, even as he protested to-day, only at that time he knew nothing of War Offices. Edith had had to be beaten into drawing her first breath; she had been able to manage life no better at its beginning than at its end. The fact remained that in Kay and Edith alone she divined an unexpressed sympathy. All the rest were Henry's children, with his energy just gone wrong. Yet when her children were babies—small, prone things, or things so young and feeble that one could sit them up in safety only by supporting their insecure heads—she, trying to compensate herself for her foregone independence, had made an effort to look forward from the day when the skull over the pulse which so terrifyingly and openly throbbed should have closed up, when their hold on life would no longer be so alarmingly precarious, when she would no longer be afraid of their drawing their last breath even as she bent over their cradle in the absence of the nurse. She had tried to look forward to the day when they would develop characters of their own; when they would hold opinions different from their parents', when they would make plans and arrangements for themselves. Even in this, she had been suppressed, thwarted. 'How amused we shall be,' she had said to Henry as they stood together looking down on Herbert netted in his cot, 'when he starts writing us letters from school.' Henry had not liked that remark; she divined his criticism instantly. Henry thought that all real women ought to prefer their children helpless, and to deplore the day when they would begin to grow up. Long-clothes should be preferable to smocks; smocks to knickers; knickers to trousers. Henry had definite, masculine ideas about women and motherhood. Although secretly proud of his rising little sons, he pretended even to himself that they were, so far, entirely their mother's concern. So, naturally, she had endeavoured to adopt those views. Herbert, at two years old, had been deposed in favour of Carrie; Carrie, at a year, in favour of Charles. Because

114

it was expected of her, the baby had always been officially her
darling. But none of these things had held any truth in them.
She had always been aware that the self of her children was as far
removed from her as the self of Henry, or, indeed, her own.

Shocking, unnatural thoughts had floated into her mind. 'If
only I had never married . . . if only I had never had any
children.' Yet she loved Henry—to the point of agony—and she
loved her children—to the point of sentimentality. She wove
theories about them, which she confided to Henry in moments
of privacy and expansion. Herbert would be a statesman, she
said, for had he not questioned her (at the age of twelve) about
problems of native government? And Kay, aged four, had asked
to be taken to see the Taj Mahal. Henry had indulged her in
these fancies, not seeing that she was, in fact, indulging him.

But all this had been as nothing compared with Henry's
ambitions which drove her down a path hedged with thorns.
Everything in Henry's conceptions of the world had run counter
to her own grain. Realist and idealist, they represented the
extreme opposites of their points of view, with the difference
that whereas Henry need make no bones about his creed, she
must protect hers from shame and ridicule. Yet there, again,
confusion swathed her. There were moments when she could
enter into the excitement of the great game that Henry was
always playing; moments when the private, specialised, intense,
and lovely existence of the artist—whose practice had been
denied her, but after whose ideal of life she still miserably and
imaginatively hankered—seemed a poor and selfish and over-
delicate thing compared with the masculine business of empire
and politics and the strife of men. There were moments when
she could understand not only with her brain but with her
sensibility, that Henry should crave for a life of action even as she
herself craved for a life of contemplation. They were indeed two
halves of one dissevered world.

Part Three

This Life we live is dead for all its breath;
Death's self it is, set off on pilgrimage,
Travelling with tottering steps the first short stage.
                                    CHRISTINA ROSSETTI

Summer over, the October days were no longer warm enough
for Lady Slane to sit in the garden. In order to get her airing she
must go for a little walk, loaded with cloaks and furs by
Genoux, who accompanied her to the front door to make sure
that she did not discard any of her wrappings in the hall on the
way. Lady Slane sometimes protested, as Genoux dragged one
garment after another from the cupboard. 'But, Genoux, you
are making me look like an old bundle.' Genoux, hanging the
last cloak firmly round her shoulders, replied, 'Miladi est
bien trop distinguée pour avoir jamais l'air d'un vieux
bundle.' 'Do you remember, Genoux,' said Lady Slane, drawing on her gloves, 'how you always wanted me to wear woollen
stockings for dinner?' It was indeed true. Genoux in cold
weather had never been willing to put out silk stockings with
her mistress's evening dress; or if she put them, after many
remonstrances, she hopefully put also a woollen pair to wear
underneath. 'Mais pourquoi pas, miladi?' said Genoux sensibly;

'dans ce temps-là les dames, même les jeunes dames, portaient les jupes convenablement longues, et un jupon par dessus le marché. Pourquoi s'enrhumer, pour des chevilles qui n'y paraissent pas? C'était la même histoire pour les combinaisons que miladi voulait à tout prix ôter pour le dîner, précisément au soir lorsqu'il fait plus froid.' She accompanied Lady Slane downstairs, talking in this strain, for all her volubility had been released since quitting Elm Park Gardens and the household of English servants with their cold discreet ways. She hovered and clucked over Lady Slane, half-scolding, half-cherishing. 'Miladi n'a jamais su se soigner. Elle ferait beaucoup mieux d'écouter sa vieille Genoux. Les premiers jours d'octobre, c'est tout ce qu'il y a de plus malin. Ça vous attrape sans crier gare. A l'âge de miladi on ne doit pas prendre de libertés.' 'Don't bury me till you need, Genoux,' said Lady Slane, escaping from her Anglicisms and pessimism alike.

She went down the steps carefully, for there had been a frost and they might be slippery. Genoux would watch her out of sight, she knew, so at the corner she must turn round to wave. Genoux would be hurt if she forgot to turn round. Yet by the gesture she would not be reassured; she would not be happy again until she had readmitted the muffled figure of the old lady to the safety of the house; drawn her in, taken off her boots, brought her slippers and perhaps a cup of hot soup, carried away her wraps, and left her to her book beside the sitting-room fire. Yet Genoux, for all her adages and croakings, was a gay and philosophical old soul, full of wisdom of the sturdy peasant kind. (She waved back to Lady Slane as Lady Slane after dutifully looking round turned the corner and pursued her way slowly towards the Heath.) Now she would go back to the kitchen and talk to the cat while she busied herself with her pots and pans. Lady Slane frequently heard her talking to the cat, 'Viens, mon bo-bo,' she would say; 'nice dinner, look, that's all for you,'—for she had an idea that English animals understood English only, and once, hearing the jackals bark round Gul-a-hek, had remarked to Lady Slane, 'C'est drôle tout de même, miladi, comme on entend tout de suite que ce ne sont pas des Anglais.' Well, it was a gentle life they led now, she and Genoux, thought Lady Slane making her way slowly up the hill towards the Heath; she and Genoux, living in such undisturbed intimacy, bound by the ties respectively of gratitude and devotion, bound also by the tie of their unspoken speculation as to which would be taken from the other first. Whenever the front door shut behind one of their rare visitors, each was conscious of a certain relief at the departure of intruders. The routine of their daily life was all they wanted—all, indeed, that they had strength for. Effort tired them both, though they had never admitted it to one another.

Fortunately, the intruders came but seldom. Lady Slane's children had come first, in rotation, as a duty, but most of them indicated to their mother so clearly the extreme inconvenience of coming as far as Hampstead that she felt justified in begging them to spare themselves the trouble, and except at intervals they took her at her word. Lady Slane was quite shrewd enough to imagine what they said to one another to appease their consciences: 'Well, we *asked* Mother to make her home with us. . . .' Edith alone had shown some disposition to come frequently and, as she called it, help. But Edith was now living in such a state of bliss in her own flat, that she had been easily able to decide that her mother didn't really want her. Kay she had not seen for some time. Last time he came, he had said after a great deal of shuffling and embarrassment that a friend of his, old FitzGeorge, wanted to be brought to call upon her. 'I think,' said Kay, poking the fire, 'that he said he had met you in India.' 'In India?' said Lady Slane vaguely. 'It's quite possible, dear, but

119

I don't remember the name. So many people came, you see. We were often twenty to luncheon. Could you put him off, do you think, Kay? I don't want to be rude, but somehow I seem to have lost my taste for strangers.'

Kay longed to ask his mother what Fitz had meant by saying he had seen him in his cradle. He had in fact come up to Hampstead determined to clear up this mystery. But, of course, he went away without asking.

No great-grandchildren. They were forbidden. The grandchildren did not count; they were insignificant as the middle distance. But the great-grandchildren, who were not insignificant, but might be disturbing, were forbidden. Lady Slane had adhered to that, with the strange firmness sometimes and suddenly displayed by the most docile people. Mr. Bucktrout was the only regular visitor, coming once a week to tea, on Tuesdays. But she was not tired by Mr. Bucktrout; they would sit on either side of the fire, not lighting the lamps, while Mr. Bucktrout's conversation ran on like a purling brook, and Lady Slane listened or not, as she felt inclined.

Meanwhile, it was very beautiful, up on the Heath, with the brown trees and the blue distance. Lady Slane sat down on a bench and rested. Little boys were flying kites; they ran dragging the string across the turf, till like an ungainly bird the kite rose trailing its untidy tail across the sky. Lady Slane remembered other little boys flying kites in China. Her foreign memories and her English present played at *chassé-croisé* often now in her mind, mingling and superimposing, making her wonder sometimes whether her memory were not becoming a little confused, so immediate and simultaneous did both impressions appear. Was she on a hillside near Pekin with Henry, a groom walking their horses up and down at a respectful distance; or was she alone, old, and dressed in black, resting on a bench on Hampstead Heath? But there were the chimney-pots of London to steady her. No doubt about it, these little boys were Cockneys in rags, not celestial urchins in blue cotton; and her own limbs, as she shifted her position a little on the hard bench, gave her a rheumatic tweak bearing no relation to her young and physical well-being as she cantered up the scorched hillside with Henry. She tried, in a dim and groping way, to revive the sensation of that well-being. She found it impossible. A dutiful inner voice summoned from the past as some old melody might float unseizable into the outskirts of recollection, reproduced for her in words the facts of that sensation without awakening any response in her dulled old body. In vain she now told herself that once she had woken up on a summer morning longing to spring from her bed and to run out for sheer exuberance of spirit into the air. In vain she tried, and most deliberately, to renew the sharpness of waiting for the moment when—their official life suspended—she would turn in the darkness into Henry's arms. It was all words now, without reality. The only things which touched reality were the routine of her life with Genoux; the tiny interests of that life—the tradesmen's ring at the back door, the arrival of a parcel of books from Mudie's, the consultation as to Mr. Bucktrout's Tuesday tea, should they buy muffins or crumpets? the agitation over an announced visit from Carrie; and then the growth of her bodily ailments, for which she was beginning to feel quite an affection. Her body had, in fact, become her companion, a constant resource and preoccupation; all the small squalors of the body, known only to oneself, insignificant in youth, easily dismissed, in old age became dominant and entered into fulfilment of the tyranny they had always threatened. Yet it was, rather than otherwise, an agreeable and interesting tyranny. A hint of lumbago caused her to rise cautiously from her chair and reminded her of the day she had ricked her back at Nervi, since when her back had never been very reliable. The small intimacies of her

121

teeth were known to her, so that she ate carefully, biting on one side rather than on the other. She instinctively crooked one finger—the third on the left hand—to save it from the pang of neuritis. An in-growing toe-nail obliged Genoux to use the shoe-horn with the greatest precaution. And all these parts of the body became intensely personal: my back, my tooth, my finger, my toe; and Genoux, again, was the only person who knew exactly what she meant by a sudden exclamation as she fell back into her chair, the bond between herself and Genoux thereby strengthening to the pitch of the bond between lovers, of an exclusive physical intimacy. Of such small things was her life now made: of communion with Genoux, of interest in her own disintegrating body, of Mr. Bucktrout's courtesy and weekly visits, of her pleasure in the frosty morning and the little boys flying kites on the Heath; even of her anxiety about slipping upon a frozen doorstep, for the bones of the aged, she knew, were brittle. All tiny things, contemptibly tiny things, ennobled only by their vast back-ground, the background of Death. Certain Italian paintings depicted trees—poplar, willow, alder—each leaf separate, and sharp, and veined, against a green translucent sky. Of such a quality were the tiny things, the shapely leaves, of her present life: redeemed from insignificance by their juxtaposition with a luminous eternity.

She felt exalted, she escaped from an obvious pettiness, from a finicking life, whenever she remembered that no adventure could now befall her except the supreme adventure for which all other adventures were but a preparation.

She miscalculated, however, forgetting that life's surprises were inexhaustible, even up to the end. On re-entering her house that afternoon she found a man's hat of peculiar square shape reposing upon the hall table, and Genoux in a state of excitement greeted her with a whisper: 'Miladi! il y a un monsieur . . . je lui ai dit que miladi était sortie, mais c'est un

122

monsieur qui n'écoute pas . . . il attend miladi au salon.
Faut-il servir le thé?—Miladi ôtera bien ses souliers,
de peur qu'ils ne soient humides?'

Lady Slane looked back upon her meeting with Mr. FitzGeorge.
So did Mr. FitzGeorge look back upon his meeting with Lady
Slane. Having waited long enough, and vainly, for Kay to bring
him, he had taken the law into his own hands and had come by
himself. Miserly in spite of his millions, he had travelled up to
Hampstead by Underground; had walked from the station; had
paused before Lady Slane's house, and with the eye of a connoisseur had appreciated its Georgian dignity. 'Ah,' he had said
with satisfaction, 'the house of a woman of taste.' He soon
discovered his error, for, having over-ridden Genoux's objec-
tions and pushed his way into the hall, he found that Lady Slane
had no taste at all. Perversely, this delighted him the more. The
room into which Genoux reluctantly showed him was simple
and comfortable. 'Arm-chairs and chintz, and the light in the
right place,' he muttered, wandering about. He was extra-
ordinarily moved at the prospect of seeing Lady Slane again. But
when she came it was obvious that she did not remember him in
the least. She greeted him politely, with a return to the viceregal
manner; apologised for her absence, asked him to sit down; said
that Kay had mentioned his name; said that tea would come in a
minute; but was manifestly puzzled as to what errand had
brought him. Perhaps she wondered whether he wished to write
her husband's life? Mr. FitzGeorge, as this reflection struck
him, cackled suddenly, and, to his hostess, inexplicably. He
could scarcely explain at once that the Vicereine and not the
Viceroy had touched his imagination, more than half a century
ago, at Calcutta.

As it was, he was compelled to explain that, as a young man,
he had come with letters of introduction to Government House

and had perfunctorily been asked to dinner. Mr. FitzGeorge, however, was not embarrassed; he was too genuinely detached from such social conventions. He accounted for himself quite simply and without evasions. 'You see,' he said, 'I was a name-less young man, to whom an unknown father had left a large fortune, with the wish that I should travel round the world. I was naturally delighted to avail myself of such an opportunity. It is always pleasant to gratify wishes which coincide with one's own. The solicitors, who were also my guardians,' he added dryly, 'commended my promptitude in complying with the wish expressed in the will. In their view, old dotards mould-ering in Lincoln's Inn, a young man who would desert London for the far East at his father's suggestion was a filial young man indeed. I suppose they thought the stage-doors of Shaftesbury Avenue a greater attraction than the bazaars of Canton. Well, they erred. Half the treasures of my collection to-day, Lady Slane, I owe to that journey round the world sixty years ago.'

It was clear that Lady Slane had never heard of his collection. She said as much. He was delighted, much as he had been delighted when he discovered that she had no taste.

'Capital, Lady Slane! My collection is, I suppose, at least twice as valuable as that of Eumorphopoulos, and twice as famous—though, I may add, I have paid a hundredth part of its present value for it. And, unlike most experts, I have never lost sight of beauty. Rarity, curiosity, antiquity are not enough for me. I must have beauty or, at any rate, craftmanship. And I have been justified. There is no piece in my collection to-day which any museum would not despoil its best show-case to possess.'

Lady Slane, knowing nothing of such things, was amused by such innocently childish boastfulness. She egged him on, this naïf old magpie, this collector of beautiful objects, who had suddenly made his way into her house, and now sat by her fire, bragging, forgetting that dinner-party at Calcutta and his friendship with Kay, which alone could have justified his intrusion. He had for her, from the first moment, the charm of a completely detached and isolated figure. The very fact that he had no known parents and no legitimate name, but was purely and simply himself, invested him with a certain legendary charm in her eyes. She had had enough, in her life, of people whose worldly status was their passport to admission. Mr. FitzGeorge had no such passport; even his wealth could scarcely be considered a passport, for his reputation as a miser instantly destroyed the hopes of the most sanguine seeker after benefit. Curiously enough, Lady Slane was not offended by his avarice as she was offended by it in her own son William. William and Lavinia were furtively avaricious; they couldn't help being stingy, since parsimony ran in their blood—she remembered thinking when they became engaged that that was the real link between them—but they were not frank about it, they tried to cover it up. Mr. FitzGeorge indulged his weakness on the grander scale, making no bones about it. Lady Slane liked people who, if they had vices, were not ashamed of them. She despised all hypocritical disguises. So when Mr. FitzGeorge told her that he hated parting with money, could only be induced to do so when irresistibly tempted by beauty, and could console himself only by the lure of a bargain, she frankly laughed and frankly gave him her respect. He looked at her across the fire. His coat, she observed, was shabby. 'I remember,' he said, 'that you laughed at me in Calcutta.'

He seemed to remember a great many things about Calcutta. 'Lady Slane,' he said, fencing, when she taxed him with his excellent memory, 'have you not yet noticed that youthful memories sharpen with advancing age?' That little 'yet' made her laugh again: he was playing the part of a man pretending to a woman that she still retained her youth. She was eighty-eight, but the man-to-woman mainspring still coiled like a cobra

125

between them. Innumerable years had elapsed since she had felt that stimulus; it came as an unexpected revival, a flicker, a farewell, stirring her strangely and awaking some echo whose melody she could not quite recapture. Had she really seen FitzGeorge before, or did his slight and old-fashioned gallantry awaken only the general memory of years when all men had looked at her with admiration in their eyes? Whichever it was, his presence disquieted her, though she could not pretend that her faint agitation was anything but pleasant, and he had looked at her, too, in such a way as to suggest that he could provide her with the explanation if he would. All the evening, after he had gone, she sat gazing into the fire, her book neglected, wondering, trying to remember, trying to put her hand on something that remained tantalisingly just round the corner, just out of reach. Something had knocked against her as the clapper might knock against a cracked old bell in a disused steeple. No music travelled out over the valleys, but within the steeple itself a tingling vibration arose, disturbing the starlings in their nests and causing the cobwebs to quiver.

Next morning she, of course, derided her evening mood. What queer freak of sentimentality had caught her? For two hours she had been as dreamy as a girl! It was FitzGeorge's fault for entering her house in that way, for sitting down beside her fire as though he had some right to be there, for talking about the past, for teasing her gently about her dignity as the young Vicereine, for looking at her as though he were saying only half of what he would say later on, for being slightly mocking, slightly gallant, wholly admiring, and, secretly, moved. Although he had preserved a surface manner, she knew that his visit had not been without import to him. She wondered whether he would come again.

If the gentleman returned, said Genoux, was he to be admitted? Next time she would be prepared for him; he should not brush her aside as though she were yesterday's newspaper and walk straight into the hall, laying his funny little hat on the table. 'Ah, mon Dieu, miladi, quel drôle de chapeau!' She doubled herself up, rubbing her hands down her thighs as she laughed. Lady Slane loved Genoux's whole-hearted enjoyment of anything that struck her as funny. In response, she permitted herself a smile at Mr. FitzGeorge's hat. Where did he get such hats? asked Genoux; car jamais je n'ai vu un pareil chapeau en devanture. Did he have them made purposely for himself alone? And his muffler—had her ladyship seen it? All checks, like a stud-groom. 'C'est un original,' Genoux concluded sagely; but, unlike an English servant, she was not interested merely in making fun of Mr. FitzGeorge. She wanted to know more about him. It was pathetic, she said, to be like that—un vieux monsieur, and all alone. Had he never been married? He did not look as though he had been married. She followed Lady Slane about, eager for the information Lady Slane was unable to provide. He had made a good tea, said Genoux; she had noticed the shabbiness of his coat, assuming an excessive poverty: 'J'ai vite couru au coin de la rue, attraper l'homme aux muffins;' and was noticeably disappointed when Lady Slane told her rather dryly that Mr. FitzGeorge, to the best of her knowledge, was a millionaire. 'Un milliardaire! et s'affubler comme ça!' Genoux could not get over it. But what was the long and short of it to be? she asked. Was she to let him in next time, or was she not?

Lady Slane said she did not suppose Mr. FitzGeorge would come again, but even as she said it she detected herself in a lie, for as he took his leave, Mr. FitzGeorge had kept her hand and had asked for permission to return. Why should she lie to Genoux? 'Yes, let him in,' she said, moving away towards her sitting-room.

There were three of them now, three old gentlemen—Mr. Bucktrout, Mr. Gosheron, and Mr. FitzGeorge. A funny trio—

127

an agent, a builder, and a connoisseur! all old, all eccentric, and all unworldly. How oddly it had come about, that the whole of her life should have fallen away from her—her activities, her children, and Henry—and should have been so completely replaced in this little interlude before the end by a new existence so satisfyingly populated! She supposed that she herself was responsible for its creation, but could not imagine how she had done it. 'Perhaps,' she said aloud, 'one always gets what one wants in the end.' And taking down an old book, she opened it at random and read:

> Cease of your oaths, cease of your great swearing,
> Cease of your pomp, cease of your vainglory,
> Cease of your hate, cease of your blaspheming,
> Cease of your malice, cease of your envy,
> Cease of your wrath, cease of your lechery,
> Cease of your fraud, cease your deception,
> Cease of your tongues making detraction.

It was surely remarkable that someone should have expressed her longing in—she looked at the date—1493?

She read the next verse:

> Flee faint falsehood, fickle, foul, and fell,
> Flee fatal flatterers, full of fairness,
> Flee fair feigning, fables of favell,
> Flee folks' fellowship, frequenting falseness,
> Flee frantic facers fulfilled of frowardness,
> Flee fools' fallacies, flee fond fantasies,
> Flee from fresh babblers, feigning flatteries.

She had fled them all, except the fond fantasies; her three old gentlemen were fond fantasies—fond fantasticks, she amended, smiling. As for pomp, vainglory, and tongues making detraction, they were things that never crossed her threshold now

128

except when Carrie brought them in on a gust of chilly air. Then she caught herself up for so readily adopting Mr. Fitz-George and adding him to her intimates: what reason had she to suppose, beyond a phrase spoken in parting civility, that he would ever come again?

He came again, and she heard Genoux welcoming him as an old friend in the hall. Yes, her ladyship was in; yes, her ladyship had said she would be delighted to receive monsieur at any time. Lady Slane listened, wishing that Genoux would not be quite so hospitable on her behalf. She was not at all sure, now, that she liked her privacy being laid open to invasion by Mr. FitzGeorge. She must ask Kay to drop him a hint.

Meanwhile she received him, rising in her soft black draperies and giving him her hand with the smile he remembered. Why should she not? After all, they were two old people, very old people, so old that they were all the time age-conscious, and being so old it was agreeable to sit like two cats on either side of the fire warming their bones, stretching out hands so transparent as to let the pink light of the flames through them, while their conversation without effort rose or fell. Lady Slane, all her life long, had made people feel that they could talk if they liked, but need not talk if disinclined—one of the reasons why Henry Holland had first decided to marry her. Having a fund of quietness within herself, she could understand that other people also enjoyed being quiet. Few women, Henry Holland said, could be quiet without being dull, and fewer women could talk without being a bore; but then Henry Holland, although he enjoyed women, had a low opinion of them and was satisfied by none except his own wife. FitzGeorge with really remarkable shrewdness had diagnosed this in Calcutta where the Viceroy, heaven knows, had been sufficiently surrounded by pretty and animated women all flatteringly deluded by the apparently close and exclusive attention he accorded to each one in turn.

129

Thank goodness, thought Mr. FitzGeorge, she has no taste. He was sick to death of women who prided themselves on their taste, and thereby assumed an understanding with him as a connoisseur. There was no relation between the two things— between 'decoration' and real beauty. His works of art belonged to a different world from the skilful interiors of women of taste. He looked almost tenderly at Lady Slane's pink shaded lamps and Turkey rug. If one wanted beauty, one had only to rest one's eyes on her, so fine and old and lovely, like an ivory carving; flowing down like water into her chair, so slight and supple were her limbs, the firelight casting a flush of rose over her features and snowy hair. Youth had no beauty like the beauty of an old face; the face of youth was an unwritten page. Youth could never sit as still as that, in absolute repose, as though all haste, all movement, were over and done with, and nothing left but waiting and acquiescence. He was glad that he had never seen her in the middle years, so that he might keep untarnished his memory of her when she was young, lively, and full of fire, completing it with this present vision of her, having arrived at the other end of the story. The same woman, but he himself in ignorance of what had happened in between.

He became aware that he had not spoken for quite five minutes. Lady Slane appeared to have forgotten him. Yet she was not asleep, for she was looking quietly into the fire, her hands lying loose in their usual attitude, and her foot resting on the fender. He was surprised that she should accept him so naturally. 'But we are old,' he thought, 'and our perceptions are muted. She takes it for granted that I should sit here as though I had known her all my life. Lady Slane,' he said aloud, 'I don't believe you took much pleasure in your viceroyalty?'

His voice was always rather harsh and sardonic, and even in her company he made no attempt to soften it. He disregarded and despised mankind so much that he seldom spoke without a sneer. Kay was his only friend, but even Kay got the rough side of his tongue oftener than the smooth.

Lady Slane stiffened, out of a reviving loyalty to Henry. 'Even viceroyalty has its uses, Mr. FitzGeorge.'

'But not for such as you,' Mr. FitzGeorge said, unrepentant. 'Do you know,' he said, leaning forward, 'I was really upset by seeing you trapped among those mummers. You submitted and did your part—oh, admirably!—but all the time you were denying your nature. I remember waiting for you and Lord Slane to appear before dinner; we were assembled in some big drawing-room, thirty of us, I daresay, people wearing jewels and uniforms, all standing about feeling more or less foolish on an immense expanse of carpet. I remember there was a huge chandelier all lit up with candles; it tinkled whenever anybody walked overhead. I wondered whether it was your footstep that made it tinkle. And then a great folding-door was thrown open and you came in with the Viceroy, and all the women curtsied. After dinner you both came round the circle of your guests, saying something to each; you wore white, with diamonds in your hair, and you asked me if I hoped to get any big-game shooting. I suppose you thought that was the right thing to say to a rich young man; you couldn't know that I abominated the idea of killing animals. I said no, I was just a traveller; but although you smiled attentively I don't believe you listened to my answer. You were thinking what you should say to the next person, and no doubt you said something just as well composed and just as inappropriate. It was the Viceroy, not you, who suggested that I should accompany you on your trip.'

'On our trip?' said Lady Slane, amazed.

'You know that easy amiable way he had of throwing out suggestions? Half the time one knew that he didn't mean what he said, and that he never expected one to act upon it. One was expected to bow and say, Thank you so much, that would be delightful, and then never to refer to it again. He would say, China? yes, I am going to China next week; very interesting country, China; you ought to come with me. But he would have been very much surprised if one had taken him at his word, though I daresay that with his perfect manners he would have concealed his surprise. Now, Lady Slane, isn't it true?'

Without waiting to hear whether it were true, he went on. 'But on this one occasion somebody did take him at his word. I did. He said, You're an antiquarian, FitzGeorge—antiquarian for him was a vague term—you're an antiquarian, he said, and you're in no hurry. Why don't you come with us to Fatihpur Sikhri?'

The broken puzzle in Lady Slane's mind shook itself suddenly down into shape. The half-heard notes reassembled themselves into their tune. She stood again on the terrace of the deserted Indian city looking across the brown landscape where puffs of rising dust marked at intervals the road to Agra. She leant her arms upon the warm parapet and slowly twirled her parasol. She twirled it because she was slightly ill at ease. She and the young man beside her were isolated from the rest of the world. The Viceroy was away from them, inspecting the mother-of-pearl mosque, accompanied by a group of officials in white uniforms and sun-helmets; he was pointing with his stick, and saying that the ring-doves ought to be cleared away from under the eaves. The young man beside Lady Slane said softly that it was a pity the ring-doves should be condemned, for if a city were abandoned by man, why should the doves not inherit it? The doves, the monkeys, and the parrots, he went on, as a flight of jade-green parakeets swept past them, quarrelling in the air; look at their green plumage against these damask walls, he added, raising his head, as the flock swirled round again like a handful of emeralds blown across the Poet's House. There was something unusual, he said, in a city of mosques, palaces, and courts,

132

inhabited solely by birds and animals; he would like to see a tiger going up Akbar's steps, and a cobra coiling its length neatly in the council chamber. They would be more becoming, he thought, to the red city than men in boots and solar topees. Lady Slane, keeping an ear pricked to observe the movements of the Viceroy and his group, had smiled at his fancies and had said that Mr. FitzGeorge was a romantic.

Mr. FitzGeorge. The name came back to her now. It was not surprising that, among so many thousands of names, she should have forgotten it. But she remembered it now, as she remembered the look he had given her when she twitted him. It was more than a look; it was a moment that he created, while he held her eyes and filled them with all the implications he dared not, or would not, speak. She had felt as though she stood naked before him.

'Yes,' he said, watching her across the fire at Hampstead; 'you were right: I *was* a romantic.'

She was startled to hear him thus audibly joining up with her recollections; the moment, then, had possessed equal significance, equal intensity, for him as for her? Its significance had indeed troubled her, and, for a while, made her more uneasy than she would acknowledge. Her loyalty to Henry was impeccable; but after the departure of FitzGeorge, that stray young traveller whose name her consciousness had scarcely registered, she had felt as though someone had exploded a charge of dynamite in her most secret cellar. Someone by a look had discovered the way into a chamber she kept hidden even from herself. He had committed the supreme audacity of looking into her soul.

'It was queer, wasn't it?' he said, still watching her.

'And after you left us at Agra,' said Lady Slane conversationally, unwilling to admit that he had shaken her, 'what did you do?'

'I went up into Cashmir,' said Mr. FitzGeorge, leaning back

133

in his chair and putting his fingertips together; 'I went up the river for a fortnight in a houseboat. I had plenty of time to think, and while I gazed over lakes of pink lotus I thought of a young woman in a white dress, so dutiful, so admirably trained, and so wild at heart. I used to flatter myself that for a minute I had come close to her, and then I remembered how after one glance she had turned away and had sauntered off towards her husband. But whether she did it because she was frightened, or because she intended to rebuke me, I could never decide. Perhaps both.'

'If she was frightened,' said Lady Slane, surprising both herself and FitzGeorge, 'it was of herself, not of you.'

'I didn't flatter myself it was of me,' said Mr. FitzGeorge; 'I knew even then that I had no charm for women, especially for lovely, eminent young women like yourself. I didn't desire it,' he said, looking at her as defiantly as his rather absurd old-maidish appearance would allow.

'Of course you didn't,' said Lady Slane, respecting this flicker of a thwarted pride.

'No,' said Mr. FitzGeorge, relapsing appeased; 'I didn't. And yet, you know,' he added, stung by some recollection to a fresh honesty, 'although I had never fallen in love with a woman before, and never have since, I fell in love with you at Fatihpur Sikhri. I suppose I really fell in love with you at that ridiculous dinner-party at Calcutta. Otherwise I should not have come to Fatihpur Sikhri. It took me out of my way, and I have never gone out of my way for man, woman, or child. I am the complete egoist, Lady Slane; you had better know it. Nothing but a work of art could tempt me out of my way. In China, where I went after Cashmir, I was so intoxicated by the works of art that I soon forgot you.'

This strange, incivil, and retarded love-making created a medley of feelings in Lady Slane. It offended her loyalty to Henry. It disturbed her old-age peacefulness. It revived the

134

perplexities of her youth. It shocked her slightly, and pleased her more than it shocked. It was the very last thing she had ever expected—she whose days were now made up of retrospect and of only one anticipation. It was as though Mr. FitzGeorge had arrived with deliberate and malicious purpose to do violence to her settled mood.

'But even in China,' Mr. FitzGeorge went on, 'I still found leisure to think of you and Lord Slane. You seemed to me ill-assorted, as one might say of biscuits, only with biscuits one always assumes that it is the other way round. By saying that you were ill-assorted I don't mean to imply that you did not do your job admirably. You did. So admirably, that it awoke my suspicions. What would you have done with your life, Lady Slane, had you not married that very delightful and disconcerting charlatan?'

'Charlatan, Mr. FitzGeorge?'

'Oh no, of course he wasn't altogether a charlatan,' said Mr. FitzGeorge; 'on the contrary, he managed to be an undisastrous Prime Minister of England during five (I am told) difficult years. Nearly all years, incidentally, are difficult. Perhaps I misjudge him. But you will admit that he was handicapped. He had more charm than any man I ever knew; and though charm pays up to a certain point, there comes a point beyond which no reasonable man can be expected to go. He went beyond it—far beyond. He was too good to be true. You yourself, Lady Slane, must often have suffered from his charm?'

The question was proffered in such a way that Lady Slane nearly replied to it truthfully and inadvertently. Mr. FitzGeorge seemed really interested; and yet, she remembered, she had often watched Henry bending his brows in interest over some human question which could not really interest him at all, withdrawn as he was into a world where human interests shrank to insignificance, and nothing but a cold, sardonic ambition lay

135

at the kernel of his mind, and if so Henry, then why not Mr. FitzGeorge? The one was a statesman, the other a connoisseur; she did not want to be examined as though she were a Tang figure which might possibly turn out to be a fake. Observation of Henry had taught her a lesson she would not easily forget. It had been terrible to live with, and to love, a being so charming, so deceptive, and so chill. Henry, she discovered suddenly, had been a very masculine man; masculinity, in spite of his charm and his culture, was the keynote of his character. He was of the world worldly, for all his scorn.

'I should have been a painter,' said Lady Slane, answering the question before last.

'Ah!' said Mr. FitzGeorge with the relief of a man who has at last secured what he wanted. 'Thank you. That gives me the key. So you were an artist, were you, potentially? But being a woman, that had to go by the board. I see. Now I understand why you sometimes looked so tragic when your face was in repose. I remember looking at you and thinking, That is a woman whose heart is broken.'

'My dear Mr. FitzGeorge!' cried Lady Slane. 'You really mustn't talk as though my life had been a tragedy. I had everything that most women would covet: position, comfort, children, and a husband I loved. I had nothing to complain of—nothing.'

'Except that you were defrauded of the one thing that mattered. Nothing matters to an artist except the fulfilment of his gift. You know that as well as I do. Frustrated, he grows crooked like a tree twisted into an unnatural shape. All meaning goes out of life, and life becomes existence—a makeshift. Face it, Lady Slane. Your children, your husband, your splendour, were nothing but obstacles that kept you from yourself. They were what you chose to substitute for your real vocation. You were too young, I suppose, to know any better, but when you chose that life you sinned against the light.'

Lady Slane put her hand over her eyes. She was no longer strong enough to bear this shock of denouncement. Mr. Fitz-George, suddenly inspired like a preacher, had overturned her placidity without any pity.

'Yes,' she said weakly, 'I know you are right.'

'Of course I am right. Old Fitz may be a comic figure, but he retains some sense of values, and I see that you have offended against one of the first canons of my creed. No wonder that I scold.'

'Don't scold me any more,' said Lady Slane, looking up and smiling; 'I assure you that if I did wrong, I paid for it. But you mustn't blame my husband.'

'I don't. According to his lights, he gave you all you could desire. He merely killed you, that's all. Men do kill women. Most women enjoy being killed; so I am told. Being a woman, I daresay that even you took a certain pleasure in the process. And now, are you angry with me?'

'No,' said Lady Slane; 'I think it is rather a relief to have been found out.'

'Of course you realise that I found you out at Fatihpur Sikhri? Not in detail, certainly, but in principle. This conversation is only a sequel to the conversation we didn't have then.'

Shaken though she was, Lady Slane laughed frankly. She felt immensely grateful to the outrageous Mr. FitzGeorge, who, now that he had ceased to scold her, sat looking at her with humour and affection.

'A conversation interrupted for fifty years,' she said.

'And now never to be resumed,' he said with surprising tact, knowing that she might dread a repeated probing of his lancet into her discovered wound; 'but there are some things which need to be said—this was one of them. Now we can be friends.'

*　　*　　*

137

Having thus arranged their friendship, Mr. FitzGeorge took it quite for granted that she should welcome his company. He arrived without warning, installed himself in what rapidly became his own chair, teased Genoux who adored him, carried on extravagant discussions with Mr. Bucktrout, imposed his habits on the house, but nevertheless fitted himself neatly in to Lady Slane's ways of life. He even accompanied her on her slow and shaky walks up to the Heath. Her capes, and his square hat, became familiar objects moving under the wintry trees. They wandered tremulously together, often sitting down on a bench, not admitting to one another that they were tired, but pretending that they desired to admire the view. When they had admired it long enough to feel rested, they agreed to get up and go a little farther. Thus they revived memories of Constable, and even visited Keats' house, that little white box of strain and tragedy marooned among the dark green laurels. Like ghosts themselves, they murmured of the ghost of Fanny Brawne and of the passion which had wrecked Keats; and all the while, just out of reach, round the corner, lurked the passion for Lady Slane which might have wrecked Mr. FitzGeorge, had he not been so wary an egoist (unlike poor Keats), just too wise to let himself float away on a hopeless love for the young Vicereine, just unwise enough to remain remotely faithful for fifty years.

Up on the Heath one day he recalled her to an incident she had forgotten.

'Do you remember,' he said—those three opening words having become so familiar to them that now they smiled whenever they used them—'that the day after that dinner-party I came back to luncheon?'

'Dinner-party?' said Lady Slane vaguely, for her mind no longer worked very quickly. 'What dinner-party?'

'At Calcutta,' he said gently, for he never grew impatient

138

when she had to be prompted. 'The Viceroy asked me back to luncheon when I had accepted to meet you at Fatihpur Sikhri. He said, we must arrange the details. I arrived rather early, and found you alone. Not quite alone, though. Kay was with you.'

'Kay?' said Lady Slane. 'Oh, but surely Kay wasn't born then.'

'He was two months old. You had him in the room with you, in his crib. Don't you remember? You were rather embarrassed at being found with your baby by a strange young man. But you got over your embarrassment at once—I remember admiring the simplicity of your manners—and asked me to look at him. You held back the curtain of his crib, and for your sake I did give one glance at the horrid little object, but what I really looked at was your hand holding back the curtain. It was as white as the muslin, and stained only with the colour of your rings.'

'These rings,' said Lady Slane, touching the bumps under her black gloves.

'If you say so. I once told Kay I had seen him in his cradle,' said Mr. FitzGeorge, chuckling. 'I had been saving up that joke against him for years. I startled him, I can tell you. But I gave him no explanation. To this day he doesn't know. Unless he asked you?'

'No,' said Lady Slane, 'he never asked me. And if he had asked me I shouldn't have been able to tell him.'

'No; one forgets, one forgets,' said Mr. FitzGeorge, staring out over the Heath. 'Yet there are some things one never forgets. I remember your hand on the curtain, and I remember your expression as you looked down on that nasty little new thing which has grown up into Kay. I remember the twisted feeling it gave me, to have stumbled into your intimacy. It didn't last long. You rang the bell, and a nurse came and removed Kay complete with his furniture.'

'Are you fond of Kay?' asked Lady Slane.

139

'Fond?' said Mr. FitzGeorge, astonished. 'Well—I'm used to him. Yes, I suppose you might say I was fond. We understand each other well enough to let each other alone. We're used to each other—put it like that. At our age, anything else would be a nuisance.'

Fondness, indeed, seemed a remote thing even to Lady Slane. She was fond of Mr. FitzGeorge, she supposed, and of Genoux, and of Mr. Bucktrout, and in a less degree of Mr. Gosheron, but it was a fondness out of which all the trouble and the agitation had departed. Even as the vitality had departed out of her old body. All emotion now was a twilight thing. She could say no more than that it was pleasant to stroll and sit on the Heath with Mr. FitzGeorge while he evoked memories of a day whose light, even through those veils, flared up too strongly for her faded eyes.

Even so, Mr. FitzGeorge had not told Lady Slane the whole of the truth. He had not reminded her that when he came that day and found her alone with Kay in his cradle in a corner of the room, he had also found her kneeling on the floor surrounded by a mass of flowers. To his idea, fresh from England, the season was winter; yet, cut from an Indian garden, roses, larkspurs, and sweet-peas lay sorted into heaps around her. Transparent glasses filled with water made points of light as they stood about all over the carpet. She had looked up at him, the unexpected visitor, catching her at an employment improbable in a Vicereine. Secretaries or gardeners should have fulfilled this function with which she preferred to deal herself. Her fingers dripping, she had looked up, pushing the hair out of her eyes. But she had pushed something else out of her eyes with the same gesture; she had pushed her whole private life out of them, and had replaced it by the perfunctory courtesy with which she rose, and, giving him her hand, wiping it first on a duster, said, 'Oh,

140

Mr. FitzGeorge,'—she had known his name then, temporarily
—'do forgive me, I had no idea it was so late.'

Down in St. James's Street, Mr. FitzGeorge's frequent absences
were noticed. Kay Holland himself observed that Fitz was now
less readily available for dinner than formerly, though the
explanation lay beyond the wildest range of his suspicion. Far
from coming near to the truth, he was full of an undeserved
solicitude for his old friend, wondering whether perhaps fatigue
or even ill-health compelled him to betake himself early to bed;
but on so ceremonious a basis had their relationship always been
placed that Kay could venture on no inquiries. He was acqu-
ainted with Mr. FitzGeorge's rooms and could form some idea
of how the old gentleman lived; could, in fact, imagine him
shuffling about in a dressing-gown and slippers among the disorder of his incomparable works of art, dissolving a soup-tablet for
his supper over the gas-ring, economising the electric light so
that one bulb alone illuminated the small Jaeger-clad figure and
touched the gilding on the stacked-up frames—or did he resort
to a candle-end stuck into a bottle? Kay was sure that Mr.
FitzGeorge did not allow himself enough to eat, nor could it be
very healthy to live among so much dust in the low, over-
crowded rooms where a daily charwoman was permitted only
the minimum of service. How Fitz himself contrived to emerge
presentably spruce and well-groomed from this sordid confusion
was a mystery to Kay, who spent a great deal of his time in
keeping his own surroundings as shiningly clean as possible. No
spinster, in fact, could be more house-proud than Kay Holland
supervising his annual spring-cleaning; washing, with his shirt-
sleeves rolled up, the more fragile of his treasures with his own
hands in a basin of water. But old Fitz! Kay supposed that those
two rooms had never been turned out since Fitz had moved into
them, untold years ago; a magpie's nest under the eaves of

141

Bernard Street, filled with the accumulation carried in, piece by piece; dumped on a chair or on the floor when the chairs gave out, stuffed into a drawer, crowded into a cupboard that would no longer shut; never touched, never dusted, except when Mr. FitzGeorge consenting to reveal his masterpieces to a visitor would blow the grimy coating away and hold picture, bronze, or carving up to the light.

And now Fitz was seldom to be seen. When he did walk into the Club, he seemed the same as usual and Kay's misgivings dwindled; if anything, he seemed a little more lively than before, abusing Kay with greater gusto, a twinkle in his eye as though he were enjoying a secret joke. Which indeed he was. Kay sat there, warmed and happy. No one had ever made fun of him as FitzGeorge made fun. But although Kay longed to revert to that conversation about having been seen in his cradle, shyness and habit forbade.

Fitz, however, had ceased asking to be introduced to Lady Slane, much to Kay's relief. He had been sure that his mother would not at all welcome the advent of a stranger in her retirement at Hampstead. He flattered himself, indeed, on his perception in this matter and on the skill he had shown in staving old Fitz off. Yet from time to time he felt a qualm: had he perhaps been rather unkindly firm in discouraging Fitz's one attempt at a new friendship? It must have cost Fitz a great effort to make the suggestion; an even greater effort to renew it. Still, his first duty was to his mother. Neither Carrie, nor Herbert, nor Charles could understand their mother's desire for retirement; but he, Kay, could understand it. It was, therefore, his duty to protect his mother in her desire. He had protected her—though he was usually overawed by Fitz—and thanks to his evasiveness Fitz had apparently forgotten all about his whim. Kay thought that he must go and see his mother one of these days and tell her how clever he had been.

142

He kept on putting off the expedition, however, for the January weather was bitterly cold, and Kay, who loved warmth and snugness as much as a cat, easily persuaded himself that draughty Underground stations were no place for a coddled person of his advancing years. Well wrapped up in overcoat and muffler, he could just undertake the walk from his rooms in the Temple across Fountain Court, through pigeons too fat to get out of his way, down the steps to the Embankment, up Northumberland Avenue and then through the Park to St. James's Street, his daily constitutional, but farther abroad than that he would not venture. He walked, not only for the sake of exercise, but because he had a lively sense of the presence of microbes in all public conveyances; a microbe to him was a horror even greater than a reptile; he seldom got through the day without imagining himself the victim of at least one deadly disease, and never drank a cup of tea without remembering thankfully that the water had been boiled into immunity. As it was, he welcomed a day of rain or sleet which gave him a pretext for remaining indoors. He quieted his conscience by writing little friendly notes to his mother, saying that he had had a cold, that he understood a great deal of influenza was about, and that he hoped Genoux was taking proper care of her. All the same, he thought, on the first fine day he must go to Hampstead and tell his mother about FitzGeorge. She would be amused. She would be grateful.

But Kay, like many a wiser man, deferred his plan just a little too long. He had forgotten Mr. FitzGeorge's twenty-five years of seniority. Eighty-one was not an age which permitted the playing of tricks with time. At twenty, thirty, forty, fifty, sixty, one might reasonably say, I will put that off until next summer—though, to be sure, even at twenty, the unexpected perils of life were always present—but at eighty-one such deferments became a mere taunt in the face of Fate. That which had been an unexpected and improbable peril in earlier years, swelled to a certainty after eighty. Kay's standards were perhaps distorted by the longevity of his own family. Certainly FitzGeorge's death came to him as a shock which he received with incredulity and resentment.

The first indication he had of it appeared on the posters: DEATH OF WEST-END CLUB-MAN. He registered this piece of news unconsciously as he walked down the Embankment and turned up Northumberland Avenue on his way to luncheon; it meant no more to him than the news of an omnibus mounting the pavement in Brixton. A little farther on he saw other posters, lunch edition: LONELY MILLIONAIRE DIES IN WEST-END. If the thought of FitzGeorge crossed his mind, he dismissed it; for Bernard Street, even by a journalist, could scarcely be described as West End. Kay had no experience of Fleet Street. Still, he bought a paper. He crossed the Park, noticing that the crocuses were beginning to show green noses above the ground. Thus had he walked a thousand times. Serene, he turned into Boodle's and ordered his bottle of Vichy water, unfolded his napkin, propped the *Evening Standard* before him, and started on his lunch—a cut from the joint, and pickles. He had no need to tell the waiter what he wanted, so regular and recurrent was daily life. There it was, in the second column on the front page: WEST-END CLUB-MAN FOUND DEAD: STRANGE LIFE-STORY OF WEALTHY RECLUSE REVEALED. (Even then, it occurred to Kay to wonder how one could be both a club-man and a recluse.) Then the name hit him: Mr. FitzGeorge. . . .

He put down his knife and fork with a clatter on his plate so that the other lunchers, who had wondered at Kay Holland's impassivity, raised their heads and whispered: 'Ah, he's heard!' Heard, when they meant read. But indeed with some justice they might say heard, since the printed name had screamed at Kay loud enough to deafen him. He felt as though someone had fetched him a box on the ear. 'Fitz dead?' he said to the man at the next table—a man he did not know, except by sight for the last twenty years, and to whom he had been accustomed to nod.

Then without knowing how he got there, except for some dim recollection of plunging into his pockets to pay the taxi, he found himself in Bernard Street, climbing the stairs to Fitz's rooms. The door into Fitz's rooms was broken in—smashed—splintered—and the police were there, two large young men, pompous and apologetic, very civil and accommodating to Kay when they learnt his name. Fitz was there too, lying on his bed in his Jaeger dressing-gown, curiously stiff. On the table were a sardine and a half, and a half-eaten piece of toast and the remains of a boiled egg, as unappetising as only the cold remains of a boiled egg can be. Fitz wore a night-cap, which was a surprise to Kay, a night-cap with a sideways tassel. He looked much the same as he had looked in life, except that he looked completely different. It was hard to say where the difference came in; the rigidity could scarcely account for it; perhaps it might be attributed to the guilty sense of eavesdropping on old Fitz, of catching him transfixed in a moment hitherto unseen by all eyes, the slippered moment, the night-cap moment, the moment when the three last sardines had been taken from the cupboard. 'We mustn't remove him, sir,' said one of the young policemen, on the watch lest Kay should go too near and touch his friend, 'before the doctors is entirely satisfied.'

Kay shrank towards the window, contrasting this death with that of his own father. They had indeed chosen very different paths in life. Fitz had scorned the world, he had lived secretly and privately, finding his pleasures within himself, betraying himself to none. Only once had Kay seen him roused, when some newspaper published an article on the eccentrics of London. 'God!' he had said, 'is it eccentric to keep oneself apart?' He had been enraged by the inclusion of his own name. He could see no reason for the curiosity commonly displayed by

145

people over other people; it seemed to him vulgar, boring, and unnecessary. All he asked was to be let alone; he had no desire to interfere in the workings of the world; he simply wanted to live withdrawn into his chosen world, absorbed in his possessions and their beauty. That was his form of spirituality, his form of contemplation. Thus the loneliness of his death held no pathos, since it was in accordance with what he had chosen.

But it worried the agents of the law and the State. They invaded his room, while Kay stood wretchedly by the window fingering the grimy curtains. This gentleman, they said, looking at the stiff and silent figure, had been extremely wealthy; in fact, it was reported that his fortune had run into seven numbers. And although they were accustomed to deal with the lonely death of paupers, no precedent told them how to deal with the lonely death of a millionaire. He must have had *some* relatives, they said, looking at Kay as though Kay were to blame. But Kay said no; so far as he knew, Mr. FitzGeorge had no relatives at all; no link with anyone on earth. 'Stay,' he added, 'the South Kensington Museum might be able to tell you something about him.'

At that the Inspector guffawed, and then put his hand over his mouth, remembering that he was in a death-chamber. A museum! he said; well, that was a pretty dreary source of information to go to about a man after he was dead. The Inspector doubtless had a comfortable wife, rows of rowdy children, and pots of red geranium on the window-sill. As a matter of fact, he said, Mr. Holland wasn't so far off the mark when he mentioned the Museum. But for the Museum, he, the Inspector, and his subordinates wouldn't be there at all. The presence of the police was most irregular, where there was no suggestion of murder or suicide. Only, thanks to the Museum ringing up Scotland Yard in what the Inspector described as a 'state,' had Scotland Yard sent police to Bernard Street to keep watch over valuable objects which might turn out to be a legacy to the nation. Much as the Inspector manifestly despised the objects, he responded with instant appreciation to the word valuable. But couldn't Mr. Holland suggest anything a bit more human than a museum? Mr. Holland couldn't. He suggested feebly that they might look Mr. FitzGeorge up in *Who's Who*.

Well, said the Inspector, getting out a note-book and settling down to business, who was his father, anyway? Keep those reporters out, he added angrily to his two subordinates. He never had a father, said Kay, feeling like a netted rabbit and wishing that he had never come near Bernard Street to be bullied by the officials of the law. He had, moreover, a suspicion that the Inspector was exceeding his duties in the interest of his curiosity by thus inquiring into the antecedents of the dead millionaire.

The Inspector stared, and a joke dawned in his eyes, but because of his self-importance he suppressed it. 'His mother, then?' he said, implying that although a man might have dispensed with a father he could scarcely dispense with a mother. But Kay had passed beyond the region of such implications; he could see FitzGeorge only as an isolated figure, fighting to maintain its independence. 'He never had a mother either,' he replied.

'Then what *did* he have?' asked the Inspector, glancing at his subordinates with an expression that summed Kay up in the sole word, Balmy.

Kay was tempted to reply, A private life; for he felt a little light-headed, and the discrepancy between FitzGeorge and the Inspector, with all that the Inspector stood for, was almost too much for him; but he compromised, and pointing to the jumble of works of art cluttering the room, said, 'These.'

'That's not enough,' said the Inspector.

'It was enough for him,' said Kay.

'That junk?' said the Inspector. Kay was silent.

One of the policemen came forward and whispered, showing the Inspector a card. 'All right,' said the Inspector after looking at the card; 'let him in.'

'There's a lot of reporters on the landing, sir, as well.'

'Keep them out, I told you.'

'They say they only want a peep at the room, sir.'

'Well, they can't have it. Tell them there's nothing to see.'

'Very good, sir.'

'Only a lot of junk.'

'Very good, sir.'

'Show in the gentleman from the Museum. Nobody else. It seems,' said the Inspector, turning to Kay, 'that we were right about this here Museum. Here it is, turning up as it might be an uncle of the corpse. Prompt.' He passed the card over to Kay, who read: 'Mr. Christopher Foljambe, Victoria and Albert Museum.'

A young man in a bowler-hat, a blue overcoat, kid-gloves, and horn-rimmed spectacles came in. He cast one glance at Mr. FitzGeorge and then averted his eyes, which roamed instead over the litter in the room, appraising, while he talked to the Inspector. His attitude, however, differed from the Inspector's, for every now and then his eye would light up and his hand would start out in an involuntary predatory movement towards some dusty but invaluable pile on chair or table. He had, more-over, greeted Kay Holland with deference, thereby increasing Kay's prestige in the Inspector's estimation. A museum, after all, was a public institution, authorised in a very practical (although meagre) way by Government subsidy; and that was the kind of thing which commanded, one might almost say bought, the Inspector's respect. He treated Mr. Foljambe with more deference than he had shown to Kay Holland. For in Kay Holland he had not recognised an ex-Prime Minister's son, whereas Mr. Foljambe had sent in a card definitely stating: 'Victoria and Albert Museum.'

Mr. Foljambe, to do him justice, was ill-at-ease. He had been dispatched by his superiors in a hurry to see that old Fitz's things were duly safeguarded. The Museum, thanks to hints thrown out by old Fitz during the past forty years, considered that they might reasonably expect to have a claim on his possible legacies. Kay Holland, again retreating to the window and again fingering the grimy curtains, gave to both the Inspector and to Mr. Foljambe the credit due to them. The Inspector had a duty to fulfil; and Mr. Foljambe had been dispatched by his museum on an uncongenial job. Old Fitz's delight in a new discovery, old Fitz's grumpy and restrained rapture over some lovely object, belonged to a different world than this practical protection of a dead man, than this interest in the dead man's dispositions. Kay knew just enough of the world to realise that it must be so. Even on behalf of his friend, he could feel no real irony. The Inspector and Mr. Foljambe were both acting according to their lights. And Mr. Foljambe, especially, was being very decent about it.

'Of course, I know we have no right to interfere,' he was saying, 'but considering the immense value of the collection, and considering the fact that Mr. FitzGeorge always gave us to understand that he would bequeath the majority of his possessions to the nation, my museum felt that some adequate steps should be taken for the safeguarding of the property. I was instructed to say that if you would like one of our men to take charge, he would be at your disposal.'

'Did I understand you to say, sir, that the collection was of immense value?'

'It runs into millions, I should say,' replied Mr. Foljambe with relish.

'Well . . .' said the Inspector. 'I don't know anything about such things myself. The room looks to me like a pawnbroker's

149

shop. But if you say so, sir, I must take your word for it. The gentleman,' he jerked his thumb at Mr. FitzGeorge, 'appears to have had no family?'

'None that I ever heard of.'

'Very unusual, sir. Very unusual for such a wealthy man.'

'Solicitors?' suggested Mr. Foljambe.

'No firm has come forward as yet, sir. Yet the news was in the lunch edition of the papers; true, there's no telephone here,' said the Inspector, looking round in disgust. 'They'd have to come in person.'

'Mr. FitzGeorge was a retiring sort of man.'

'So I understand, sir—a real solitary, you might say. Can't understand it myself; I like a bit of company. All right up here, sir?' asked the Inspector, tapping his forehead.

'A bit eccentric perhaps; nothing more.'

'You would expect a gentleman of his sort to be a J.P., or something, wouldn't you, sir? To have some public work, I mean—hospital committees, or something.'

'I don't think Mr. FitzGeorge was very publicly minded,' said Mr. Foljambe in such a tone that Kay could not decide whether he was being sympathetic or censorious. 'And yet,' he added, 'I oughtn't to say that about a man who can leave such a priceless collection to the nation.'

'You don't know for sure that he has,' said the Inspector.

Mr. Foljambe shrugged. 'His hints were pretty clear. And if he hasn't left it to the nation, who could he leave it to? Unless he's left it all to you, Mr. Holland,' he said, turning to Kay, pleased by his own joke.

But Mr. FitzGeorge had left his collection neither to the nation nor to Kay Holland. He had left it all, including the whole of his fortune, to Lady Slane. The will was written on a half-sheet of paper, but it was perfectly lucid, perfectly in order, duly witnessed, and left no loophole for other interpretation. It revoked a previous will, by which the fortune went to charity and the collection to be divided between various museums and the National and Tate Galleries. It stated expressly that Lady Slane's possession was to be absolute, and that no obligation was imposed on her as to the ultimate disposal.

This news was made public amid general consternation. The rage and dismay of the museums were equalled only by the astonishment and delight of Lady Slane's own family, which gathered at once and in force round Carrie's tea-table. Carrie was in the strong and enviable position of having seen her mother that very afternoon; she had, in fact, rushed straight up to Hampstead. 'Dear Mother,' she said, 'I couldn't leave her alone with that great responsibility thrust upon her. You know how little fitted she is to deal with that kind of thing.' 'But how on earth,' said Herbert, particularly explosive that day, 'how on earth did it all come about? How did she know this man FitzGeorge? And what had Kay to do with it? We know Kay and FitzGeorge were friends; we never knew that Mother knew him so much as by sight. I never heard her mention his name.' Herbert's explosiveness crackled like a heath fire.

'It was a plot, that's what it was; and Kay was at the bottom of it. Kay wanted the old man's things for himself. Well, Kay at any rate has been nicely sold.'

'But has he?' said Charles. 'How do we know that Kay hasn't got some private arrangement with Mother? Kay always kept himself apart from us; I always felt that Kay might be a little unscrupulous.'

'Oh, surely,' began Mabel.

'Be quiet, Mabel,' said Herbert. 'I agree with Charles; certainly Kay has always been a bit of a dark horse. And Mother has never said anything to any of us about her will.'

'Up to now,' said Edith, who had joined her relations,

151

though she despised herself for doing so, 'she has never had anything to leave.'

Edith's remark passed unnoticed as usual.

'I disagree with all of you,' said William, who was respected in his family for having the best grasp of practical considerations; 'if Kay and Mother had had an understanding between them, they would not have arranged for this FitzGeorge's fortune to go first to Mother. Think of the duties.'

'Death-duties?' said Edith, tactless as usual, uttering the unpleasant word.

'Half a million at least,' said William. 'No. Much better that it should all have gone straight to Kay.'

'But Mother is so unpractical,' said Carrie with a sigh.

'Tragically unpractical,' said William. 'Why didn't she consult one of us? But it's done now,' he resumed more philosophically, 'and what in Heaven's name will she do with it all?'

'She seemed to take no interest in it,' said Carrie. 'I found her reading a book while Genoux fed scraps to the cat in the corner. I don't believe she was really reading it, for when I asked her the title—just trying to make conversation, you know—she couldn't tell me. She said it was something Mudie had sent, but, as you know, Mother always makes up her lists most carefully, and never leaves it to Mudie. I had some difficulty in getting in, because, it appears, the house had been so besieged by newspaper men that Mother had forbidden Genoux to answer the door-bell. I had to go round into the garden and shout "Mother!" under the window.'

'Well,' said Herbert, as Carrie paused, 'and when you had got in, what explanation did she give you?'

'None. She had known this FitzGeorge in India, it appears, and he had been to call on her once or twice recently. So she told me. But I am sure she was keeping something back. When she said FitzGeorge had been to call on her, Genoux, who was hovering about, began to cry and went out of the room. She picked up her apron and began to sniff into it. As she went she said something about "Un si gentil monsieur." From which I assume that he had always given her a tip.''

'And what about Mother? Did she seem upset?'

'She was quiet,' said Carrie after a pause, judicially. 'Yes, on the whole, I'm sure she was keeping something back. She kept trying to change the subject. As though one could change the subject! She hadn't seen the posters in London; that was evident. Dear Mother, I was only trying to help her. I did feel it was a little hard to be so misunderstood. She seemed to want to keep me out of it—to keep me at arm's length.'

'But,' said Lavinia, 'what could one want to keep back, at your mother's age? Not . . .?

'Well,' said Carrie, 'one never knows, does one?'

'No,' said Herbert, 'no! I can't believe *that*!' He spoke righteously, as the head of the family.

'Perhaps not,' said Carrie, deferring to him; 'I'm sure your judgment is best, Herbert. And yet, you know, a very strange idea struck me.'

They all edged forward to hear Carrie's very strange idea.

'No, I really can't say it,' said Carrie, delighted at having aroused so much interest; 'I really can't, not even here where I know it would go no further.'

'Carrie!' said Herbert, 'you know we always had a pact that we would never start a sentence unless we meant to finish it.'

'When we were children,' said Carrie, keeping up her reluctance.

'Of course, if you would rather not . . .' said Herbert.

'Well, if you insist,' said Carrie. 'This is what struck me. None of us ever knew of Mother's friendship with this old man—this old FitzGeorge. She never mentioned him to any of us. Now it turns out that she knew him in India—just about the time when Kay was born—perhaps before. And he always took an interest in Kay. Then he dies, leaving everything to Mother—not to Kay, it's true. But that's no reason why Mother shouldn't leave it all in turn to Kay. And perhaps he always meant Kay to have it. He merely short-circuited Kay. Who knows that that may not have been a kind of bluff? Eccentric old men like that, you know, are always terrified of scandal.'

'Because . . .' said Herbert.

'Exactly. Because.'

'Oh no, no!' said Edith, 'it's horrible, Carrie, it's monstrous. Mother loved Father, she never would have deceived him.'

'Dear Edith!' said Carrie. 'So naïve! seeing everything in terms of black or white!' But already she regretted having spoken in the presence of Edith, who might betray her to their mother. She had the best of reasons for wishing to remain on good terms with her mother at present.

Edith took her departure in indignation, leaving a united family behind her. They drew their chairs a little closer.

'And then,' said Carrie, going on with her story, 'a young man came—a most unpleasant young man. Foljambe, from some museum. Genoux behaved most unsuitably. I suppose that he had given her his card, instead of merely giving her his name; anyway, she announced him as Monsieur Follejambe. I suspect that she did it on purpose. But I soon saw that it served him right. It was quite clear that he and his museum had designs on poor Mother's inheritance. He pretended that he had come with an offer from his museum to house the collection if Mother hadn't room for it. Mother, for once, was quite sensible. She would make no promises. She said she hadn't decided what to do. She looked at Foljambe as though he weren't there. And then, of course, Genoux burst in as she always does, asking

154

whether Mother would rather have cutlets or a chicken for dinner. A chicken, she said, was less economical, but it could be finished up next day. And Mother with at least eighty thousand a year!'

Lavinia groaned.

'But Mother was just as reticent with me as with the young man,' Carrie continued. 'I kept on assuring her that I only wanted to help—and you all know me well enough to believe that that was the simple truth—but she looked at me just as vaguely as she looked at Foljambe. She seemed to be thinking of something else all the time. Sentimental memories, perhaps,' said Carrie viciously. 'She didn't even ask me to stay to dinner, when Genoux came in again to say the chicken was nearly ready and would spoil. I had to leave with Foljambe finally, and, of course, I had to offer him a lift in the car. He tells me that the collection, apart from the fortune, is estimated at a couple of million.'

'Poor Father,' said Herbert; 'for the first time I feel glad that he is no longer alive.'

'Yes, that's a great comfort,' said Carrie. 'Poor Father. He never knew.'

They silently digested this comforting fact.

'But,' said William, ever practical, resuming the conversation, 'what will Mother do with all those things—all that money? Eighty thousand a year! And two million or so locked up in works of art! Why, if she sold them, she'd have a hundred and sixty thousand a year—more, if she invested it at five per cent. As she easily could.' His voice became shrill, as it always did over any question of money. 'One never knows, with Mother. Look at the casual way she behaved over the jewels. She seems to have no idea of value, no idea of responsibility. For all we know, she may hand over the whole collection to the nation.'

155

Terror descended upon Lady Slane's family.

'You don't really believe that, William? Surely she must have *some* feeling for her children?'

'I do believe it,' said William, working himself up. 'Mother is like a child who treats rubies as though they were pebbles. She has never learnt; she has merely wandered through life. You know we have always tacitly felt that Mother wasn't quite like other people. One doesn't like to say that sort of thing about one's mother, but at moments like this one can't afford to be over-delicate. At any moment she may do something erratic, something which makes one wring one's hands in despair. And we are powerless. Powerless!'

'Nonsense, William,' said Carrie, feeling that William was dramatising the situation; 'Mother has always been amenable to reason.'

'Even when she went to live at Hampstead?' said William gloomily. 'I can't agree that people who strike out a new line for themselves at Mother's age are amenable to reason. Even when she gave away the jewels in that ridiculous way?' He looked at Mabel, who nervously tried to cover up the pearls by some stringy lace. 'No, Carrie. Mother is a person who has never had her feet on the ground. Cloud-cuckoo-land—that's Mother's natural home. And, unfortunately, she has met with another inhabitant: Mr. FitzGeorge.'

'And what about Bucktrout?' said Carrie.

'What, indeed?' said William. 'Bucktrout may well induce her to make the whole fortune over to him. Poor Mother—so simple, so unwise. A prey. What is to be done?'

Meanwhile, Mr. Bucktrout had called on Lady Slane to condole with her over this sudden responsibility.

'You see, Mr. Bucktrout,' said Lady Slane, who was looking ill and troubled, 'Mr. FitzGeorge couldn't have known what he was doing. He wanted me to enjoy his beautiful things—I realise

156

that. But what did he imagine I could do with so much money? I have quite enough for my wants. I knew a millionaire once, Mr. Bucktrout, and he was the most unhappy of men. He was so much afraid of assassination that he lived surrounded by detectives. They were like mice in the walls. He wouldn't allow himself to make a friend, because he couldn't get ulterior motives out of his mind. When one sat beside him at dinner, he was all the time fearing that one would end by asking him for a subscription to a favourite charity. Most people disliked him. I liked him very much. I have seen a great deal of men who mistrusted others because they scented ulterior motives, Mr. Bucktrout, and I don't want to be put into the same position. It seems absurd that Mr. FitzGeorge, of all men, should have put me into it. I don't think he can have known what he was doing.'

'In the eyes of the world, Lady Slane,' said Mr. Bucktrout, 'Mr. FitzGeorge has conferred an enormous benefit upon you.'

'I know, I know,' said Lady Slane, deeply worried and distressed, and not wishing to appear ungrateful.

All her life long, she was thinking, people had conferred benefits on her, benefits she did not covet. Henry by making her first into a Vicereine, and then into a political hostess, and now FitzGeorge by heaping her quiet life with gold and treasures.

'I never wanted anything, Mr. Bucktrout,' she said, 'but to stand aside. One of the things, it appears, that the world doesn't allow! Even at the age of eighty-eight.'

'Even the smallest planet,' said Mr. Bucktrout sententiously, 'is compelled to circle round the sun.'

'But does that mean,' asked Lady Slane, 'that we must all, willy-nilly, circle round wealth, position, possessions? I thought Mr. FitzGeorge knew better. Don't *you* understand?' she said, appealing to Mr. Bucktrout in desperation. 'I thought I had escaped at last from all those things, and now Mr. FitzGeorge,

157

of all people, pushes me back into the thick of them. What am I to do, Mr. Bucktrout? What am I to do? I believe Mr. Fitz-George collected very beautiful things, but I know nothing of such things. I always preferred the works of God to the works of man. The works of God, I always felt, were given freely to anyone who could appreciate them, whether millionaire or pauper, whereas the works of man were reserved for the million-aires. Unless, indeed, the works of man were sufficient to the man who made them; then, it wouldn't matter what millionaire bought them in after years. Not that Mr. FitzGeorge,' she added, 'bought the works of man because of their value. He was an artist in appreciation. Besides, he was a miser. Far from paying the market value of a work of art, it amused him to discover a work of art for less that its market value. Then he felt he had got it on terms of a work of God rather than a work of man, if you follow me.'

'I follow you perfectly,' said Mr. Bucktrout.

'Few people would,' said Lady Slane. 'You encourage me to think that you sympathise with my position as few people would sympathise. I don't want all these valuable things, beau-tiful though they may be. It would worry me to think that I had upon my mantelpiece a terra-cotta Cellini, which Genoux would certainly break, dusting one morning before breakfast. No, Mr. Bucktrout. I would rather go up on to the Heath, if I want something to look at, and look at Constable's trees.'

'Rather than own a Constable?' asked Mr. Bucktrout shrewdly. 'I believe that Mr. FitzGeorge's collection includes a very fine Constable of Hampstead Heath.'

'Well,' said Lady Slane, relaxing, 'I might perhaps keep that.'

'But for the rest, Lady Slane,' said Mr. Bucktrout, 'excluding a few pieces that you might be willing to keep for personal reasons, what shall you decide to do?'

158

'Give them away,' said Lady Slane wearily, not energetically. 'Let the nation have them. Let the hospitals have the money. As Mr. FitzGeorge first intended. Let me be rid of it all. Only let me be rid of it! Besides,' she added, with the twist to which Mr. Bucktrout had become accustomed, 'think how much I shall annoy my children!'

He fully appreciated the subtlety of the practical joke that Lady Slane was playing on her children. Practical jokes, in principle, did not amuse Mr. Bucktrout; he dismissed them as childish and silly; but this particular joke tickled his sense of humour. He had formed a shrewd idea of Lady Slane's children, although he had never seen them.

'But when you die,' said Mr. Bucktrout, with his usual forthrightness, 'your obituary notices will point to you as a disinterested benefactor of the public.'

'I shan't be there to read them,' said Lady Slane, who had learnt enough from Lord Slane's obituary notices about the possibilities of false interpretation.

Mr. Bucktrout walked away genuinely concerned with the perplexity of his old friend. It never occurred to him that most people would regard Lady Slane's wistful regrets as very peculiar regrets indeed. He accepted quite simply the fact that Lady Slane disagreed with the world's customary values, and accordingly it seemed natural to him that she should resent having them so constantly forced upon her. Moreover, he now knew all about her early ambitions, and their complete variance with her actual life. Mr. Bucktrout, although simple in many ways—most people thought him a little mad—was also endowed with a direct and unprejudiced wisdom of his own: he knew that standards must be altered to fit the circumstances, and that it was absurd, although usual, to expect the circumstances to adjust themselves to ready-made standards. Lady Slane thus, in his opinion, deserved as much sympathy in the frustration of her life as an

159

athlete stricken with paralysis. It was an unconventional view to take, no doubt, but Mr. Bucktrout never questioned its rightness.

Genoux, however, was struck with horror when she heard what Lady Slane proposed to do. Her French soul was appalled. For a couple of days she had walked on air, and in order to celebrate this sudden, this unbelievable, accretion of wealth had bought some extra pieces of fish for the cat. Her ideas of the fortune bequeathed to Lady Slane—she had read the amount in the papers, and had counted the zeros on her fingers, incredulously doing the sum several times over—were curiously mixed: she knew well enough what a million was, what two millions were, but in practical application she decided only that she might now venture to ask Lady Slane for the charwoman three times a week instead of twice. Hitherto, in the interests of economy, she had not spared herself even when her rheumatism made her stiffer than usual. She had simply doubled her coverings of brown paper, had put on an extra petticoat, and gone about her business hoping for relief. She knew miladi was not rich, and would rather suffer herself than add to miladi's expenses. But with Lady Slane's decision, casually communicated to her one evening as she came to remove the tray, all visions of future extravagance vanished. 'C'est pas possible, miladi!' she exclaimed. 'Et moi qui pensais voir revenir nos plus beaux jours!' Genoux was really in despair. Moreover, she had been delighted by the light of publicity turned once more on Lady Slane. Both the daily papers and the weekly illustrated papers had flaunted Lady Slane's photograph; the photographs had been very out-of-date, it was true, since nothing recent was available; they had shown Lady Slane as Vicereine, as Ambassadress, young, bejewelled, in evening dress, a tiara crowning her elaborate *coiffure*, seated under a palm; curiously old-fashioned; holding an open book in which

160

she was not reading; surrounded by her children, Herbert in his sailor suit, Carrie in her party frock—how well Genoux remembered it!—leaning affectionately over their mother's shoulders, looking down at the baby—was it Charles? was it William?—she held upon her knee. One paper even, accepting the impossibility of getting a photograph of Lady Slane to-day, had boldly made the best of a bad job and had reproduced a photograph taken in her wedding dress seventy years ago. The companion picture was of Lord Slane in jodhpurs, rifle in hand, one foot resting on a tiger. These things, which Lady Slane so inexplicably did not like, satisfied Genoux' sense of fitness. It was not for her to dictate to miladi, she said, but had miladi considered her position and what was due to it? miladi, who had been accustomed to all those aides-de-camp, all those servants—'bien que ce n'était que des nègres'—all those orderlies, ready to run at any moment with a note or a message? 'Dans ce temps-là, miladi était au moins bien servie.' Then, in the midst of her despair, a thought struck Genoux which caused her to double up suddenly and rub her hands up and down her thighs. 'Ah, mon Dieu, miladi, c'est Lady Charlotte qui va être contente! Et Monsieur William, donc! Ah, la belle plaisanterie!'

Lady Slane was lonely, now that Mr. FitzGeorge had gone. The excitement aroused by her gift to the nation, and the frenzy displayed by her own children, all passed over her without making much impression. She forbade Genoux to bring a newspaper into the house until the headlines should have dwindled to a mere paragraph, and she refused to see any of her children until they would consent to treat the matter as though it had never happened. Carrie wrote a carefully composed and dignified letter; a few weeks, possibly even a few months must elapse, she said, before this terrible wound could heal sufficiently to allow her to observe her mother's condition of silence. Until then she could not trust herself. When she had recovered a little she would write again. Meanwhile it was clear that Lady Slane must consider herself in the direst disgrace.

But although this left her unmoved, and although, thanks to Kay and to Mr. Bucktrout, she had had very little trouble with the authorities, beyond appending her signature to a few documents, she felt tired now and emptied in spirit. Her friendship with FitzGeorge had been strange and lovely—the last strange and lovely thing that was ever likely to happen to her. She desired nothing more. She desired only peace and the laying-down of vexation.

From time to time she came across allusions to her family in the papers. Carrie had opened a bazaar. Carrie's granddaughter was taking part in a charity matinée. Charles had succeeded in getting one of his letters into *The Times*. Richard—Herbert's eldest grandson—had won a point-to-point race. Deborah, his sister, had become most suitably engaged to the eldest son of a duke. Herbert himself had been delivered of a speech in the House of Lords. It was rumoured that the next vacant Governor-generalship would be awarded to Herbert. As it was, he had received the K.C.M.G. in the New Year Honours. . . . From the immense distance of her years Lady Slane contemplated these happenings, tiny and far-off, bringing with them some echo of the events mixed up with her own life. 'How weary, flat, stale, and unprofitable,' she said to herself, going carefully downstairs with the help of a stick and the banisters, and wondering why, at the end of one's life, one should ever trouble to read anything but Shakespeare; or, for the matter of that, at the beginning of one's life either, since he seemed to have understood both exuberance and maturity. But it was only in maturity, perhaps, that one could fully appreciate his deeper understanding.

162

She looked upon this group of people, sprung from her own loins, and saw them in mid-career or else starting out upon their course. Young Deborah, she supposed, was happy in her engagement, and young Richard felt himself filled to the brim with life as he rode across country. She smiled quite tenderly as she thought of the two young creatures. But they would harden, she thought, they would harden when their warm youth grew chilled; they would become worldly-wise, self-seeking; the rash generosity of youth would be replaced by the prudence of middle-age. There would be no battle for them, no struggle in their souls; they would simply set hard into the moulds prepared for them. Lady Slane sighed to think that she was responsible, though indirectly, for their existence. The long, weary serpent of posterity streamed away from her. She felt sick at heart, and looked forward only to release.

Still, she did an inexplicable thing. After she had done it— after she had written the letter, stamped it, and given it to Genoux to post—she looked back upon her action and decided that she had acted in a trance. She could not say what impulse had moved her, what strange desire had tugged at her to recreate a link with the life she had abjured. Perhaps her loneliness was greater than any human courage could stand; perhaps she had overrated her own fortitude. Only a very strong soul could stand quite alone. Be that as it might, she had written to a press-cutting agency with the instruction that any references to her own family should be supplied to her. Privately, she knew that she wanted only the references to her great-grandchildren. She cared very little what happened to Carrie, Herbert, Charles, and William; the path that they followed and would continue to follow was clearly marked, offering no surprises, no delights. But even in her trance she shrank from betraying herself to the eyes of an agency in Holborn: she disguised her real desire under the extravagance of a general order. When the little green packets began to arrive, however, all references to her own children went straight into the waste-paper basket, and references to her great-grandchildren only were pasted very carefully by Lady Slane into an album bought from the stationer round the corner.

She derived an extraordinary pleasure from this occupation, carried on every evening under the shade of the pink lamp. Every evening, for, realising that a fresh supply would not arrive more than twice or thrice a week, she economised her little hoard, and would allow herself the luxury of pasting in only a proportion of the cuttings every day, so that one or two might always remain left over for the morrow. Fortunately, out of Lady Slane's great-grandchildren, two were grown-up, and their activities manifold. They were, in fact, among the prominent young people of the day, and in the gossip columns they had their news-value. Many pleasant hours were spent by Lady Slane in constructing their characters and personalities from these snippets, reinforced by her previous knowledge of them; a recreation for their great-grandmother of which the children themselves were entirely ignorant, an ignorance which added considerably to Lady Slane's half-mischievous, half-sentimental pleasure, for pleasure to her was entirely a private matter, a secret joke, intense, redolent, but as easily bruised as the petals of a gardenia. Genoux alone knew of her nightly occupation, but Genoux was no intrusion, being as much a part of Lady Slane as her boots or her hot-water bottle, or as the cat John, who sat bunched with incomparable neatness and dignity before the fire. Genoux indeed shared Lady Slane's interest in the young Hollands, though from a different point of view. She had been quick to guess and to welcome Lady Slane's reviving interest, and trotted in with a green packet as soon as it had fallen through the letter-box. 'Voilà, miladi! c'est arrivé!' and she would stand by expectantly while Lady Slane stripped off the wrapper and revealed the print. They were futile enough, heaven knows,

164

these paragraphs. Treasure-hunting in Underground stations; a ball; a party; sometimes a photograph, of Richard in riding-breeches or of Deborah representing Mary Queen of Scots at a fancy-dress ball. Futile, but young and harmless. Lady Slane turned them over, and who should presume to analyse her feelings? But Genoux frankly clasped her hands in ecstasy. 'Ah, miladi, qu'il est donc beau, Monsieur Richard! Ah, miladi, qu'elle est donc jolie!' That was Deborah. Lady Slane would smile, pleased by Genoux' admiration. She was, after all, an old woman, and small things pleased her now. 'Yes,' she said, looking at a photograph of Richard, muddy, holding a silver cup under one arm and a riding whip under the other, 'he is a well-built young man—pas si mal.' 'Pas si mal!' cried Genoux in indignation, 'he is superb, a god; such elegance, such chic. All the young women must be mad about him. And he will follow in the footsteps of his great-grandfather,' added Genoux, who had a wholesome appreciation of worldly prestige; 'he will be Viceroy, Prime Minister, Dieu sait quoi encore; miladi verra.' For Genoux had never estimated Lady Slane's contempt for such things. 'No, Genoux,' said Lady Slane; 'I shan't be there to see.'

She would see only, and at so queer a remove, their lovely, silly youth. Thank God, she would not be there to see their hardening into an even sillier adult life, redeemed not even by this wild, foolish, but decorative quality. 'Nymphs and shepherds, come away,' she murmured, looking at the thick hair, the slim elastic limbs. 'Ah, Genoux,' she said, 'it was good to be young.'

That depends, said Genoux sagely, on what sort of a youth one had. It was not good to be the twelfth child of poor parents, and to be sent to live with farmers near Poitiers; to sleep on straw in a barn; never to see one's parents; to get up at five every morning, winter and summer; to be beaten if one didn't do one's work properly; to know that one's brothers and sisters were growing up as strangers. Genoux had been with Lady Slane for nearly seventy years, yet Lady Slane had never heard this revelation. She turned to Genoux with curiosity. 'And when you did see your brothers and sisters again, Genoux, did it feel very strange to you?'

Not a bit, said Genoux; blood counted. One's own family was one's own family. She had walked into the little flat in Paris, at the age of sixteen, as though she belonged there by right. The farm near Poitiers had vanished, and she never thought of it again, though she knew better than anybody where the straying hens laid their eggs. She had walked straight into the lives of her brothers and sisters and had taken up her place there as though she had never been away. She had had a little trouble with one of her sisters, who had given birth to twins just after her elder child had died of diphtheria. They had tried to conceal the death from her, Genoux said, but she had guessed it somehow, and leaping straight out of bed had rushed as she was, in her nightgown, to the cemetery, there to fling herself upon the grave. Genoux had been sent to fetch her back, nor had it apparently struck her as odd that a girl of her age should be employed on such a mission. Necessity ruled; and her mother had to stay at home to look after the twins. But her sojourn with her family had been but a brief interlude. Her father had already put down her name at a registry office, and the next thing she knew was that she was crossing the Channel to England, to take service with miladi.

Lady Slane listened with some emotion to this simple and philosophical recital. She blamed herself for never having questioned Genoux before. She had taken Genoux for granted, all these years; yet a wealth of experience was locked up in that sturdy breast. It must have been a curious transition, from the farm near Poitiers, where she slept on straw and was beaten, to the magnificence of Government House and Viceregal

Lodge. . . . The experiences of her great-grandchildren seemed shallow indeed by comparison; her own experiences seemed thin and over-civilised, lacking any contact with reality. She, who had brooded in secret over an unfulfilled vocation, had never been obliged to tear a distraught sister away from a newly-dug grave. Watching Genoux, who stood there imperturbably relating these trials out of the past, she wondered which wounds went the deeper: the jagged wounds of reality, or the profound invisible bruises of the imagination?

Since those days Genoux had never had any personal life, she supposed. Her life was in her service, with self submerged. Lady Slane suddenly condemned herself as an egoistic old woman. Yet, she reflected, she also had given her life away, to Henry. She need not blame herself overmuch for the last indulgence of her melancholy.

She returned to Genoux. The Holland family had replaced Genoux' own family, absorbing everything that Genoux possessed of pride, ambition, snobbery. She remembered Genoux' paeans of delight when Henry had been given a peerage. Over every child she had watched as though it were her own, and nothing but her fierce protectiveness of Lady Slane could have drawn from her a word of criticism about the Holland children. Now she transferred her interest to the great-grandchildren, making no difference since the day they had ceased to come to the house. Her loyal soul had momentarily been torn in half by Lady Slane's refusal to receive Deborah and Richard. But when Lady Slane explained that youthful vitality was too tiring for an old lady, she had at once readjusted her notions. 'Bien sûr, miladi; la jeunesse, c'est très fatigant.'

She welcomed, however, this suitable revival of family pride typified in the green packets and the album. Deep down in her peasant wisdom, she recognised the wholesome instinct for perpetuation in posterity. Her own womanhood unfulfilled, she

167

clung pathetically to a vicarious satisfaction through the medium of her adored Lady Slane. 'Ça me fait du bien,' she said, tears in her eyes, 'de voir miladi s'occuper avec son petit pot of Stickphast.' And once she lifted up John, the cat, to look at a full-page photograph of Richard in the *Tatler*. 'Regarde, mon bobo, le beau gars.' John struggled and would not look. She set him down again, disappointed. 'C'est drôle, miladi; les animaux, c'est si intelligent, mais ça ne reconnaît jamais les images.'

Common sense rarely laid its fingers on Lady Slane, these days. It did occur to her to wonder, however, what the young people had thought of her renunciation of FitzGeorge's fortune. They had been indignant probably; they had cursed their great-grandmother soundly for defrauding them of a benefit which would eventually have been theirs. They would certainly have given her no credit for romantic motives. Perhaps she owed them an explanation, though not an apology? But how could she get into touch with them, now especially? Pride caught her wrist even as she stretched her pen out towards the ink. She had, after all, behaved towards them in what to any reasonable person must seem a most unnatural way; first she had refused to see them, and then she had eliminated from their future the possibility of great and easy wealth. She must appear to them as the incarnation of egoism and inconsideration. Lady Slane was distressed, yet she knew that she had acted according to her convictions. Had not FitzGeorge himself once taken her to task for sinning against the light? And suddenly, in a moment of illumination, she understood why FitzGeorge had tempted her with this fortune: he had tempted her only in order that she should find the strength to reject it. He had offered her not so much a fortune as a chance to be true to herself. Lady Slane bent down and stroked the cat, whom as a rule she did not much like. 'John,' she said, 'John—how fortunate that I did what he wanted, before I realised what he wanted.'

After that she was happy, though her qualms about her young

descendants continued to worry her. By a curious twist, her qualms of conscience about them increased now that she had satisfactorily explained her own action to herself, as though she blamed herself for some extravagant gesture of self-indulgence. Perhaps she had come too hastily to her decision? Perhaps she had treated the children unfairly? Perhaps one should not demand sacrifices of others, consequent upon one's own ideas? She had consulted her own ideas entirely, with the added spice of pleasure, she must admit, in annoying Carrie, Herbert, Charles, and William. It had seemed wrong to her that private people should own such possessions, such exaggerated wealth; therefore she had hastened to dispose of both, the treasures to the public and the money to the suffering poor; the logic was simple though trenchant. Stated in these terms, she could not believe in her own wrong-doing; but on the other hand, should she not have considered her great-grandchildren? It was a subtle problem to decide alone; and Mr. Bucktrout, to whom she confided it, gave her no help, for not only was he entirely in sympathy with her first instinct but, moreover, in view of the approaching end of the world, he could not see that it mattered very much one way or the other. 'My dear lady,' he said, 'when your Cellinis, your Poussins, your grandchildren, and your great-grandchildren are all mingled in planetary dust your problem of conscience will cease to be of much importance.' That was true rather than helpful. Astronomical truths, enlarging though they may be to the imagination, contain little assistance for immediate problems. She continued to gaze at him in distress, a distress which at that very moment had been augmented by a sudden thought of what Henry, raising his eyebrows, would have said.

'Miss Deborah Holland,' said Genoux, throwing open the door. She threw it open in such a way as to suggest that she was retrospectively aping the manner of the grand major-domo at the Paris Embassy.

169

Lady Slane rose in a fluster, with the usual soft rustle of her silks and laces; her knitting slipped to the floor; she stooped ineffectually to retrieve it; her mind swept wildly round, seeking to reconcile this improbable encounter between her great-grand-daughter, Mr. Bucktrout, and herself. The circumstances were too complicated for her to govern successfully in a moment's thought. She had never been good at dealing with a situation that demanded nimbleness of wit; and, considering the conversations she had had with Mr. Bucktrout about her great-grand-children, of whom Herbert's granddaughter thus suddenly presented herself as a specimen, the situation demanded a very nimble wit indeed. 'My *dear* Deborah,' said Lady Slane, scurrying affectionately, dropping her knitting, trying to retrieve it, abandoning the attempt midway, and finally managing to kiss Deborah on the cheek.

She was the more confused, for Deborah was the first young person to enter the house at Hampstead since Lady Slane had removed herself from Elm Park Gardens. The house at Hampstead had opened its doors to no one but Mr. FitzGeorge, Mr. Bucktrout, and Mr. Gosheron—and, of course, on occasion, to Lady Slane's own children, who, although they might be unwelcome, were at any rate advanced in years. Deborah came in the person of youth knocking at the doors. She was pretty, under her fur cap; pretty and elegant; the very girl Lady Slane would have expected from her photographs in the society papers. In the year since Lady Slane had seen her, she had changed from a schoolgirl into a young lady. Of her activities in the fashionable world since she became a young lady, Lady Slane had had ample evidence. This observation reminded Lady Slane of her press-cutting album, which was lying on the table under the lamp; releasing Deborah's hand, she hurriedly removed the album to a dark place, as though it were a dirtied cup of tea. She put the blotter over it. A narrow escape; narrow and unforeseen;

but now she felt safe. She came back and introduced Deborah formally to Mr. Bucktrout.

Mr. Bucktrout had the tact to take his leave almost immediately. Lady Slane, knowing him, had feared that he might plunge instantly into topics of the deepest import, with references to her own recent and eccentric conduct, thereby embarrassing both the girl and herself. Mr. Bucktrout, however, behaved most unexpectedly as a man of the world. He made a few remarks about the beginning of spring—about the reappearance of flowers on barrows in the London streets—about the longevity of anemones in water, especially if you cut their stems—about the bunches of snowdrops that came up from the country, and how soon they would be succeeded by bunches of primroses—about Covent Garden. But about cosmic catastrophes or the right judgment of Deborah Holland's great-grandmother he said nothing. Only once did he verge on an indiscretion, when he leant forward, putting his finger against his nose, and said, 'Miss Deborah, you bear a certain resemblance to Lady Slane whom I have the honour to call my friend.' Fortunately, he did not follow up the remark, but after the correct interval merely rose and took his leave. Lady Slane was grateful to him, yet it was with dismay that she saw him go, leaving her face to face with a young woman bearing what had once been her own name.

She expected an evasive and meaningless conversation as a start, dreading the chance phrase that would fire it into realities, growing swiftly like Jack's beanstalk into a tangle of reproaches; she expected anything in the world but that Deborah should sit at her knee and thank her with directness and simplicity for what she had done. Lady Slane made no answer at all, except to lay her hand on the girl's head pressed against her knee. She was too much moved to answer; she preferred to let the young voice go on, imagining that she herself was the speaker, reviving her adolescent years and deluding herself with the fancy that she had at last found a confidant to whom she could betray her thoughts. She was old, she was tired, she lost herself willingly in the sweet illusion. Was it an echo that she heard? or had some miracle wiped out the years? were the years being played over again, with a difference? She allowed her fingers to ruffle Deborah's hair, and, finding it short instead of ringleted, supposed vaguely that she had put her own early plans for escape into execution. Had she then really run away from home? had she, indeed, chosen her own career instead of Henry's? Was she now sitting on the floor beside a trusted friend, pouring out her reasons, her aspirations, and her convictions, with a firmness and a certainty lit as by a flame from within? Fortunate Deborah! she thought, to be so firm, so trustful, and by one person at least so well understood; but to which Deborah she alluded, she scarcely knew.

She had told herself after FitzGeorge's death that no strange and lovely thing would ever enter her life again, a foolish prophecy. This unexpected confusion of her own life with that of her great-granddaughter was as strange and as lovely. FitzGeorge's death had aged her; at her time of life people aged suddenly and alarmingly; her mind was, perhaps, no longer very clear; but at least it was clear enough for her to recognise its weakness, and to say, 'Go on, my darling; you might be myself speaking.' Deborah, in her young egoism, failed to pick up the significance of that remark, which Lady Slane, indeed, had inadvertently let slip. She had no intention of revealing herself to her great-grand-daughter; her hand upon the latch of the door of death, she had no intention of troubling the young with a recital of her own past problems; enough for her, now to submerge herself into a listener, a pair of ears, though she might still keep her secrets running in and out of her mind according to her fancy—for it must be remembered that Lady Slane had always relished the

172

privacy of her enjoyments. This enjoyment was especially private now, though not very sharp; it was hazy rather than sharp, her perceptions intensified and yet blurred, so that she could feel intensely without being able or obliged to reason. In the deepening twilight of her life, in the maturity of her years, she returned to the fluctuations of adolescence; she became once more the reed wavering in the river, the skiff reaching out towards the sea, yet blown back again and again into the safe waters of the estuary. Youth! youth! she thought; and she, so near to death, imagined that all the perils again awaited her, but this time she would face them more bravely, she would allow no concessions, she would be firm and certain. This child, this Deborah, this self, this other self, this projection of herself, was firm and certain. Her engagement, she said, was a mistake; she had drifted into it to please her grandfather; (Mother doesn't count, she said, nor does Granny—poor Mabel!) her grandfather had ambitions for her, she said; he liked the idea of her being, some day, a duchess; but what was that, she said, compared with what she herself wanted to be, a musician?

When she said 'a musician,' Lady Slane received a little shock, so confidently had she expected Deborah to say 'a painter.' But it came to much the same thing, and her disappointment was quickly healed. The girl was talking as she herself would have talked. She had no prejudice against marriage with someone who measured his values against the same rod as herself. Understanding was impossible between people who did not agree as to the yard and the inch. To her grandfather and her late fiancé, wealth and so great a title measured a yard— two yards—a hundred yards—a mile. To her, they measured an inch—half an inch. Music, on the other hand, and all that it implied, could be measured by no terrestrial scale. Therefore she was grateful to her great-grandmother for reducing her value in the worldly market. 'You see,' she said amused, 'for a week I

173

was supposed to be an heiress, and when it was found that I wasn't an heiress at all it became much easier for me to break off my engagement.'

'When did you break it off?' asked Lady Slane, thinking of her newspaper cuttings which had not mentioned the fact.

'The day before yesterday.'

Genoux came in with the evening post, glad of a pretext to take another look at Deborah. Lady Slane slipped the green packet under her knitting. 'I didn't know,' she said, 'that you had broken it off.'

And such a relief it was, said Deborah, wriggling her shoulders. She would have no more to do, she said, with that crazy world. 'Is it crazy, great-grandmother,' she asked, 'or am I? Or am I merely one of the people who can't fit in? Am I just one of the people who think a different set of things important? Anyhow, why should I accept other people's ideas? My own are just as likely to be right—right for me. I know one or two people who agree with me, but they are always people who don't seem to get on with grandfather or great-aunt Carrie. And another thing'—she paused.

'Go on,' said Lady Slane, moved to the heart by this stumbling and perplexed analysis.

'Well,' said Deborah, 'there seems to be a kind of solidarity between grandfather and great-aunt Carrie and the people that grandfather and great-aunt Carrie approve of. As though cement had been poured over the whole lot. But the people I like always seem to be scattered, lonely people—only they recognise each other as soon as they come together. They seem to be aware of something more important than the things grandfather and great-aunt Carrie think important. I don't yet know exactly what that something is. If it were religion—if I wanted to become a nun instead of a musician—I think that even grandfather would understand dimly what I was talking about. But it

174

isn't religion; and yet it seems to have something of the nature of religion. A chord of music, for instance, gives me more satisfaction than a prayer.'

'Go on,' said Lady Slane.

'Then,' said Deborah, 'among the people I like, I find something hard and concentrated in the middle of them, harsh, almost cruel. A sort of stone of honesty. As though they were determined at all costs to be true to the things that they think matter. Of course,' said Deborah dutifully, remembering the comments of her grandfather and her great-aunt Carrie, 'I know that they are, so to speak, very useless members of society.' She said it with a childish gravity.

'They have their uses,' said Lady Slane; 'they act as a leaven.'

'I never know how to pronounce that word,' said Deborah; 'whether to rhyme with even or seven. I suppose you are right about them, great-grandmother. But the leaven takes a long time to work, and even then it only works among people who are more or less of the same mind.'

'Yes,' said Lady Slane, 'but more people are really of the same mind than you would believe. They take a great deal of trouble to conceal it, and only a crisis calls it out. For instance, if you were to die,'—but what she really meant was, If I were to die— 'I daresay you would find that your grandfather had understood you (me) better than you (I) think.'

'That's mere sentimentality,' said Deborah firmly; 'naturally, death startles everybody, even grandfather and great-aunt Carrie—it reminds them of the things they prefer to ignore. My point about the people I like, is not that they dwell morbidly on death, but that they keep continually a sense of what, to them, matters in life. Death, after all, is an incident. Life is an incident too. The thing I mean lies outside both. And it doesn't seem compatible with the sort of life grandfather and great-aunt Carrie think I ought to lead. Am I wrong, or are they?'

175

Lady Slane perceived one last opportunity for annoying
Herbert and Carrie. Let them call her a wicked old woman! she
knew that she was no such thing. The child was an artist, and
must have her way. There were other people in plenty to carry
on the work of the world, to earn and enjoy its rewards, to
suffer its malice and return its wounds in kind; the small and rare
fraternity to which Deborah belonged, indifferent to gilded
lures, should be free to go obscurely but ardently about its
business. In the long run, with the strange bedlam always in
process of sorting itself out, as the present-day became history,
the poet: and the prophets counted for more than the con-
querors. Christ himself was of their company.

She could form no estimate of Deborah's talents; that was
beside the point. Achievement was good, but the spirit was
better. To reckon by achievements was to make a concession to
the prevailing system of the world; it was a departure from the
austere, disinterested, exacting standards that Lady Slane and her
kindred recognised. Yet what she said was not at all in accordance with her thoughts; she said, 'Oh dear, if I hadn't given
away that fortune I could have made you independent.'

Deborah laughed. She wanted advice, she said, not money.
Lady Slane knew very well that she did not really want advice
either; she wanted only to be strengthened and supported in her
resolution. Very well, if she wanted approval, she should have
it. 'Of course you are right, my dear,' she said quietly.

They talked for a while longer, but Deborah, feeling herself
folded into peace and sympathy, noticed that her great-grandmother's mind wandered a little into some maze of confusion to
which Deborah held no guiding thread. It was natural at Lady
Slane's age. At moments she appeared to be talking about herself, then recalled her wits, and with pathetic clumsiness tried to
cover up the slip, rousing herself to speak eagerly of the girl's
future, not of some event which had gone wrong in the distant

176

past. Deborah was too profoundly lulled and happy to wonder much what that event could be. This hour of union with the old woman soothed her like music, like chords lightly touched in the evening, with the shadows closing and the moths bruising beyond an open window. She leaned against the old woman's knee as a support, a prop, drowned, enfolded, in warmth, dimness, and soft harmonious sounds. The hurly-burly receded; the clangour was stilled; her grandfather and her great-aunt Carrie lost their angular importance and shrivelled to little gesticulating puppets with parchment faces and silly wavering hands; other values rose up like great archangels in the room, and towered and spread their wings. Inexplicable associations floated into Deborah's mind; she remembered how once she had seen a young woman in a white dress leading a white borzoi across the darkness of a southern port. This physical and mental contact with her great-grandmother—so far removed in years, so closely attuned in spirit—stripped off the coverings from the small treasure of short experience that she had jealously stored away. She caught herself wondering whether she could afterwards recapture the incantation of this hour sufficiently to render it into terms of music. Her desire to render an experience in terms of music transcended even her interest in her great-grandmother as a human being; a form of egoism which she knew her great-grandmother would neither resent nor misunderstand. The impulse which had led her to her great-grandmother was a right impulse. The sense of enveloping music proved that. On some remote piano the chords were struck, and they were chords which had no meaning, no existence, in the world inhabited by her grandfather and her great-aunt Carrie; but in her great-grandmother's world they had their value and their significance. But she must not tire her great-grandmother, thought Deborah, suddenly realising that the old voice had ceased its maunderings and that the spell of an hour was broken. Her great-grandmother

177

was asleep. Her chin had fallen forward on to the laces at her breast. Her lovely hands were limp in their repose. As Deborah rose silently, and silently let herself out into the street, being careful not to slam the door behind her, the chords of her imagination died away.

Genoux, bringing in the tray an hour later, announcing 'Miladi est servie,' altered her formula to a sudden, 'Mon Dieu, mais qu'est-ce que c'est ça—Miladi est morte.'

'It was to be expected,' said Carrie, mopping her eyes as she had not mopped them over the death of her father; 'it was to be expected, Mr. Bucktrout. Yet it comes as a shock. My poor mother was such a very exceptional woman, as you know— though I'm sure I don't see how you should have known it, for she was, of course, only your tenant. A correspondent in *The Times* described her this morning as a rare spirit. Just what I always said myself: a rare spirit.' Carrie had forgotten the many other things she had said. 'A little difficult to manage some-times,' she added, stung by a sudden thought of FitzGeorge's fortune; 'unpractical to a degree, but practical things are not the only things that count, are they, Mr. Bucktrout?' *The Times* had said that too. 'My poor mother had a beautiful nature. I don't say that I should always have acted myself as she some-times acted. Her motives were sometimes a little difficult to follow. Quixotic, you know, and—shall we say?—injudicious. Besides, she could be very stubborn. There were times when she wouldn't be guided, which was unfortunate, considering how unpractical she was. We should all be in a very different position now had she been willing to listen to us. However, it's no good crying over spilt milk, is it?' said Carrie, giving Mr. Bucktrout what was meant to be a brave smile.

Mr. Bucktrout made no answer. He disliked Carrie. He wondered how anyone so hard and so hypocritical could be the

178

daughter of someone so sensitive and so honest as his old friend. He was determined to reveal to Carrie by no word or look how deeply he felt the loss of Lady Slane.

'There is a man downstairs who can take the measurements for the coffin, should you wish,' he said.

Carrie stared. So they had been right about this Mr. Bucktrout: a heartless old man, lacking the decency to find one suitable phrase about poor Mother; Carrie herself had been generous enough to repeat those words about the rare spirit; really, on the whole, she considered her little oration over her mother to be a very generous tribute, when one remembered the tricks her mother had played on them all. She had felt extremely righteous as she pronounced it, and according to her code Mr. Bucktrout ought to have said something graceful in reply. No doubt he had expected to pull some plums out of the pudding himself, and had been embittered by his failure. The thought of the old shark's discomfiture was Carrie's great consolation. Mr. Bucktrout was just the sort of man who tried to hook an unsuspecting old lady. And now, full of revengefulness, he fell back on bringing a man to make the coffin.

'My brother, Lord Slane, will be here shortly to make all the necessary arrangements,' she replied haughtily.

Mr. Gosheron, however, was already at the door. He came in tilting his bowler hat, but whether he tilted it towards the silent presence of Lady Slane in her bed, or towards Carrie standing at the foot, was questionable. Mr. Gosheron in his capacity as an undertaker was well accustomed to death; still, his feeling for Lady Slane had always been much warmer than for a mere client. He had already tried to give some private expression to his emotion by determining to sacrifice his most treasured piece of wood as the lid for her coffin.

'Her ladyship makes a lovely corpse,' he said to Mr. Bucktrout. They both ignored Carrie.

'Lovely in life, lovely in death, is what I always say,' said

179

Mr. Gosheron. 'It's astonishing, the beauty that death brings out. My old grandfather told me that, who was in the same line of business, and for fifty years I've watched to see if his words were true. "Beauty in life," he used to say, "may come from good dressing and what-not, but for beauty in death you have to fall back on character." Now look at her ladyship, Mr. Bucktrout. Is it true, or isn't it? To tell you the truth,' he added confidentially, 'if I want to size a person up, I look at them and picture them dead. That always gives it away, especially as they don't know you're doing it. The first time I ever set eyes on her ladyship, I said, yes, she'll do; and now that I see her as I pictured her then I still say it. She wasn't never but half in this world, anyhow.'

'No, she wasn't,' said Mr. Bucktrout, who, now that Mr. Gosheron had arrived, was willing to talk about Lady Slane, 'and she never came to terms with it either. She had the best that it could give her—all the things she didn't want. She considered the lilies of the field, Mr. Gosheron.'

'She did, Mr. Bucktrout; many a phrase out of the Bible have I applied to her ladyship. But people will stand things in the Bible that they won't stand in common life. They don't seem to see the sense of it when they meet it in their own homes, although they'll put on a reverent face when they hear it read out from a lectern.'

Oh goodness, thought Carrie, will these two old men never stop talking across Mother like a Greek chorus? She had arrived at Hampstead in a determined frame of mind: she would be generous, she would be forgiving—and some genuine emotion had come to her aid—but now her self-possession cracked and her ill-temper and grievances came boiling up. This agent and this undertaker, who talked so securely and so sagaciously, what could they know of her mother?

'Perhaps,' she snapped, 'you had better leave my mother's

funeral oration to be pronounced by one of her own family.'

Mr. Bucktrout and Mr. Gosheron both turned gravely towards her. She saw them suddenly as detached figures; figures of fun certainly, yet also figures of justice. Their eyes stripped away the protection of her decent hypocrisy. She felt that they judged her; that Mr. Gosheron, according to his use and principle, was imagining her as a corpse; was narrowing his eyes to help the effort of his imagination; was laying her out upon a bed, examining her without the defences she could no longer control. That phrase about the rare spirit shrivelled to a cinder. Mr. Bucktrout and Mr. Gosheron were in league with her mother, and no phrases could cover up the truth from such an alliance.

'In the presence of death,' she said to Mr. Gosheron, taking refuge in a last convention, 'you might at least take off your hat.'

THE END

181

THE RETURN OF
THE SOLDIER

Rebecca West

REBECCA WEST

(1892–1983) was born Cicely Isabel Fairfield in London. Her father had come from County Kerry, Ireland, and she acquired her early education in Edinburgh. She adopted her pen name, Rebecca West, from the strong-willed character of that name in Ibsen's social drama, *Rosmersholm*, in which she once acted in her late teens. She began to appear in print as a journalist and political writer in London as early as 1911, in *The Freewoman*, and was soon deeply involved in the causes of feminism and social reform. Some of her early writings (1911–1917) have been collected into one volume, *The Young Rebecca*, published by Virago.

Rebecca West's first book, *Henry James*, was published in 1916; she went on to write novels, criticism, satire, biography, travel and history. Her works of fiction include *The Return of the Soldier* (1918—now a major British film), *The Judge* (1922), *Harriet Hume: A London Fantasy* (1929), *The Harsh Voice* (1935), *The Thinking Reed* (1936), *The Fountain Overflows* (1956), *The Birds Fall Down* (1966) and *Sunflower* (1986). Other notable works include *The Strange Necessity* (1928), her biography of St Augustine (1933), her two-volume magnum opus, *Black Lamb and Grey Falcon* (1937), *The Meaning of Treason* (1949), *A Train of Powder* (1955) and *The Court and the Castle* (1957).

Her only child, Anthony West (b. 1914), is the son of the novelist H. G. Wells. In 1930 she married Henry Maxwell Andrews, the banker, and began a lifelong companionship at their country house at Ibstone, in Buckinghamshire, with visits to London and many travels together, including her journey to Yugoslavia that inspired *Black Lamb and Grey Falcon*. Rebecca West was created a Dame Commander of the British Empire in 1959. After her husband's death in 1968 she returned to London where she lived until her death.

Virago publishes nine of Rebecca West's fictional works and five works of non-fiction, including her memoir *Family Memories*. In forthcoming years Virago will be editing and issuing her other unpublished writings.

INTRODUCTION

Rebecca West was 24 in 1918, when *The Return of the Soldier* was published. She was already well established as a journalist, and this was her second book; her first was *Henry James*, a short but assured and lively study that had come out two years before.

The Return of the Soldier too is a short book; on a first reading it is a simple and bitter-sweet tale turning on the loss of memory of Chris Baldry, the central male character, which makes him forget his charming wife and their ten years of marriage and remember only an earlier, humbler love. Loss of memory is a fictional device that is frequently abused in stories and films to facilitate mediocre plotting. It is important to remember that it was a frequent and frightening symptom of what is technically called 'hysterical fugue', the 'shell-shock' suffered by some soldiers as a result of the horrors of the trenches in the First World War. Rebecca West was writing her novel during that war; there was nothing fanciful or expedient in her use of such trauma.

Chris's fugue, or flight, was not only from the grim realities of war; it was from the apparently pleasant reality of his marriage. It seems to me that he himself, seen in the novel only through the uncritical eyes of love, is not an interesting character; he is the epitome of English masculine fineness, virtue and charm, a love-object. The interest and the tension of the book lie

185

in the three women who, in their crucially different ways, care about him.

The background of Baldry Court, where Kitty his wife and Jenny his cousin—the narrator—wait for Chris's return, is built up like a stage-set. A gracious house full of 'brittle beautiful things'—Kitty has 'decorative genius'—and an atmosphere of comfort and ease where everything, even the crocuses along the drive, are planned and ordered. It would have been easy for the author to have introduced a note of satire from the very beginning at the expense of so much good taste and luxury. But the reader is drawn into the magic circle of Baldry Court and accepts Jenny, and even spoilt Kitty, who is associated only with delicate silken garments and rosebuds—even if she does look 'so like a girl on a magazine cover that one expected to find a large ''7d'' somewhere attached to her person'.

Into this exquisitely arranged Eden comes Margaret, with the news of Chris's condition and the revelation of his illusion: it is Margaret he wants to come home to, having blotted his marriage from his mind. To Kitty and Jenny it seemed inconceivable that Christ could ever have loved this plain, shabby woman, 'repulsively furred with neglect and poverty', with her 'deplorable umbrella, her unpardonable raincoat'. Social snobbery is too flimsy a term for what they feel. Sexual jealousy and tribal instinct combine into hatred; Jenny 'hated her as the rich hate the poor, as insect things that will struggle out of the crannies that are their decent home, and introduce ugliness to the light of day'. For ugliness, at Baldry Court, is kept at bay by all the means that money and manner can muster. Margaret's intrusion was like 'a spreading stain on the fabric of our life'.

When Chris comes home and is faced with the unremembered Kitty, the thought of Margaret 'made him unable to breathe, sent the blood running under his skin'. Jenny, who is—though she never quite admits it—in love with Chris,

186

feels 'stunned with jealousy'. 'I suppose the truth is that I was physically so jealous of Margaret that it was making me ill.' In *Henry James*, Rebecca West had written of the master's technique of significant omission: 'that if one had a really "great" scene one ought to leave it out and describe it simply by the full relation of its consequences'. When Margaret is reunited with Chris in the garden of Baldry Court, Jenny watches from a top window, but covers her eyes so as not to witness their first embrace; and no one hears what they say. After, Jenny feels 'utterly cut off' from Chris, and thinks of him 'with the passion of exile'. In his marriage to Kitty he had never thus excluded her. Now that he is regularly visited and comforted by Margaret, Kitty is like 'a broken doll'; she 'holds a review of her underclothing', looking 'wanly at the frail luminous silks' like a speculator who has cornered a commodity for which there is no demand.

Jenny, in spite of her jealousy, perceives Margaret's quality—her simplicity, her serene, ecstatic goodness. She comes upon them in the woods—Chris peacefully sleeping, Margaret squatting protectively at his side—both 'englobed in peace as in a crystal sphere'. She feels that Margaret's 'was the most significant as it was the loveliest attitude in the world':

> It means that the woman has gathered the soul of the man into her soul and is keeping it warm in love and peace so that his body can rest quiet for a little time. That is a great thing for a woman to do.

That may seem an unlikely opinion for the young, independent and feminist Rebecca West to endorse, as she surely does. What in fact she is celebrating is goodness, the creative, life-giving goodness that is independent of intellect, or of art as it is usually understood. The passage goes on:

> I know there are things at least as great for those women whose independent spirits can ride fearlessly and with interest

187

outside the home park of their personal relationships, but independence is not the occupation of most of us. What we desire is greatness such as this which had given sleep to the beloved.

Rebecca West herself was one of the 'independent spirits', but she has always had a robust and catholic understanding of creativity; the person who can make a good cake may be as creative as the person who can write a story. It is Margaret's self, her soul, that Chris loves. Jenny spells it out:

> I suppose that the subject of our tragedy, written in spiritual terms, was that in Kitty he had turned from the type of woman that makes the body conqueror of the soul and in me from the type that mediates between the soul and the body . . . and had given himself to a woman whose bleak habit it was to champion the soul against the body.

Kitty made the body 'conqueror of the soul' only in one sense. She and Jenny were 'images of Chris's conception of women': 'Exquisite we were according to our equipment; unflushed by appetite or passion, even noble passion . . . and he had known none other than us. With such a mental habit a man could not help but wince at Margaret,' thinks Jenny, wrongly as it happens. She is nearer the mark when she says, 'we are as we are and there is nothing more to us. The whole truth about us is in our material seeming.'

For in spite of their attractiveness she and Kitty are as passionless as flowers. Margaret, who 'champions the soul against the body', can express her soul in a sexuality that answers Chris's own—his 'body and soul were consumed with desire for her'. When the Freudian doctor surmises that Chris turned to sex 'with a peculiar need', it is Margaret who answers, to the discomfiture of the other two, 'Yes, he was always very dependent.'

188

One of Rebecca West's themes has been the sacrifice made by men (and therefore by society) of the sexual woman to the non-sexual woman. Here it comes about because it must. Margaret consents to cooperate in curing Chris—'making him ordinary', as she puts it—because the situation he so desires is not true. He was in reality married to Kitty, and Margaret was married to the dim Mr Grey. The world 'will not suffer magic circles to endure'. Truth must be faced at all costs. 'I knew quite well,' says Jenny, 'that when one is adult one must raise to one's lips the wine of the truth . . . or else walk for ever queer and small like a dwarf.' If Chris is allowed to stay in the magic circle of a past truth he 'would not be quite a man'. So by a heart-breaking device he is 'cured', and walks back into his marriage with 'a dreadful decent smile', 'every inch a soldier'.

Margaret, one imagines, in the dignity of a requited and renounced love, will continue to mother her husband. Jenny, the mediator, has reached new understanding. And Kitty, whom Jenny sees towards the end as 'the falsest thing on earth, who was in tune with every kind of falsity', Rebecca West acknowledges, through Jenny, the role of all the Kitties of this world, watching her demeanour as she prepares to meet the new doctor. Kitty was 'glowing', because she was going to meet a new man:

> Beautiful women of her type lose, in this matter of admiration alone, their otherwise tremendous sense of class distinction; they are obscurely aware that it is their civilising mission to flash the jewel of their beauty before all men, so that they shall desire it and work to get the wealth to buy it, and thus be seduced by a present appetite to a tilling of the earth that serves the future. There is, you know, really room for all of us; we each have our peculiar use.

In the last sentence of that quotation lies one of the characteristically ironic and characteristically humane illuminations that can be gleaned from *The Return of the Soldier*.

The sources of the novel are necessarily complex. Gordon N. Ray, in his *H. G. Wells and Rebecca West*, offers an interpretation that connects Kitty with Jane Wells. Rebecca West was living during the writing of the book in some anxiety and discomfort, and the ease and security of Baldry Court may well seem like a reflection of the ease and security—and perhaps the falsity—of Wells's domestic life. But she wrote to Ray on 14 July 1971 that although he had given 'a most brilliant explanation', such thoughts had not been at the forefront of her mind:

> The story was written round the personality of Mrs Vernon, a very nice woman, who was our landlady at Claverton Street over several years. . . . She was the complete Margaret, and she had once been to Monkey Island on an unspecified occasion, which was of great importance to her, and speculations on what this might have been gave me the idea for the story. Kitty is not at all my idea of Jane . . . The original of Kitty was a woman I met only once, when someone took me to a house said to be the original of the house Galsworthy describes as being built by Bosinney for Soames in the Forsyte Saga.

The Monkey Island setting (on the Thames, near Bray) of the early idyll between Chris and Margaret was one that was well known to the author. In the descriptions in this book it is always dusk on Monkey Island when the young man and girl meet: 'In the liquefaction of colours which happens on a summer evening, when the green grass seemed like a precious fluid poured out on the earth and dripping over to the river, and the chestnut candles were no longer proud flowers . . . but just wet lights in the humid mass of the trees. . . .' Rebecca West has a painter's eye,

190

and can trace the mood of landscape in words as effectively as a poet. To readers more used to her analytic trenchancy and her deflationary wit her lyrical writing may cause a subtle unease: it is like seeing a panther playing very tenderly with a butterfly.

She had been happy herself at the Monkey Island Inn, which she makes Margaret's home. H. G. Wells too had known the place since he was a boy, when he used to pay summer visits to his uncle at the Surly Hall Inn, half a mile down river. Chris in the novel walks through the fields to visit Margaret from an uncle's house: 'From Uncle Ambrose's gates one took the field-path across the meadow . . .' The quarrel on which Chris and Margaret so disastrously part was about the over-familiarity of one 'Bert Wells, nephew to Mr Wells who keeps the inn at Surly Hall'. This was just a private joke, as perhaps was the Wellsian appearance of the doctor at the end of the novel: 'He was a little man with winking blue eyes, a flushed and crumpled forehead, a little grey moustache that gave him the profile of an amiable cat, and a lively taste in spotted ties . . .'

These are superficialities, grace-notes, but illustrative of the ease with which the author manipulates material in a book that is prodigal of insights and observations that a lesser writer would have made more of: as in a glancing sketch, for example, of the way Chris would talk to a pretty visitor, with 'that detached attention, such as an unmusical man pays to good music, which men of anchored attentions give to attractive women'.

Samuel Hynes has rightly written that *The Return of the Soldier* is 'a small masterpiece'; and added, 'but it is more nearly a "woman's novel" . . . than anything else Dame Rebecca wrote . . . For it comes too close to being *merely* a woman's novel, and so confirming the notions about women that exist in a man-governed world.' The plot may lead one to that conclusion; but it is an inadequate reading of the book as a whole, which has sharp things to say about truth and falsity, about

191

confronting reality, about different modes of love and about the nature of goodness. In her later work Dame Rebecca has tended to concentrate on a complementary topic, the nature of evil. But the really striking thing about *The Return of the Soldier* is the way in which the preoccupations and the convictions of the mature writer are already discernible in this short, dramatic and very readable piece of fiction written in her early twenties.

Victoria Glendinning, 1980

I

'Ah, don't begin to fuss!' wailed Kitty; 'if a woman began to worry in these days because her husband hadn't written to her for a fortnight——! Besides, if he'd been anywhere interesting, anywhere where the fighting was really hot, he'd have found some way of telling me instead of just leaving it as ''Somewhere in France.'' He'll be all right.'

We were sitting in the nursery. I had not meant to enter it again after the child's death, but I had come suddenly on Kitty as she slipped the key into the lock and had lingered to look in at the high room, so full of whiteness and clear colours, so unendurably gay and familiar, which is kept in all respects as though there were still a child in the house. It was the first lavish day of spring, and the sunlight was pouring through the tall arched windows and the flowered curtains so brightly that in the old days a fat fist would certainly have been raised to point out the new translucent glories of the rose-buds; it was lying in great pools on the blue cork floor and the soft rugs, patterned with strange beasts; and it threw dancing beams, that should have been gravely watched for hours, on the white paint and the blue distempered walls. It fell on the rocking-horse which had been Chris's idea of an appropriate present for his year-old son and showed what a fine fellow he was and how tremendously dappled; it picked out Mary and her little lamb on the chintz

ottoman. And along the mantelpiece, under the loved print of
the snarling tiger, in attitudes that were at once angular and
relaxed—as though they were ready for play at their master's
pleasure but found it hard to keep from drowsing in this warm
weather—sat the Teddy Bear and the chimpanzee and the
woolly white dog and the black cat with the eyes that roll.
Everything was there, except Oliver. I turned away so that I
might not spy on Kitty revisiting her dead.

But she called after me:

'Come here, Jenny. I'm going to dry my hair.'

And when I looked again I saw that her golden hair was all
about her shoulders and that she wore over her frock a little
silken jacket trimmed with rosebuds. She looked so like a girl on
a magazine cover that one expected to find a large '7d.' somewhere attached to her person. She had taken Nanny's big basket-
chair from its place by the high chair and was pushing it over to
the middle window.

'I always come in here when Emery has washed my hair; it's
the sunniest room in the house. I wish Chris wouldn't have it
kept as a nursery when there's no chance——'

She sat down, swept her hair over the back of the chair into
the sunlight, and held out to me her tortoise-shell hairbrush.

'Give it a brush now and then like a good soul. But be careful.
Tortoise snaps so.'

I took the brush and turned to the window, leaning my forehead against the glass and staring unobservantly at the view.
You probably know the beauty of that view; for when Chris
rebuilt Baldry Court after his marriage, he handed it over to
architects who had not so much the wild eye of the artist as the
knowing wink of the manicurist, and between them they mas-
saged the dear old place into matter for innumerable photographs in the illustrated papers.

The house lies on the crest of Harrowweald, and from its

windows the eye drops to miles of emerald pastureland lying wet and brilliant under a westward line of sleek hills blue with distance and distant woods, while nearer it ranges the suave decorum of the lawn and the Lebanon cedar whose branches are like darkness made palpable, and the minatory gauntnesses of the topmost pines in the wood that breaks downward, its bare boughs a close texture of browns and purples, from the pond on the hill's edge.

That day its beauty was an affront to me, because like most Englishwomen of my time I was wishing for the return of a soldier. Disregarding the national interest and everything except the keen prehensile gesture of our hearts towards him, I wanted to snatch my cousin Christopher from the wars and seal him in this green pleasantness his wife and I now looked upon. Of late I had had bad dreams about him. By night I saw Chris running across the brown rottenness of No Man's Land, starting back here because he trod upon a hand, not even looking there because of the awfulness of an unburied head, and not till my dream was packed full of horror did I see him pitch forward on his knees as he reached safety—if it was that. For on the war-films I have seen men slip down as softly from the trench parapet, and none but the grimmer philosophers would say that they had reached safety by their fall. And when I escaped into wakefulness it was only to lie stiff and think of stories I had heard in the boyish voice, that rings indomitable yet has most of its gay notes flattened, of the modern subaltern.

'We were all of us in a barn one night, and a shell came along. My pal sang out, "*Help me, old man, I've got no legs!*" and I had to answer, "*I can't, old man, I've got no hands!*" '

Well, such are the dreams of Englishwomen to-day; I could not complain. But I wished for the return of our soldier.

So I said: 'I wish we could hear from Chris. It is a fortnight since he wrote.'

195

And then it was that Kitty wailed, 'Ah, don't begin to fuss,' and bent over her image in her hand-mirror as one might bend for refreshment over scented flowers.

I tried to build about me such a little globe of ease as always ensphered her, and thought of all that remained good in our lives though Chris had gone. My eye followed the mellow brick of the garden wall through the trees, and I reflected that by the contriving of these gardens that lay, well-kept as a woman's hand, on the south side of the hill, Kitty and I had proved ourselves worthy of the past generation that had set the old house on this sunny ledge, overhanging and overhung by beauty. And we had done much for the new house.

I could send my mind creeping from room to room like a purring cat, rubbing itself against all the brittle beautiful things that we had either recovered from antiquity or dug from the obscure pits of modern craftsmanship, basking in the colour that glowed from all our solemnly chosen fabrics with such pure intensity that it seemed to shed warmth like sunshine. Even now, when spending seemed a little disgraceful, I could think of that beauty with nothing but pride. I was sure that we were preserved from the reproach of luxury because we had made a fine place for Chris, one little part of the world that was, so far as surfaces could make it so, good enough for his amazing goodness.

Here we had nourished that surpassing amiability which was so habitual that one took it as one of his physical characteristics, and regarded any lapse into bad temper as a calamity startling as the breaking of a leg. Here we had made happiness inevitable for him. I could shut my eyes and think of innumerable proofs of how well we had succeeded, for there never was so visibly contented a man: the way he lingered with us in the mornings while the car throbbed at the door, delighting just in whatever way the weather looked in the familiar frame of things, how our

196

rooms burned with many coloured brightness on the darkest winter day, how not the fieriest summertime could consume the cool wet leafy places of our garden; the way that in the midst of entertaining a great company he would smile secretly to us, as though he knew we would not cease in our task of refreshing him; and all that he did on the morning just a year ago, when he went to the front. . . .

First he had sat in the morning-room and talked and stared out on the lawn that already had the desolation of an empty stage although he had not yet gone; then broke off suddenly and went about the house, looking into many rooms. He went to the stables and looked at the horses and had the dogs brought out; he refrained from touching them or speaking to them, as though he felt himself already infected with the squalor of war and did not want to contaminate their bright physical well-being. Then he went to the edge of the wood and stood staring down into the clumps of dark-leaved rhododendra and the yellow tangle of last year's bracken and the cold winter black of the trees. (From this very window I had spied on him.) Then he moved broodingly back to the house to be with his wife until the moment of his going, when I stood with her on the steps to see him motor off to Waterloo.

He kissed us both; as he bent over me I noticed once again how his hair was of two colours, brown and gold. Then he got into the car, put on his Tommy air, and said, 'So long! I'll write you from Berlin!' and as he spoke his head dropped back and he set a hard stare on the overarching house. That meant, I knew, that he loved the life he had lived with us and desired to carry with him to the dreary place of death and dirt the completest picture of everything about his home, on which his mind could brush when things were at their worst, as a man might finger an amulet through his shirt. This house, this life with us, was the core of his heart.

'If he could come back!' I said. 'He was so happy here.'

And Kitty answered: 'He could not have been happier.'

It was important that he should have been happy, for, you see, he was not like other city men. When we had played together as children in that wood he had always shown great faith in the imminence of the improbable. He thought that the birch tree would really stir and shrink and quicken into an enchanted princess, that he really was a Red Indian and that his disguise would suddenly fall from him at the right sundown, that at any moment a tiger might lift red fangs through the bracken; and he expected these things with a stronger motion of the imagination than the ordinary child's make-believe. And from a thousand intimations, from his occasional clear fixity of gaze on good things as though they were about to dissolve into better, from the passionate anticipation with which he went to new countries or met new people, I was aware that this faith had persisted into his adult life.

He had exchanged his expectation of becoming a Red Indian for the equally wistful aspiration of becoming completely reconciled to life. It was his hopeless hope that some time he would have an experience that would act on his life like alchemy, turning to gold all the dark metals of events, and from that revelation he would go on his way rich with an inextinguishable joy.

There had been, of course, no chance of his ever getting it. Literally there wasn't room to swing a revelation in his crowded life. First of all, at his father's death, he had been obliged to take over a business that was weighted by the needs of a mob of female relatives who were all useless either in the old way with anti-macassars or in the new way with golf clubs.

Then Kitty had come along and picked up his conception of normal expenditure and carelessly stretched it as a woman stretches a new glove on her hand. Then there had been the

198

difficult task of learning to live after the death of his little son. It had lain on us, as the responsibility that gave us dignity, to compensate him for his lack of free adventure by arranging him a gracious life. But now, just because our performance had been so brilliantly adequate, how dreary was the empty stage. . . .

We were not, perhaps, specially contemptible women, because nothing could ever really become a part of our life until it had been referred to Chris's attention. I remember thinking, as the parlourmaid came in with a card on the tray, how little it mattered who had called and what flag of prettiness she flew, since there was no chance that Chris would come in and stand over her, his fairness red in the firelight, and show her that detached attention, such as an unmusical man pays to good music, which men of anchored affections give to attractive women.

Kitty read from the card, ' "Mrs. William Grey, Mariposa, Ladysmith Road, Wealdstone." I don't know anybody in Wealdstone.' That is the name of the red suburban stain which fouls the fields three miles nearer London than Harrowweald. One cannot now protect one's environment as one could in the old days. 'Do I know her, Ward? Has she been here before?'

'Oh, no, ma'am.' The parlourmaid smiled superciliously. 'She said she had news for you.' From her tone one could deduce an over-confidential explanation made by a shabby visitor while using the door mat almost too zealously.

Kitty pondered and said, 'I'll come down.' As the girl went she took up the amber hairpins from her lap and began swathing her hair about her head. 'Last year's fashion,' she commented; 'but I fancy it'll do for a person with that sort of address.' She stood up and threw her little silk dressing-jacket over the rocking-horse. 'I'm seeing her because she may need something, and I specially want to be kind to people while Chris is away. One wants to deserve well of Heaven.'

199

For a minute she was aloof in radiance, but as we linked arms and went out into the corridor she became more mortal with a pout.

'The people that come breaking into one's nice quiet day,' she moaned reproachfully, and as we came to the head of the broad staircase she leaned over the white balustrade to peer down on the hall, and squeezed my arm. 'Look!' she whispered.

Just beneath us, on one of Kitty's prettiest chintz arm-chairs, sat a middle-aged woman. She wore a yellowish raincoat and a black hat with plumes whose sticky straw had but lately been renovated by something out of a little bottle bought at the chemist's. She had rolled her black thread gloves into a ball on her lap, so that she could turn her grey alpaca skirt well above her muddy boots and adjust its brushbraid with a seamed red hand which looked even more horrible when she presently raised it to touch the glistening flowers of the pink azalea that stood on a table beside her.

Kitty shivered and muttered, 'Let's get this over,' and ran down the stairs. On the last step she paused and said with a conscientious sweetness, 'Mrs. Grey?'

'Yes,' answered the visitor.

She lifted to Kitty a sallow and relaxed face whose expression gave me a sharp, pitying pang of prepossession in her favour; it was beautiful that so plain a woman should so ardently rejoice in another's loveliness.

'Are you Mrs. Baldry?' she asked, almost as if she were glad about it, and stood up.

The bones of her cheap stays clicked as she moved. Well, she was not so bad. Her body was long and round and shapely and with a noble squareness of the shoulders; her fair hair curled diffidently about a good brow; her grey eyes, though they were remote, as if anything worth looking at in her life had kept a long way off, were full of tenderness; and though she was

200

slender there was something about her of the wholesome endearing heaviness of the draught-ox or the big trusted dog. Yet she was bad enough. She was repulsively furred with neglect and poverty, as even a good glove that has dropped down behind a bed in a hotel and has lain undisturbed for a day or two is repulsive when the chambermaid retrieves it from the dust and fluff.

She flung at us as we sat down:

'My general is sister to your second housemaid.'

It left us at a loss. 'You've come about a reference?'

'Oh, no. I've had Gladys two years now, and I've always found her a very good girl. I want no reference.' With her fingernail she followed the burst seam of the dark pigskin purse that slid about on her shiny alpaca lap. 'But girls talk, you know. You mustn't blame them. . . .'

She seemed to be caught in a thicket of embarrassment, and sat staring up at the azalea.

Kitty said, with the hardness of a woman who sees before her the curse of women's lives, a domestic row, that she took no interest in servants' gossip.

'Oh, it isn't'—her eyes brimmed as though we had been unkind—'servants' gossip that I wanted to talk about. I only mentioned Gladys'—she continued to trace the burst seam of her purse—'because that's how I heard you didn't know.'

'What don't I know?'

Her head dropped a little.

'About Mr. Baldry. Forgive me, I don't know his rank.'

'Captain Baldry,' supplied Kitty wonderingly. 'What is it that I don't know about him?'

She looked far away from us, to the open door and its view of dark pines and pale March sunshine, and appeared to swallow something.

'Why, that he's hurt,' she gently said.

'Wounded, you mean?' asked Kitty.

201

Her rusty plumes oscillated as she moved her mild face about with an air of perplexity.

'Yes,' she said, 'he's wounded.'

Kitty's bright eyes met mine and we obeyed that mysterious human impulse to smile triumphantly at the spectacle of a fellow-creature occupied in baseness. For this news was not true. It could not possibly be true. The War Office would have wired to us immediately if Chris had been wounded. This was such a fraud as one sees recorded in the papers that meticulously record squalor, in paragraphs headed 'Heartless Fraud on Soldier's Wife.'

Presently she would say that she had gone to some expense to come here with her news, and that she was poor, and at the first generous look on our faces there would come some tale of trouble that would disgust the imagination by pictures of yellow wood furniture that a landlord oddly desired to seize and a pallid child with bandages round its throat.

I turned away my eyes and tried to be inattentive. Yet there was something about the physical quality of the woman, unlovely though she was, which preserved the occasion from utter baseness. I felt sure that had it not been for the tyrannous emptiness of that evil, shiny, pigskin purse that jerked about on her trembling knees, the poor driven creature would have chosen ways of candour and gentleness. It was, strangely enough, only when I looked at Kitty and marked how her brightly coloured prettiness arched over this plain criminal, as though she were a splendid bird of prey and this her sluggish insect food, that I felt the moment degrading.

She was, I felt, being a little too clever over it.

'How is he wounded?' she asked.

The caller traced a pattern on the carpet with her blunt toe.

'I don't know how to put it. . . . He's not exactly wounded . . . . A shell burst. . . .'

'Concussion?' suggested Kitty.

202

She answered with an odd glibness and humility, as though tendering us a term she had long brooded over without arriving at comprehension, and hoping that our superior intelligences would make something of it. 'Shell-shock.' Our faces did not illumine so she dragged on lamely. 'Anyway, he's not well.' Again she played with her purse. Her face was visibly damp.

'Not well? Is he dangerously ill?'

'Oh, no!' She was too kind to harrow us. 'Not dangerously ill.'

Kitty brutally permitted a silence to fall. Our caller could not bear it, and broke it in a voice that nervousness had turned to a funny diffident croak.

'He's in the Queen Mary Hospital at Boulogne.' We did not speak, and she began to flush and wriggle on her seat, and stooped forward to fumble under the legs of her chair for her umbrella. The sight of its green seams and unveracious tortoise-shell handle disgusted Kitty into speech.

'How do you know all this?'

Our visitor met her eyes. This was evidently a moment for which she had steeled herself, and she rose to it with a catch of her breath.

'A man who used to be a clerk along with my husband is in Mr. Baldry's regiment.' Her voice croaked even more piteously and her eyes begged, 'Leave it at that! Leave it at that! If you only knew——'

'And what regiment is that?' pursued Kitty.

The poor sallow face shone with sweat.

'I never thought to ask!' she said.

'Well, your friend's name. . . .'

Mrs. Grey moved on her seat so suddenly and violently that the pigskin purse fell from her lap and lay at my feet. I supposed that she cast it from her purposely because its emptiness had brought her to this humiliation, and that the scene would close presently in a few quiet tears.

203

I hoped that Kitty would let her go without scaring her too much with words and would not mind if I gave her a little money. There was no doubt in my mind but that this queer ugly episode, in which this woman butted like a clumsy animal at a gate she was not intelligent enough to open, would dissolve and be replaced by some more pleasing composition in which we would take our proper parts; in which, that is, she should turn from our rightness ashamed.

Yet she cried, 'But Chris is ill!'

It took a second for the compact insolence of the moment to penetrate: the amazing impertinence of the use of his name, the accusation of callousness she brought against us, whose passion for Chris was our point of honour, because we would not shriek at her false news, the impudently bright indignant gaze she flung at us, the lift of her voice that pretended she could not understand our coolness and irrelevance.

I pushed the purse away from me with my toe and hated her as the rich hate the poor, as insect things that will struggle out of the crannies which are their decent home, and introduce ugliness to the light of day. And Kitty said, in a voice shaken with pitilessness:

'You are impertinent. I know exactly what you are doing. You have read in the *Harrow Observer* or somewhere that my husband is at the front, and you come to tell this story because you think that you will get some money. I've read of such cases in the papers. You forget that if anything has happened to my husband the War Office would have told me. You should think yourself very lucky that I don't hand you over to the police.' She shrilled a little before she came to the end. 'Please go!'

'Kitty!' I breathed.

I was so ashamed that such a scene should spring from Chris's peril at the front that I wanted to go out into the garden and sit by the pond until the poor thing had removed her deplorable umbrella, her unpardonable raincoat, her poor frustrated fraud. But Mrs. Grey, who had begun, childishly and deliberately, 'It's *you* who are being . . .' and had desisted, simply because she realized that there were no harsh notes on her lyre and that she could not strike these chords that others found so easy, had fixed me with a certain wet, clear, patient gaze. It is the gift of animals and those of peasant stock. From the least regarded, from an old horse nosing over a gate or a drab in a workhouse ward, it wrings the heart. From this woman . . . I said checkingly, 'Kitty!' and reconciled her in an undertone ('There's some mistake. Got the name wrong, perhaps). Please tell us all about it, Mrs. Grey.'

Mrs. Grey began a forward movement like a curtsey. She was grovelling after that purse. When she rose her face was pink from stooping and her dignity swam uncertainly in a sea of half-shed tears. She said:

'I'm sorry I've upset you. But when you know a thing like that it isn't in flesh and blood to keep it from his wife. I am a married woman myself and I know. I knew Mr. Baldry fifteen years ago.' Her voice freely confessed that she had taken a liberty. 'Quite a friend of the family he was.' She had added that touch to soften the crude surprisingness of her announcement. It hardly did. 'We lost sight of each other. It's fifteen years since we last met. I had never seen or heard of him, nor thought to do again till I got this a week ago.'

She undid the purse and took out a telegram. I knew suddenly that all she said was true; for that was why her hands had clasped that purse.

'He isn't well! He isn't well!' she said pleadingly. 'He's lost his memory, and thinks—thinks he still knows me.'

She passed the telegram to Kitty, who read it and laid it on her knee.

'See,' said Mrs. Grey, 'it's addressed to Margaret Allington,

205

my maiden name, and I've been married these ten years. And it was sent to my old home, Monkey Island at Bray. Father kept the inn there. It's fifteen years since we left it. I never should have got this telegram if me and my husband hadn't been down there a little while back and told the folks who keep it now who I was.'

Kitty folded up the telegram and said in a little voice:

'This is a likely story.'

Again her grey eyes brimmed. People are rude to one, she visibly said, but surely not nice people like this. She simply continued to sit.

Kitty cried out, as though arguing:

'There's nothing about shell-shock in this wire.'

She melted into a trembling shyness.

'There was a letter too.'

Kitty held out her hand.

She gasped. 'Oh, no! I couldn't do that.'

'I must have it,' said Kitty.

The caller's eyes grew great, she rose and dived clumsily for her umbrella, which had again slipped under the chair. 'I can't,' she cried, and scurried to the open door like a pelted dog. She would have run down the steps at once had not some tender thought arrested her. She turned to me trustfully and stammered, 'He is at that hospital I said,' as if, since I had dealt her no direct blow, I might be able to salve the news she brought from the general wreck of manners. And then Kitty's stiff pallor struck to her heart, and she cried comfortingly across the distance, 'But I tell you I haven't seen him for fifteen years.' She faced about, pushed down her hat on her head, and ran down the steps on to the gravel. 'They won't understand,' we heard her sob.

For a long time we watched her as she went along the drive, her yellowish raincoat looking sick and bright in the sharp

206

sunshine, her black plumes nodding like the pines above, her cheap boots making her walk on her heels; a spreading stain on the fabric of our life. When she was quite hidden by the dark clump of rhododendra at the corner Kitty turned and went to the fire-place. She laid her arms against the oak mantelpiece and cooled her face against her arms.

When at last I followed her she said,

'Do you believe her?'

I started. I had forgotten that we had ever disbelieved her.

'Yes.'

'What can it mean?' She dropped her arms and stared at me imploringly. 'Think, think of something it can mean which isn't detestable!'

'It's all a mystery,' I said; and added mildly, because nobody has ever been cross with Kitty, 'You didn't help to clear it up.'

'Oh, I know you think I was rude,' she petulantly moaned, 'but you're so slow, you don't see what it means. Either it means that he's mad, our Chris, our splendid sane Chris, all broken and queer, not knowing us. . . . I can't bear to think of that. It can't be true. But if he isn't . . . Jenny, there was nothing in that telegram to show he'd lost his memory. It was just affection—a name that might have been a pet name—things that it was a little common to put in a telegram. It's queer he should have written such a message, queer that he shouldn't have told me about knowing her, queer that he ever should have known such a woman. It shows there are bits of him we don't know. Things may be awfully wrong. It's all such a breach of trust. I resent it.'

I was appalled by this stiff dignified gesture that seemed to be plucking Chris's soul from his body. She was hurt, of course. But there are ways pain should not show itself. . . .

'But Chris is ill,' I said.

She stared at me. 'You're saying what she said.'

Indeed there seemed no better words than those Mrs. Grey had used. I repeated. 'But he is ill.'

She laid her face against her arms again. 'What does that matter?' she said. 'If he could send that telegram, he. . . .' She paused, breathed deeply, and went on with the sick delight the unhappy sometimes find in ungraciousness. 'If he could send that telegram he isn't ours any longer.'

II

I was sorry, the next morning, that the post comes too late at Harrowweald to be brought up with the morning tea and waits for one at the breakfast table; for under Kitty's fixed gaze I had to open a letter which bore the Boulogne postmark and was addressed in the writing of Frank Baldry, Chris's cousin, who is in the Church.

'Dear Jenny,' it began, 'I am sorry to have to tell you that poor Chris has been disabled. He has had shell-shock and although not physically wounded is in a very strange state indeed. I got a wire from him on Thursday saying he was in hospital about a mile from Boulogne and that he wanted to see me. The telegram had not been sent direct to me, but to Ollenshaws, although I left the Ollenshaws curacy for Pentmouth nearly fifteen years ago. Sumpter is still there, luckily, and forwarded it on at once. I started that evening and looked hard for you and Kitty on the boat, naturally expecting to see you. But as you now know you were not there. I found the hospital in a girl's school which had been taken over by the Red Cross. The Red Cross is everywhere here.

'I found Chris in a nice room with a southern exposure with three other officers, who seemed very decent. He was better than I had expected but did not look quite himself. For one thing he was oddly boisterous in his greeting. He seemed glad to see

209

me, and told me he could remember nothing about his concussion, but that he wanted to get back to Harrowweald. He said things about the wood and the upper pond that seemed sentimental but not so much out of the way. He wanted to know if the daffies were out yet, and when he would be allowed to travel, because he felt that he would get well at once if only he could get home. And then he was silent for a minute as though he was holding something back. When he did begin to let out what he was holding back I was amazed. I will try and set it down as far as possible in the order in which it occurs. He informed me—with just the boyish manner he might have used fifteen years ago—that he was in love with a girl called Margaret Allington, who is the daughter of the man who keeps the inn on Monkey Island at Bray on the Thames. I gasped, "How long has this been going on?" He laughed at my surprise, and said, "Ever since I went down to stay with Uncle Ambrose at Dorney after I'd got my degree." Fifteen years ago! I was still staring at him, unable to believe this bare-faced admission of a deception carried on for years, when he went on to say that though he had wired to her and she had wired a message in return, she hadn't said anything about coming over to see him. "Now," he said quite coolly, "I know old Allington's had a bad season—oh, I'm quite well up in the innkeeping business these days!—and I think it may quite possibly be a lack of funds that is keeping her away. I've lost my cheque-book somewhere in the scrim and so I wonder if you'd send her some money. Or better still, for she's a shy country thing, you might fetch her." '

'I stared. "Chris," I said, "I know the war is making some of us very lax, and nobody could be more broadminded than I am. But there are limits. And when it comes to asking me to go over to England and fetch a woman. . . ." He interrupted me with a sneer that we parsons are inveterately eighteenth century

210

and have our minds perpetually inflamed by visions of squires' sons seducing country wenches, and declared that he meant to marry this Margaret Allington. "Oh, indeed," I said. "And may I ask what Kitty says to this arrangement?" "Who the devil is Kitty?" he asked blankly. "Kitty is your wife," I said quietly, but firmly. He sat up and exclaimed, "I haven't got a wife! Has some woman been turning up with a cock-and-bull story of being my wife? Because it's the damnedest lie!" '

'I determined to settle the matter by sharp common-sense handling. "Chris," I said, "you have evidently lost your memory. You were married to Kitty Ellis at St. George's, Hanover Square, on the third, or it may have been the fourth"—you know my wretched memory for dates—"of February in 1906." He turned very pale and asked what year this was. "1916," I told him. He fell back in a fainting condition. The nurse came and said I had done it all right this time, so she at least seemed to have known that he required a rude awakening, although the doctor (a very nice man, Winchester and New) told me he had known nothing of Chris's delusions.

'An hour later I was called back into the room. Chris was looking at himself in a hand mirror, which he threw on the floor as I entered. "You are right," he said. "I'm not twenty-one, but thirty-six." He said he felt lonely and afraid, and that I must bring Margaret Allington to him at once or he would die. Suddenly he stopped raving and asked, "Is Father all right?" I prayed for guidance and answered, "Your father passed away twelve years ago." He said, "Good God, can't you say he *died?*" and he turned over and lay with his back to me. I have never before seen a strong man weep and it is indeed a terrible sight. He moaned a lot and began to call for this Margaret. Then he turned over again and said "Now tell us all about this Kitty that I've married." I told him she was a beautiful little woman and mentioned that she had a charming and cultivated soprano

211

voice. He said very fractiously, "I don't like little women and I hate everybody, male or female, who sings. O God, I don't like this Kitty. Take her away." And then he began to rave again about this woman. He said that his body and soul were consumed with desire for her and that he would never rest until he once more held her in his arms. I had no suspicion that Chris had this side to his nature and it was almost a relief when he fainted again.

'I have seen him since and it is evening. But I have had a long talk with the doctor, who says that he has satisfied himself that Chris is suffering from a loss of memory extending over a period of fifteen years. He says that though of course it will be an occasion of great trial to us all he thinks that in view of Chris's expressed longing for Harrowweald he ought to be taken home, and advises me to make all arrangements for bringing him back some time next week. I hope I shall be upheld in this difficult enterprise.

'In the meantime I leave it to you to prepare Kitty for this terrible shock. How to do that you will know better than I. I wish she could be spared the experience, but since he is coming back and is certain to betray his real forgetfulness of her—for I am convinced there is no shamming in the business, there is a real gap in his memory—she must of course be made to understand. I hope she may have strength in the time of trial that lies before her and if I can be of any help to her no one will be more glad than I to render it. Tell me if I can run over now or any time either to talk to her or to help, so far as I can help, with him. You know how much I have always cared for dear old Chris. Yours ever, FRANK.'

Over my shoulder Kitty muttered, 'And he always pretended he liked my singing. . . .' And then gripped my arm and cried in a possessive fury. 'Bring him home! Bring him home!'

And so, a week later, they brought Chris home.

From breakfast-time that day the house was pervaded with a day-before-the-funeral feeling: although all duties arising from the occasion had been performed one could settle to nothing else. Chris was expected at one, but there then came a telegram to say he was delayed till the late afternoon. So Kitty, whose beauty was as changed in grief from its ordinary seeming as a rose in moonlight is different from a rose by day, took me down after lunch to the greenhouses and had a snappishly competent conversation about the year's vegetables with Pipe the gardener. After she had said many such horticulturally scandalous things as 'I know Queen Mary's prolific, but she isn't sweet,' she tugged at my hand and we went back to the house and found a great piece of the afternoon still on our hands. So Kitty went into the drawing-room and filled the house with the desolate merriment of an inattentively played pianola while I sat in the hall and wrote letters and noticed how sad dance music has sounded ever since the war began. And then she started a savage raid of domestic efficiency and made the housemaids cry because the brass handles of the tallboys were not bright enough and because there was only a ten to one instead of a hundred to one risk of breaking a leg on the parquet. After that she had tea, and hated the soda-cake. She was a little shrunk thing, huddled in the arm-chair farthest from the light, when at last the big car came nosing up the drive through the dusk.

We stood up. Through the thudding of the engines came the sound of Chris's great male voice, that always had in it a note like the baying of a big dog. 'Thanks, I can manage by myself. . . .' I heard, amazed, his step ring strong upon the stone, for I had felt his absence as a kind of death from which he would emerge ghostlike impalpable. And then he stood in the doorway, the gloom blurring his outlines like fur, the faint clear candle-light catching the fair down on his face. He did not see me, in my dark dress, nor huddled Kitty, and with the sleepy

213

smile of one who returns to a dear familiar place to rest, he walked into the hall and laid down his stick and his khaki cap beside the candlestick on the oak table. With both his hands he felt the old wood and stood humming happily through his teeth.

I cried out, because I had seen that his hair was of three colours now—brown and gold and silver.

With a quick turn of the head he found me out in the shadows. 'Hullo, Jenny!' he said, and gripped my hands.

'Oh, Chris, I am so glad,' I stuttered, and then could say no more for shame that I was thirty-five instead of twenty. For his eyes had hardened in the midst of his welcome as though he had trusted that I at least would have been no party to this conspiracy to deny that he was young, and he said: 'I've dropped Frank in town. My temper's of the convalescent type.' He might as well have said, 'I've dropped Frank, who has grown old, like you. . . .'

'Chris,' I went on, 'it's so wonderful to have you safe. . . .'

'Safe,' he repeated. He sighed very deeply and continued to hold my hands. There was a rustle in the shadows, and he dropped my hands.

The face that looked out of the dimness to him was very white; her upper lip was lifted over her teeth in a distressed grimace. And it was immediately as plain as though he had shouted it that this sad mask meant nothing to him. He knew, not because memory had given him any insight into her heart but because there is an instinctive kindliness in him which makes him wise about all suffering, that it would hurt her if he asked if this was his wife, but his body involuntarily began a gesture of inquiry before he realized that that too would hurt her and he checked it half-way. So, through a silence, he stood before her slightly bent, as though he had been maimed.

'I am your wife.' There was a weak, wailing anger behind the words.

214

'Kitty,' he said, softly and kindly. He looked round for some graciousness to make the scene less wounding, and stooped to kiss her. But he could not. The thought of another woman made him unable to breathe, sent the blood running under his skin.

With a toss, like a child saying, 'Well, if you don't want to, I'm sure I wouldn't for the world!' Kitty withdrew from the suspended caress. He watched her retreat into the shadows, as though she were a symbol of this new life by which he was baffled and oppressed, until the darkness outside became filled with the sound like the surf which we always hear at Harrowweald on angry evenings, and his eyes became distant and his lips smiled. 'Up here . . . in this old place . . . how one hears the pines. . . .'

She cried out from the other end of the room, as though she were speaking with someone behind a shut door. 'I've ordered dinner at seven. I thought you'd probably have missed a meal or two. Or would want to go to bed early.' She said it very smartly, with her head one one side like a bird, as if she was pleading that he would find her very clever about ordering dinner and thinking of his comfort.

'Good,' he said. 'I'd better dress now, hadn't I?' He looked up the staircase and would have gone up had I not held him back. For the little room in the south wing with the fishing-rods and the old books went in the rebuilding, absorbed by the black and white magnificence that is Kitty's bedroom.

'Oh, I'll take you up!' Kitty rang out efficiently. She pulled at his coat sleeve, so they started level on the lowest step. But as they went up the sense of his separateness beat her back; she lifted her arms as though she struggled through a fog, and fell behind. When he reached the top she was standing half-way down the stairs, her hands clasped under her chin. But he did not see her. He was looking along the corridor and saying, 'This

215

house is different.' If the soul has to stay in its coffin till the lead
is struck asunder, in its captivity it speaks with such a voice.

She braced herself with a gallant laugh. 'How you've forgotten,' she cried, and ran up to him, rattling her keys and
looking grave with housewifery, and I was left alone with the
dusk and the familiar things. The dusk flowed in wet and cool
from the garden as if to put out the fire of confusion lit on our
hearthstone, and the furniture, very visible through the soft
evening opacity with the observant brightness of old well-
polished wood, seemed terribly aware. Strangeness had come
into the house and everything was appalled by it, even time. For
the moments dragged. It seemed to me, half an hour later, that I
had been standing for an infinite period in the drawing-room,
remembering that in the old days the blinds had never been
drawn in this room because old Mrs. Baldry had liked to see the
night gathering like a pool in the valley while the day lingered as
a white streak above the farthest hills; and perceiving in pain that
the heavy blue blinds, which shroud the nine windows because a
lost Zeppelin sometimes clanks like a skeleton across the sky
above us, would make his home seem even more like prison.

I began to say what was in my mind to Kitty when she came
in, but she moved past me, remote in preoccupation, and I was
silent when I saw that she was dressed in all respects like a bride.
The gown she wore on her wedding-day ten years ago had been
cut and embroidered as this white satin was, her hair had been
coiled low on her neck as it was now. Around her throat were
her pearls, and her longer chain of diamonds dropped, looking
cruelly bright, to her white small breasts; because she held some
needlework to her bosom I saw that her right hand was stiff
with rings and her left hand bare save for her wedding-ring. She
dropped her load of flannel on a work-table and sat down,
spreading out her skirts, in an arm-chair by the fire. With her
lower lip thrust out, as if she were considering a menu, she

216

lowered her head and looked down on herself. She frowned to see that the high lights on the satin shone scarlet from the fire, that her flesh glowed like a rose, and she changed her seat for a high-backed chair beneath the furthest candle sconce. There were green curtains close by, and now the lights on her satin gown were green like cleft ice. She looked cold as moonlight, as virginity, but precious; the falling candlelight struck her hair to bright, pure gold. So she waited for him.

There came suddenly a thud at the door. We heard Chris swear and stumble to his feet, while one of the servants spoke helpfully. Kitty knitted her brows, for she hates gracelessness and a failure of physical adjustment is the worst indignity she can conceive. 'He's fallen down those three steps from the hall,' I whispered. 'They're new. . . .' She did not listen, because she was controlling her face into harmony with the appearance of serene virginity upon which his eyes would light when he entered the room.

His fall had ruffled him and made him look very large and red, and he breathed hard like an animal pursued into a strange place by night, and to his hot consciousness of his disorder the sight of Kitty, her face and hands and bosom shining like the snow, her gown enfolding her and her gold hair crowning her with radiance and the white fire of jewels giving a passion to the spectacle, was a deep refreshment. She sat still for a time, so that he might feel this well. Then raised her ringed hand to her necklaces.

'It seems so strange that you should not remember me,' she said. 'You gave me all these.'

He answered kindly. 'I am glad I did that. You look very beautiful in them.' But as he spoke his gaze shifted to the shadows in the corners of the room. He was thinking of another woman, of another beauty.

Kitty put up her hands as if to defend her jewels.

In that silence dinner was announced, and we went into the

dining-room. It is the fashion at Baldry Court to use no electric light save when there is work to be done or a great company to be entertained, and to eat and talk by the mild clarity of many candles. That night it was a kindly fashion, for we sat about the table with our faces veiled in shadow and seemed to listen in quiet contentment to the talk of our man who had come back to us. Yet all through the meal I was near to weeping because whenever he thought himself unobserved he looked at the things that were familiar to him. Dipping his head he would glance sideways at the old oak panelling; and nearer things he fingered as though sight were not intimate enough a contact, his hand caressed the arm of his chair, because he remembered the black gleam of it, stole out and touched the recollected salt-cellar. It was his furtiveness that was heartrending; it was as though he were an outcast and we who loved him stout police-men. Was Baldry Court so sleek a place that the unhappy felt offenders there? Then we had all been living wickedly and he too. As his fingers glided here and there he talked bravely about noncommittal things; to what ponies we had been strapped when at the age of five we were introduced to the hunting-field; how we had teased to be allowed to keep swans in the pond above the wood, and how the yellow bills of our intended pets had sent us shrieking homewards; and all the dear life that makes the bland English countryside so secretly adventurous. 'Funny thing,' he said, 'All the time I was at Boulogne I wanted to see a kingfisher. That blue, scudding down a stream. Or a heron's flight round a willow.' . . . He checked himself suddenly; his head fell forward on his chest. 'You have no herons here, of course,' he said drearily, and fingered the arm of his chair again. Then raised his head again, brisk with another subject. 'Do they still have trouble with foxes at Steppy End?'

Kitty shook her head. 'I don't know. . . .'

'Griffiths will know,' Chris said cheerily and swung round

218

on his seat to ask the butler, and found him osseous where Griffiths was rotund, dark where Griffiths had been merrily mottled, strange where Griffiths had been a part of home, a condition of life. He sat back in his chair as though his heart had stopped.

When the butler who is not Griffiths had left the room he spoke gruffly.

'Stupid of me, I know. But where is Griffiths?'

'Dead seven years ago,' said Kitty, her eyes on her plate.

He sighed deeply in a shuddering horror. 'I'm sorry. He was a good man.'

I cleared my throat. 'There are new people here, Chris, but they love you as the old ones did.'

He forced himself to smile at us both, to a gay response. 'As if I didn't know that to-night!'

But he did not know it. Even to me he would give no trust, because it was Jenny the girl who had been his friend and not Jenny the woman. All the inhabitants of this new tract of time were his enemies, all its circumstances his prison bars. There was suspicion in his gesture with which, when we were back in the drawing-room, he picked up the flannel from the work-table.

'Whose is this?' he said curiously; his mother had been a hard riding woman, not apt with her needle.

'Clothes for one of the cottagers,' answered Kitty breathlessly. 'We—we've a lot of responsibilities, you and I. With all the land you've bought there's ever so many people to look after. . . .'

He moved his shoulders uneasily, as if under a yoke, and after he had drunk his coffee pulled up one of the blinds and went out to pace the flagged walk under the windows. Kitty huddled carelessly by the fire, her hands over her face, unheeding that by its red glow she looked not so virginal and bridelike, so I think she was too distracted even to plan. I went to the piano.

219

Through this evening of sentences cut short because their completed meaning was always sorrow, of normal life dissolved to tears, the chords of Beethoven sounded serenely.

'So like you, Jenny,' said Kitty suddenly, 'to play Beethoven when it's the war that's caused all this. I could have told that you would have chosen to play German music, this night of all nights.'

So I began a sarabande by Purcell, a jolly thing that makes one see a plump, sound woman dancing on a sanded floor in some old inn with casks of good ale all about her and a world of sunshine and May lanes without. As I played I wondered if things like this happened when Purcell wrote such music, empty of everything except laughter and simple greeds and satisfactions and at the worst the wail of unrequited love. Why had modern life brought forth these horrors that make the old tragedies seem no more than nursery shows? Perhaps it is that adventurous men have too greatly changed the outward world which is life's engenderment. There are towns now, and even the trees and flowers are not as they were; the crocuses on the lawn, whose blades showed white in the wide beam let out by the window Chris had opened, should have pierced turf on Mediterranean cliffs; the golden larch beyond should have cast its long shadows on little yellow men as they crossed a Chinese plain. And the sky also is different. Behind Chris's head, as he halted at the open window, a searchlight turned all ways in the night like a sword brandished among the stars.

'Kitty.'

'Yes, Chris.' She was sweet and obedient and alert.

'I know my conduct must seem to you perversely insulting.' Behind him the searchlight wheeled while he gripped the sides of the window. 'But if I do not see Margaret Allington I shall die.'

She raised her hands to her jewels and pressed the cool globes of her pearls into her flesh. 'She lives near here,' she said easily. 'I will send the car down for her to-morrow. You shall see as much of her as you like.'

His arms fell to his side. 'Thank you,' he muttered. 'You're all being so kind——' he disengaged himself into the darkness.

I was amazed at Kitty's beautiful act and more amazed to find that it had made her face ugly. Her eyes snapped as they met mine. 'That dowd!' she said, keeping her voice low so that he might not hear it as he passed to and fro before the window. 'That dowd!'

This sudden abandonment of beauty and amiability means so much in our Kitty, whose law of life is grace, that I went over and kissed her. 'Dear, you're taking things all the wrong way,' I said. 'Chris is ill——'

'He's well enough to remember her all right,' she replied unanswerably.

Her silver shoe tapped the floor, she pinched her lips for some moments. 'After all, I suppose I can sit down to it. Other women do. Teddy Rex keeps a Gaiety girl and Mrs. Rex has to grin and bear it.'

She shrugged in answer to my silence. 'What else is it, do you think? It means that Chris is a man like other men. But I did think that bad women were pretty. I suppose he's had so much to do with pretty ones that a plain one's a change. . . .'

'Kitty! Kitty! how can you?' But her little pink mouth went on manufacturing malice. 'This is all a blind,' she said at the end of an unpardonable sentence. 'He's pretending. . . .' I was past speech then, who had felt his agony all the evening like a wound in my own body, and I did not care what I did to stop her. I gripped her small shoulders with my large hands and shook her till her jewels rattled and she scratched my fingers and gasped for breath. But I did not mind so long as she was silent.

Chris spoke from the darkness. 'Jenny!'

I let her go. He came in and stood over us, running his hand

221

through his hair unhappily. 'Let's all be decent to each other,' he said heavily. 'It's all such a muddle and it's so rotten for all of us. . . .'

Kitty shook herself neat and stood up. 'Why don't you say, "Jenny, you mustn't be rude to visitors?" It's how you feel, I know.' She gathered up her needlework. 'I'm going to bed. It's been a horrid night.'

She spoke so pathetically, like a child who hasn't enjoyed a party as much as it had thought it would, that both of us felt a stir of tenderness towards her as she left the room. We smiled sadly at each other as we sat down by the fire, and I perceived that, perhaps because I was flushed and looked younger, he felt more intimate with me than he had yet done since his return. Indeed in the warm friendly silence that followed he was like a patient when tiring visitors have gone and he is left alone with his trusted nurse; smiled under drooped lids and then paid me the high compliment of disregard. His limbs relaxed, he sank back into his chair. I watched him vigilantly and was ready at that moment when thought intruded into his drowsings and his face began to twitch.

'You can't remember her at all?' I asked.

'Oh, yes,' he said, without raising his eyelids. 'In a sense. I know how she bows when you meet her in the street, how she dresses when she goes to church. I know her as one knows a woman staying in the same hotel. Just like that.'

'It's a pity you can't remember Kitty. All that a wife should be she's been to you.'

He sat forward, warming his palms at the blaze and hunching his shoulders as though there was a draught. His silence compelled me to look at him and I found his eyes on me, cold and incredulous and frightened. 'Jenny, is this true?'

'That Kitty's been a good wife?'

'That Kitty is my wife. That I am old. That——' he waved a hand at the altered room—'all this.'

222

'It is all true. She is your wife and this place is changed—and it's better and jollier in all sorts of ways, believe me—and fifteen years have passed. Why, Chris, can't you see that I have grown old?' My vanity could hardly endure his slow stare but I kept my fingers clasped on my lap. 'You see?'

He turned away with an assenting mutter. But I saw that deep down in him, not to be moved by any material proof, his spirit was incredulous.

'Tell me what seems real to you,' I begged. 'Chris, be a pal—I'll never tell——'

'Mmm,' he said. His elbows were on his knees, and his hands stroked his thick tarnished hair; I could not see his face, but I knew that his skin was red and that his grey eyes were wet and bright. Then suddenly he lifted his chin and laughed, like a happy swimmer breaking through a wave that has swept him far inshore. He glowed with a radiance that illuminated the moment till my blood tingled and I began to run my hands together and laugh too. 'Why, Monkey Island's real. But you don't know old Monkey. Let me tell you——'

I have lived so long with the story which he told me that I cannot now remember his shy phrases. But this is how I have visualized his meeting with love on his secret island. I think it is the truth.

223

III

From Uncle Ambrose's gates one took the field-path across the meadow where Whiston's cows are put to graze and got through the second stile, the one between the two big alders, into a long straight road that ran, very tedious in the trough of hot air that is the Thames valley, across the flat lands to Bray. After a mile or so there branched from it a private road which followed a line of noble poplars that led to the pretentiously simple porch of a *cottage ornée* called 'The Hut.' One passed that and went on to a group of outbuildings which gave, as it seemed impossible that bricks and wood and plaster should give, an impression that they were knock-kneed. There was a shed that let in the rain through its mossy tiles and sported a board 'Garage'; there was a glasshouse containing a pinched and sulky vine; there was a hasty collection of planks set askew over an agricultural machine of some sort; there were three barrels of concrete and an empty and rusting aviary. 'Margaret's father,' said Chris, 'had bought them at sales.' Past these marched the poplars and lifted their strong yet tremulous silver spires on each side of the gravel slope which went down to the ferry; between two of them—he described it meticulously as though it were of immense significance—there stood a white hawthorn. In front were the dark green glassy waters of an unvisited backwater; and beyond them a bright lawn set with many walnut trees and a

224

few great chestnuts, well lit with their candles, and to the left of that a low white house with a green dome rising in its middle and a veranda whose roof of hammered iron had gone verdigris colour with age and the Thames weather. This was the Monkey Island Inn. The third Duke of Marlborough had built it for a 'folly,' and perching there with nothing but a line of walnut trees and a fringe of lawn between it and the fast full shining Thames it had a grace and silliness that belonged to the eighteenth century.

Well, one sounded the bell that hung on a post, and presently Margaret in a white dress would come out of the porch and would walk to the stone steps down to the river. Invariably, as she passed the walnut tree that overhung the path, she would pick a leaf and crush it and sniff the sweet scent; and as she came near the steps she would shade her eyes and peer across the water. 'She is a little near-sighted; you can't imagine how sweet it makes her look.' (I did not say that I had seen her, for indeed this Margaret I had never seen.) A sudden serene gravity would show that she had seen one, and she would get into the fourfoot punt that was used as a ferry and bring it over very slowly, with rather stiff movements of her long arms, to exactly the right place. When she had got the punt up on the gravel her serious brow would relax and she would smile at one and shake hands and say something friendly, like, 'Father thought you'd be over this afternoon, it being so fine, so he's saved some ducks' eggs for tea.' And then one took the pole from her and brought her back to the island, though probably one did not mount the steps to the lawn for quite a long time. It was so good to sit in the punt by the landing-stage while Margaret dabbled her hands in the black waters and forgot her shyness as one talked. 'She's such good company. She's got an accurate mind that would have made her a good engineer, but when she picks up facts she kind of gives them a motherly hug. She's charity and love itself.'

225

(Again, I did not say that I had seen her.) If people drifted in to tea one had to talk to her while she cut the bread and butter and the sandwiches in the kitchen, but in this year of floods few visitors cared to try the hard rowing below Bray Lock. So usually one sat down there in the boat, talking with a sense of leisure, as though one had all the rest of one's life in which to carry on this conversation, and noting how the reflected ripple of the water made a bright vibrant mark upon her throat and other effects of the scene upon her beauty; until the afternoon grew drowsy and she said, 'Father will be wanting his tea.' And they would go up and find old Allington, in white ducks, standing in the fringe of long grasses and cow-parsley on the other edge of the island, looking to his poultry or his rabbits. He was a little man with a tuft of copper-coloured hair rising from the middle of his forehead like a clown's curl, who shook hands hard and explained very soon that he was a rough diamond. Then they all had tea under the walnut tree where the canary's cage was hanging, and the ducks' eggs would be brought out, and Mr. Allington would talk much Thameside gossip: how the lock-keeper at Teddington had had his back broken by a swan, mad as swans are in May, and how they would lose their licence at the Dovetail Arms if they were not careful, and how the man who kept the inn by Surly Hall was like to die, because after he had been cursing his daughter for two days for having run away with a soldier from Windsor Barracks, he had suddenly seen her white face in a clump of rushes in the river just under the hole in the garden fence. Margaret would sit quiet, round-eyed at the world's ways, and shy because of Chris.

So they would sit on that bright lawn until the day was dyed with evening blue, and Mr. Allington was more and more often obliged to leap into the punt to chase his ducks, who had started on a trip to Bray Lock, or to crawl into the undergrowth after rabbits similarly demoralized by the dusk. And then Chris would say he had to go, and they would stand in a communing silence while the hearty voice of Mr. Allington shouted from midstream or under the alder-boughs a disregarded invitation to stay and have a bit of supper. In the liquefaction of colours which happens on a summer evening, when the green grass seemed like a precious fluid poured out on the earth and dripping over to the river, and the chestnut candles were no longer proud flowers, but just wet white lights in the humid mass of the tree, when the brown earth seemed just a little denser than the water, Margaret also participated. Chris explained this part of his story stumblingly, but I too have watched people I loved in the dusk and I know what he meant. As she sat in the punt while he ferried himself across it was no longer visible that her fair hair curled diffidently and that its rather wandering parting was a little on one side; that her straight brows, which were a little darker than her hair, were nearly always contracted in a frown of conscientious speculation; that her mouth and chin were noble yet delicate as flowers; that her shoulders were slightly hunched because her young body, like a lily stem, found it difficult to manage its own tallness. She was then just a girl in white who lifted a white face or drooped a dull gold head. And as that she was nearer to him than at any other time. That he loved her, in this twilight which obscured all the physical details which he adored, seemed to him a guarantee that theirs was a changeless love which would persist if she were old or maimed or disfigured. He stood beside the crazy post where the bell hung and watched the white figure take the punt over the black waters, mount the grey steps and assume their greyness, become a green shade in the green darkness of the foliage-darkened lawn, and he exulted in that guarantee.

How long this went on he had forgotten; but it continued for some time before there came the end of his life, the last day he could remember. I was barred out of that day. His lips told me of its physical appearances, while from his wet, bright eyes and his flushed skin, his beautiful signs of a noble excitement, I tried to derive the real story. It seemed that the day when he bicycled over to Monkey Island, happy because Uncle Ambrose had gone up to town and he could stay to supper with the Allingtons, was the most glorious day the year had yet brought. The whole world seemed melting into light. Cumulus clouds floated very high, like lumps of white light against a deep, glowing sky, and dropped dazzling reflections on the beaming Thames. The trees moved not like timber shocked by wind, but floatingly, like weeds at the bottom of a well of sunshine. When Margaret came out of the porch and paused, as she always did, to crush and smell the walnut leaf and shade her eyes with her hand, her white dress shone like silver.

She brought the punt across the said very primly, 'Dad will be disappointed, he's gone up to town on business,' and answered gravely, 'That is very kind of you,' when he took the punt-pole from her and said laughingly, 'Never mind. I'll come and see you all the same.' (I could see them as Chris spoke, so young and pale and solemn, with the intense light spilling all around them.) That afternoon they did not sit in the punt by the landing-stage, but wandered about the island and played with the rabbits and looked at the ducks, and were inordinately silent. For a long time they stood in the fringe of rough grass on the other side of the island and Margaret breathed contentedly that the Thames was so beautiful. Past the spit of sand at the far end of the island, where a great swan swanked to the empty reach that it would protect its mate against all comers, the river opened to a silver breadth between flat meadows stretching back to far rows of pin-thick black poplars, until it wound away to Windsor behind a line of high trees whose heads were bronze with unopened buds and whose flanks were hidden by a hedge of copper-beech and crimson and white hawthorn. Chris said he

228

would take her down to Dorney Lock in the skiff, and she got in very silently and obediently, but as soon as they were out in midstream she developed a sense of duty and said she could not leave the inn with just that boy. And then she went into the kitchen and, sucking in her lower lip for shyness, very conscientiously cut piles of bread and butter in case some visitors came to tea. Just when Chris was convincing her of the impossibility of any visitors arriving they came; a fat woman in a luscious pink blouse and an old chap who had been rowing in a tweed waistcoat. Chris went out, though Margaret laughed and trembled and begged him not to, and waited on them. It should have been a great lark but suddenly he hated them, and when they offered him a tip for pushing the boat off he snarled absurdly and ran back, miraculously relieved, to the bar-parlour.

Still Margaret would not leave the island. 'Supposing,' she said, 'that Mr. Learoyd comes for his Bass.' But she consented to walk with him to the wild part of the island, where poplars and alders and willows grew round a clearing in which white willow herb and purple figwort and here and there a potato flower, last ailing consequence of one of Mr. Allington's least successful enterprises, fought down to the fringe of iris on the river's lip. In this gentle jungle was a rustic seat, relic of a reckless aspiration on the part of Mr. Allington to make this a pleasure garden, and on it they sat until a pale moon appeared above the green cornfield on the other side of the river. 'Not six yet,' he said, taking out his watch. 'Not six yet,' she repeated. Words between them seemed to bear a significance apart from their meaning. Then a heron flapped gigantic in front of the moon and swung in wide circles round the willow tree before them. 'Oh, look!' she cried. He seized the hand she flung upwards and gathered her into his arms. They were so for long while the great bird's wings beat above them.

Afterwards she pulled at his hand. She wanted to go back

229

across the lawn and walk round the inn, which looked mournful as unlit houses do by dusk. They passed beside the green and white stucco barrier of the veranda and stood on the three-cornered lawn that shelved high over the stream at the island's end, regarding the river, which was now something more wonderful than water, because it had taken to its bosom the rose and amber glories of the sunset smouldering behind the elms and Bray church-tower. Birds sat on the telegraph wires that span the river there as the black notes sit on a stave of music. Then she went to the window of the parlour and rested her cheek against the glass, looking in. The little room was sad with twilight, and there was nothing to be seen but Margaret's sewing-machine on the table and the enlarged photograph of Margaret's mother over the mantelpiece, and the views of Tintern Abbey framed in red plush, and on the floor, the marigold pattern making itself felt through the dusk, Mr. Allington's carpet slippers. 'Think of me sitting in there,' she whispered, 'not knowing you loved me.' Then they went into the bar and drank milk, while she walked about fingering familiar things with an absurd expression of exaltation, as though that day she was fond of everything, even the handles of the beer engine.

When there had descended on them a night as brilliant as the day, he drew her out into the darkness, which was sweet with the scent of walnut leaves, and they went across the lawn, bending beneath the chestnut boughs, not to the wild part of the island, but to a circle of smooth turf divided from it by a railing of wrought iron. On this stood a small Greek temple, looking very lovely in the moonlight. He had never brought Margaret here before because Mr. Allington had once told him, spatulate forefinger at his nose, that it had been built by the Dook for his excesses, and it was in the quality of his love for her that he could not bear to think of her in connection with anything base. But to-night there was nothing anywhere but beauty. He lifted her in his arms and carried her within the columns and made her stand in a niche above the altar. A strong stream of moonlight rushed upon her there; by its light he could not tell if her hair was white as silver or yellow as gold, and again he was filled with exultation because he knew that it would not have mattered if it had been white. His love was changeless. Lifting her down from the niche, he told her so. And as he spoke her warm body melted to nothingness in his arms. The columns that had stood so hard and black against the quivering tide of moonlight and starlight tottered and dissolved. He was lying in a hateful world where barbed-wire entanglements showed impish knots against a livid sky full of booming noise and splashes of fire and wails for water, and the stretcher bearers were hurting his back intolerably.

Chris fell to blowing out the candles, and I, perhaps because the egotistical part of me was looking for something to say that would make him feel me devoted and intimate, could not speak.

Suddenly he desisted, stared at a candle flame, and said: 'If you had seen the way she rested her cheek against the glass and looked into the little room, you'd understand that I can't say, "Yes, Kitty's my wife, and Margaret somehow just nothing at all." '

'Of course you can't,' I murmured.

We gripped hands, and he brought down on our conversation the finality of darkness.

231

IV

Next morning it appeared that the chauffeur had to take the Rolls-Royce up to town to get a part replaced, and Margaret could not be brought from Wealdstone till the afternoon. It fell to me to fetch her. 'At least,' Kitty had said, 'I might be spared that.' Before I started I went to the pond on the hill's edge. It is a place where autumn lives half the year, for even when the spring lights tongues of green fire in the undergrowth and the valley shows sunlit between the tree trunks, here the pond is fringed with yellow bracken and tinged bramble, and the water flows amber over last winter's leaves. Through this brown gloom, darkened now by a surly sky, Chris was taking the skiff, standing in the stern and using his oar like a gondolier. He had come down here soon after breakfast, driven from the house by the strangeness of all but the outer walls, and discontented with the ground because everywhere but this wet intractable spot bore the marks of Kitty's genius. After lunch there had been another attempt to settle down, but, with a grim glare at a knot of late Christmas roses bright in a copse that fifteen years ago had been dark, he went back to the russet-eaved boat-house and this play with the skiff. It was a boy's sport, and it was dreadful to see him turn a middle-aged face as he brought the boat inshore.

'I'm just going down to fetch Margaret,' I said.

He thanked me for it.

'But, Chris, I must tell you. I've seen Margaret. She came up here, so kind and gentle, to tell us you were wounded. She's the greatest dear in the world. But she's not as you think of her. She's old, Chris. She isn't beautiful any more. She's drearily married. She's seamed and scored and ravaged by squalid circumstances. You can't love her when you see her.'

'Didn't I tell you last night,' he said, 'that that doesn't matter?' He dipped his oar to a stroke that sent him far away from me. 'Bring her soon. I shall wait for her down here.'

Wealdstone is not, in its way, a bad place; it lies in the lap of open country and at the end of every street rise the green hill of Harrow and the spires of Harrow School. But all the streets are long and red and freely articulated with railway arches, and factories spoil the skyline with red angular chimneys, and in front of the shops stand little women with backs ridged by cheap stays, who tapped their upper lips with their forefingers and made other feeble, doubtful gestures as though they wanted to buy something and knew that if they did they would have to starve some other appetite. When we asked them the way they turned to us faces sour with thrift. It was a town of people who could not do as they liked. And here Margaret lived, in a long road of red brick boxes, flecked here and there with the pink blur of almond blossom, which debouched on a flat field where green grass rose up rank through clay mould blackened by coal dust from the railway line and the adjacent goods yard. Mariposa, which was the last house in the road, did not even have an almond tree. In her front garden, which seemed to be imperfectly reclaimed from the greasy field, yellow crocus and some sodden squills just winked, and the back, where a man was handling a spade without mastery, presented the austere appearance of an allotment. And not only did Margaret live in this place; she belonged to it. When she opened the door she gazed at me with watering eyes and in perplexity stroked her disordered

233

hair with a floury hand. Her face was sallow with heat, and beads of perspiration glittered in the deep dragging line between her nostrils and the corners of her mouth.

She said, 'He's home?'

I nodded.

She pulled me inside and slammed the door. 'Is he well?'

'Quite,' I answered.

Her tense stare relaxed. She rubbed her hands on her overall and said, 'You'll excuse me. It's the girl's day out. If you'll step into the parlour. . . .'

So in her parlour I sat and told her how it was with Chris and how greatly he desired to see her. And as I spoke of his longing I turned my eyes away from her, because she was sitting on a sofa, upholstered in velveteen of a sickish green, which was so low that her knees stuck up in front of her and she had to clasp them with her seamed floury hands; and I could see that the skin of her face was damp. And then my voice failed me as I looked round the room, because I saw just what Margaret had seen that evening fifteen years ago when she had laid her cheek to the parlour window at Monkey Island. There was the enlarged photograph of Margaret's mother over the mantelpiece; on the walls were the view of Tintern Abbey, framed in red plush; between the rickety legs of the china cupboard was the sewing-machine; and tucked into the corner between my chair and the fender were a pair of carpet slippers. All her life long Margaret, who in her time had partaken of the inalienable dignity of a requited love, had lived with men who wore carpet slippers in the house. I turned my eyes away again and this time looked down the garden at the figure that was not so much digging as exhibiting his incapacity to deal with a spade. He was sneezing very frequently, and his sneezes made the unbuckled straps at the back of his waistcoat wag violently. I supposed him to be Mr. William Grey.

234

I had finished the statement of our sad case; and I saw that though she had not moved, clasping her knees in a set hideous attitude, the tears were rolling down her cheeks. 'Oh, don't! Oh, don't!' I exclaimed, standing up. Her tear-stained immobility touched the heart. 'He's not so bad—he'll get quite well. . . .'

'I know, I know,' she said miserably. 'I don't believe that anything bad would be allowed to happen to Chris for long. And I'm sure,' she said kindly, 'you're looking after him beautifully. But when a thing you had thought had ended fifteen years ago starts all over again, and you're very tired. . . .' She drew one of those dreadful hands across her tears, her damp skin, her rough, bagging overall. 'I'm hot. I've been baking. You can't get a girl nowadays that understands the baking.' Her gaze became remote and tender, she said in a manner that was at once argumentative and narrative, as though she were telling the whole story to a neighbour over the garden wall, 'I suppose I ought to say that he isn't right in his head and I'm married—but oh!' she cried, and I felt as though after much fumbling with damp matches and many doubts as to whether there was any oil in the wick I had lit the lamp at last, 'I want to see him so! It's wrong—I know it's wrong, but I am so glad Chris wants to see me too!'

'You'll do him good!' I found myself raising my voice to the pitch she had suddenly attained as though to keep her at it. 'Come now!'

She dipped suddenly to compassion. 'But the young lady?' she asked timidly. 'She was upset last time I went. I've often wondered if I did right in going. Even if Chris has forgotten her,' she gave out with an air of exposition, 'he'll want to do what's right. He couldn't bear to hurt her.'

'That's true,' I said. 'You do know our Chris. He watches her out of the corner of his eye, even when he's feeling at his

235

worst, to see she isn't wincing. But she sent me here to-day.'

'*Oh!*' cried Margaret, glowing. 'She must have a lovely nature!'

I lost suddenly the thread of the conversation. I could not talk about Kitty. She appeared to me at that moment a faceless figure with flounces, just as most of the servants at Baldry Court appear to me as faceless figures with caps and aprons. There were only two real people in the world, Chris and this woman whose personality was sounding through her squalor like a beautiful voice singing in a darkened room, and I was absorbed in a mental vision of them. You know how the saints and the prophets are depicted in the steel engravings in old Bibles; so they were standing, in flowing white robes, on rocks against a pitch black sky, a strong light beating on their eyes up-turned in ecstasy, and their hands out-stretched to receive the spiritual blessing of which the fierce rays were an emanation. Into that rapt silence I desired to break, and I whispered irrelevantly, 'Oh, nothing, nothing is too good for Chris,' while I said to myself, 'If she were really like that, solemn and beautified,' and my eyes returned to look despairingly on her ugliness. But she was really like that. She had responded to my irrelevant murmur of adoration by just such a solemn and beatified appearance as I had imagined. Her grave eyes were up-turned, those terrible hands lay palm upwards on her knees as though to receive the love of which her radiance was an emanation. And then, at a sound in the kitchen, she snatched my exaltation from me by suddenly turning dull. 'I think that's Mr. Grey come in from his gardening. You'll excuse me. . . .'

Through the open door I heard a voice saying in a way which suggested that its production involved much agitation of a prominent Adam's apple. 'Well, dear, seeing you had a friend I thought I'd better slip up and change my gardening trousers.' I do not know what she said to him, but her voice was soft and comforting and occasionally girlish and interrupted by laughter, and I perceived from its sound that with characteristic gravity she had accepted it as her mission to keep loveliness and excitement alive in his life. 'An old friend of mine has been wounded,' was the only phrase I heard, but when she drew him out into the garden under the window she had evidently explained the situation away, for he listened docilely as she said, 'I've made some rock-cakes for your tea. And if I'm late for supper there's a dish of macaroni cheese you must put in the oven and a tin of tomatoes to eat with it. And there's a little rhubarb and shape.' She told them off on her fingers, and then whisked him round and buckled the wagging straps at the back of his waistcoat. He was a lank man with curly grey hairs growing from every place where it is inadvisable that hairs should grow, from the inside of his ears, from his nostrils, on the back of his hands; but he looked pleased when she touched him and said in a devoted way, 'Very well, dear. Don't worry about me. I'll trot along after tea and have a game of draughts with Mr. Podds.' She answered, 'Yes, dear. And now get on with those cabbages. You're going to keep me in lovely cabbages just as you did last year, won't you, darling?' She linked arms with him and took him back to his digging.

When she came back into the parlour again she was wearing that yellowish raincoat, that hat whose hearse plumes nodded over its sticky straw, that grey alpaca skirt. I first defensively clutched my hands. It would have been such agony to the finger tips to touch any part of her apparel. And then I thought of Chris, to whom a second before I had hoped to bring a serene comforter. I perceived clearly that that ecstatic woman lifting her eyes and her hands to the benediction of love was Margaret as she existed in eternity; but this was Margaret as she existed in time, as the fifteen years between Monkey Island and this damp day in Ladysmith Road had irreparably made her. Well, I had promised to bring her to him.

She said, 'I'm ready,' and against that simple view of her condition I had no argument. But when she paused by the painted drain pipe in the hall and peered under contracted brows for that unveracious tortoise-shell handle, I said hastily, 'Oh, don't trouble about an umbrella.'

'I'll maybe need it walking home,' she pondered.

'But the car will bring you back.'

'Oh, that will be lovely!' She laughed nervously, looking very plain. 'Do you know, I know the way we're coming together is terrible, but I can't think of a meeting with Chris as anything but a kind of treat. I've got a sort of party feeling now!'

As she held the gate open for me she looked back at the house. 'It is a horrid little house, isn't it?' she asked. She evidently desired sanction for a long suppressed discontent.

'It isn't very nice,' I agreed.

'They put cows sometimes into the field at the back,' she went on, as if conscientiously counting her blessings. 'I like that. But otherwise it isn't much.'

'But it's got a very pretty name,' I said, laying my hand on the raised metal letters that spelt 'Mariposa' across the gate.

'Ah, isn't it!' she exclaimed, with the smile of the inveterate romanticist. 'It's Spanish, you know, for butterfly.'

Once we were in the automobile she became a little sullen with shyness because she felt herself so big and clumsy, her clothes so coarse against the fine upholstery, the silver vase of Christmas roses, and all the deliberate delicacy of Kitty's car. She was afraid of the chauffeur, as the poor are always afraid of menservants, and ducked her head when he got out to start the car. To recall her to ease and beauty I told her that though Chris had told me all about their meeting he knew nothing of their parting, and that I wished very much to hear what had happened. And in a deep, embarrassed voice she began to tell me

238

about Monkey Island. It was strange that both Chris and she spoke of it as though it were not a place, but a magic state which largely explained the actions performed in it. Strange too that both of them should describe meticulously the one white haw-thorn that stood among the poplars by the ferryside; I suppose that a thing that one has looked at with somebody one loves acquires for ever after a special significance. She said that her father had gone there when she was fourteen. After Mrs. Allington had been taken away by a swift and painful death the cheer of his Windsor hostelry had become intolerable to the man. He regarded the whole world as her grave; and the tipsy sergeants in scarlet and the carter crying for a pint of four-half, and the horses dipping their mild noses to the trough in the courtyard, all seemed to be defiling it by their happy, silly appetites. So they went to Monkey Island, whose utter differ-ence was a healing, and settled down happily in its green silence. All the summer was lovely; quiet kind people, schoolmasters who fished, men who wrote books, married couples who still loved solitude, used to come and stay in the bright little inn. And all the winter was lovely too; her temperament could see an adventure in taking up the carpets because the Thames was coming into the coffee-room. That was the tale of her life for four years. With her head on one side, and an air of judging this question by the light of experience, she pronounced that she had then been happy.

Then, one April afternoon, Chris landed at the island, and by the first clean quick movement of tying up his boat made her his slave. I could imagine that it would be so. He was so wonderful when he was young; he possessed in great measure the loveliness of young men, which is like the loveliness of the spry foal or the sapling, but in him it was vexed into a serious and moving beauty by the inhabiting soul. When the sunlight lay on him, discerning the gold hairs on his brown head, or when he was

239

subject to any other physical pleasure there was always reserve in his response to it; from his eyes, which though grey were somehow dark with speculation, one perceived that he was distracted by participation in some spiritual drama. To see him was to desire intimacy with him so that one might intervene between this body which was formed for happiness and this soul which cherished so deep a faith in tragedy. . . . Well, she gave Chris ducks' eggs for tea. 'No one ever had ducks' eggs like father did. It was his way of feeding them. It didn't pay, of course, but they *were* good.' Before the afternoon was out he had snared them all with the silken net of his fine manners; he had talked to father about his poultry and walked about the runs, and then as on many succeeding days he had laid his charm at the girl's feet. 'But I thought he must be someone royal, and when he kept on coming I thought it must be for the ducks' eggs.' Then her damp, dull skin flushed suddenly to a warm glory, and she began to stammer.

'I know all about that,' I said quickly. I was more afraid that I should feel envy or any base passion in the presence of this woman than I have ever been of anything in my life. 'I want to hear how you came to part.'

'Oh,' she cried. 'It was the silliest quarrel. We had known how we felt for just a week. Such a week. Lovely weather we had, and father had noticed nothing. I didn't want him to, because I thought father might want the marriage soon and think any delay a slight on me, and I knew we would have to wait. Eh, I can remember saying to myself, "Perhaps five years," trying to make it as bad as I could so that if we could marry sooner it would be a lovely surprise.' She repeated it with soft irony. 'Perhaps five years!'

'Well, then, on Thursday afternoon I'd gone on the back-water with Bert Wells, nephew to Mr. Wells who keeps the inn at Surly Hall. I was laughing out loud because he did row so

240

funny. He's a town chap, and he was handling those oars for all the world as though they were teaspoons. The old dinghy just sat on the water like a hen on its chicks and didn't move, and he so sure of himself! I just sat and laughed and laughed. Then all of a sudden—*clang-clang!* the bell at the ferry. And there was Chris, standing up there under the poplars, his brows straight and black and not a smile on him. I felt very bad. We picked him up in the dinghy and took him across, and still he didn't smile. He and I got on the island and Bert, who saw there was something wrong, said, "Well, I'll toddle off." And there I was on the lawn with Chris, and he angry and somehow miles away. I remember him saying, "Here I am, coming to say good-bye because I must go away to-night, and I find you larking with that bounder," and I said, "Oh, Chris! I've known Bert all my life, through him coming to his uncle for the holidays, and we weren't larking. It was only that he couldn't row." And he went on talking and then it struck me he wasn't trusting me as he would trust a girl of his own class, and I told him so, and he went on being cruel. Oh, don't make me remember the things we said to each other! It doesn't help. . . . At last I said something awful and he said, "Very well, I agree. I'll go," and he walked over to where the boy was chopping wood and got him to take him over in the punt. As he passed me he turned away his face. Well, that's all.'

I had got the key at last. There had been a spring at Baldry Court fifteen years ago which was desolate for all that there was beautiful weather. Chris had lingered with Uncle Ambrose in his Thameside rectory as he had never lingered before, and old Mr. Baldry was filling the house with a sense of hot, apoplectic misery. All day he was up in town at the office and without explanation he had discontinued his noontide habit of ringing up his wife. All night he used to sit in the library looking over his papers and ledgers; the housemaids often found him in the

morning asleep across his desk, very red, yet looking dead. The
men he brought home to dinner treated him with a kindness and
consideration which was not the tribute that that victorious and
trumpeting personality was accustomed to exact; in the course
of conversation with them he dropped braggartly cheerful hints
of impending ruin, which it would have been humiliating to
address to us directly. At last there came one morning when
he said to Mrs. Baldry across the breakfast table, 'I've sent
for Chris. If the boy's worth his salt . . .' It was an
appalling admission, like the groan of an old ship as her tim-
bers shiver, from a man who doubted the capacity of his son as
fathers always doubt the capacity of the children of their old age.
It was that evening, as I went down to see the new baby at the
lodge, that I met Chris coming up the drive. Through the blue
twilight his white face had a drowned look. I remember it well
because my surprise that he passed me without seeing me had
made me perceive for the first time that he had never seen me
at all save in the most cursory fashion; on the eye of his mind,
I realized thenceforward. I had hardly impinged. That night he
talked till late with his father and in the morning he had
started for Mexico, to keep the mines going through the
revolution, to keep the firm's head above water and Baldry
Court sleek and hospitable, to keep everything bright and
splendid save only his youth, which after that was dulled by
care.

Something of this I told Margaret, to which she answered,
'Oh, I know all that,' and she went on with her story. On
Sunday, three days after their quarrel, Mr. Allington was found
dead in his bed. 'I wanted Chris so badly, but he never came, he
never wrote,' and she fell into a lethargic disposition to sit all
day and watch the Thames flow by, from which she was hardly
roused by finding that her father had left her nothing save
an income of twenty pounds a year in unrealizable stock. She

negotiated the transfer of the lease of the inn to a publican and, after exacting a promise from the new hostess that she would forward all letters that might come, embarked upon an increasingly unfortunate career as a mother's help. First she fell into the hands of a noble Irish family in reduced circumstances named Murphy, whose conduct in running away and leaving her in a Brighton hotel with her wages and her board unpaid, still distressed and perplexed her. 'Why did they do it?' she asked. 'I liked them so. The baby was a darling and Mrs. Murphy had such a nice way of speaking. But it almost makes one think evil of people when they do a thing like that.' After two years of less sensational but still uneasy adventures, she had come upon a large and needy family called Watson who lived at Chiswick, and almost immediately Mr. William Grey, who was Mrs. Watson's brother, had begun a courtship that sounded to me as though it had consisted of an incessant whining up at her protective instinct. 'Mr. Grey,' she said softly, as though stating his chief claim to affection, 'has never been very successful.' And still no letter ever came.

So, five years after she left Monkey Island, she married Mr. William Grey. Soon after their marriage he lost his job and was for some time out of work; later he developed a weak chest that needed constant attention. 'But it all helped to pass the time,' she said cheerfully and without irony. So it happened that it was not for many years that she had the chance of revisiting Monkey Island. At first there was no money and later there was the necessity of seeking the healthful breezes of Brighton or Bognor or Southend, which were the places in which Mr. Grey's chest oddly elected to thrive. And when those obstacles were removed she was lethargic; and also she had heard that the inn was not being managed as it ought to be, and she could not have borne to see the green home of her youth defiled. But then there had come a time when she had been very much upset; she glared a little wildly at me as she said this, as if she would faint if I asked her any questions. And then she had suddenly become obsessed with a desire to see Monkey Island once more.

'Well, when we got to the ferry Mr. Grey says, "But mercy, Margaret, there's water all round it!" and I said, "But, William, that's just it!" ' They found that the island was clean and decorous again, for it had but recently changed hands. 'Father and daughter the new people are, just like me and dad, and Mr. Taylor's something of dad's cut, too, but he comes from the North. But Miss Taylor's much handsomer than I ever was; a really big woman she is, and such lovely golden hair. They were very kind when they heard who I was; gave us duck and green peas for lunch and I did think of dad. They were nothing like as good as his ducks, but then I expect they paid. And then Miss Taylor took William out to look at the garden. I could see he didn't like it, for he's always shy with a showy woman, and I was going after them when Mr. Taylor said, "Here, stop a minute, I've got something here that many interest you. Just come in here," and he led me to the roller desk in the office. Out of a drawer he took twelve letters addressed to me in Chris's handwriting.

'He was a kind man. He put me into a chair and called Miss Taylor in and told her to keep William out in the garden as long as possible. At last I said, "But Mrs. Hitchcock did say she'd send my letters on." And he said, "But Mrs. Hitchcock hadn't been three weeks before she bolted with a bookie from Bray. And after that Hitchcock mixed his drinks and got careless." The Taylors had found these stuffed into the desk when they came.'

'And what was in them?'

'For a long time I did not read them. I thought it was against my duty as a wife. But when I got that telegram saying he was wounded I went upstairs and read those letters. Oh, those letters. . . .'

She bowed her head and wept.

As the car swung through the gates of Baldry Court she sat up and dried her eyes. She looked out at the strip of turf, so bright that one would think it wet, and lit here and there with snowdrops and scillas and crocuses, that runs between the drive and the tangle of silver birch and bramble and fern. There is no aesthetic reason for that border; the common outside looks lovelier where it fringes the road with dark gorse and rough amber grasses. Its use is purely philosophic; it proclaims that here we estimate only controlled beauty, that the wild will not have its way within our gates, that it must be made delicate and decorated into felicity. Surely she must see that this was no place for beauty that has been not mellowed but lacerated by time, that no one accustomed to live here could help wincing at such external dinginess as hers. . . . But instead she said, 'It's a big place. How poor Chris must have worked to keep it up.' The pity of this woman was like a flaming sword. No one had ever before pitied Chris for the magnificence of Baldry Court. It had been our pretence that by wearing costly clothes and organizing a costly life we had been the servants of his desire. But she revealed the truth that although he did indeed desire a magnificent house, it was a house not built with hands.

But that she was wise, that the angels would of a certainty be on her side, did not make her any the less physically offensive to our atmosphere. All my doubts as to the wisdom of my expedition revived in the little time we had to spend in the hall waiting for the tea which I had ordered in the hope that it might help Margaret to compose her distressed face. She hovered with her back to the oak table, fumbling with her thread gloves, winking her tear-red eyes, tapping with her foot on the carpet, throwing her weight from one leg to the other, and constantly contrasted her appearance with the new acquisition of Kitty's decorative genius which stood so close behind her on the table that I was

245

afraid it might be upset by one of her spasmodic movements.
This was a shallow black bowl in the centre of which crouched
on hands and knees a white naked nymph, her small head
intently drooped to the white flowers that floated on the black
waters all around her. Beside the pure black of the bowl her
rusty plumes looked horrible; beside that white nymph, eternally innocent of all but the contemplation of beauty, her opaque
skin and her suffering were offensive; beside its air of being the
coolly conceived and leisurely executed production of a hand and
brain lifted by their rare quality to the service of the not absolutely necessary, her appearance of having but for the moment
ceased to cope with a vexed and needy environment struck one
as a cancerous blot on the fair world. Perhaps it was absurd to
pay attention to this indictment of a woman by a potter's toy,
but that toy happened to be also a little image of Chris's conception of women. Exquisite we were according to our equipment;
unflushed by appetite or passion, even noble passion; our small
heads bent intently on the white flowers of luxury floating on
the black waters of life; and he had known none other than us.
With such a mental habit a man could not help but wince at
Margaret. I drank my tea very slowly because I previsioned what
must happen in the next five minutes. Down there by the pond
he would turn at the sound of those heavy boots on the path, and
with one glance he would assess the age of her, the rubbed surface of her, the torn fine texture, and he would show to her
squalid mask just such a blank face as he had shown to Kitty the
night before. Although I have a gift for self-pity I knew her case
would then be worse than mine; for it would be worse to see, as
she would see, the ardour in his eyes give place to kindliness than
never to have seen ardour there. He would hesitate, she would
make one of her harried gestures and trail away with that wet
patient look which was her special line. He would go back to his
boyish sport with the skiff; I hoped the brown waters would not

seem too kind. She would go back to Mariposa, sit on her bed, and read those letters. . . .

'And now,' she said brightly, as I put down my cup, 'may I see Chris?' She had not a doubt of the enterprise.

I took her into the drawing-room and opened one of the French windows. 'Go past the cedars to the pond,' I told her. 'He is rowing there.'

'That is nice,' she said. 'He always looks so lovely in a boat.'

I called after her, trying to hint the possibility of a panic breakdown to their meeting, 'You'll find he's altered. . . .'

She cried gleefully, 'Oh, I shall know him.'

As I went upstairs I became conscious that I was near to a bodily collapse; I suppose that the truth is that I was physically so jealous of Margaret that it was making me ill. But suddenly, just like a tired person dropping a weight they know is precious but that they cannot carry for another moment, my mind refused to consider the situation any longer and turned to the perception of material things. I leant over the banisters and looked down at the fineness of the hall: the deliberate figure of the nymph in her circle of black water, the clear pink and white of Kitty's chintz, the limpid surface of the oak, the gay reflected colours in the panelled walls. I said to myself, 'If everything else goes there is always this to fall back on,' and I went on, pleased that I was wearing delicate stuffs and that I had a smooth skin, pleased that the walls of the corridor were so soft a twilight blue, pleased that through a far-off open door came a stream of light that made the carpet blaze its stronger blue. And when I saw that it was the nursery door that was open, and that in Nanny's big chair at the window Kitty sat, I did not care about the peaked face she lifted, its fairness palely gilt by the March sunlight, nor the tremendous implications of the fact that she had come to the dead child's nursery though she had not washed her hair. I said sternly, because she had forgotten that we lived in

247

the impregnable fortress of a gracious life, 'Oh, Kitty, that poor battered thing outside.'

She stared so grimly out into the garden that my eyes followed her stare.

It was one of those draggled days, so common at the end of March, when a garden looks at its worst. The wind that was rolling up to check a show of sunshine had taken away the cedar's dignity of solid shade, had set the black firs beating their arms together and had filled the sky with glaring grey clouds that dimmed the brilliance of the crocus. It was to give gardens a point on days such as these, when the planned climax of this flower bed and that stately tree goes for nothing, that the old gardeners raised statues in their lawns and walks, large things with a subject, mossy Tritons or nymphs with an urn, that held the eye. Even so in this unrestful garden one's eye lay on the figure in the yellow raincoat that was standing still in the middle of the lawn.

How her near presence had been known by Chris I do not understand, but there he was, running across the lawn as night after night I had seen him in my dreams running across No Man's Land. I knew that so he would close his eyes as he ran; I knew that so he would pitch on his knees when he reached safety. I assumed that at Margaret's feet lay safety, even before I saw her arms brace him under the armpits with a gesture that was not passionate, but rather the movement of one carrying a wounded man from under fire. But even when she had raised his head to the level of her lips, the central issue was not decided. I covered my eyes and said aloud, 'In a minute he will see her face, her hands.' But although it was a long time before I looked again they were still clinging breast to breast. It was as though her embrace fed him, he looked so strong as he broke away. They stood with clasped hands, looking at one another (they looked straight, they looked delightedly!), and then, as if

248

resuming a conversation tiresomely interrupted by some social obligation, drew together again and passed under the tossing branches of the cedar to the wood beyond. I reflected, while Kitty wept, how entirely right Chris had been in his assertion that to lovers innumerable things do not matter.

V

After the automobile had taken Margaret away Chris came to us as we sat in the drawing-room and, after standing for a while in the glow of the fire, hesitantly said, 'I want to tell you that I know it is all right. Margaret has explained to me.'

Kitty crumpled her sewing into a white ball. 'You mean, I suppose, that you know I'm your wife. I'm pleased that you describe that as knowing ''it's all right,'' and grateful that you have accepted it at last—on Margaret's authority. This is an occasion that would make any wife proud.' Her irony was as faintly acrid as a caraway seed, and never afterwards did she reach even that low pitch of violence, for from that mild forward droop of the head with which he received the mental lunge she realized suddenly that this was no pretence and that something as impassable as death lay between them. Thereafter his proceedings evoked no comment but suffering. There was nothing to say when all day, save for those hours of the afternoon which Margaret spent with him, he sat like a blind man waiting for his darkness to lift. There was nothing to say when he did not seem to see our flowers, yet kept till they rotted on the stalk the daffodils which Margaret brought from the garden that looked like an allotment. So Kitty lay about like a broken doll, face downward on a sofa with one limp arm dangling to the floor, or protruding stiff feet in fantastic slippers from the end of her curtained bed; and I tried to make my permanent wear that mood which had mitigated the end of my journey with Margaret, a mood of intense perception in which my strained mind settled on every vivid object that came under my eyes and tried to identify myself with its brightness and its lack of human passion. This does not mean that I passed my day in a state of joyous appreciation; it means that many times in the lanes of Harrowweald I have stood for long looking up at the fine tracery of bare boughs against the hard, high spring sky while the cold wind rushed through my skirts and chilled me to the bone, because I was afraid that when I moved my body and my attention I might begin to think. Indeed grief is not the clear melancholy the young believe it. It is like a siege in a tropical city. The skin dries and the throat parches as though one were living in the heat of the desert; water and wine taste warm in the mouth and food is of the substance of the sand; one snarls at one's company; thoughts prick one through sleep like mosquitoes.

A week after my journey to Wealdstone I went to Kitty to ask her to come for a walk with me and found her stretched on her pillows, holding a review of her underclothing. She refused bitterly and added, 'Be back early. Remember Dr. Gilbert Anderson is coming at half-past four, He's our last hope. And tell that woman she must see him. He says he wants to see everybody concerned,' and continued to look wanly at the frail luminous silks her maid brought her, as a speculator who had cornered the article for which there had been no demand might look at his damnably numerous, damnably unprofitable freights. So I went out alone into a soft day, with the dispelled winter lurking above in high dark clouds under which there ran quick fresh currents of air, and broken shafts of insistent sunshine that spread a grey clarity of light in which every colour showed sharp

and strong. On the breast that Harrowweald turns to the south
they had set a lambing-yard, whose pale lavender hurdles and
gold strewn straw and orange drinking-trough were new gay
notes on the opaque winter green of the slope, and the apprehen-
sive bleatings of the ewes wound about the hill like a river of
sound as they were driven up a lane hidden by the hedge. The
lines of bare elms darkening the plains below made it seem as
though the tide of winter had fallen and left this promontory
bare and sparkling in the spring. I liked it so much that I opened
the gate and went and sat down on a tree that had been torn up
by the roots in the great gale last year, but had not yet resigned
itself to death and was bravely decking itself with purple elm-
flowers. That pleased me too, and I wished I had someone with
me to enjoy this artless little show of the new year. I had not
really wanted Kitty; the companions I needed were Chris and
Margaret. Chris would have talked as he loved to do when he
looked at leisure on a broad valley, about ideas which he had to
exclude from his ordinary hours lest they should break the
power of business over his mind, and Margaret would have
gravely watched the argument from the shadow of her broad hat
to see that it kept true, like a housewife watching a saucepan of
milk lest it should boil over. They were naturally my friends,
these gentle speculative people. Then suddenly I was stunned
with jealousy. It was not their love for one another that caused
me such agony at that moment; it was the thought of the things
their eyes had rested upon together. I imagined that white
hawthorn among the poplars by the ferry on which they had
looked fifteen years ago at Monkey Island, and it was more than
I could bear. I thought how even now they might be exclaiming
at the green smoke of the first buds on the brown undergrowth
round the pond, and at that I slid off the tree-truck and began
walking very quickly down the hill. The red cows drank from
the pond cupped by the willow roots, a raw-boned stallion

252

danced clumsily because warmth was running through the ground, I found a stream in the fields and followed it till it became a shining dyke embanked with glowing green and gold mosses in the midst of woods; and the sight of those things was no sort of joy, because my vision was solitary. I wanted to end my desperation by leaping from a height, and I climbed on a knoll and flung myself face downwards on the dead leaves below.

I was now utterly cut off from Chris. Before, when I looked at him I knew an instant ease in the sight of the short golden down on his cheeks, the ridge of bronze flesh above his thick fair eyebrows. But now I was too busy reassuring him by showing a steady, undistorted profile crowned by a neat proud sweep of hair instead of the tear-darkened mask he always feared, ever to have enough vitality left over to enjoy his presence. I spoke in a calm voice full from the chest quite unfluted with agony; I read *Country Life* with ponderous interest; I kept my hands, which I desired to wring, in doeskin gloves for most of the day; I played with the dogs a great deal and wore my thickest tweeds; I pretended that the slight heaviness of my features is a correct indication of my temperament. The only occasion when I could safely let the sense of him saturate me as it used was when I met Margaret in the hall as she came or went. She was very different now; she had a little smile in her eyes as though she were listening to a familiar air played far away, her awkwardness seemed indecision as to whether she should walk or dance to that distant music, her shabbiness was no more repulsive than the untidiness of a child who had been so eager to get to the party that it has not let its nurse fasten its frock. Always she extended a hand in an unbuttoned black thread glove and said, 'It's another fine day again,' or diffidently, as Kitty continued to withhold her presence, 'I hope Mrs. Baldry is keeping well.' Then as our hands touched he was with us, invoked by our common adoration;

253

I felt his rough male texture and saw the clear warmth of his brown and gold colouring. I thought of him with the passion of exile. To Margaret it was a call, and she moved past me to the garden, holding her hands in front of her as though she bore invisible gifts, and pausing on the step of the French window to smile to herself, as if in her heart she turned over the precious thought, 'He is here. This garden holds him.' My moment, my small sole subsistence, ended in a feeling of jealousy as ugly and unmental as sickness. This was the saddest spring.

Nothing could mitigate the harshness of our rejection. You may think we were attaching an altogether fictitious importance to what was merely the delusion of a madman. But every minute of the day, particularly at those trying times when he strolled about the house and grounds with the doctors, smiling cour-teously, but without joy, and answering their questions with the crisp politeness of a man shaking off an inquisitive commer-cial traveller in a hotel smoking-room, it became plain that if madness means liability to wild error about the world, Chris was not mad. It was our peculiar shame that he had rejected us when he had attained to something saner than sanity. His very loss of memory was a triumph over the limitations of language which prevent the mass of men from making explicit statements about their spiritual relationships. If he had said to Kitty and me, 'I do not know you,' we would have gaped; if he had expanded his meaning and said, 'You are nothing to me; my heart is separate from your hearts,' we would have wept at an unkindness he had not intended. But by the blankness of those eyes which saw me only as a disregarded playmate and Kitty not at all save as a stranger who had somehow become a decorative presence in his home and the orderer of his meals he let us know completely where we were. Even though I lay weeping at it on the dead leaves I was sensible of the bitter rapture that attends the discov-ery of any truth. I felt, indeed, a cold intellectual pride in his

254

refusal to remember his prosperous maturity and his determined dwelling in the time of his first love, for it showed him so much saner than the rest of us, who take life as it comes, loaded with the inessential and the irritating. I was even willing to admit that this choice of what was to him reality out of all the appearances so copiously presented by the world, this adroit recovery of the dropped pearl of beauty, was the act of genius I had always expected from him. But that did not make less agonizing this exclusion from his life.

I could not think clearly about it. I suppose that the subject of our tragedy, written in spiritual terms, was that in Kitty he had turned from the type of woman that makes the body conqueror of the soul and in me from the type that mediates between the soul and the body and makes them run even and unhasty like a well-matched pair of carriage horses, and had given himself to a woman whose bleak habit it was to champion the soul against the body. But I saw it just as a fantastic act of cruelty that I could only think of as a conjunction of calamitous images. I think of it happening somewhere behind the front, at the end of a straight road that runs by a line of ragged poplars between mud flats made steel-bright with floods pitted by the soft slow rain. There, past a church that lacks its tower, stand a score of houses, each hideous with patches of bare bricks that show like sores through the ripped-off plaster and uncovered rafters which stick out like broken bones. There are people still living here. A slut sits at the door of a filthy cottage, counting some dirty linen and waving her bare arms at some passing soldiers. And at another house there is a general store with strings of orange onions and bunches of herbs hanging from the roof, a brown gloom rich with garlic and humming with the flies that live all the year round in French village shops, a black cat rubbing her sleekness against the lintel. It is in there that Chris is standing, facing across the counter an old man in a blue blouse, with a scar running white into the grey thickets of his beard, an old man with a smile at once lewd and benevolent, repulsive with dirt and yet magnificent by reason of the Olympian structure of his body. I think he is the soul of the universe, equally cognisant and disregardful of every living thing, to whom I am no more dear than the bare-armed slut at the neighbouring door. And Chris is leaning on the counter, his eyes glazed. (This is his spirit; his body lies out there in the drizzle at the other end of the road.) He is looking down on two crystal balls that the old man's foul strong hands have rolled across to him. In one he sees Margaret; not in her raincoat and her nodding plumes but as she is transfigured in the light of eternity. Long he looks there; then drops a glance to the other, just long enough to see that in its depths Kitty and I walk in bright dresses through our glowing gardens. We had suffered no transfiguration, for we are as we are and there is nothing more to us. The whole truth about us lies in our material seeming. He sighs a deep sigh of delight and puts out his hand to the ball where Margaret shines. His sleeve catches the other one and sends it down to crash in a thousand pieces on the floor. The old man's smile continues to be lewd and benevolent, he is still not more interested in me than in the bare-armed slut; and Chris is wholly enclosed in his intentness on his chosen crystal. No one weeps for this shattering of our world. . . .

I stirred on the dead leaves as though I had really heard the breaking of the globe and cried out, 'Gilbert Anderson, Gilbert Anderson must cure him.' Heaven knows that I had no reason for faith in any doctor, for during the past week so many of them, sleek as seals with their neatly brushed hair and their frock-coats, had stood round Chris and looked at him with the consequenceless deliberation of a plumber. Their most successful enterprise had been his futile hypnotism. He had submitted to it as a good-natured man submits to being blindfolded at a

256

children's party and under its influence had recovered his memory and his middle-aged personality, had talked of Kitty with the humorous tenderness of the English husband and had looked possessively about him. But as his mind came out of the control he exposed their lie that they were dealing with a mere breakdown of the normal process by pushing away this knowledge and turning to them the blank wall, all the blanker because it was unconscious, of his resolution not to know. I had accepted that it would always be so. But at that moment I had so great a need to throw off my mood of despair, so insupportably loaded with all the fantastic images to which my fevered mind transmuted the facts of our tragedy, that I filled myself with a gasping, urgent faith in this new doctor. I jumped up and pushed through the brambles to the hedge that divided the preserves in which I was trespassing from our own woods, breathless because I had let it go past four and I had still to find Chris and Margaret for the doctor's visit at the half-hour.

There had been a hardening of the light during the afternoon that made the dear familiar woods rich and sinister and, to the eye, tropical. The jewel-bright buds on the soot-black boughs, and the blue valley distances, smudged here and there with the pink enamel of villa roofs and seen between the black and white intricacies of the birch-trunks and the luminous grey pillars of the beeches, hurt my wet eyes as might beauty blazing under an equatorial sun. There was a tropical sense of danger too, for I walked as apprehensively as though a snake coiled under every leaf, because I feared to come on them when he was speaking to her without looking at her, or thinking in silence while he played with her hand. Embraces do not matter; they merely indicate the will to love and may as well be followed by defeat as victory. But disregard means that now there needs to be no straining of the eyes, no stretching forth of the hands, no pressing of the lips, because theirs is such a union that they are no

257

longer conscious of the division of their flesh. I know it must be so; a lonely life gives one opportunities of thinking these things out. I could not have borne to see signs of how he had achieved this intimacy with the woman whom a sudden widening of the downward vista showed as she leant her bent back, ridged by those cheap stays, against a birch that some special skill of the forester had made wonderful for its straight slenderness. Against the clear colours of the bright bare wood her yellow raincoat made a muddy patch, and as a dead bough dropped near her she made a squalid dodging movement like a hen. She was not so much a person as an implication of dreary poverty, like an open door in a mean house that lets out the smell of cooking cabbage and the screams of children. Doubtlessly he sat somewhere close to her, lumpishly content. I thought distractedly how necessary it was that Gilbert Anderson should cure him, and tried to shout to her but found my throat full of sobs. So I broke my way down through the fern and bramble and stood level with them, though still divided by some yards of broken ground.

It was not utter dullness not to have anticipated the beauty that I saw. No one could have told. . . . They had taken the mackintosh rug out of the dinghy and spread it on this little space of clear grass, I think so that they could look at a scattering of early primroses in a pool of white anemones at an oak-tree's foot. She had run her dreadful hands over the rug so that it lay quite smooth and comfortable under him when at last he felt drowsy and turned on his side to sleep. He lay there in the confiding relaxation of a sleeping child, his hands unclenched and his head thrown back so that the bare throat showed defencelessly. Now he was asleep and his face undarkened by thought one saw how very fair he really was. And she, her mournfully vigilant face pinkened by the cold river of air sent by the advancing evening through the screen of rusted gold bracken was sitting beside him, just watching.

I have often seen people grouped like that on the common outside our gates, on Bank Holidays. Most often the man has a handkerchief over his face to shade him from the sun and the woman squats beside him and peers through the undergrowth to see that the children come to no harm as they play. It has sometimes seemed to me that there was a significance about it. You know when one goes into the damp odorous coolness of a church in a catholic country and sees the kneeling worshippers, their bodies bent stiffly and reluctantly and yet with abandonment as though to represent the inevitable bending of the will to a purpose outside the individual, or when under any sky one sees a mother with her child in her arms, something turns in one's heart like a sword and one says to oneself, 'If humanity forgets these attitudes there is an end to the world.' But people like me, who are not artists, are never sure about people they don't know. So it was not until now, when it happened to my friends, when it was my dear Chris and my dear Margaret who sat thus englobed in peace as in a crystal sphere, that I knew that it was the most significant as it was the loveliest attitude in the world. It means that the woman has gathered the soul of the man into her soul and is keeping it warm in love and peace so that his body can rest quiet for a little time. That is a great thing for a woman to do. I know there are things at least as great for those women whose independent spirits can ride fearlessly and with interest outside the home park of their personal relationships, but independence is not the occupation of most of us. What we desire is greatness such as this which had given sleep to the beloved. I had known that he was having bad nights at Baldry Court, in that new room with the jade-green painted walls and the lapis lazuli fire-place, which he had found with surprise to be his instead of the remembered little room with the fishing-rods. But I had not been able to do anything about it.

It was not fair that by the exercise of a generosity which

seemed as fortuitous a possession as a beautiful voice a woman should be able to do such wonderful things for a man. For sleep was the least of her gifts to him. What she had done in leading him into this quiet magic circle out of our life, out of the splendid house which was not so much a house as a vast piece of space partitioned off from the universe and decorated partly for beauty and partly to make our privacy more insolent, out of the garden where the flowers took thought as to how they should grow and the wood made formal as a pillared aisle by forestry, may be judged from my anguish in being left there alone. Indeed she had been generous to us all, for at her touch our lives had at last fallen into a pattern; she was the sober thread whose interweaving with our scattered magnificences had somehow achieved the design that otherwise would not appear. Perhaps even her dinginess was part of her generosity, for in order to fit into the pattern one sometimes has to forgo something of one's individual beauty. That is why women like us do not wear such obviously lovely dresses as cocottes, but clothe themselves in garments that by their slight neglect of the possibilities of beauty declare that there are such things as thrift and restraint and care for the future. And so I could believe of Margaret that her determined dwelling in places where there was not enough of anything, her continued exposure of herself to the grime of squalid living, was unconsciously deliberate. The deep internal thing that had guided Chris to forgetfulness had guided her to poverty so that when the time came for her meeting with her lover there should be not one intimation of the beauty of suave flesh to distract him from the message of her soul. I looked upward at this supreme act of sacrifice and glowed at her private gift to me. My sleep, though short, was now dreamless. No more did I see his body rotting into union with that brown texture of corruption which is No Man's Land, no more did I see him slipping softly down the parapet into the trench, no more did I hear voices talking in a void: '*Help me, old man, I've got no legs. . . .*'—'*I can't, old man, I've got no hands. . . .*' They could not take him back to the Army as he was. Only that morning as I went through the library he had raised an appalled face from the pages of a history of the war. 'Jenny, it can't be true—that they did *that*—to Belgium? Those funny, quiet, stingy people. . . .' And his soldierly knowledge was as deeply buried as this memory of that awful August. While her spell endured they could not send him back into the hell of war. This wonderful kind woman held his body as safely as she held his soul.

I was so grateful that I was forced to go and sit down on the rug beside her. It was an intrusion, but I wanted to be near her. She did not look surprised when she turned to me her puckered brows, but smiled through the ugly fringe of vagrant hairs the weather had plucked from under the hard rim of her hat. It was part of her loveliness that even if she did not understand an act she could accept it.

Presently she leant over to me across his body and whispered, 'He's not cold. I put the overcoat on him as soon as he was fairly off. I've just felt his hands and they're as warm as toast.' If I had whispered like that I would have wakened him.

Soon he stirred, groped for her hand and lay with his cheek against its rough palm. He was awake by then but liked to lie so.

In a little she shook her hand away and said, 'Get up and run along to the house and have some hot tea. You'll catch your death lying out here.'

He caught her hand again. It was evident that for some reason the moment was charged with ecstasy for them both.

It seemed as though there were a softer air in this small clearing than anywhere else in the world. I stood up with my back against a birch and said negligently, knowing now that nothing could really threaten them, 'There is a doctor coming at half-past four who wants to see you both.' It cast no shadow on their serenity. He smiled upward, still lying on his back, and hailed me, 'Hallo, Jenny.' But she made him get up and help her fold the rug. 'It's not right to keep a doctor waiting in these times,' she declared, 'so overworked they are, poor men, since the war. . . .' As I led the way up through the woods to the house I heard her prove her point by an illustrative anecdote about something that had happened down her road. I heard, too, their footsteps come to a halt for a space. I think her grey eyes had looked at him so sweetly that he had been constrained to take her in his arms.

VI

I felt—I remember it with the little perk of self-approbation with which one remembers any sort of accurate premonition even if its fulfilment meant disaster—a cold hand close round my heart as we turned the corner of the house and came on Dr. Gilbert Anderson. I was startled, to begin with, by his unmedical appearance. He was a little man with winking blue eyes, a flushed and crumpled forehead, a little grey moustache that gave him the profile of an amiable cat, and a lively taste in spotted ties, and he lacked that appetiteless look which is affected by distinguished practitioners. He was at once more comical and more suggestive of power than any other doctor I had ever seen, and this difference was emphasized by his unexpected occupation. A tennis ball which he had discovered somewhere had roused his sporting instincts, and he was trying at what range it was possible to kick it between two large stones which he had placed close together in front of the steps up to the house. It was his chubby absorption in this amusement which accounted for his first gape of embarrassment. 'Nobody about in there—we professional men get so little fresh air——' he said bluffly, and blew his nose in a very large handkerchief, from whose folds he emerged with perfect self-possession. 'You,' he said to Chris, with a naïve adoption of the detective tone, 'are the patient.' He rolled his blue eye on me, took a good look, and

263

as he realized I did not matter shook off the unnecessary impression like a dog coming out of water. He faced Margaret as though she were the nurse in charge of the case and gave her a brisk little nod. 'You're Mrs. Grey. I shall want to talk to you later. Meantime—this man. I'll come back.' He indicated by a windmill gesture that we should go into the house and swung off with Chris.

She obeyed; that sort of woman always does what the doctor orders. But I delayed for a moment to stare after this singular specialist, to side-track my foreboding by pronouncing him a bounder, to wish, as my foreboding persisted, that like a servant I could give notice because there was 'always something happening in the house.' Then, as the obedient figure at the top of the stairs was plainly shivering under its shoddy clothes in the rising wind that was polishing the end of the afternoon to brightness, I hastened to lead her into the hall. We stood about uneasily in its gloaming. As usual the shining old panelling seemed aware of all that was going on and conscious that it was older and better than the people who owned it; the white nymph drooped over the black waters of the bowl and reminded one how nice, how neat and nice, life used to be; the chintz sang the vulgar old English country-house song. Margaret looked round her and said, in a voice slightly flattened by the despondency which she evidently shared with me, 'It is nice to have everything ready that people can want, and everything in its place. I used to do it at Monkey Island Inn. It was not grand like this, of course, but our visitors always came back a second time.' Abstractedly and yet with joy she fingered the fine work of the table leg.

There was a noise above us like the fluttering of doves. Kitty was coming downstairs in a white serge dress against which her hands were rosy; a woman with such lovely little hands never needed to wear flowers. By her kind of physical discipline she had reduced her grief to no more than a slight darkening under the eyes, and for this moment she was glowing. I knew it was because she was going to meet a new man and anticipated the kindling of admiration in his eyes, and I smiled, contrasting her probable prefiguring of Dr. Anderson with the amiable rotundity we had just encountered. Not that it would have made any difference if she had seen him. Beautiful women of her type lose, in this matter of admiration alone, their otherwise tremendous sense of class distinction; they are obscurely aware that it is their civilizing mission to flash the jewel of their beauty before all men, so that they shall desire it and work to get the wealth to buy it, and thus be seduced by a present appetite to a tilling of the earth that serves the future. There is, you know, really room for all of us; we each have our peculiar use.

'The doctor's talking to Chris outside,' I said.

'Ah,' breathed Kitty. I found, though the occasion was a little grim, some entertainment in the two women's faces, so mutually intent, so differently fair, the one a polished surface that reflected light, like a mirror hung opposite a window, the other a lamp grimed by the smoke of careless use but still giving out radiance from its burning oil. Margaret was smiling wonderingly up at this prettiness; but Kitty seemed to be doing some brainwork.

'How do you do, Mrs. Grey?' she said suddenly, shaking out her cordiality as one shakes out a fan. 'It's very kind of you to come. Won't you go upstairs and take off your things?'

'No, thank you,' answered Margaret shyly, 'I shall have to go away so soon.'

'Ah, do!' begged Kitty prettily.

It was, of course, that she did not want Margaret to meet the specialist in those awful clothes, but I did not darken the situation by explaining that this disaster had already happened. Instead I turned to Margaret an expression which conveyed that this was an act of hospitality the refusal of which we would find

265

wounding, and to that she yielded as I knew she would. She followed me upstairs and along the corridors very slowly, like a child paddling in a summer sea; she enjoyed the feeling of the thick carpet underfoot, she looked lingeringly at the pictures on the wall, occasionally she put a finger to touch a vase as if by that she made its preciousness more her own. Her spirit, I could see, was as deeply concerned about Chris as was mine, but she had such faith in life that she retained serenity enough to enjoy what beauty she came across during her period of waiting. Even her enjoyment was indirectly generous; when she came into my room the backward flinging of her head and her deep 'Oh!' recalled to me what I had long forgotten, how fine were its proportions, how clever the grooved arch above the window, how like the evening sky my blue curtains. . . .

'And the lovely things you have on your dressing-table,' she commented. 'You must have very good taste.' The charity, that changed my riches to a merit! As I helped her to take off her raincoat, and reflected that Kitty would not be pleased when she saw that the removal of the garment disclosed a purple blouse of stuff called moirette that servants use for petticoats, she exclaimed softly Kitty's praises. 'I know I shouldn't make personal remarks, but Mrs. Baldry is lovely. She has three circles round her neck. I've only two.' It was a touching betrayal that she possessed that intimate knowledge of her own person which comes to women who have been loved. I could not for the life of me have told you how many circles there were round my neck. Plainly discontented with herself in the midst of all this fineness she said diffidently, 'Please, I would like to do my hair,' so I pulled the arm-chair up to the dressing-table and leant on its back while she, sitting shyly on its very edge, unpinned her two long braids, so thick, so dull.

'You've lovely hair,' I said.

'I used to have nice hair,' she mourned, 'but these last few years I've let myself go.' She made half-hearted attempts to smooth the straggling tendrils on her temples, but presently laid down her brush and clicked her tongue against her teeth. 'Tchk! I hope that man's not worrying Chris.'

There was no reassurance ready, so I went to the other side of the room to put her hat down on a chair, and stayed for a moment to pat its plumes and wonder if nothing could be done with it. But it was, as surgeons say, an inoperable case. So I just gloomed at it and wished I had not let this doctor interpose his plumpness between Chris and Margaret, who since that afternoon seemed to me as not only a woman whom it was good to love, but as a patron saint must appear to a catholic, as an intercessory being whose kindliness could be daunted only by some special and incredibly malicious decision of the Supreme Force. I was standing with eyes closed and my hands abstractedly stroking the hat which was the emblem of her martyrdom, and I was thinking of her in a way that was a prayer to her, when I heard her sharp cry. That she should cry out sharply, whose essence was a patient silence . . . I turned very quickly.

She was standing up, and in her hand she held the photograph of Oliver that stands on my dressing-table. It is his last photograph, the one taken just a week before he died.

'Who is this?'

'The only child Chris ever had. He died five years ago.'

'Five years ago?'

Why did it matter so?

'Yes.'

'He died five years ago, my Dick.' Her eyes grew great. 'How old was he?'

'Just two.'

'My Dick was two. . . .' We both were breathing hard. 'Why did he die?'

'We never knew. He was the loveliest boy, but delicate from his birth. At the end he just faded away, with the merest cold.'

'So did my Dick. A chill. We thought he would be up and about the next day, and he just——'

Her awful gesture of regret was suddenly paralysed. She seemed to be fighting her way to a discovery.

'It's—it's as if,' she stammered, 'they each had half a life. . . .'

I felt the usual instinct to treat her as though she were ill, because it was evident that she was sustained by a mystic interpretation of life. But she had already taught me something, so I stood aside while she fell on her knees, and wondered why she did not look at the child's photograph, but pressed it to her bosom as though to staunch a wound. I thought, as I have often thought before, that the childless have the greatest joy in children, for to us they are just slips of immaturity lovelier than the flowers and with a power over the heart, but to mothers they are fleshy cables binding one down to such profundities of feeling as the awful agony that now possessed her. For although I knew I would have accepted it with rapture, because it was the result of intimacy with Chris, its awfulness appalled me. Not only did it make my body hurt with sympathy, it shook the ground beneath my feet. For that her serenity, which a moment before had seemed as steady as the earth and as all-enveloping as the sky, should be so utterly dispelled made me aware that I had of late been underestimating the cruelty of the order of things. Lovers are frustrated; children are not begotten that should have had the loveliest life, the pale usurpers of their birth die young. Such a world will not suffer magic circles to endure.

The parlourmaid knocked at the door. 'Mrs. Baldry and Dr. Anderson are waiting in the drawing-room, ma'am.'

Margaret reassumed her majesty, and put her white face close to the glass as she pinned up her braids. 'I knew there was a

268

something,' she moaned, and set the hairpins all awry. She said nothing more; but the slow gesture with which, as we were about to leave the room, she laid her hand across the child's photograph, somehow convinced me that we were not to be victorious.

When we went into the drawing-room we found Dr. Anderson, plump and expository, balancing himself on the balls of his feet on the hearthrug and enjoying the caress of the fire on his calves, while Kitty, showing against the dark frame of her oak chair like a white rosebud that was still too innocent to bloom, listened with that slight reservation of the attention customary in beautiful women.

'A complete case of amnesia,' he was saying, as Margaret, white-lipped yet less shy than I had ever seen her, went to a seat by the window and I sank down on the sofa. 'His unconscious self is refusing to let him resume his relations with his normal life, and so we get this loss of memory.'

'I've always said,' declared Kitty, with an air of good sense, 'that if he would make an effort. . . .'

'Effort!' He jerked his round head about. 'The mental life that can be controlled by effort isn't the mental life that matters. You've been stuffed up when you were young with talk about a thing called self-control—a sort of barmaid of the soul that says, "Time's up, gentlemen," and "Here, you've had enough." There's no such thing. There's a deep self in one, the essential self, that has its wishes. And if those wishes are suppressed by the superficial self—the self that makes, as you say, efforts and usually makes them with the sole idea of putting up a good show before the neighbours—it takes its revenge. Into the house of conduct erected by the superficial self it sends an obsession. Which doesn't, owing to a twist that the superficial self, which isn't candid, gives it, seem to bear any relation to the suppressed wish. A man who really wants to leave his wife develops a hatred

269

for pickled cabbage which may find vent in performances that lead straight to the asylum. But that's all technical!' he finished bluffly. 'My business to understand it, not yours. The point is, Mr. Baldry's obsession is that he can't remember the latter years of his life. Well——' his winking blue eyes drew us all into a community we hardly felt—'what's the suppressed wish of which it's the manifestation?'

'He wished for nothing,' said Kitty. 'He was fond of us, and he had a lot of money.'

'Ah, but he did!' countered the doctor gleefully. He seemed to be enjoying it all. 'Quite obviously he has forgotten his life here because he is discontented with it. What clearer proof could you need than the fact you were just telling me when these ladies came in—that the reason the War Office didn't wire to you when he was wounded was that he had forgotten to register his address? Don't you see what that means?'

'Forgetfulness,' shrugged Kitty, 'he isn't business-like.' She had always nourished a doubt as to whether Chris was really, as she put it, practical; his income and his international reputation weighed as nothing against his so evident inability to pick up pieces at sales.

'One forgets only those things that one wants to forget. It's our business to find out why he wanted to forget this life.'

'He can remember quite well when he is hypnotized,' she said obstructively. She had quite ceased to glow.

'Oh, hypnotism's a silly trick. It releases the memory of a dissociated personality which can't be related—not possibly in such an obstinate case as this—to the waking personality. I'll do it by talking to him. Getting him to tell his dreams.' He beamed at the prospect. 'But you—it would be such a help if you could give me any clue to this discontent.'

'I tell you,' said Kitty, 'he was not discontented till he went mad.'

270

He caught at last the glint of her rising temper. 'Ah,' he said, 'madness is an indictment not of the people one lives with, only of the high gods! If there was anything it's evident that it was not your fault——' A smile sugared it, and knowing that where he had to flatter his dissecting hand had not an easy task he turned to me, whose general appearance suggests that flattery is not part of my daily diet. 'You, Miss Baldry, you've known him longest. . . .'

'Nothing and everything was wrong,' I said at last. 'I've always felt it. . . .' A sharp movement of Kitty's body confirmed my deep, old suspicion that she hated me.

He went back further than I thought he would. 'His relations with his father and mother, now?'

'His father was old when he was born, and always was a little jealous of him. His mother was not his sort. She wanted a stupid son, who would have been satisfied with shooting.'

He laid down a remark very softly, like a hunter setting a snare.

'He turned, then, to sex with a peculiar need.'

It was Margaret who spoke, shuffling her feet under her chair.

'Yes, he was always very dependent.' We gaped at her, who said this of our splendid Chris, and I saw that she was not as she had been. There was a directness of speech, a straight stare, that was for her a frenzy. 'Doctor,' she said, her mild voice roughened, 'what's the use of talking? You can't cure him.' She caught her lower lip with her teeth and fought back from the brink of tears. 'Make him happy, I mean. All you can do is to make him ordinary.'

'I grant you that's all I do,' he said. It queerly seemed as though he was experiencing the relief one feels on meeting an intellectual equal. 'It's my profession to bring people from various outlying districts of the mind to the normal. There seems to be a general feeling it's the place where they ought to be. Sometimes I don't see the urgency myself.'

She continued without joy. 'I know how you could bring him back. A memory so strong that it would recall everything else—in spite of his discontent.'

The little man had lost in a moment his glib assurance, his knowingness about the pathways of the soul. 'Well, I'm willing to learn.'

'Remind him of the boy,' said Margaret.

The doctor ceased suddenly to balance on the balls of his feet. 'What boy?'

'They had a boy.'

He looked at Kitty. 'You told me nothing of this!'

'I didn't think it mattered,' she answered, and shivered and looked cold as she always did at the memory of her unique contact with death. 'He died five years ago.'

He dropped his head back, stared at the cornice, and said with the soft malignity of a clever person dealing with the slow-witted, 'These subtle discontents are often the most difficult to deal with.' Sharply he turned to Margaret. 'How would you remind him?'

'Take him something the boy wore, some toy they used to play with.'

Their eyes met wisely. 'It would have to be you that did it.'

Her face assented.

Kitty said, 'I don't understand. Why does it matter so much?' She repeated it twice before she broke the silence that Margaret's wisdom had brought down on us. Then Dr. Anderson, rattling the keys in his trouser pockets and swelling red and perturbed, answered, 'I don't know why. But it does.'

Kitty's voice soared in satisfaction. 'Oh! Then it's very simple. Mrs. Grey can do it now. Jenny, take Mrs. Grey up to the nursery. There are lots of things up there.'

Margaret made no movement, but continued to sit with her heavy boots resting on the edge of their soles. Dr. Anderson searched Kitty's face, exclaimed, 'Oh, well!' and flung himself into an armchair so suddenly that the springs spoke.

Margaret smiled at that and turned to me, 'Yes, take me to the nursery, please.' Yet as I walked beside her up the stairs I knew this compliance was not the indication of any melting of this new steely sternness. The very breathing that I heard as I knelt beside her at the nursery door and fitted the key in the lock, seemed to come from a different and a harsher body than had been hers before. I did not wonder that she was feeling bleak, since in a few moments she was to go out and say the words that would end all her happiness, that would destroy all the gifts her generosity had so difficultly amassed. Well, that is the kind of thing one has to do in this life.

But hardly had the door opened and disclosed the empty sunny spaces swimming with motes before her old sweetness flowered again. She moved forward slowly, tremulous and responsive and pleased, as though the room's loveliness was a gift to her; she stretched out her hands to the clear sapphire walls and the bright fresco of birds and animals with a young delight. So, I thought, might a bride go about the home her husband had secretly prepared for her. Yet when she reached the hearth and stood with her hands behind her on the fireguard, looking about her at all the exquisite devices of our nursery to rivet health and amusement on our reluctant little visitor, it was so apparent that she was a mother that I could not imagine how it was that I had not always known it. It has sometimes happened that painters who have kept close enough to earth to see a heavenly vision have made pictures of the Assumption of the Blessed Virgin, which do indeed show women who could bring God into the world by the passion of their motherhood. 'Let there be life,' their suspended bodies seem to cry out to the universe about

273

them, and the very clouds under their feet change to cherubim. As Margaret stood there, her hands pressed palm to palm beneath her chin, and a blind smile on her face, she looked even so.

'Oh, the fine room!' she cried. 'But where's his cot?'

'It isn't here. This is the day nursery. The night nursery we didn't keep. It's just a bedroom now.'

Her eyes shone at the thought of the cockered childhood this had been. 'I couldn't afford to have two nurseries. It makes all the difference to the wee things.' She hung above me for a little as I opened the ottoman and rummaged among Oliver's clothes. 'Ah, the lovely little frocks! Did she make them? Ah, well, she'd hardly have the time, with this great house to see to. But I don't care much for baby frocks. The babies themselves are none the happier for them. It's all for show.' She went over to the rocking-horse and gave a ghostly child a ride. For long she hummed a tuneless song into the sunshine and retreated far away into some maternal dream. 'He was too young for this,' she said. 'His daddy must have given him it. I knew it. Men always give them presents above their age. They're in such a hurry for them to grow up. We like them to take their time, the loves. But where's his engine? Didn't he love puffer-trains? Of course, he never saw them. You're so far from the railway station. What a pity! He'd have loved them so. Dick was so happy when I stopped his pram on the railway bridge on my way back from the shops, and he could sit up and see the puffers going by.' Her distress that Oliver had missed this humble pleasure darkened her for a minute. 'Why did he die! You didn't overtax his brain? He wasn't taught his letters too soon?'

'Oh, no,' I said. I couldn't find the clothes I wanted. 'The only thing that taxed his little brain were the prayers his Scotch nurse taught him, and he didn't bother much over them. He would say "Jesus, tender leopard," instead of "Jesus, tender

274

shepherd,'' as though he liked it better that way. . . .'

'Did you ever! The things they say! He'd a Scotch nurse. They say they're very good. I've read in the papers the Queen of Spain has one.' She had gone back to the hearth again and was playing with the toys on the mantelpiece. It was odd that she showed no interest in my search for the most memorable garment; a vivacity which played above her tearwet strength, like a ball of St. Jacob's fire on the mast of a stout ship, made me realize she still was strange. 'The toys he had! His nurse didn't let him have them all at once. She held him up and said, ''Baby, you must choose!'' and he said, ''Teddy—please—Nanny!'' and wagged his head at every word.'

I had laid my hand on them at last. I wished, in the strangest way, that I hadn't. Yet of course it had to be. 'That's just what he did do.'

As she felt the fine kid skin of the clockwork dog her face began to twitch. 'I thought perhaps my baby had left me because I had so little to give him. But if a baby could leave all this——.' She cried flatly, as though constant repetition in the night had made it as instinctive a reaction to suffering as a moan. 'I want a child! I want a child!' Her arms invoked the life that had been squandered in this room. 'It's all gone so wrong!' she fretted, and her voice dropped to a solemn whisper. 'They each had only half a life. . . .'

I had to steady her. She could not go to Chris and shock him, not only by her news, but also by her agony. I rose and took her the things I had found in the ottoman and the toy cupboard. 'I think these are the best things to take. This is one of the blue jerseys he used to wear. This is the red ball he and his father used to play with on the lawn.'

Her hard hunger for the child that was not melted into a tenderness for the child that had been. She looked broodingly at what I carried, then laid a kind hand on my arm. 'You've chosen

275

the very things he will remember. Oh, you poor girl. . . .'

I found that from her I could accept even pity.

She nursed the jersey and the ball, changed them from arm to arm and held them to her face. 'I think I know the kind of boy he was. A man from the first.' She kissed them, folded up the jersey and neatly set the ball upon it on the ottoman, and regarded them with tears. 'There, put them back. That's all I wanted them for. All I came up here for.'

I stared.

'To get near Chris's boy,' she moaned. 'You thought I meant to take them out to Chris?' She wrung her hands, her weak voice quavered at the sternness of her resolution. 'How can I?'

I grasped her hands. 'Why should you bring him back?' I said.

I might have known there was deliverance in her yet.

Her slow mind gathered speed.

'Either I never should have come,' she pleaded, 'or you should let him be.' She was arguing not with me, but with the whole hostile reasonable world. 'Mind you, I wasn't sure if I ought to come the second time, seeing we both were married and that. I prayed and read the Bible, but I couldn't get any help. You don't notice how little there is in the Bible really till you go to it for help. But I've lived a hard life and I've always done my best for William, and I know nothing in the world matters so much as happiness. If anybody's happy you ought to let them be. So I came again. Let him be. If you knew how happy he was just pottering round the garden. Men do love a garden. He could just go on. It can go on so easily.' (But there was a shade of doubt in her voice; she was pleading not only with me but with fate.) 'You wouldn't let them take him away to the asylum. You wouldn't stop me coming. The other one might, but you'd see she didn't. Oh, do just let him be. . . .

'Put it like this.' She made such explanatory gestures as I have seen cabmen make over their saucers of tea round a shelter. 'If my boy had been a cripple—he wasn't; he had the loveliest limbs—and the doctors had said to me, ''We'll straighten your boy's legs for you, but he'll be in pain all the rest of his life,'' I'd not have let them touch him. . . .

'I seemed to have to tell them that I knew a way. I suppose it would have been sly to sit there and not tell them. I told them anyhow. But oh! I can't do it. Go out and put an end to the poor love's happiness! After the time he's had, the war and all. And then he'll have to go back there! I can't! I can't!'

I felt an ecstatic sense of ease. Everything was going to be right. Chris was to live in the interminable enjoyment of his youth and love. There was to be a finality about his happiness which usually belongs only to loss and calamity; he was to be as happy as a ring cast into the sea is lost, as a man whose coffin has lain for centuries beneath the sod is dead. Yet Margaret continued to say, and irritated me by the implication that the matter was not settled, 'I oughtn't to do it, ought I?'

'Of course not! Of course not!' I cried heartily, but the attention died in her eyes. She stared over my shoulder at the open door, where Kitty stood.

The poise of her head had lost its pride, the shadows under her eyes were black like the marks of blows, and all her loveliness was diverted to the expression of grief. She held in her arms her Chinese sleeve dog, a once prized pet that had fallen from favour and now was only to be met whining upward for a little love at every passer in the corridors, and it sprawled leaf-brown across her white frock, wriggling for joy at the unaccustomed embrace. That she should at last have stooped to lift the lonely little dog was a sign of her deep unhappiness. Why she had come up I do not know, nor why her face puckered with tears as she looked in on us. It was not that she had the slightest intimation of our decision, for she could not have conceived that we could follow any course but that which was obviously to her advantage. It was simply that she hated to see this strange ugly woman moving about among her things. She swallowed her tears and passed on, to drift like her dog about the corridors.

Now, why did Kitty, who was the falsest thing on earth, who was in tune with every kind of falsity, by merely suffering somehow remind us of reality? Why did her tears reveal to me what I had learned long ago, but had forgotten in my frenzied love, that there is a draught that we must drink or not be fully human? I knew that one must know the truth. I knew quite well that when one is adult one must raise to one's lips the wine of the truth, heedless that it is not sweet like milk but draws the mouth with its strength, and celebrate communion with reality, or else walk for ever queer and small like a dwarf. Thirst for this sacrament had made Chris strike away the cup of lies about life that Kitty's white hands held to him, and turn to Margaret with this vast trustful gesture of his loss of memory. And helped by me she had forgotten that it is the first concern of love to safeguard the dignity of the beloved, so that neither God in his skies nor the boy peering through the hedge should find in all time one possibility for contempt, and had handed him the trivial toy of happiness. We had been utterly negligent of his future, blasphemously careless of the divine essential of his soul. For it we left him in his magic circle there would come a time when his delusion turned to a senile idiocy; when his joy at the sight of Margaret disgusted the flesh, because his smiling mouth was slack with age; when one's eyes no longer followed him caressingly as he went down to look for the first primroses in the wood, but flitted here and there defensively to see that nobody was noticing the doddering old man. Gamekeepers would chat kindly with him and tap their foreheads as he passed through the copse, callers would be tactful and dangle bright talk before him.

278

He who was as a flag flying from our tower would become a queer-shaped patch of eccentricity on the country-side, the stately music of his being would become a witless piping in the bushes. He would not be quite a man.

I did not know how I could pierce Margaret's simplicity with this last cruel subtlety, and turned to her stammering. But she said, 'Give me the jersey and the ball.'

The rebellion had gone from her eyes and they were again the seat of all gentle wisdom.

'The truth's the truth,' she said, 'and he must know it.'

I looked up at her, gasping yet not truly amazed, for I had always known she could not leave her throne of righteousness for long, and she repeated, 'The truth's the truth,' smiling sadly at the strange order of this earth.

We kissed, not as women, but as lovers do; I think we each embraced that part of Chris the other had absorbed by her love. She took the jersey and the ball and clasped them as though they were a child. When she got to the door she stopped and leaned against the lintel. Her head fell back, her eyes closed, her mouth was contorted as though she swallowed bitter drink.

I lay face downwards on the ottoman and presently heard her poor boots go creaking down the corridors. Through the feeling of doom that filled the room as tangibly as a scent I stretched out to the thought of Chris. In the deep daze of devotion which followed recollection of the fair down on his cheek, the skin burnt brown to the rim of his grey eyes, the harsh and diffident masculinity of him, I found comfort in remembering that there was a physical gallantry about him which would still, even when the worst had happened, leap sometimes to the joy of life. Always, to the very end, when the sun shone on his face or his horse took his fences well, he would screw up his eyes and smile that little stiff-lipped smile. I nursed a feeble glow at that. 'We must ride a lot,' I planned. And then Kitty's heels tapped on the

279

polished floor and her skirts swished as she sat down in the arm-chair, and I was distressed by the sense, more tiresome than a flickering light, of someone fretting.

She said, 'I wish she would hurry up. She's got to do it sooner or later.'

My spirit was asleep in horror. Out there Margaret was breaking his heart and hers, using words like a hammer, looking wise, doing it so well.

'Aren't they coming back?' asked Kitty. 'I wish you'd look.'

There was nothing in the garden. Only a column of birds swimming across the lake of green light that lay before the sunset.

A long time after Kitty spoke once more. 'Jenny, do look again.'

There had fallen a twilight which was a wistfulness of the earth. Under the cedar boughs I dimly saw a figure mothering something in her arms. Almost had she dissolved into the shadows; in another moment the night would have her. With his back turned on this fading happiness Chris walked across the lawn. He was looking up under his brows at the over-arching house as though it were a hated place to which, against all his hopes, business had forced him to return. He stepped aside to avoid a patch of brightness cast by a lighted window on the grass; lights in our house were worse than darkness, affection worse than hate elsewhere. He wore a dreadful decent smile; I knew how his voice would resolutely lift in greeting us. He walked not loose limbed like a boy, as he had done that very afternoon, but with the soldier's hard tread upon the heel. It recalled to me that, bad as we were, we were yet not the worst circumstance of his return. When we had lifted the yoke of our embraces from his shoulders he would go back to that flooded trench in Flanders under that sky more full of flying death than

280

clouds, to that No Man's Land where bullets fall like rain on the rotting faces of the dead. . . .

'Jenny, aren't they there?'

'They're both there.'

'Is he coming back?'

'He's coming back.'

'Jenny, Jenny! How does he look?'

'Oh. . . .' How could I say it? 'Every inch a soldier.'

She crept behind me to the window, peered over my shoulder and saw.

I heard her suck her breath with satisfaction. 'He's cured!' she whispered slowly. 'He's cured!'

TWO DAYS IN ARAGON

M.J. Farrell

M. J. FARRELL

is the pseudonym for Molly Keane. She was born in Co. Kildare, Ireland, in 1904 into 'a rather serious Hunting and Fishing and Church-going family' who gave her little education at the hands of governesses. Her father originally came from a Somerset family and her mother, a poetess, was the author of 'The Songs of the Glens of Antrim'. Molly Keane's interests when young were 'hunting and horses and having a good time': she began writing only as a means of supplementing her dress allowance, and chose the pseudonym M. J. Farrell 'to hide my literary side from my sporting friends'. She wrote her first novel, *The Knight of the Cheerful Countenance*, at the age of seventeen.

Molly Keane published ten novels between 1928 and 1952: *Young Entry* (1928), *Taking Chances* (1929), *Mad Puppetstown* (1931), *Conversation Piece* (1932), *Devoted Ladies* (1934), *Full House* (1935), *The Rising Tide* (1937), *Two Days in Aragon* (1941), *Loving Without Tears* (1951) and *Treasure Hunt* (1952). She was also a successful playwright, of whom James Agate said 'I would back this impish writer to hold her own against Noel Coward himself.' Her plays, with John Perry, always directed by John Gielgud, include *Spring Meeting* (1938), *Ducks and Drakes* (1942), *Treasure Hunt* (1949) and *Dazzling Prospect* (1961).

The tragic death of her husband at the age of thirty-six stopped her writing for many years. It was not until 1981 that another novel—*Good Behaviour*—was published, this time under her real name. Molly Keane has two daughters and lives in Co. Waterford. Her latest novel, *Time After Time*, was published in 1983 and her cookery book, *Nursery Cooking*, was published in 1985.

Virago publishes *Devoted Ladies*, *The Rising Tide*, *Two Days in Aragon*, *Mad Puppetstown*, *Full House* and *Taking Chances*. *Loving Without Tears* and *Young Entry* are forthcoming.

INTRODUCTION

Two Days in Aragon was Molly Keane's ninth novel and is perhaps her most ambitious. Written in 1941 when the passage of time and events had cast the traumatic and dreadful events of the Irish Civil Wars of the 1920s into a new perspective, the book, on one level, is a threnody, or lamentation, for the great houses of Ireland and the end of a way of life. On another, it is a celebration of those same houses, and the life that was lived in them—and there too on different levels—by the Anglo-Irish and their Catholic servants alike; but it is also, and most satisfactorily I think, a special kind of record of the social system that pertained among the Ascendancy in the South of Ireland and a close look at those golden beehives that such 'big' houses were. This social system, based on the existence of a separate, large and ostensibly powerful Ascendancy finally perished in the time of the Troubles, but it had begun to crumble with the demise of Landlordism many years before, and in the destruction or abandonment of many of the great houses its epitaph was composed.

Yet if it seems merely a shocking act of vandalism that such beautiful monuments should have been put to the torch, one must remember that to the mass of the Irish, whose forbears had been dispossessed to make way for the great demesnes over which these houses presided, they were more than great buildings. It was not easy for the Irish to perceive them as beautiful

artefacts, ornaments to the countryside. They were establish-
ments, symbols, more like Residencies than residences, and as
such, when the smouldering resentments of centuries flamed
into open rebellion, became targets for the flame—in every
sense. And the simile of the Residency can be carried further
since the English Government regarded the Irish uprising of
1916 ('The Easter Rising') as mutiny and executed nearly all its
leaders.

The ways of life conducted within these Anglo-Irish houses
were alien to the Irish way of life. It was not merely a question of
class differences, although it was certainly that too. There was
no question of anyone from the Anglo-Irish side crossing the
great social divide that lay between what are sometimes called
'the races'. The Anglo-Irish had allegiance to the British
Crown; England was their mother country, though Ireland may
have been their native land: and it was English manners, mores,
modes that pertained among them. Perhaps most of all the
dividing line was religion: the Anglo-Irish were to a man
Protestant—Catholicism or Romanism was 'common'. 'Even
so late as 1932 an Irish Peer who showed leanings towards
Rome was taken by his father to look at the Sunday congrega-
tion streaming out of the Catholic church on the estate and
asked how he could ally himself with them.' (Terence de Vere
White, *The Anglo-Irish*, Gollancz 1972). There is hostility there,
and there always was hostility, though it was cloaked on one
side by patronage, on the other by subservience or evasion. The
way of life in the 'big houses' was superimposed on the other
way of life in Ireland—that of the vast majority of the popula-
tion who were Catholics, spoke English as a foreign tongue and
whose accent was called a brogue (the other meaning of which,
interestingly enough, was a cheat), and who led lives that were
more impenetrable, secret and unknowable than those of their
Ascendancy masters. What is extraordinary is that so many of

286

the Anglo-Irish, whilst recognising the irredeemable spaces between them and the mass of the people, did not admit to their otherness. Stephen Gwynn, an ardent Irish nationalist, born in a rectory, and who felt himself to be Irish to the backbone, wrote 'The new nationalism describes me and the likes of me as Anglo-Irish. So all my life I have been spiritually hyphenated without knowing it.' It's as good a description as any, and that other hyphen joining the separate existences of the Anglo-Irish and the Irish on Irish soil was wiped out in the Troubles and their aftermath.

Molly Keane, almost inadvertently one might suppose, and one would be quite wrong to do so (for she is artful in her modesty), has preserved as much of the minutiae of the last days of the Irish Raj as any writer with more pretension to posterity. She did not mean to be a writer, never mind a social historian, and claims not to have set out to do anything other than to escape the bonds of her extraordinary upbringing in a large house in County Wexford where her parents lived in a way that was both eccentric yet typical of the gentry of that time. They ignored their children for the most part save for insisting on their skill in horsemanship, which was an essential accomplishment.

Molly Keane—or Skrine, her maiden name—was educated in fits and starts by a series of governesses, and in the gaps in between them, by her mother, whom she now recalls as a remarkable linguist and musician, and who under the pseudonym Moira O'Neil was a successful rhymster writing about the countryside and people of Ireland with charm and sentimentality. 'She made no attempt to pass any of her interests or accomplishments on to her children. I now think what an interesting woman she must have been. But I chiefly remember being alone as a child—my elder sister was away at a High School in Oxford and my brothers were at school in England. I never *did* go to school there.'

When she was older there was an attempt to formalise her

287

education and she went to a French school in Bray, outside Dublin, until a doctor diagnosed incipient T.B., in those days a killing disease. She was sentenced to bed for an indefinite period and out of sheer boredom started to write; or that, at least, is one of the legends. The other is that she wrote, in desperation, to earn pin money to supplement her tiny dress allowance. From the beginning she used a pseudonym, M.J. Farrell. Like mother, like daughter, though her mother never recognised it.

Startled though she was, to discover herself a writer, once started Molly Keane never looked back, and over three decades, in intense and painful bouts of writing, crammed into a few months taken off from her precious hunting, she wrote eleven novels and four plays (in collaboration with John Perry) which were great successes in the West End. Margaret Rutherford made her name in one and John Gielgud directed all four. Her last play *Dazzling Prospect*, produced in 1961, at a time when the spate of Angry Young Men plays had changed the conventions of West End theatre, was a failure.

Sarah Miles, straight out of RADA, had her first professional role in it and she once ruefully remembered, 'Never was there a less apt title than *Dazzling Prospect*. It marked one of the last times that people actually threw spoiled fruit at actors in a West End production.' Times had changed. As they had for M.J. Farrell whose beloved husband Bobbie Keane died suddenly, tragically aged only thirty-six. She stopped writing; not till the 1980's did she resurrect herself as a writer, this time under her own name, with the novels *Good Behaviour*, a wild success, and *Time After Time*, a dazzling *tour de force*. (She tells a good story of how, at a dinner party in her honour in Paris, the guests expressed their horror of Jasper the hero of the book 'Quel bête' they said, and congratulated her on her ferocious imagination at conjuring up such a horror. 'But Jasper' she said, smiling gently, 'c'est moi.')

288

Two Days in Aragon was one of the last books to be written in her great creative period between the wars. It was written after her marriage to Bobbie Keane 'a witty, happy man who loved old furniture, me, his daughters, good food and talk'. *Two Days in Aragon* sets out to be more deliberately serious than her other books and though it is occasionally portentous and sentimental it is also sympathetic to the Irish cause. It also tackles head on what is either implicit in her earlier work or avoided: the enormous, vexed problem that was Ireland's turbulent relationship with England which was coming to a horrid head in the times of which she was writing. These years of rebellion and fighting are known as the Troubles, though god knows the troubles had been going on for centuries, but by 1920 the fighting was 'a dreary record of reprisals and counter reprisals, burnings, murders and outrages, not between armies but between expert gunmen on both sides' (Edmund Curtis, *A History of Ireland*, Methuen 1961). The gunman became the new symbol for Ireland.

Molly Keane wrote *Two Days in Aragon* partly for her beloved husband who, she said, was far more open-minded than she, and saw things more clearly at the time they were happening. But the book was also written as a kind of atonement for her contemporaneous attitude, her condemnations and her lack of understanding. An understandable lack of understanding and one shared by so many of her class, epitomised by the attitude of her mother, who, Molly Keane once surmised, 'would have dismissed Yeats as just another Irish patriot. She couldn't think that the English had ever done anything wrong whereas of course they had behaved appallingly for generation after generation.'

As an artist, Molly Keane saw both sides of the tragic Irish question. She perceived, too, that the young Irishmen her friends thought of simply as murderers and fanatics, were fighting for their basic right to be self-governing. She gives excuses for their behaviour though they believed that they had reasons, moral imperatives, which, were they not to be fulfilled, would constitute treachery not only to their country but to themselves as Irishmen. This was something outside her experience but she accommodated it. Indeed throughout the book one gets the feeling of the author giving her imagination a specific imaginative wrench, jolting it to sympathy and forgiveness.

Two Days in Aragon is a precise title. The novel relates the tragic sequence of events over the last two days of Aragon, a great house by a large river in County Westmeath. Molly Keane took the name from a mountain—Araglin—near where she lived, but its name inevitably invokes the close connections that have always existed between Spain and Ireland; a strange empathy based as much on emotional affinities as on their shared, rabidly Catholic history and heritage.

Aragon is a spectacularly beautiful house, an amalgam of houses Molly Keane knew and loved, many of which were destroyed in the Troubles, and she delivers it marvellously, lying golden and rich in its demesne and valley, its inhabitants living apparently effortlessly in a way that, though long doomed, is still flourishing. Her details are so engaging; the things people eat (she describes the meals with a delicious relish that bespeaks a great cook) the way the house is furnished: the joy of cupboards full of fine linen, the sprawl of a house that is clean and grand and spacious. And, as in all the houses in her books, history and portent hang heavy in all the rooms. 'The past doesn't dwell in people's minds now in the way that it did' she says, and it's a sentiment she voices strongly in *Two Days in Aragon*.

What was there then in the air of the houses that is not now? Was it more stirred by the emotions of the past than now, when the life of the present is gay and firm in the ether with the radio ministering to the loneliest? Radio has stirred away the hauntings and stillness in the old rooms. The waves of the past cannot lap and lap, quietly encroaching onto the solid sands of now. Houses and memories have less power to injure, less power to assuage.

In all her books houses play an *active* part—she treats them as though they had an actual awful power for good or ill. Aragon's power appears benign but occasionally Molly Keane twitches aside the serene veil and shows the malevolence that has accumulated behind the aftermath of evil done there, as in the discovery of a torture chamber built by a sadistic forbear of the Foxes, the family who have always lived in the house.

Mrs Fox, fluffy-headed, childish and widowed since her husband died after a hunting accident, and her two children Sylvia and Grania, are the owners of the house, but at the pivot of the novel is its true inheritor Nan O'Neill. Molly Keane has drawn in Nan O'Neill a powerful portrait of a powerful woman, standing at the centre of the book as she does of Aragon. Our first glimpse of her is as solid and sure as a figure in Chardin or a Brueghel painting as she emerges from the shadows of Aragon into the reader's vision in a blue blouse and full black skirt and white apron, 'its sure soothing shape as sure a shape as a sail'. Nan O'Neill is a melodramatic figure, histrionic, obsessive and compulsive. As its housekeeper, guardian and protector she is the living embodiment of Aragon, which she literally worships. Aragon is her temple, her shrine, and the people who live in it are sacred to her, except for Miss Pigeon, an ancient Fox aunt and scapegoat for Nan's complex pent-up virulence and cruelties. Not surprising, since the same blood that flowed in the veins of the builder of the torture chamber flows in Nan's veins. For she is the illegitimate daughter of the father of Hugh Fox, dead father of Sylvia and Grania, and is therefore a cousin.

291

Molly Keane is firing on all barrels in her outrageous portrait of Miss Pigeon, who is in fact the kind of eccentric gentlewoman who used to lurk, backwatered in the great houses, not just of Ireland, but all over Europe from Sicily to Scotland. 'It was extraordinary how many old aunts there were everywhere in all the houses, getting dottier all the time, utterly arrogant and absolutely certain of their right to *be* there. They were there because they never married—there was a great shortage of men. The arrogance they were born with. I took such things for granted then, as one took so much—the whole of life is so different. None of the owners of these houses worked—they never thought of working. They had their horses, a pack of hounds, shooting, fishing—it was a hard day's work just keeping up with those things—and one needed so much less money. When I think of how Bobbie [Keane] and I lived at Belleville, I really believe that you would need at least twenty times the income now.' Belleville was the beautiful house near the Blackwater river where Molly Keane and her husband spent their happy married life. Belleville was not the model for Aragon, though the Blackwater is the same river that Aragon looks down on. She remembers that 'everything went up and down the river, starting with the Phoenicians—little steamers and boats plying between Youghal and Cappoquin. My father-in-law started up a boat service—the boat was called 'The Happy Harry'. Of course the service *cost* money rather than made it and during the Troubles the Republicans took the boat over—I suppose they thought it was bringing soldiers in. It got caught between the two warring parties and was sunk. That kind of thing is what happened to many houses—Woodrooff for example [where Molly Keane spent a formative time away from her parents] was only burnt down because it was on a strategic point between Clare and Clonmel and was caught in the crossfire.'

Aragon as painted by Molly Keane is a representative of these great houses, lived in by people who felt themselves at one with the country, who counted themselves Irish, who were looked after by Irish servants, but who might have come from a different planet as regards how the Irish viewed and regarded them. In *Two Days in Aragon* Molly Keane inclined to the view that these houses had come to the end of their useful lives, that their span was over, and that their burning was a cremation. Just as many people, looking back, see the 1914 War as inevitable in a way, if only to put an end to a way of life that was inappropriate to the twentieth century, so it appears that the demise of Aragon—and all such houses—was historically inevitable. Ireland after the signing of the Treaty and for many years after it, might be likened to China in the throes of the Cultural Revolution, save that the killing was done. The way of life that loomed ahead had no place in it for gracious living.

The burning of their houses was an enormous shock to the Anglo-Irish who believed themselves to be Irish and believed too that they commanded the loyalty of those who lived around them and worked for them. They deceived themselves. There was loyalty and love, certainly, but of a kind, and it was ambivalent. The Conquered Celt has never been straightforward in his dealing with those who consider themselves to be socially superior. This attitude is perhaps best summed up in David Thomson's great book *Woodbrook* in which he speaks about the servants of an Irish house, 'They secretly cherished hatred for the major, their present landlord and employer, whom in day to day relationships they loved—cherished this hatred because of his ancestors and theirs and because it might help their advancement.'

Nan of Aragon is not of this ilk . . . her devotion to the house and its family is total. She serves it like a slave, proud of her chains, and though she herself is a Fox she regards the family as so far removed from her that an alliance is unthinkable. Indeed the leap that Grania, the younger of the two Fox daughters, makes in taking a native Irishman for her lover is almost unimaginably daring and damning. The appalled exclamation in *Two Days in Aragon* 'that a Fox, a daughter of Aragon, should carry on an affair with an O'Neill from the mountain, was as wrong, Grania knew, to Nan as the love of black and white people seemed to her' is utterly in context with such an atmosphere. And even though this particular O'Neill is Nan's own son, she is as shocked as though she has discovered some arcane form of miscegnation. 'A person like that, what can anybody nice think of you if this gets known—it's a deeply terrible shocking thing, my child, to let a man like that touch you, and of course if anybody gets to know you have then it's too dreadful, it's too dreadful then.' This is to do with class. Distinctions were absolute and constituted even more of a chasm in Ireland than pertained in England.

Molly Keane has an acute ear for Irishisms, things that Irish people said that were often treasured up by those who heard them and recounted at dinner for fond patronising amusement. But hers are classic and funny and make absolute sense in their paradox, as in Nan's comment as she looks in horror at a ferret. 'Everyone has their favourite animal that they hate.'

Molly Keane herself seems an amalgam of Grania and Sylvia. Grania is the wild, poetic creature who makes the leap over convention and Sylvia the cool, swift elder sister, sharp as a lemon, willingly locked into a conventional way of life that could as easily be lived in England as in Ireland. Grania, silly, artless, without a grain of common sense, is fired by ignorant, useless bravery. She is culpably innocent; a girl who causes trouble because she ignores convention and because she cannot help it. She is open-hearted and uncalculatingly gullible, a fat little slut who is a great hand at curling her hair but not too good at washing—the reverse of the impeccable, shining Sylvia, street-wise, elegant, calculating, who knows the cost of everything and finds out the price of love.

Yet it is not golden Grania, who would have died for love, who comes nearest to death, but Sylvia, and that because of the code by which she lives, a code which is so much a part of her existence that it impels her to the impossible. Sylvia, the perfect little deputy mistress of Aragon, as one day she plans to be the perfect Lady Purvis in Norfolk, is an unlikeable, though admirable character. Just once does she become human, when she makes that remarkable pact of love with the other side, the enemy. As a result her perfectly ordered life, rigid in its perfection, can never be the same again, nor can her belief in the correctness of things, in good behaviour. Even her attitude towards the man who is to be her husband will be coloured by her secret, shocking knowledge that the call of man to woman is beyond class divide, though it is she who is the cruellest snob in the book.

In *Two Days in Aragon* Molly Keane looks at the rights and wrongs of a series of traumatic events in the course of two days of Irish history in an Irish house. In doing so she has made a miniature of something very large and sad, the history of Ireland and the people who lived there and loved her. It is a fictional account of bitter events and sad truths. Elizabeth Bowen, her great friend and owner of Bowen's Court, a house in spirit much like the one called Aragon, concluded sadly at the end of her own Anglo-Irish family history, 'The stretches of the past I have to cover have been on the whole painful. My family got their position and drew their power from a situation that shows an inherent wrong. In the grip of that situation England and Ireland each turned to the other a closed, hash, distorted face, a face their lovers would hardly know.' Molly Keane saw both faces very clearly on both days in Aragon.

Polly Devlin, Somerset, 1985

I

Grania Fox was eighteen. She was alone in a wood she knew
very well, far beyond the house and above the river. She was waiting. But she never projected herself from one moment into the
next, from one day into another, because she had no imagination.

Now she took in through her body the streaming pallor of
the spring light spread across the wide shallow valley beneath
the woods; the river without any glare on its smooth, lit flowing; the fields, warm and living as flesh under the sun; the smells
of honey and gum from the blue larches and the gorse. She knew
of a little dog's hunting lust, and ditches of primroses dry for
sitting down, sheltered for love. She had a bunch of primroses,
their pink stalks damp in her hand, fisted as in childhood to hold
them—their scent was dry as powder—the lightest most affecting scent. Where was her dog now? Where was Soo, her little
black bitch?

'Soo, Soo, Soo, naughty one, Soo!'

A little black deer came flying through its forest of game, a
little black unicorn without its horn; flying back from its other
life, its great and wild life where it was a terror and a menace to
the wood things, the birdies, the bunnies, the mice, the moles;
back to her slave-love life—eyes shining, unknowing of Grania.
A spring into her arms, into her heart, but Grania has no claim
on her now. A kiss for a wild hunter and freedom of woods and

297

coverts till the hunter grows weary, and then come back, my little Pompey, my slave love.

Grania had no repose. She flew about doing things all the time. Now she thought she had time to get some watercress before her lover came to her. In the ditch just outside the wood there was plenty of watercress, excellent watercress, growing cleanly and richly in the steep dark ditch. She had better get some watercress.

Grania was a fat little blonde with pretty bones under her flesh; rather a slut, and inclined to wear party shoes with old tweeds. She would be in her bath, and forget to wash very much, but she was a great hand at curling up her blonde hair, of which she was very vain. Three of the most marriageable young men in the County Westcommon had asked her to marry them; but they had no skill for love-making so she refused them all, and returned to Foley O'Neill, who embraced her in woods and other out-of-the-way places, whereas the eligible young men seldom did more than hold her hand before they proposed. Foley O'Neill did not propose. He was so much her social inferior. A fantastic reason perhaps, but good enough for him, as he did not really want to marry her.

This evening Grania did not see him until he was beside her, she was so occupied with her watercress. He smiled and said to her in that quiet voice, neither quite of the common people nor quite of Grania's people.

'Aren't you going to talk to me at all to-day?'

'How long have you been here?'

'Hours and hours——'

'And hours—What a lie! I must get this bit of cress. Wait a minute.'

Instead of saying, 'I can't wait,' or 'It's not a lie,' he got down in the ditch too and picked cress neatly and seriously beside her. He could put love away while it was closer than at present.

Foley had always been a person of importance. When he was four years old his father died and his mother left the mountain farm and went back to Aragon, where she had been nurse to the Fox's before she married—there was Fox blood in her and she could not leave the place. Dymphnia O'Neill was her name, but they called her Nan at Aragon.

Foley's Aunt Gipsy, his father's sister, looked after him through his childhood, flattering and coaxing him as 'the young Master,' 'the young Boss.' Aunt Gipsy managed the farm in a sort of a way under Nan's direction from Aragon.

Nan had always hated the poor twist of mountainy farm she had married into. But when she lived there she had worked and striven on it with all her power, civilising it a little more every year.

Nan never wanted her son to be a farmer. She spent far beyond her means on his education. From his youngest days she had horses in her mind for him—such horses were his life and his trade now. He was brave, hardworking and lucky, and, insofar as maybe in this precarious way of living, he now made a success of horse dealing.

Foley loved and feared his mother. He would discuss the twists of people's characters and circumstances with her if he wished to get the better of them in a deal. His respect for her opinion was strong. He was very much afraid of her knowing about this love affair with Grania, which she would have condemned utterly.

'Where's that silly little dog of yours to-day?' Foley thought they had picked enough watercress for the present. They sat together on the bank.

'Hunting. She's not silly.' Grania always rose in defence of her dog—her beautiful little black bitch.

'Silly and useless. She hasn't even got a tail.'

'Oh, how dare you! She's not meant to have one. Who ever

saw a Schipperke with a tail. Don't be silly,'

'Well, what is she good for?'

'Good for love—they're love dogs.'

'No good. They're a rotten breed of dog.'

'They're the Barge dogs of Holland. You know, they pull the barges up and down the canals.'

'You're telling lies,' he picked up her hand and bit her wrist gently. Deeply. Real pain.

'Oh, Foley, poor Grania.'

'You're telling lies and you have to be punished.' The shadows of leaves were flickering across her fat white neck, trembling at a certain depth within her eyes.

He said, 'I've got a present for you.'

'What is it?' She tried to keep her voice steady. But this was too much—this breaking off from love. She had no experience.

'A new ferret. It's in the car.'

His triangular blue eyes held hers. He was speaking across his pause in love-making.

She answered with difficulty. 'Oh, how lovely. Shall we go and talk to him?'

He laughed, putting his arms round her.

'Do you think we need him now?'

'No——No——'

It's not me. It's not myself. Grania was transcended, purged of all fret, or small unhappy thought, running home through the woods to her house built above the river. Soo ran beside her, leaping for the ferret that dangled horrid and malign from her hand. Across the valley the woods reached strange evening heights and deeps of shadows. Near her path were little pale blue mosses and water-green patches of bracken. Love sang at her heart no more. She had made a moment's peace with love, and now she was planning how to get a box arranged for this ferret before dinner.

II

Down on the dark kept paths nearer the house Grania met her Aunt Pigeon. Aunt Pigeon was old. She was an invalid they said. She had her own bedroom and sitting-room, and Nan Foley looked after her. She had been tall and fat once but now she looked to be a small old woman, the flesh all fallen from her elegant bones—her body huddled together and dressed in absurdly old clothes.

'We really must get Aunt Pigeon a new dress,' Grania's mother had been saying distractedly for the last ten years. With her voice she had a way of making almost anything seem impossible of accomplishment; 'I must rush to the garden for one instant and try to plant this primrose before it quite dies.' Everything was like that. 'I wonder if that tiresome child ought to have a tonic? Cod liver oil? Do try to remind me, darling, if you possibly can.'

Certainly there had never been a new dress for Aunt Pigeon. It was too difficult. She was wearing a waisted black jacket this evening, sticking out over her thin behind and trimmed with braid. She had a yellow-brown skunk fur on her shoulders with topaz yellow eyes, and an elaborate fastening system. The long skirt nearly covered those thick boots that Nan Foley bought in the village, and which were so heavy on her exquisitely made but perfectly flat little feet—and then you had to lace them up. It was a terrible business every morning, every morning of your life. Aunt Pigeon's face was as white as a sheep's face. Her eyes still held a little of the blue they had been, so she always liked to wear a blue scarf or a bit of blue trimming somewhere to bring out their colour. To Grania and Sylvia she was part of life. They could never remember a time when they had not known she was more childish than themselves. They were not particularly kind to her. Darling Nan looked after her, and they knew she did not like Nan. Poor Nan had some terrible times with her; for instance, when she would not sleep in bed on account of catching leprosy. The only way to avoid leprosy was to sleep on the stairs. She took terrible fancies when she got a glass of port, Nan said, oh terrible. Such talk of Heathen Gods then, you couldn't believe it; and saucers of milk for the fairies tripping you up wherever you went. Since earliest days the children could remember finding those little offerings, hidden under leaves, left behind stones or in nooks of trees for her Diblins, as she called them. Dolls' saucers of curds and jam, scraps of buttered toast from breakfast, sometimes the children ate them, sometimes the dogs. Aunt Pigeon wagged her head solemnly when she could remember where she had put the saucers and saw them emptied.

Finding her this evening in the darkness of the towering rhododendron, among the glossy darkness of the laurel leaves, Grania had a chill moment before the customary way of seeing Aunt Pigeon came back to her, and she was blinded again by custom to that moment's vision of a different creature; alive, rather wild, strong in its desires. Aunt Pigeon was putting something away in her pocket which she wore hung on a tape round her waist. Complicated explorations were in progress among skirt and petticoat, a prolonged grope for what she called her sporran.

'I keep everything most precious just here,' she would say,

302

patting the hiding-place with a calm and unembarrassed gesture. 'You'd be surprised how many people have been after this little pattern of mine. You'd be amazed. It's so nice for when I travel. Oh, and such a comfort to think there's one place nobody can pry into.'

To-day Grania detected a good deal of bustle and confusion as Aunt Pigeon stowed away some treasure. It might be an old ring or a letter or some morsel for the Diblins, over which she had been brooding by herself among the dark evergreens.

'What have you got in your sporran to-night, Aunt Pigeon?' she asked. Aloof, benignant, patronising, she spoke from the distance of a world away—from her different star.

'Hush.' Aunt Pigeon came nearer and whispered. 'It's a surprise for my Diblins.'

'What is it?'

'I've been bird's nesting,' Aunt Pigeon said in a tough buccaneering tone of voice. 'Three Thrushes' eggs and two Blackbirds', what d'you think o' that?'

'But did you take the eggs away?'

'Safe in my sporran.'

'And take care they don't hatch there.'

'Ah, they may hatch and flutter their wings, they can't get out of my sporran.'

'But the poor big Birdies?'

'Oh, they can lay more eggs.'

'Hard on them.'

'Fun for them. It's nature.'

'And Aunt Pigeon won't take any more eggs?'

'Aunt Pigeon will come creeping—creeping up to their nests.' She gave an imitation of herself that was a little frightening, moving without a sound on the soft path. 'Pigeon will find a brown nest in the silver holly, she will put her hand into it, quiet as a mouse. Oh, it's so smooth and hot in there, and three warm

303

little eggs all ready for her. She can't see them, no ! but she can touch them——'

'Only three?'

'Much better three, better for eating, my darling. If there were four those nasty little birds might be hatching up in them.'

'Oh, Aunt Pigeon, do put them back.'

'Nothing ever gets out of my sporran.'

'Think of the birds, they'll be in such a state.'

'Let them cry. Let them cry. We all have a cross to bear. We can't all expect the best of everything.'

III

Nan Foley was coming down the path from the house. She had not yet plunged into the shades and thicknesses of the laurel and the common rhododendron. She was walking in the sun through the flame and salmon and honey-yellow of the azaleas and the great house was long and pale behind her. Straight behind her were the big pillars of the carriage porch. They made a powerful frame behind her, if you had been coming towards her it would have seemed a gorgeous descent. For Nan Foley was a beautiful woman, and as strong as one of the pillars of the Corinthian porch. She was tall, with such wide shoulders that her hips seemed neat and narrow. She had a wide forehead and her grey hair curled strongly on her head. The bones round her eyes were of that full exciting shape which age makes more true and regular. The skin was thick and healthy still, and hardly lined for a woman of fifty (in 1920 she must have been fifty at least). She wore a blue blouse with her full black skirt and a great white apron, white as an advertisement for soap; its pure soothing shape was as sure a shape as a sail seen on the sea.

She turned to her left out of the bright sun, and started walking down some steps cut in the side of the hill, they led to the lower path through the rhododendrons where Grania and Aunt Pigeon were talking. Nan had not heard them, but some sensible instinct always led her directly to her charge's most frequented places. As she walked along she paused now and then to pull out a weed or twist back an encroaching bough. The actions were strong and neat and calculated to a nicety. She accomplished each little effort with a minimum outlay of strength.

'Ah, now I have you,' she exclaimed gaily as she turned into the staight dark path and bore down on Aunt Pigeon and Grania. 'Now I have you located, imagine! And do you know how long it is past your time for supper?'

'I know you want to pack me off to bed. You needn't tell me that, Nan.'

'No, dear, no, but it's time for you to come in all the same.'

Nan gave Grania a glance while she spoke, a glance of confidence, suggesting that they were two sensible people who must indulge the tiresome whims of a spoilt child. They two were of another life entirely, the sane life, outside poor Miss Pigeon's.

'Do go in, Aunt Pidgie,' Grania said, returning Nan's look with a knowing smile. 'I'm sure Nan has a lovely supper ready for you.'

'What's for the dining-room dinner?' Aunt Pigeon asked eagerly.

'Clear soup.'

'Strong clear soup?'

'Made of the best of shin beef and reduced to pure goodness.'

'Ah, that will do their insides good. After that?'

'Salmon, and lettuce hearts.'

'A nice salmon?'

'Lepping fresh from the sea, imagine.'

'And then?'

'The shoulder of lamb and the first green peas.'

'Was it a black-faced lamb?'

'I believe so.'

'Are they those nasty tasteless Pilot peas?'

'No, the juicy Little Marvel.'

'And a little butter and mint with them, of course?'

'Of course, yes.'

'And the sweet—— Don't tell me, I'll guess—bottled plums?'

'No.'

'Rhubarb fool?'

'No,'

'Don't tell me, don't tell me! Jam puffs and cream?'

'You're getting warmer.'

'Is it a gooseberry tart from the early bush on the left-hand side of the asparagus bed?'

'It is.'

'Ah, ah, I knew I'd get it right. Oh, that sounds a very nice dinner.' The voice changed. The life in it when she had questioned Nan about the dining-room dinner died, and she said in a voice like the small voice of the smallest bear.

'But what's for my supper?'

'Oh, a delicious little supper. Come in now and see.'

'I'm coming, I'm coming. Oh, the hill is so steep and my feet are so tired.'

Nan gave Aunt Pigeon one of those strong commanding looks of hers, a look that would have put life back in the dead by its compulsion to action.

'No delay now, Miss Pigeon, or I'll let the Diblins in to eat your supper.'

'No, Nan, no. I'll leave them each a little piece, but not all Nan, please not all my supper.'

She started pegging away up the warm path towards the house at an absurd rate; such was her haste that she almost forgot to use her stick as she bundled out of sight round the corner past which Nan had come to find her.

As she disappeared Nan burst into a laugh of indulgent annoyance, the sort of laugh with which one admits a misdemeanour in an old dog.

'Well, isn't she a caution? Now Miss Grania it's time you were in too. The dressing-gong sounded as I came out. Oh, goodness, child, what's that awful thing in your hand?'

'It's a ferret, Nanny darling. Can you get me a box to put it in?'

'O Jesu! Ferrets of all things. I imagine they give me the oh's—keep away from me with it, will you now, will you, will you, Miss Grania.'

'I can't put it in among the others yet. It's a stranger to them, so do find me a cosy box for the night; one we can close up, Nan, mind. I wouldn't lose it for the world.'

'Where did you get it?—the dirty thing—keep off from me like a good child.'

'I got it, I got it from a tinker on the hill.'

Grania had no intention of telling Foley's mother where the love gift came from. Nan would be on to this affair if she got so much as a breath, as a hint, as a whisper on the breeze, and the strength of her disapproval, Grania truly felt, would be well matched by the strength and weight of her opposition in the matter. For a Fox, a daughter of Aragon, to carry on an affair with an O'Neill from the Mountain was as wrong, Grania knew, to Nan as the love of black and white people seemed to her. But her secret, her joy and her thrilling refuge, were still her unshared delights. Her foot was set now in a strange country, and its ways were before her. She was not going to share her speculations or tell her present joy.

'God forgive me, I hate them. I think everyone has their favourite animal that they hate—look at the spot on its back—I thought it was only Foley had the breed of the white ferrets with the spot on them.'

Grania held the ferret up, its horrid little hands hung down, its neck lifted and twisted a little as it peered about it with red eyes. Soo, who had been sitting trembling with disgust, made a spring towards it. It was the diversion Grania had played for. Screams from Nan. Screams from Soo. Screams from Grania, and awful hissings from the ferret, mingled under the dark thin boughs of the laurels and rhododendrons.

'Indeed, Soo, I wouldn't blame you, Petty. Who's a love? Who's a little wee? Who didn't like a dirty ferret? Come to me, love. Kiss for Nanny? Now, pet! Now! I'll go on and get the box for you, Miss Grania.'

Nan went striding away carrying Soo in her arms as if she was a baby, and for the moment the ferret's resemblance to Foley's breed seemed to be forgotten. Grania was glad to be alone again. She went slowly with a delicious weariness up the path, and when she got back into the sunlight she felt overcome by her own well-being and happiness.

The scent of azaleas caught in the back of her nose like a fog of honey and pepper. The harsh almost animal breath that is behind its scent was not here yet, only the wild pungent sweet of its earliest flowers. Great groups almost grown to the size of trees flowered along the wide grass borders of the avenue towards the house. They were above the trees that dropped down the steep bank of the valley. Rooks were flying to and from their nests in the tree tops below. Above the house again, the hill climbed up nursing the sun in its hollows and elbows, sheltering the rare trees, and the rhododendrons, and tender magnolias, and camellias that flowered so freely along the side of this valley.

Aragon stood high above a tidal river. So high and so near that there was only a narrow kind of garden between house and water. It was almost a hanging garden, as Spanish as the strange name Aragon. There was a path under the long line of windows, then a wide short flight of steps with little stone foxes, flying along, stretched brushes out in the air behind them, at the top and the bottom of the steps. Below the steps there were no flower-beds, but a narrow piece of dark grass, and another path, and a very low wall built above the drop to the river. If you sat on the wall you looked down into a grove of ilex and beech and cherry trees. You looked down into the highest places of the trees familiarly from above. Into rooks' nests and into the stone pine where herons built, you might sit and stare, and breathe up the fogged white scent of Portugal laurel flowers on the heavy river air.

Directly underneath the house and this grove, the river swelled and shrank with the tides. You could look deep into the river bed, and up its slow turns towards the mountains and down its straighter way to the sea. Small ships could come up above Aragon, and it was nice to watch them go up and down on the tides.

You sat on the wall above the steep fall of ground as on a balcony. Leaning, you looked down the full river, and across the shining country of fields and woods and mountains. You looked directly down on wet trees and on the bright backs of flying birds—they seemed to be swimming across the air below.

The house itself was long and pale, but it did not share in the coldness and obscure gloom proper to so many beautiful houses of the Georgian age in Ireland. Perhaps because of the deep shelter that surrounded it there was a calm and a kindness about its lines; lines that had all the strict flow and balance of their period. Beauty so correct and satisfactory since then there has never been; nor so much dignity with so little heaviness. The great stone carriage porch of Aragon was not pompous; the balustrade round the roof edge, with its cut stone urns at regular intervals, had the severity belonging rightly to decoration.

Above the house, and above the wall of the castle that had been here before the house, the pleasure grounds were made. There you went up and down half-circular flights of steps and breathed the hushed air in grassy spaces. You walked among towering rhododendrons, great red castles of flower, and saw

310

the air blue in the bamboos and eucalyptus, and golden in the sticky apricot of azaleas. It was the quietest, most solemn garden. The parliaments of rooks in the woods below, only an echo here, a ring for the circle of quiet.

IV

'Oh, Grania, my dear child, you naughty thing, why are you so late? Where have you been dear, really? It's five minutes to dinner, and have I got time to run out and give my Canary Birds a drop of water before the gong sounds?'

Grania's mother met her in the hall. She was little and pretty and distracted, always on the point of doing some tremendous thing and never having time to accomplish it. Her two passions in life were cards and her garden, and she would sacrifice any one or anything for either. She was a bad gardener and a bad gambler. Yet no disasters ever disgusted her of her two pursuits. Of course, plants were difficult and would sometimes refuse to grow; if cards would not always come your way, what of it? Next time would be different.

Grania and Sylvia were fond of their mother in an unpositive kind of way, but Nan Foley adored and served her with a sort of passion.

'Oh, Mummy, I won't really truly be a moment, not a second.'

'Well, not too quick perhaps, darling, or I shan't have time for my watering. I'll just rush——'

They ran away from each other, Mrs. Fox still talking, and flying out of doors in her mauve tulle teagown with all the bows, her bronze beaded evening shoes hurrying comfortably along towards the newly planted primulas.

312

Grania went bundling up the wide staircase to her bedroom.

As she reached the landing one of the tall lightly-curved mahogany doors opened and Sylvia came out.

'My dear Grania, how late, aren't you? And, oh, my dear, how you do smell.' She nipped her thin nose between finger and thumb and continued to talk, holding her skirt away from Grania with the other hand. 'You smell of musk and, oh, every conceivable awfulness. Put a drop of something in your bath, but not my Rose Geranium.'

'I wouldn't touch your filthy Rose Geranium.'

'Then who, one rather wonders, half-emptied the bottle?' Sylvia let go her nose and the question at the same instant.

'I suppose you mean I did.'

'Perhaps—perhaps not.'

'You don't believe me?'

'Did I say so?'

'As good as.'

'Oh, my dear child,' Sylvia laughed her cold nonplussing little laugh, 'have it your own way, and use the rest too if it's going to mask this very curious smell.'

'Shut up, shut up, shut up.'

'Certainly, certainly, certainly.'

Grania opened and slammed the door of her bedroom. In three words Sylvia could stir hatred and passion in her so that she sweated and cried with rage. Now she tore off her clothes, all her peace forgotten, and rushed to the bathroom determined to pour the rest of the Rose Geranuim down the drain, only to find that Sylvia had removed the bottle and left a small tin of Jeyes Fluid in its place.

Neatly and arrogantly Sylvia walked down the stairs; unstirred by her little contest with Grania; cool and charming in her pale grey dress; a string of river pearls round her neck; a string of

313

pearls which she had collected singly since childhood, to which she still added and substituted better for less perfect little pearls with untiring interest. The poachers on the river would bring her the odd mussel pears they found, and for these she would drive the shrewdest and most good-humoured bargains. She would often go pearl fishing herself, compelling any biddable girl friend to fish with her, and long and cold and unsuccessful these outings usually were. But Sylvia had the gift of making any labour she undertook a sort of excitement, more important than a game, more enthralling than a party—there was a fire somewhere within her cool artistry, a thin scented flame, sharp as a frosty star.

She went into the drawing-room now and sat down to wait for dinner, for her Mother and for Grania. With a nice calculation of their probable lateness she decided that she would just have time to finish the wing of a swan in the exquisite and elaborate piece of tapestry work on which she was working. Head bent to lifted hands she sat in the full spring light, her needle digging and darting with such skill and certainty that she seemed to be drawing the very bones behind the feathers in her work.

The drawing-room at Aragon was a particularly beautiful room—in a long and very fully curved wall tall windows looked out over the river below. The river light swelled up to the windows in great swimming reflections on the air.

In winter time this light was as cold as the water. Although it was too wide a light for melancholy or petty depression, it was empty, it retreated to darkness and the water. But in summer and in springtime there was another quality in its taking of this beautiful room. A possession of light, of soft airs familiar with the room for many years. There was a very old paper on the walls, a dark rococo design striping them formally, dark and gold against white. It was not a pretty paper, but it was peculiar and valuable. A carpet had once been woven to follow the circle of the room. It

gave you the feeling of a large pale pond with wreaths of faint
ghostly flowers on its round margins. Two knife-thin marble
mantelpieces stood one to each side of the inside wall, a high
mahogany door marking the centre between them. Thin buff
marble was inlaid in their pillars. Delicate plaques and swinging
wreaths decorated them. Portraits of ancestors in dresses and
coats of maroon and pink and plum and pale pearly green, were
hung, far too high, on the walls; over doors and above mirrors,
squeezed upwards and closer together as the generations progressed onwards. There was a quantity of china in the room,
most of it Dresden and not all particularly good, little flowers
curling as tight as cauliflowers and plentiful as gravel thrown on
cement on many of the pieces. But there was a pair of fine horses,
pallid yet fierce, standing on one of the mantelpieces.

It was a difficult room in which to arrange furniture. The
largest tables looked islanded and isolated, and smaller ones were
like desolate sea anemones stuck here and there in space. Even the
grand piano (in 1920 still magnificently shawled and bephoto-
graphed) had a pathetic spinet-like appearance. The room indeed
was made for parties only, parties in the grand manner. It was in
no sense of the word a sitting-room and refused to allow its
grandeur to be in any way cajoled or modernised. The Bucks and
Belles of Ireland had danced here, the windows open to the river
and candles burning in the darkly bright clusters of the chandeliers and wall brackets. There had been plenty of the best claret
drunk at Aragon in those days; routs and card parties with lands
all gone on the throw of the dice, at the same tables where now
they played a silly game of the moment called 'Put and Take,'
and Mrs. Fox sat late into the night when she could get people to
play bridge with her.

To-night ten minutes after the gong had rung, Mrs. Fox came
bundling in from the garden, some of her bows a little moist and
drabbled, and those bronze shoes rather dirty where their sharp

curved heels had dug their half-moons in the grass.

'Oh, Frazer,' she said in the most abject way to the butler, who was standing rather reprovingly in the hall. 'Oh, Frazer, how naughty of me, I am sorry. I had intended to be really punctual to-night. Are the young ladies down yet?'

'Miss Sylvia is down since five minutes to eight, Madam.'

'Oh, you must really give Miss Grania a good scolding for me. She's never in time for anything. There you are, precious,' as Grania came hurrying down stairs. 'Come on—let's get into the dining-room, and Sylvia'll think we were in time. She's just too punctual for anything. Just go in and tell her we're finishing our soup, Frazer.'

Frazer came quietly up to Sylvia as she was clipping off the thread at the completion of her swan's wing. He stood behind her for a just perceptible pause before he spoke.

'Mrs. Fox and Miss Grania, Miss, have just this moment gone into the dining-room. Excuse me, Miss Sylvia, but I fancy a little joke is intended—the idea being that they have finished their soup, Miss.'

'Thank you, Frazer.' Sylvia rose neatly and briskly. As she walked through the room she paused to alter, to its distinct improvement, the position of a bowl of roses. She crumpled up the wrapping torn off a newspaper and threw it in a waste basket as she passed by a writing table. Frazer followed her into the dining-room, knowing that she would get the better of her mother and Grania without giving him away over the soup joke.

'So sorry,' Sylvia said as she came into the dining-room and went across to her chair. 'Very stupid of me.' Frazer pulled back her chair and she sat down. 'Where have you got to? Soup over? Please go straight on, Frazer. I don't want any soup, thank you.'

Frazer looked towards Mrs. Fox with tolerant compassion and mild inquiry as to whether the joke was to proceed. An access of dignity suddenly succeeded her childish nonsense.

316

'I'll have some more soup, please, Frazer.' She turned to Grania, 'Have a little more, dear, too, just to keep me company.'

Sylvia was always driving them into such undignified corners.

Dinner proceeded as described by Nan to Aunt Pigeon. Grania and her mother ate with pleasure, commenting on the new peas, the crispness of the lettuce hearts, the goodness of the salmon. Sylvia ate very little and very neatly but her enjoyment was higher and stricter than theirs, although she said nothing about the food and its cooking. Actually she had visited the peas daily for the last fortnight, and compelled the gardener to pick them before they reached maturity. She had obtained, after an endless correspondence, the seed of this lettuce from France, and had ordained the butchery of the black-faced lamb. She spared herself comment on any of these subjects.

For what was Sylvia saving up? That was the question. Towards what end was that store of secret energy directed. When would the expense of spirit begin? And if she found no object, either man or thing, on which to expend herself, what then? And where would it drive her?

Of course Sylvia had her admirers among the young soldiers who were quartered in the garrison town. Why not. She rode well, played tennis well, and though she had not Grania's blonde, untidy beauty, she had a birdlike tidy prettiness which was very attractive. Also with a competent restraint she seldom made intelligent remark except now and then on the subject of horses. But that was allowed, it was admirable. But beyond this Sylvia had her love—her love was still untold. Schooled and strict and clear as an unpicked lemon among its leaves, her love was there for her to take some day.

No one knew yet but he and she, and they, in knowing themselves exactly matched, kept silence still with one another, because of the life and strength of their secret. They would play the exquisite game out, meeting and parting without a word of

317

love spoken; keeping each a cool length of distance from the other, crossing the distance with a glance, contradicting the glance with a word, a pause, a carefree sentence to show how far was the mind from this deeper look given. They had their own language, their own subjects in common; their fishing, their horses, their dogs. And each collected glass and knew enough of the subject to venture to back his knowledge by buying. Glass and horses are curious bonds, but through such things they spoke to one another. There was no reason why they should not have been enagaged and married six months ago, but they had not, and in this kept distance and brittle restraint had grown the fonder. His name was Michael Purvis, and he came from Norfolk. He would leave the army when his father died. He would be rich and a good match for Miss Fox of Aragon. Sylvia only waited for her hour.

'Who is coming to play tennis to-morrow?' Sylvia asked her mother, and listened attentively to her reply, sorting, planning, piecing out her own intentions in regard to the party, should he be there.

'Colonel and Mrs. Ingram.'

'Bridge for you.'

'Well dear, yes, but do you mind?'

Grania said, 'Darling, you won't take Tony Craye to make a fourth, now angel, promise.'

Sylvia said, 'Of course she will—anyhow he's not a very exciting tennis player.'

'He's just my form.'

'Oh, you can manage a rabbity game without him.' Sylvia said gently.

'Grania's tennis is never going to improve, poor pet, if she's always put with the duds.'

'I don't want to improve.'

'She likes flopping about and screaming.'

'I don't scream. You shut up.'

318

'Oh, all right. We'll give her Tony, Mummy.'

'Yes, darling, of course I will. I'll try out that new Major Radley for bridge.'

'He looked a dreary old heap. Michael Purvis likes bridge.'

'Oh, I don't know if he's coming. I said, just any of the Boys——'

They came in dozens every Sunday afternoon to Aragon, the soldiers from the barracks. They were institutions, those tennis parties that ended in supper, and cars that wouldn't start pushed down the avenue late into the night. They had been going on as long as any one could remember. All the Aunts, except Aunt Pigeon (and there had been six Miss Foxs in the previous generation) had married into smart cavalry regiments on the strength of these parties. Cider cup and moonlight on the river succeeding long long games of tennis, played out in sweeping strokes from the base line, and underhand serves from the elegant spoon-like racquets.

But enough of easy jeering at the first tennis players. They got their men, and they kept these men either with skill, or tenacity, or because of a curious ignorant charm which they had, a reserve, a dignity, a power to ignore . . .

They still came to Aragon, the successors of these officers, although in 1920 the roads in the South of Ireland were hardly the most sensible places for Ireland's enemies on Sunday or any other afternoons.

Dinner at Aragon came to its decorous end. Coffee with sugar candy and cream was handed in the drawing-room, and then Grania and Sylvia and Viola sat reading and sewing by the green-shaded gas light. The windows were still open, and the full evening tide swelled the river to greater, fuller widths below.

Grania put down her paper soon, and went across to the window. She knelt on a stool leaning out, her fat white arms cold and dented on the window ledge. She kept very still, holding in

319

her mind the troubled and secret delight that belonged to her. She was frightened by the thought of all that was happening to her, and the inexorable calm flowing of the river gave her a false sense of strength and peace. Of all people, she longed to discuss the matter most with Nan, Nan who was so strong, so wise, so gay in her councils, but of all people alive she could less let Nan know than any other. Foley was afraid of her too, exceedingly afraid of her sensible anger.

But Foley did not know this little fearfulness that was not sure at all which was now on Grania's mind. She had not told him. She could not say anything yet. She must wait another week at least before she told him what she feared. Or did she fear? There was a warmth and an importance about her suspicion. Like all women when they think themselves with child Grania saw all things in focus only to this tremendous happening. The idea would grow to a certainty of importance when she was alone. Sometimes it frightened her. But her love was so ignorant, her trust so complete, that she only put off the time for telling Foley because she promised herself a divine hour of love and comfort with him when she could say this beyond doubt. It was all so easy to her. The simplest way in which to say, Now Foley we can be married. Her dream ended and began in marriage. Of course they would be married. They would go to Dublin together and come back and say, Now we're married. Well, what could be simpler?

Grania was absolutely confident in Foley's love for her. She did not for a moment doubt that she filled the thoughts of his days and nights with the same agonizing strength and sweetness that was in her thoughts of him. She was a wild-blooded but a single-hearted child. There was nothing light or easy about this loving of hers. The idea that there could be a successor to Foley in her life never trembled on the edge of her mind. He only was her love, and if they parted she would die. She was as sure of this as of anything, as sure indeed as she was of his love.

320

And now she was tired. She turned from the window and rubbed the chill of the river air in her cold fat arms and thought of her bed where she would sleep away this exquisite mindless exhaustion, and of the morning when she was to meet him early and ride out with him. . . . Already her plans were laid for it, her lies were told. And now, good-night. Good-night to these poor cold creatures outside the ring of her thoughts. Good-night to that spry and secret Sylvia, who had no secret like Grania's to keep to herself. Say good-night to the silly sweetie your mother, and how she would cry and go on, beg, persuade and forbid if she knew the truth, and then hurry away to confide the whole thing in Nan. Nan again, Nan all the time. She was the beginning and the end of Aragon.

Except to Sylvia, and Sylvia had always kept her own secrets, and Nan as well as everyone else respected her for it. Sylvia had put away her embroidery now, and she and her mother were playing a game of Bezique, snapping the little score boards up and down, dealing out the cards with quick precision. Sylvia didn't much like playing Bezique but she was as concentrated on this occupation as any other.

'I'm going to bed,' Grania said after her wordless rehearsed good-nights, and came over from the window to kiss her mother good-night.

'You're looking pale, darling. Are you tired? Try to remind me to write off for some more of that expensive tonic. Now what was its name? I can't remember names—Bezique, I think, dear, that's another 100. Good-night, Lammy. The child *is* looking pale. . . .'

'Bezique,' said Sylvia.

Grania went up to bed.

V

Much later Mrs. Fox sat in front of her dressing-table while Nan brushed her feathery grey hair. She put her hands up to her mouth yawning luxuriously. Then she slipped off her rings and settle down to a good gossip with Nan.

It was never admitted to be a gossip, of course. It was a sort of grave council on the affairs of Aragon, and only as though by accident shaded off into the provocative, 'Well, I know I shouldn't say,' prelude to luscious detail and unbrindled confidence.

Mrs. Fox loved the feeling of the brush in her hair with Nan's strength behind it, she could lie back relaxed, in no great hurry to speak, when she did speak her words came in a calm easy flow, without trouble, without trying.

'Do you think, Nan, Miss Grania should take that tonic again —what was its name?'

'Syrup of Phosphates.'

'*Of course*, does she look a little pale? Of course it's the weather too. My primulas, they were limp to-night, quite limp. If I hadn't slipped out to water them before dinner, well, I ask myself—Now that reminds me, what's the good of telling Kane anything? Only this afternoon I said to him he was to be *sure* to water my primulas.'

'You know what ails him, or perhaps I shouldn't say it, *Nellie McVeagh*.'

'That ugly little thing. Are you sure, Nan?'

'And her mind's not on her work for one five minutes either. "Nellie," I said to her to-day, or was it yesterday, maybe it was Tuesday, "Nellie," I said, "Your mind's not on your work, and where is it, Nellie?" I said. Well, she went the colour of a peony, so I said no more.'

Mrs. Fox settled the faintly grubby little cape of lace and bows that she wore for these hair brushings, and pursed her mouth at her reflection.

'Keep your eye on her, Nan. I don't like to even *think* it, but those McVeaghs . . .'

Nan said, with resignation, but with a condemnation in her voice that was a little frightening:

'Ah, those McVeaghs—they were bred to be hot.'

Mrs. Fox nodded regretful agreement. That condemnation of the joy of sex, that forgetting of their own past joys, and heats, fears and failures, left a curious blank streak of cruelty equally in her and Nan. Love and the mating of bodies, was really vile to their minds, they could not avoid this mental attitude. It was as much a part of them as their own noses.

Of course when everything was circumspect, restrained and satisfactory, love was quite another thing, spoken of in another language. Its relation to any natural heats and lusts transcended, forgotten in the glorious mists and romanticism of veils and tears and orange blossoms, and the happy solidity of marriage portions, and a nice sense of permanence. But that attitude of mind, though real enough, was not so straight from their souls and stomachs as the first revulsion from the obscenity of sex. In the second there was a loathed thing to forget. In the first there was nothing but the loathed thing to remember. But it was nice to play with the idea, in the proper spirit of disgust, of course.

'Do you think . . .?'

Mrs. Fox said, now raising her eyebrows in a horrid query:

323

'Well, last Thursday evening when I was passing down by the grove to post a letter, what did I see by the giant rhododendrons but two bicycles, and one, if you'll pardon the expression, was a man's bicycle. Yes, indeed.'

It sounded most unutterably dirty. What was not said about the embraces enacted in the shelter of the giant rhododendrons was implied by nods and ghastly pauses. A stretching of a silence, a withdrawal, a faintly renewed implication.

'Oh, dear.' Mrs. Fox sighed, a sigh of luscious disapproval. 'And was to-day her afternoon? My goodness, Nan, of course, it's Thursday again to-day.'

'Aha, no wonder those primulas went dry.'

They stared at each other for a moment in the glass. Nan's lips grew tight. She picked up a ribbon, and put it round Mrs. Fox's pretty feathers of grey hair. Knotted the bow with cruel decision.

'I'll keep my eyes open,' was all she said.

Mrs. Fox went back to the subject of Grania without bothering where her thought led from.

'Pale. She does look pale. Nan, what did you say the tonic was called?'

'Syrup of Phosphates. I'll order it. But she's well, ma'am. She was always that kind of colour. She's healthy.'

'Girls are difficult, Nan—one never knows.'

'Ah, you and I would remark it, dear. . . .'

'She asked me to leave Mr. Craye out of the bridge to-morrow.'

'She'd never have asked that if it meant anything.'

'Oh, dear, I suppose not indeed. He's such a nice boy, Nan, and I was presented at the same court as his mother.'

'Perhaps it's not my place to say it . . ?'

'No . . . What, Nan?'

I've been thinking lately that Miss Sylvia and Captain Purvis . . .'

'Now, that would be nice, what makes you think so, Nan?'

'Well, now, it's very few Miss Sylvia'd ask advice from on the subject of a horse, unless it's my Foley. Still, she and Captain Purvis were about a half-hour up in her show horses's box last Sunday. Why I know is I was up to the garden for a couple of heads of lettuce Kane forgot to leave in, and there they were and I going up. So I stopped up to gather green gooseberries for the Fool, and when I was coming down, yes, indeed, imagine, there they were still in it.'

'Well, Nan!'

'Well, indeed. "Well" is right.'

'We'll watch it, but tact of course.'

'Oh, tact, ma'am, tact is the thing indeed.'

'And how do you think, Miss Pigeon, has been the last few days, Nan?'

'Tch, Tch, Tch. Oh, I've had some terrible times with her. You'll excuse me, pardon, ma'am, but would she sleep in her bed last night? No. She said she'd get leprosy sleeping in a bed, and it was out on the stairs in her nightgown, with an eiderdown and a pillow, imagine! Well (not that it would signify one bit), but I lost the best part of my night's sleep before I got her back to her room.'

'Poor Nan, what a time she does give you.'

'Oh, I wouldn't grudge the time, or the trouble, but the way she'd take against me over every little thing is cruel.'

'And you are so sweet to her. Nan, I wonder if you could, tactfully, keep her away from the tennis party to-morrow. You know, sometimes she can be so embarrassing.'

'Oh, I'll think up some excuse. I'll tell her there's a black man coming. She has a horror of those blacks. If you tell her you heard there was a black man seen about the woods she won't put a foot out of the house for a week.'

'Well, tell her anything you like. But, of course, don't frighten her, Nan.'

'Is it me to frighten her and she the only baby I have left? Ready

325

for bed now? Don't forget to drink your milk, and there's a new kind of biscuit in your box. Try one. Don't let the crumbs in your sheets. Is your bottle nice and hot? Well, good-night, now ma'am.'

'Good-night Nan, bless you.'

VI

Nan turned out the gas, and shut the door with comfortable assurance. Out in the dark passage above the well of the staircase she stood alone with her candle in her hand. She was less alone now than at any time. For here she was close as flesh can be to spirit with all the dead Fox's of Aragon; as close and comfortable with them as she was with the living Fox's, as unsurprised by her own strange consciousness of their crowding presences as she was unsurprised by her strong powers with the living. Nan was the only person who knew the ghosts at Aragon familiarly. It was like nothing to her to go into a room and know the movement, the fullness, the stirring of air that told of its occupation. Now, as she went down the shallow steps of the stairs, candlestick held carefully in one hand, she reached down her other hand to a certain height for she felt that one she called 'the Child' was with her, and it was late and dark for the creature to be about. She did not pay much attention, for she was searching by the light of her candle for the cobwebs invisible by day. Three she counted, and pursed her lips thinking of what she could say to Nellie McVeagh in the morning. That such a slut should let cobwebs and dust gather on the pictures of dead Fox's was abhorrent to Nan. She went on down to the servants' hall, where she made herself a nice little bit of supper. The other servants had gone to bed so she got the end of the gooseberry tart and some thick cream. A nice little piece of lamb first and then a cup of tea, strong Indian tea with rich cream in it.

Upstairs Aunt Pidgie, waiting for Nan to come up, lay on her face in bed, a shawl was knotted tightly round her stomach, and a pillow doubled and put between her body and her mattress; she found this a good way to appease the hunger that so often overcame her at night, so that she was sometimes sorely tempted to eat up the morsels she had saved from supper for her Diblins. To-night she thought longingly of the backbone of a herring and a small quantity of cold boiled rice stored away in her sporran for their breakfast in the morning. There had been three blackbirds' eggs in her sporran this evening too, but these she had eaten herself with the bathroom door locked on such a shocking exhibition of greed.

VII

Foley O'Neill's house was up near the mountains. Near, but not very near. There was a little valley with a stream at the bottom and a wild hill covered in bracken and gorse and crowned wildly in dark fir trees between his house and farm, and the real mountains. Once there had been a rocky little laneway deep between loose stone walls leading from the main road up to the O'Neills' house. But Foley and Nan had civilised the approach. There were solid bright white gates now, with a latch that could be opened easily from a horse's back, and inside the dark walls that sank to the depths of the lane were white timber rails, rather like a racecourse, this partly for the safety of a couple of brood mares and their foals, and partly because Nan admired the smart look they gave the place.

The house was on the left of the laneway. It had been a steep grey farm-house of infinite squalor, standing undivided from its wet steep yard where fowl scratched morosely at the steaming manure heaps, and housed calves bayed for food, and chopped furze was laid thickly in the slush so that you walked dry-footed round the house on dark winter days.

Things were different now. Two gay, villa like bow windows were built on to the south face of the house. A square of garden was divided off from the yard by a whitewashed wall. Two neat grass plots, parted cleanly by a gravelled path, squared each side of the hall door. Two beds of begonias were there carefully minded because they looked so well. But hydrangeas flowered untended and bluer than any summer mountain because they have a tiresome preference for such situations.

When you opened the hall door you looked straight down a narrow passage to the kitchen. If both the inner and outer kitchen doors happened to be open at the same time you looked right across into the mountains. The intervening land and the yard at the back were cut out by the height on which the house stood. It was as if there was a house and mountains in grand isolation. The two things that counted. The mountains for wildness and cold hours. The house for shelter.

Foxes' masks, ruffed by faded brushes, were hung on the walls of the passage-way. A couple of hunting prints, divorced from their series, took the place of the holy pictures that might have been there. The parlour door was on the right, the dining-room door on the left. The parlour was papered in brownish cream with a gay dado of cornflowers. There were panes of blue and red glass in the sides of its bow window. Dampish chintz clung to the intricate outlines of the elaborate suite of furniture spaced accurately round the room. Paraffin oil lamps with globes moulded and frosted in red and white glass stood high among forests of photographs of Nan's aristocratic patients and nurslings. Foxes of all ages were well represented, from Mrs. Fox in her court dress bouqueted and feathered, to Grania, photographed in her vest by Speight. But there were plenty of other treasures, including a couple of coroneted ladies, with fondest Love to Dearest Nan; scattered through the collection were pictures of Foley's progressive moments of triumph in the horse-world. From the time a smart little boy sat his show jumping pony with stylish ease, to the time when a rigidly nonchalant young man was taken on a Dublin show champion —that most dreadful and triumphant of all horse pictures—

330

Nan had kept and framed them all. Her pride in Foley's horse-manship and all it meant was as strong in her as a well grounded hate is strong.

Across the other side of the passage was the dining-room. It was bow-windowed to correspond exactly with the parlour. There, one picture of the Pope, and a few common family photographs, were allowed on the walls, wedding groups, the brides all wearing navy gabardine and roses in their hats and the grooms with collars swallowing their ears and one large posses-sive hand laid on the bride's shoulder as they stood to attention behind her chair. The walls were papered in red. Both lace and red velvet curtains shrouded the windows into the proper gloom for dining. The silver cups Foley's horses had won in shows decorated the sideboard. In a couple of the slenderest shape, bouquets of imitation carnations had been arranged.

VIII

Donatia, Foley's cousin, was sixteen. She would have been at her convent school, but her prayers to the saints, her horrid influence on her fellow pupils, and her disregard of the Sisters' and Reverend Mother's holy influences or spiteful punishment, had set her free from the fifth of these sacred prisons, and here she was in April back with her mother and Foley at Mountain Brig. That was the name of this house now, although in its less smart days it had been called Clonamore. But Nan thought Mountain Brig sounded much more civilised, as indeed it did.

Donatia was a small strong black little gipsy. She was deeply religious, a terrible liar, and a tireless worker, a tireless worker for Foley because she loved him with the worship of childhood turning into the sad passion of the adolescent.

Sixteen and possessed of herself in a curiously simple way. You could see it in the air and swing with which she wore her clothes, in the confidence of her walk. She had been the spoilt child of older men, men who belonged to the world of horse-dealing, or to the racing world, whose business it was to know people and horses. Such men have a sophistication of outlook so complete that they can turn their own simplicity to account, and hardly know they do so. They have a confidence, and a right confidence, in the importance of their trade, which is not acquired from any association with a sophisticated aristocracy of

customers, but grows from within. It is acquired through hardship and gambles that go wrong, and successes sometimes, and a
life where perception is keyed to an abnormal pitch and quickness is all. That quickness of eye and ear and sharpness of mind
had been alive in Donatia since the age of ten when Foley had
first taken her about looking at horses, or to a summer race-
meeting, or a point-to-point, perhaps, if he was not riding, or in
later years if he was. She would ride out on her pony with him in
the mornings when the early silence hung hollow as a bell over
cold fields, and she knew enough at ten years old to keep her
mouth shut, and to keep herself and her pony out of his way at
these times. If she made a mistake she was cursed with cold
emphasis, and she would a great deal sooner have been beaten.

When she was thirteen she was a well-known person to
Foley's friends and customers. As sharp as a needle and as bright
as paint, she never stuck herself into a conversation unless
invited. She called all his older friends 'Uncle,' 'Uncle Charley,'
'Uncle Jack,' When she was litle they would send her ponies to
school before they were sold to the parents of rich little boys and
girls. She did not really civilise them completely, but they could
be sold as hunted by a child. Now she seldom rode a horse except
one of Foley's. She was his stable slave and gloried in her
usefulness to him. She was a marvel to catch the boys out if they
idled. There was no horse he put her on that she would not ride,
in the pathetic confidence that if Foley said she could ride the
horse, to do so was well within her powers.

But now, now at sixteen, the proudest age of all, a very
terrible and darkly secret thing was happening to Donatia. It
was eating the heart out of her, though so far no one knew. She
was growing frightened of horses. All the strong bright unruly
horses she had ridden were only like ghosts to her. No strength
came from the knowledge that she had ruled their strength.

In Donatia's room there was a little plaster stoup of holy

333

water, a dusty sprig of palm stuck behind it since last Palm Sunday, and on the little table below was a very imposing statue of the Blessed Virgin. So blue, so white her robes as clouds and summer skies; so unreal those folded plaster hands, they would have made a fable of any story. And it was to her Donatia prayed unceasingly for strength against her sinful cowardice. From her praying she would turn to that picture of Foley (the same one that his mother had in her bedroom, the picture of Foley on Teltaletit. Superb in confidence and strength and ease). It seemed to her as if she caught her heart in her teeth as she told herself that he must never know. At sixteen you do not own that you love your gods—you are contented to worship them.

IX

Six o'clock on an April morning and the birds shouting in ecstasy when Donatia woke in her hard familiar little bed. She lay quietly, accepting a consciousness of fear, new every morning after the night, measured out to her in small realities; the cold sound of stirrup-irons touching in the half-dark morning air came from below; horses moving in their boxes and the muffled voices of the boys still heavy and sullen with sleep, as they began another day's work.

There was an ugly taste in Donatia's mouth as she got out of her bed, she must get up now if she wanted to get a cup of tea for Foley and herself before they rode out. She shivered as she sat on the edge of her bed, her feet feeling for the slippers underneath it. Donatia was as small as a girl of twelve, but she was as tough and muscular as any gipsy boy. Her strong black hair was twisted into a little bun on the top of her head in an unaffectedly female and untidy curve, small straight pieces escaping pathetically to fall on the collar of her striped pyjamas, a present from Foley when she had won a jumping competition. They were too long by far for the strong small body they covered. Cuffs were turned back and trousers roped in folds round her waist. Her face had the inscrutability of a head carved on a very small walking stick; precise features set carefully, a sphinx-like straightness of line. If there had been some abandon, some break, some wildness, some mistake, there might have been some fascination too, but everything was closed in and shut down in the terrible reserve of youth.

She took off her pyjamas and stood, a dark naked little image in the cold early air, the holy medal she wore on a chain round her neck gleamed in its pale circle above her bare breasts, and swung out on the length of its chain as she stooped for her clothes.

'Mother, have you our tea for us?' She was dressed and down in the kitchen where a lamp still burned in the daylight, and Mrs. Bohane, a great overgrown gipsy, bent across the table reading the advertisements on the back of a week-old paper. Her black hair was still in curling pins, and her white skin greasy from sleeping. She had put on a tweed skirt and jumper over her nightdress, and there were no stockings on her beautiful legs. She was a gorgeously shameless slattern, an ageing beauty whose riotous blood perforce subdued its excitement to shoppings and gossipings and local births (the more difficult the better), deaths (preferably by cancer) and love affairs which she investigated with a bitter condemnatory enthralment.

'Have I your tea, love? Of course. There you are now, take the blue cup up to Foley. Look, wasn't it the luck of God I took a glance at this paper, I had it in the fire itself when I caught a sight of this hat . . .' her voice followed Donatia out of the kitchen door and paused comfortably poised in narrative until her return. . . .

He was in his shirt sleeves and shaving—why shaving?—when she came in, pulling his face into terrible angles and preoccupied with more than morning silence. She put the cup down beside him. A blue shirt and his new jodhpurs—why not his red jersey and old breeches? He gave her a smile, half a 'thank you, child,' and as she was going out he said, 'Would you like a surprise?'

'I would, Foley.'

'Well, you can ride out the Knight of Aragon horse this morning.'

Her hands shut into fists and her eyes for a second closed too —Mother of God be near me.

'Would you be able for him?' the voice went on teasing and affectionate. He had no doubt as to her ability, the hardy little thief.

'I'll tell them to change my saddle, they have it on the pony.'

She nearly whispered, her voice was so dry—the Knight of Aragon horse, oh, dear Mother of God, didn't he fire Mickey Brown in two small shots of bucks only yesterday? Why not the pony? Ah, why not the pony?

'Then tell Mickey to lead the pony on—there's a lady wants to ride him at school, we'll go down through Tin-a-curry bog,'

A lady? At this hour of the morning? It was no hour of the morning for ladies—or for questions, Donatia knew. No doubt one of those dream-like creatures, pearls, tweeds, glamour and shooting sticks, who stood rounds of drink at race-meetings and leaned and whispered to Foley after they had 'had a couple' (how well Donatia knew the signs of slight intoxication in the aristocracy), and drove away in rich pale-coloured motor cars, back into their own soft lives, had taken a crazy fancy for riding out when she could be in her bed—well she'd get her fill of it schooling over the Tin-a-curry fences—Oh, Jesu, had she forgotten? Even for a moment had she forgotten?

'And will you ride the Aragon into the Bog double for me.'

It was her thought spoken for her but turned into such a sweet intention of flattery that she was warmed and powerless to speak of fear.

'I will, of course.'

'You will? Great little girl. Run on now and hurry the boys.'

He picked up his watch and frowned as he buckled the strap, his mind for a moment occupied with a thought of Donatia, his little Donatia. I wonder is she able for him? Ah, she is, I think, she is. Anyway I couldn't give Grania anything but the pony. He was knotting his tie, very tight and neat and pinning the end with a worn gold safety pin, smooth and sharp from all its years of use. He would sooner lose £3 than lose that pin, though he could scarcely remember now how he got it. He would wear his second good coat, it would look too remarkable if he wore his good coat as well as his new jodhpurs. He reached it down from its hanger in the cupboard, and put it on with that strained carefulness that the least vain men show when it comes to their coats, and Foley was vain enough in a simple way. He liked a good coat, but if it was *his* coat (or horse, or dog, or woman), it became good any way. He was very faithful and undoubting in possession and careful about things too, this morning he had said his prayers before he dressed so that he would not have to kneel down in his good jodhpurs. He drank his tea now and went downstairs, his mind on what was immediately to do, not so far on as meeting Grania again.

In the kitchen Aunt Gipsy was still reading the advertisements on the table, and her voice rose again from where it had ceased for the second time that morning when Donatia went out to the yard.

'And do you know, Foley, I always find it very hard to buy a hat. Why it is I don't know, but the styles now aren't what they were, and when you do chance to see a thing that would suit you, you should nip to it quickly, wouldn't you say that yourself?'

'I would, Aunt Gipsy.'

'Maybe I could get a drive into town then on Tuesday, maybe. There's a nice sale on at Aherns.'

'You could, Aunt Gip, if any one was going.'

That was the way to take Aunt Gipsy, easy, and leave yourself a way of escape, don't let her pin you down.

'I might bring Miss Grania back to breakfast with us. She's trying out the pony.'

'Oh, Holy Hour! I'll have to hurry myself, child.'

She would too, he knew Aunt Gipsy. Everything would be nice and a credit to him when they came back. There would be fresh eggs, and fresh bread, and sweet salty butter, and good strong tea in the flowered china pot Aunt Gipsy had bought at an auction, taking a passionate leave of her senses and bidding against a Dublin dealer. Yes, everything in Foley's house was all right. He was pleased with it.

He crossed the yard slowly, not at that almost trotting little walk that men whose lives have been spent with horses mostly adopt. Everyone was very grave in the morning before riding out, everyone in the grip of himself, and horses unfriendly and set in their minds away from any kindness between horses and men. They stood darkly and crookedly in their boxes. No boy whistled yet or spoke cheerfully—the reality of to-day was present and unpitying.

Donatia was leaning where the sun struck a patch on the wall of the Knight of Aragon horse's box (leaning on her lion's cage). She was yawning, as she felt very very sick, and the collar of her dark coat was turned up against the green thin line of her jaw. Her mind and her body seemed to stand apart coldly afraid for each other.

'Doatie, ride your pony down to the bog, and let Micky get up on that laddo first.'

Mickey said, 'I have Miss Doatie's saddle on him, sir.'

A wave of fury towards Micky swept through her, Micky who didn't care what horse he rode or how often he got fired, to crucify her like this. She was stretched in pain while Foley paused, before he said, carelessly.

'Ah, swop your leathers.'

He did not know why he had suddenly changed his mind

about Donatia's ability for the horse. It wasn't that exactly. She was well able to ride him, but that hardy little thief, Micky, might as well soften him for her first. The child looked sick this morning, any way.

Reprieved, Donatia felt the full heat of the sun again, felt life in her hands again, and the loosening of a cruel knot within her. A tide of gratitude flowed through her. She caught her breath to steady herself. If she had acted with freedom then she would have reached out to touch Foley's coat; to kiss its stuff in love and gratefulness. But she stood quietly against the wall, and he never guessed she was so much afraid, and he knew nothing at all of that flame of adoring gratitude that rose in her beside him.

Because of her relief she mounted the pony with forgotten confidence, she did not remember how she had lain awake the night before thinking and seeing with taut hands how dangerous the pony could be.

Micky ran into the saddle room to look for his stick, and the big horse was led out and round the yard—to Donatia he looked infinite in strength and evil. Cold as a snake's eye his was. The early sun shuddered across his bright and beautiful body. Donatia knew he was filled as full of bad intentions as a horse could be. She had seen one of the boys cross himself in the dark of the stable before mounting him. This was not Micky, who came out swinging and fastening his coat, his own little stick in his hand, stepping lightly towards the horse and speaking easily, gathering up his reins, and holding up a leg to Foley.

'Right?'

'Right, sir.'

Up through the air with the greatest of ease, in the saddle away by yourself from the help of man, and to think it might have been herself up there on the cold bad horse's back; but she was saved, saved for a time. They had four miles to go before they got to the bogs, and Micky would have the worst edge worn off him by then.

340

Foley was mounting now, like a gentleman from the ground, one foot in his stirrup, for this horse was going to England. Donatia turned her pony's head, and rode warily down the deep lane. She could hear Micky's voice growling a threat to his horse, and knew without looking behind how the horse's back was in an iron bow under the saddle, and his neck straining to drive his head away and down beyond control. Her pony stopped to shy at nothing inside the field, and Micky's voice came urgently from behind her.

'Keep going, Miss Doatie.'

She caught hold of the pony and sent her on again.

Out on the wider road Foley rode up beside her.

'I thought Micky was gone when the pony stopped in the lane—the horse was gathered up under him ready to pelt him.'

'Imagine, was he?' Donatia answered politely while her heart turned in sympathy for Micky. And Foley was laughing. He always laughed when people were in danger from horses. He was so seldom in danger himself. With strength and confidence and the little ways he had, he would fool horses into doing his will. He had lovely ways with horses. Even when they hated him they appeared kind and easy when he rode them.

'Oh, look, look! Poor Micky. Stay there, Mick, you're all right boy!'

A goat in the hedge raising her drab ivory face, struggling with spancled legs, was enough to set the big horse swerving and bucketing across the road.

'Ah, Micky, I thought he had you that time.'

And Micky, smiling and patting the lion's arched neck, saying:

'The beggar's only watching his chance, sir.'

The sun shone out more kindly as they rode along. The little unawakened houses looked like toy farms unpacked out of a box, as definite and unliving in the earliness. The blackthorn

341

blossom was laid along the banks thick and quiet as wreaths on a grave. Willow trees flowered and dropped their yellow dust sadly on the low shine of water beneath them. A grass road as old as anything in Ireland took them past the arches and broken towers of a castle. It was flung up high against the sky, and the hills. Sky and hills were framed like light cold water-colours in its windows and doorways. Rooks flew across and through the airy roofless heights of walls and towers. Brave, bold and elegant the horses strode by under the castle walls.

Foley looked up at a certain window as he passed, but he saw no sign or message there for him to-day. In these troubled times he was so far involved with Ireland's Republican Army that he knew where to look for such signs.

Beyond food, shelter and silence for any flying column that might call for these things at his house, he held to a thorny neutrality in this war between the English, from whom he made his money, and the Irish who sought to drive the English out of Ireland. He betrayed neither one side nor the other, but maintained a tricky balance between the two. To-night, two tired boys on the run might have the food and the shelter of his house. Tomorrow afternoon, two smart hardy young British officers would be schooling horses with him, and standing him a drink after the school was ridden. That was the situation. He might as well accommodate the boys pleasantly as be bullied and beaten up, perhaps shot for refusing them a refuge when they needed one. And most certainly he was not going to abandon his trade with the soldiers before he could help it.

Much of Nan's passion and skill for the intrigues and situations of life was in Foley too, he loved a good reason for diplomacy, it was like a game of cards to him. But just lately, from whispers he had heard, only whispers, he was getting a little watchful and nervy. He was glad to see no sign or signal at the castle for him to-day. They went on by a track a little paler

than the sallow fields. They rode through a line of gaps in walls
built thinly of the castle stones. Foley and Donatia talked a little.
He said:

'Aunt Gipsy's wild to buy a hat. She saw a very nice hat in the
paper this morning.'

'We have to take her in to get Confession some day soon. She
could try the hat then.'

'And we could go to the pictures.'

'Will she ever get her hat, and the pictures, and Confession
all on the one day?'

'We'll go to the pictures while she'll be at the hat.'

'Oh, she'd die if she didn't see this fellow that is on this
week, what's this his name is?'

'I wouldn't know.'

'I wouldn't either, but she's stone mad about him.'

'If that's the way it is we'll never get out of town. Will we
give these horses a canter? It's what they want.'

A wild field sloped up and away from them. Here many a
contest had been won or lost under cold grey skies with wind
and rain driving, and on bright hot mornings with flowers in
the drenching grass and the grey and gold of honeysuckle along
the banks and groups of foxglove spires all furred in dew. And
mornings like to-day where nothing was yet but promise and
those black and white grave-wreaths of thorn to show that
promises ended in death, and primroses in all the sheltered places
growing on for ever in soft placid contradiction.

'Right, Micky?'

'Right, Sir!'

The big horse moved crookedly, his head to the east, his tail
to the west, fighting his bit, waiting his chance, his eye cold
and his neck black with sweat. A bird in the hedge gave him
his chance. One—two—three—with the grace and quickness of a
panther and the strength of a bull he fired the bucks out of his

343

wicked body, and at the third Micky was gone, shot out of the saddle to land uncannily on his feet with the reins in his hand.

'Hold on to him now, Micky,' Foley said quietly as he dismounted and gave his horse to Donatia, Donatia trembling and pricking with a sweat of sympathy—her own pony unruly in the fracas. And Micky, poor lion tamer of the circus, brave, stupid slave, standing again as he had stood in the yard, patting the untamed strength of that neck, ready to be thrown up again, even to death.

'Are you right, Mick?'

'Right, Sir.'

He was up again and the horse trembled in the light air as Foley led him on half-threatening, half-cajoling, round and round in a circle.

'I'll take him around the field now, sir. I'll soberize the beggar.'

Micky edged away from the other two horses and set going up the long slope of the field.

'That's a great boy,' Foley said to Donatia, watching them over the rise of the hill.

'He is.' A great pang of envy rose in Donatia's heart to take the place of the awful pity she had felt for Micky.

Foley lit a cigarette, his eyes watching all the time to see Micky reappear, before he took his horse from her.

'Would you be very cross with me if I asked you something,' he said.

'I would I suppose.' She was so used to the unmeaning caress in his voice. She had known it since she was eight years old, as long as she had loved him.

'Ah, you'd be mad with me, I think.'

'Go on. What is it?'

'I think I'll leave Micky school that fellow to-day. I wouldn't mind him being green, but the beggar's too rough for you.'

'Ah, Foley.'

He mistook that cry of relief for disappointment.

'Well, we'll see,' he said.

'Whatever you say yourself, of course.'

'You wouldn't be real mad with me, Doatie?'

'No. I wouldn't care.'

'You can ride him to-morrow. We'll let Micky knock him round to-day.'

'Who's the lady you have for the pony?'

He hesitated.

'One of the Miss Fox's. I think it's Grania they said would try him.'

'I wonder Aunt Dymphnia didn't mention it. She was over yesterday.'

'They're getting big girls now—maybe they don't tell their Nanny everything.'

'Ah, go on, Aunt Dymphnia wouldn't wait to be told.'

Foley laughed, a faint acquiescence in his mother's ability to find out what she wanted to know. He picked up his reins and rode off across the field, riding away from Donatia and her questions. He wondered if he had laid up trouble for himself in this lie about Grania buying the pony. Doatie was so sharp and so close. You couldn't tell what was in her mind, and it was such an easy explanation of Grania's early morning appearance, he was a master of the easy word.

Out of the fields where Micky and a quieter horse waited at the gate, and down a steep lane through gorse and heather to a crossroads where the wind blew clean and naked across the sallow bog land.

Grania's hair was blown back like the grass behind her head. Hair and grass had the same strange shining life in their pallor as the wind caught and turned them in the light. She leant against a bank, her little black bitch sat on the bank and leant against her cheek. Grania looked so bold and uncaring leaning there, her

345

coat was full of mends and holes, her boots and breeches very clean and expensive. She gazed on Foley and spoke to him only, after a faint good-morning to Donatia and Micky.

'Oh,' she cried, 'I thought you were never coming. Poor Grania! Do you know she bicycled all the way here? Yes, really, honestly. Do you think the bicycle will be safe if we pop it inside the gate? Don't let me if it's going to be stolen?'

'It wouldn't be a big loss,' Foley was standing beside her, he had given his horse to Donatia to hold with not a glance. 'That's a dangerous yoke.' He was considering the bicycle. 'Look! not a brake on it, and the back wheel nearly off.'

'It was all I could find and I thought I'd be late.' She had dropped heavy eyelids and her mouth trembled as he stood near her.

'You'll be safer on my pony.'

'Yes, Foley.'

X

'You'll be safer on my pony.' What was there in that absent insistent voice of Foley's that bred in Donatia such a gush of venom towards Grania—'My pony,' why not, 'Doatie's pony?' It was always called Doatie's pony? The ponies were all called that, always. Donatia was well used to his politely caressing ways with the ladies who came to buy horses, the ladies who fêted him on the race courses of Ireland, but these were strange ladies, often married ladies, with their bold, uncaring, gentry ways. This eagerness in his meeting with Grania was another thing. He had known Grania for years. Foley's mother was Grania's nurse. There was no need for her to live at Aragon and work for Fox money, but so she did. Donatia could always remember when she was Nannie in the nursery before she became friend and counsellor, and those afternoons when she was taken for a great treat to have tea with *Miss* Grania and *Miss* Sylvia. Her mother would bring her over, and both she and Aunt Dymphnia would watch her all the time to see that she did not disgrace herself or them by common word or rude vulgar act. Doatie was not very old before she knew that Aunt Dymphnia watched her mother in the same way dreading that she would betray herself in over-politeness to the other servants, that she would not keep a distance as befitted Nannie's sister-in-law, or that some slight grossness in feeding would be observed

347

and retold in the servants' hall. But she was always nice to her sister-in-law, if a little eager to speak for her in society to which she was unaccustomed, and to hint in invitations to nursery tea at Aragon what clothes she and Donatia should wear for the treat.

Later than nursery days Donatia's skill and bravery with her ponies and her success in children's classes at shows had put her in a position to which the two Misses Fox, inept but ambitious equestrians, looked with envy and respect. Donatia always saw the hunts they could not see, and caught the judge's eye on ponies infinitely inferior to their own. It was rather grand to be seen talking horse to Donatia in show grounds, and they were not ashamed to give her their ponies to civilise when they proved beyond their own powers. Then in school days they drifted away from any familiar contact with her, and now at seventeen Grania came out to meet Foley with such gay challenge as Donatia could not mistake.

Donatia could not name the jealousy that pierced her and shook her with an anger she had never known, an anger that purged her of fear and left her in a state of hot intention. She would show the fat, shameless thing the kind of girl you had to be to please Foley, the hardy useful kind that he approved. Soft blondes were but by the way, no matter how kindly he looked on them, or sweetly smiled.

It was while Foley mounted Grania on the pony with every care and watchful attention that Micky (and not sorry either) threw Donatia up on the big horse. She walked him off down the road, feeling her way with him, strong and confident in her new anger.

Foley was delighted when he saw what she had done. There was a kink in him which liked to see Donatia in danger, liked other people to see her surmount that danger, the skill and courage in her little body triumphant. Together with Donatia he resented Grania's spoilt softness, resented that she had never had to work for anything, remotely disliked the knowledge that his mother worked for hers. Though he did not know it Foley was on Donatia's side and against Grania this morning.

'You're a very bold girl,' he said to her and she laughed, recognising the indulgence in his voice. She rode first through the gate that Micky held open, the gate that led into the waste bog-lands where death might be her portion.

Donatia did not care. She was freed from her fear she had taken it wholly upon herself and now it was gone. Her horse plunged under her as Grania's little black bitch flew screaming across their path, her rabbit prey in view. Donatia caught up that wicked strength between her hands and her knees, and thrilled to know she ruled him.

'You could leave her at home another day,' Foley had said, surly. 'I hate dogs around young horses.'

'Another day . . . another day . . .' was this not the first and the only day? Donatia's heart turned with the gull that wheeled chalk white in the strong air: the wind across the bog blew on her coldly, but the wind never blows warm across a bog, and far off the mountains turned a chill indigo. A wave of evil intention came from her horse, so strong that it brought the edge of fear to life in her again. He knew it. He knew it. He was looking for his chance again. Anything might give it to him. Grania jostling along carelessly on the pony, her dog splashing its way after a bird through bright sparkling pools in the rushes, a bird alone, or the shadow of a cloud across the bare land. Why had she got up on him? What did anything matter except the far-off warmth of safety, the comfort of being on your own feet? Now she would have given everything she had twice over to be safe again and out of this cold purgatory of waiting for danger.

'All right, Doatie?' Foley asked as he had called to Micky earlier and:

'Right, Foley,' she answered as they jogged down the edge of a field and he reached for his bit and leaned heavy in her hands. Down in the corner was the first fence they jumped in this school. He remembered it and the remembrance excited him, but she was strong enough for him still; hold him, present him, and pop him up on the bank, and into the next field with style. Ah, she was warmer then, she could feel her confidence sub-duing the power set against her. Brave again for the next bank and the next, but now between each fence he would make a drive to be off. She knew she had only to weaken by a very little and he, not she, would be in charge, but still she was not tired, she could ride him.

Foley and Grania rode together, talking quietly, the pony hopping on and off the banks like a dog, and who had taught her to jump so well, and so neatly? Doatie, poor Doatie alone in her danger now, and no one in the world to care at what moment disaster would overtake her.

It was Grania's Soo that caused the trouble, Soo screaming in pursuit of a rabbit running under his tail as he fidgeted on the far side of a fence that Foley's horse refused behind him. The dog and the sound of Foley's stick together were too much. He gave one sickening plunge and flew down the field.

Now it had come, now danger was here, she had no fear, yet she could not stop him. She could not turn him. She must not tire herself yet, drop her hands, cod him, deceive him, talk to him. The field was wide, she could turn him round and back to the other horses, keep him going round the field, Ah, but she couldn't turn him. His neck was set like a neck of iron, and he gathered strength below her like a big ship, like an engine, and can you stop it? But she was not tired yet. Time to steady him still, and only a little wall with bushes laid on the top of it between them and the next field. No, but she could not stop or steady him. They galloped into it, hit all the bushes, sent loose

350

stones flying, and landed anyway in the farther field. A stirrup gone now, and the wind knocked out of her, she sobbed to him in panic anger. Could nothing give him a second's kindness? She caught her stirrup again as they galloped through a rough gap. Better, she had got her breath back; now he nearly slipped-up down the side of a little hill; two quiet asses grazing and a stream at the bottom—picture of another world. Recovery unbalanced, and on out of control through another gap, up a laneway, whirling up it, swerving and driving on.

Tired, oh tired, and he forever strength, wicked, bloody strength beyond her, beyond all compassing. Sick and silly and full of a terrible loathing, riding him worse each minute, she was finished. She saw the lane ending, ending in a high black barrier of thorns, built strong and high for her destruction in the bright field, and the bright cruel morning beyond. She dropped her hands and caught up the reins again, pulling the bit through his mouth with a last sobbing effort before he galloped into the fence. Then violence beyond all violence struck her and there was nothing more.

XI

Grania came flying down the lane on Donatia's pony, tears poured down her face, and sobs blew back in gusts through the air behind her. It was her fault, all her fault. She had killed little Doatie with her stupidity bringing Soo and all. She screamed with rage at Soo who screamed back, thrilled and flying along like a little black whippet beside her. Lovely, Soo thought, it was the best morning for a long time. Birdies and bunnies and horses all flying before her. She had frightened the life out of everything she met to-day.

There was a great breach in the obstacle that fenced the lane's end. Bushes and stones and an iron bar all burst out into the field beyond, and Foley was stooping over a terrifying little huddled bundle on the short grass, and the Knight of Aragon horse was standing with a foot up like a dog, afar off; staring and raging with reins hanging straight down from his upflung head and his tail out behind him like a horse on a monument on a hill-top. Oh, it was a dreadful scene of confusion, and frighteningly quiet, with a horrid after battle subsidence in the air, a dip towards unreality.

'I don't like moving her,' Foley said to Grania. 'I think her collar bone's gone, and she's clean out. Go and get a door some place and a blanket.'

He was taking off his coat to put over her, and Grania hurried

off hers, delighted that he seemed to have forgotten the dreadful
things he had said to her and Soo not five minutes before; now
he spoke quite naturally, his hands feeling over poor little Doatie
like a doctor's.

A man came running heavily down the side of the hill to
them, the splendid thrill of disaster bore him to them as surely as
a land-coming wave. He was disappointed that disaster's victim
was still alive, he had viewed the fall, and thought she had no
business to be.

'She set spurs to him, and she whipped into it,' he told Foley.
'Look see, look see, he flew through the bars of iron like a
pigeon through smoke, and he tumbled his body three times
through the air before ever he hit the land—oh, it was noble.'

Grania redeemed herself a little by catching the horse. But the
redemption turned a little sour in her mouth when she saw how
he hobbled beside her. Foley would have something more to say
about that. But he said nothing. He was smoking a cigarette and
looking down at Doatie's dead little face, flat on the ground in
the sunny shelter of the bank. He stooped down often to wrap
the coats more snugly round her, and often looked over the hill
behind to see if there was any sign of the man's return with door
or blanket. It is the isolation and slowness of competing with
such disasters that unnerves the waiters. Doors are not lying
about, waiting to carry the wounded to hospital, nor do blankets or doctors grow on the bushes, and there is always the
inconvenient horse which cannot be left to its own device and
wild purpose. You must wait and watch the still, suffering
creature until help comes, pieced so slowly and clumsily
together from sources foreign to the accident.

To-day the kind vulture man returned soon with a company
of helpers, and Doatie was carried to a house where a priest had
been summoned. There was every circumstance of tragedy until
the doctor's arrival, and his disappointing opinion that she was

not too bad, and had better be got home and to bed as soon as possible. She was put in the doctor's car with Foley holding her.

Grania and Micky took the three horses home, Micky riding Foley's and leading the wounded lion, while Grania (though very worried as to how she was to get her bicycle back to Aragon) rode the pony.

They talked ceaselessly.

'Well, wasn't it a fright, Miss?'

'Oh, it was too shattering.'

'A holy fright to God.'

'Ghastly, and all Soo's fault. Oh, Soo, you naughty, wicked——'

'It's little troubles her, and mind you a bird in the air would do the same with this beggar, if he choose, he choose and Miss Doatie's not equal to the likes of him.'

'And poor Soo, really she didn't do so much. Just a little dash out after a rabbit, poor sweetie.'

'Dogs is a black and bloody nuisance around horses.'

'Do you hear that, Soo? Now you know.'

'And I suppose the little she done was why he soared through the air with buck, lep and kick, and away with him into the firmaments, I suppose?'

'Oh, it was terrible. He was gone in a flash, and then Foley couldn't get his horse over the fence and didn't know what to do, and Soo was barking like a mad woman, and then if you only heard the crack he hit the wall—I don't know how Miss Doatie stayed on him.'

'Ah, she's hardy. But she's not hardly enough for the likes of he. God help her she shouldn't be so venturesome.'

They turned in at the gate of Foley's house and rode down the deep lane. The dark walls were alive with little ferns wedged in the shade as bright as lizards in the sun. A group of five cherries held their flowers pretty as dancers' skirts on the dark edge of a grove. Cherry is the only white flower with gaiety and none of the ominous waxen quality implicit in white flowers.

Foley was waiting in the yard. He took no heed of Grania but gently led the lame horse into his stable and closed the door.

Grania was in a state. What to do next? Did Foley not take in her difficulties? Where was the bicycle? Where was the doctor, who would surely report where he had seen her? And no matter either if she had not lied about it. Fishing for minnows indeed, a queer story to tell Nan. Oh, what should she do? and what had come of this daring morning outing but disgrace with Foley. She felt furious with Soo, but could not resist her when she came mimbling along for love, she must come into your arms again, little sweetness. Grania sat on the wooden stump of mounting block, her short hair pouring over Soo as she bent her head, dividing at the back of her neck as cleanly as water parts.

She lost herself in thoughts of Soo. Soo was like so many things. Smooth as a blackbird, supple as a cat, fast as a tiny deer. When she laid herself down to gallop a thrill would pierce Grania to see that flashing speed, those jinks and turnings. Filled with hunting lusts her gait of going was different, the procedure tremendously thought out. Then she mimbled about carefully in sight with her ears laid back flat against her head, she would edge up to the mate chosen for the day's sports and give him sly and wicked looks; saying, watch me, keep your eye on me, I'll give the signal. Waiting until, even for a breath, Grania's attention was distracted; even a breath is long enough, and like a horse jumping into its bridle, she would be off at a wicked bullet-like speed, tucking herself into herself and firing herself along, a black bee with no wings. A passion that knows no conscience possessing her, savage and extreme in her desire, she must reach the coverts and the wild, and pursue the game, which she so seldom captured. If, one day out of a year of days, she did by some chance turn of speed, or by some immemorial dig get her teeth fastened in the choking stink of bunny fur and flesh, her mouth, alas, was too weak to hold her prize. A moment there may be with fulfilment in her grasp, paradise between the teeth, then a couple of bounding kicks from her prey and he is gone from her, lost to her. Only frustration owns the cruel moment.

Who can tell, there may be other times, when a nest of blind and naked baby rabbits falls to her share, and she can bloat herself on their succulent delicacy. But she never returned full-stomached and bloody from her hunting—or if she was bloody, blood cannot be seen against her blue-black coat. One thing is sure, she never came back other than spindle-boiled and hungry. Her belly touching her backbone. There are bracelets of platinum bound round her bird-thin forelegs where traps and snares, the wicked gins of men, have snapped into her flesh in dark rabbit runs, where for hours she has striven and suffered while Grania searched and called for her fruitlessly.

There was once such a night when the trapper went his rounds, and a tough tinker he was, but to Soo a man, and men are kind. As she saw him approach her agony held her silent in anticipation of mercy and release. Now it was dusk and her torment would soon cease. He was coming to her through the wet, blood-red bracken, through the cold, through the pain. He came nearer. He paused. Soo's black back was arched in her pain and terror.

He turned away and left her. A black cat, he thought. I'll bring my gun and shoot her in the morning. For black cats touch no chord of pity in any poacher's heart.

None can ever know or tell about the night that followed. A new height of suffering and terror must have reached its pain up towards the chill stars and screamed, mercy, to the night.

The next morning she was loosed, in such a cold extremity of exhaustion that she could hardly make her way home. Two hours it took her to cover a distance that she could have done in twenty minutes. And when she got back to her house, to Aragon, no, she could not even cry; but crouched and licked her wound in the cold dewed grass near to the dark of the rhododendrons, there she was found and succoured with passionate and healing love.

So Grania dwelt and dreamed on the thought of Soo, and held her and forgave her foolishness, and murmured to her, What shall we do now, Soo? We're lost. What fools we were.

Then Foley was standing at her shoulder saying coldly, 'I wonder would you go in and give Aunt Gipsy a hand with Doatie?' Saying then with an intention that left her breathless in its promise and forgiveness:

I'm going to drive you back to your bicycle after breakfast. Don't fret about the horse, he's all right.'

He picked Soo up. 'Weren't you a very naughty girl. Give us a kiss now and say you're sorry,' his eyes at that trick of holding hers across what he was saying. 'I must go back to my patient,' as Micky came out of the kitchen door with a pail of hot water. 'Run along now, and don't be keeping my mind from my work.'

Freed and insolent, knowing she was restored to her place in his love again Grania walked across the yard, away from the smart line of boxes and towards the house.

The old yard sloped up towards the back of the house which, unadorned by bow-windows or porches of coloured glass, had the tall dismal dignity of a narrow old farmhouse. Low white walls came up to each corner of the house and thick fuschia hedges, clipped year after year to impenetrable sturdiness, jutted roundly above the curved wall coping. The windows in the back of the house were small, small-paned and dark looking, set with purpose and carefulness in the walls, flat to the extreme outside of the thick walls. You thought the house to be higher than it was, the drop of the yard below gave it a faintly towerlike look.

The outer walls were so sour and flat you supposed them to be thin, but they were built as solid as a castle. The back of Foley's house was so unlike the front of it that the contrast gave you as quick a shock as the sight of a skeleton sitting on a sofa might give, or the geniality of a friend suddenly turned to bitterness and accusation.

Grania opened the high latched door that led into the kitchen, and stood within, looking about her in the quiet gloom of a farm kitchen where for years food had been prepared for people and for animals, and where many people had lived in the poverty and dignity of daily life, before the idea of masters feeding apart from their men was known, or the dreadful style of parlours.

Aunt Gipsy's voice came calling down the stairs for someone to boil a kettle, and Grania called back, 'I'll do it.' She put the kettle on and stirred the fire, alone and responsible for this slight act. She was curiously excited, it was absurd for there could not be a smaller thing to do, but the air in the long dim kitchen seemed full of presage as the stars, the whitened walls leaned inwards and towards her. Light rode down a lean beam from a window deeply dug in the thick wall. Such light never came directly in, the windows were too high and deep sunk to the outer wall, but there was a softness and warmth of light that melted against the limed walls and poured back from them into the air. On the table there was a wide bowl, pale brown outside and white inside. Nine fresh eggs it held. They were so new that a sort of bloom lay on their shells. A smell of bread came strongly from the oven. She opened the door, and found a cloth hanging on a chair to turn the pan of bread. A sweet volume of warmth came from the open oven door.

She felt drunk with this contrast to her morning of danger and hardihood. The warmth enclosed within walls, the delight of a house, the sweetness of new bread, all these things touched the realm of the exotic now. Common joys were new to her, making bread or making love. She was awed and enchanted by them newly, and deeply ignorant of both. She was beyond and outside herself and reality, in a world of different wonders and unguessed at values.

Grania was far too young and inexperienced to take love at all lightly. The idea of passing love, was not born in her. It had not dawned on her that Foley's love could mean only a little. She thought everything in him and of him was for her, as he was the breath of life and the only meaning of love to her, so she must be to him. She had no doubts of him whatever. She was only unquestioningly wildly glad that by a miracle he had found her to love. She pinched her fat arms now, hurting herself into the knowledge of reality. She was well lost indeed, a fat beautiful blonde.

Now the boiling kettle checked her pleasant dreaming and she lifted it clumsily off the fire, and called up the stairs:

'Mrs. Bohane! Mrs. Bohane!' and only the gabble of quick praying came down, in a hammer-like mutter, in answer to her calling. How she wished Nan and not Mrs Bohane were in charge of poor Doatie. There would be more nursing than praying done by Nan in such a case.

The praying went on. You could not hear any words, only the rhythm that repeated prayers make on the empty air, despairingly mechanical.

She took the kettle and went up the steep stairs, a feeling of carefulness and responsibility alive in her. She opened the room through which the sound of praying came. Mrs. Bohane, smartly dressed in mauve for her breakfast party, was kneeling by Doatie's bed, and a young and dirty girl knelt a little apart, as was fit. Mrs. Bohane led the prayer and the girl responded. Doatie moved a little and waved her poor head from side to side on the pillow. She was no more than half-conscious.

'Oh, Miss Grania, my heavens, you'll have to excuse us, oh,

359

really, you will,' Mrs. Bohane sprang to her feet and began to drag the curlers out of her hair, her toilet not having progressed to its conclusion before catastrophe was sprung on her.

'The kettle boiled so I brought it up.'

'My heavens, will you ever excuse us? Mary, what are you thinking of? Take the kettle from Miss Fox. Oh, we all need a cup of tea, don't we? Go down and make it, Mary.'

'How is poor Doatie?'

Mrs. Bohane shook her dark head despairingly.

'Oh, the doctor said he'd be back in a couple of hours. Indeed, my great heavens, look at her. She might be gone by then, wouldn't you say so yourself? It's the priest we might be calling, don't you think so?'

'Oh, Mrs. Bohane, I thought the doctor said she wasn't as bad as we thought.'

'Oh, doctors say this and doctors say that, but I can see the Blue Shadow on her face, and we all know what that means.'

'Oh, no!'

'Oh, yes, indeed, and a corpse in my tea cup on a Friday, don't tell me she'll ever leave that bed again but in her little coffin. A child's coffin would nearly do her, perhaps. Indeed I'll have to get into town to see about it.'

All this conversation streamed in a galloping whisper from Mrs. Bohane, and Grania's answers had been murmured back, so when Foley came into the room and said in a low but natural voice :

'Breakfast's ready. How's poor Doatie?' it really seemed as though he brought with him the possibility of life. He stepped over to her bed and stood there considering for a moment before he found her hand, with a half-yard of striped sleeve below it and felt her pulse. Then he felt under the bed clothes for her feet.

'What about a hot bottle?' he said, 'Two in fact. She's perished. Her little feet are like stones in a river.'

'Oh, my God, I had the kettle boiling and I forgot what I had it for, imagine! I sent it down for the tea.'

'I suppose you were laying plans for the funeral party.'

'Oh, Jesu, what a rap!'

'Go on and get the two bottles now as quick as you can.'

'There's but the one in the house, dear, I'll have to get into town and buy another.'

Foley tucked the clothes gently round poor Doatie and went down to the kitchen.

'Mary,' he said, 'get me a hot bottle. Have you only the one?'

'I have an old jar some place.'

'Quick now, good girl.'

He had a great way of getting things done; small necessary things. Cosy fundamentals, and he used people without bullying them. Grania watched him, back in Donatia's room in five minutes after he had left it, wrap the jar and the rubber bottle in two vests of Doatie's and put them in her bed, felt a surprised respect for such handiness. Suddenly she saw his likeness to Nan. Just so did Nan deal with things. The same hard, quick strength and dexterity; more comforting when you were ill than all the warmth and kind chatter in the world. Seeing this likeness so plainly frightened her a little. For a flashing moment she saw that there were things that mattered to her which would be no more to him than to Nan. She might keep many things she loved a secret for always. The way she thought of the silent pleasure-ground at Aragon, of the still river air feeling its way with watery quiet into the drawing-room, poems of De La Mare, poems of Grania Fox, ah, but what had love to do with such cold things? How compare those joys belonging essentially to your loneliness to this glory, and this longing shared.

He held the door of Donatia's room open for her and walked after her down the stairs at a cool and courtly distance. She was so vulnerable to him that even this could hurt and surprise her. She walked through the kitchen with her fair head reared up, swallowing tears and spit. She wanted to say, I did boil the kettle. I turned the bread, I'm not useless.

In the dining-room Mrs. Bohane sat importantly behind her teapot facing the Pope.

Foley said, 'I told Mary to stay with Doatie till you go back to her. She shouldn't be left alone.'

'Oh, pardon and excuse me, Foley, Doctor said leave her perfectly quiet, and if there was ever a bull in a thunder shop that's Mary.'

'Well I'm going into town after breakfast, and I'll bring out a nurse.'

'A nurse, indeed! You'll excuse me, Miss Grania, but whose daughter is Doatie? And who should nurse her but her mother? Not one of those brats in a white bib, I suppose, from the County home, imagine, making work for nobody through the house, don't tell me.'

'Well, she may be your daughter, Aunt Gip, but whose horse was it nearly killed her, poor child? and who should get her a nurse?'

'And whose dog nearly killed her?' Grania suddenly felt impelled to a share in Doatie's misfortune.

'Oh, don't think of it, Miss Grania. Look, what am I doing? You haven't a bit to eat, do you take sugar in your tea? Really I'm so nervous I'm getting quite forgetful.'

'You're not fit to nurse her after the shock, Aunt Gip.'

'Indeed it must have been a great shock for you, Mrs. Bohane.'

'Shock, dear? When I saw the doctor's car from this window, Oh, I said to myself, what will I do, if he's come to break it to me she's gone? Now, I wonder, I said to myself, what will I do. I could see myself at the little grave, Miss Grania—really

362

now I could—all in black and a black hat. Isn't it well, I said to myself, I never saw that nice little flowered hat on the paper till this very morning, or it would be up there now in its box, and I'd never knock a turn out of it the summer long.'

'Aunt Gip——'

'A broken collar bone, Mrs. Bohane, the doctor said.

'Is that only all, I said. I knew it was only softening the blow he was——'

'Aunt Gip——'

'Well, there's a touch of concussion too, he said, and with that my head commenced to reel and it's reeling yet.'

'Aunt Gip, you'll let me bring the nurse out now, won't you? It's for your sake as much as Doatie.'

'Very well, dear. I'll come in with you and see have they the little hat yet at McBirney's, and get a few little things for poor Doatie.'

'Milk and water's all poor Doatie'll want for the next few days, and I'll tell them to keep the hat for you, Aunt Gip.'

'Ah, Foley, how would you know it from the picture? I'll have to see it my own self.' Aunt Gip was getting desperate.

'Now, listen, when I bring the nurse out to Doatie I'll bring you in to Ahern's. Will that satisfy you?'

'Now, it's not for any pleasure attached to it, but I do find it very hard, imagine, to buy a hat that suits me, and it's only an economy to buy one hat that suits you, where you could be buying three you couldn't wear.'

'That's a fact, Aunt Gip . . . Look'—he put in a smile instead of 'Miss Grania'—'we must be off. I dont want to hurry you but I have a lot to do.'

'Are you driving Miss Grania back to Aragon, Foley? Will you see your mother?'

'No,' he said shortly, 'I won't.'

'Oh,' said Aunt Gip, and she sat in a surprising silence and stillness staring at the Pope for at least a minute before she wove her complicated good-byes and excuses and compliments round Grania. But there were no messages for Nan.

Foley noticed this. He said to himself, 'The old bitch is on the line, God blast her. . . . I'll not do a thing about the hat or she'll get more suspicious if I'm too nice with her.'

XII

'Miss Pigeon, up, now, it's time to get up and dress yourself, and your bath morning too.'

Aunt Pidgie curled herself down in her bed. She longed to be a sitting hen that no one could disturb for twenty-one days, no one could throw her off her eggs. Ah, but they did come and throw the hens from their nests, the poor birdies, but I would steal my nest some place where no one could find me, Aunt Pidgie decided. In the old ice-house perhaps or maybe a nice empty manger, a sturdy deep manger of worm-eaten wood. She saw herself blinking in the blue seedy light of an empty stable; the quiet stuffiness; the light coming through slatted windows in dusty bars. She would purr to herself, spreading her feathers, and tap gently on a hot egg with her bill, pushing it back beneath her heavy flattened body. Her body would cling to those hot eggs and she would be steeped in quiet and queen of quietness and warmth.

'Miss Pigeon, are you never going to get out of bed? And such a glorious day it's a shame for you to be wasting it. Come on now, your bath's none too hot, and it's not getting hotter.'

Nan spoke in a voice in which cajoling and threats were equally balanced. A nurse's voice, a voice that knows the body well and cares nothing for the extravagances of the mind.

Aunt Pidgie bundled herself desperately to the edge of her bed

365

and stretched down those tiny blue veined feet for her slippers.

'My slippers, Nan, my slippers.'

'They're there,' Nan was collecting towels and soap.

'They're not.'

They were, of course. Nan came over and clapped them on her feet as if they were irons. Clapped in irons. That's what the pirates did to you, and there was something else, a shadow on her mind about irons. Who did they put in irons?

'Who do they put in irons, Nan?'

'Who's been talking to you about irons, Miss Pigeon? Wait till I meet them. No, you'll never come to that, dear, indeed no, not while you have Nan to look after you.'

It was a terrifying little speech delivered with goulish becks and nods and veiled understanding of possible horrors not to be explained. It was by such innuendos that Nan kept Miss Pigeon in order and alive in her a recognition of Nan's protective power. Miss Pidgie knew there were things Nan could tell that would get her locked away for ever in the asylum, that terrible prison on the hill where you never saw a fire or felt the soft yielding heat of a hot-water bottle (such as Nan sometimes very kindly gave her on particularly cold nights, not every night of course), where terrible people called Brutal Warders knocked you about, and you got stewed mice every second Thursday for your dinner, and there were lice in the beds and bars on the windows. . . . Oh, hurry, hurry to your bath and no moaning and shivering about it if it ran cold, for if you were not good you might find yourself taken away from Aragon, and out of Nan's care, so you had to be very careful not to annoy Nan, and never, never to complain about her or about anything she might say or do.

Nan washed Miss Pigeon with firm carefulness and left her floating in the warm water, her body nearly as transparent as a frog's, while she went down to get the breakfast tray.

'But only a minute now, Miss Pigeon, and you're to be dry when I get back. There's your hot towel, and there's your vest.'

Alone in hot water, and it was hot to-day, Aunt Pidgie lay back and luxuriated at her ease. Oh, delicious warmth, soaking into her bones, why was one always cold? The torture of coldness, now she wondered if she couldn't be a little hotter, how comfortable to have the water one degree hotter and one inch deeper. Nan would not know. Miss Pigeon pulled herself up and carefully with both hands turned on the hot tap. An exquisite dribble enlivened the temperature of the water. Aunt Pidgie sat near the tap, sponging the hotter water over her shoulders, holding hot spongefuls on the back of her thin neck, smiling with ease and pleasure, forgetting all the worries and responsibilities of her life.

Suddenly she heard Nan's returning step, quick and loud and busy, and at the sound her hands flew to the tap to turn it off. Even if she was not dried and in her vest she could not be found committing this iniquity in her bath. And now the tap would not turn off. She twisted at it with weak fury but it would not budge. Regardless of her effort the water ran on, deepening her crime, comfortably cruelly running into the bath, already far deeper and hotter than Nan permitted. Aunt Pidgie was in a terrible state. She splashed and clattered about in the water trying to deaden the sound of the running tap until she found some means to stop it flowing. It was too late when she saw that she had been twisting at COLD not HOT, for Nan was back again, a ferocious mixture of wrath and injured trustfulness.

'And so this is what happens when I leave you and trust you! Giving yourself a good boil the way you'll catch every chill of the day when you go out.' Nan came whirling in. 'Have you no conscience, have you no thought for others, living here at your ease in the Mansion of Aragon?'

'Oh, Nan, Nan, I'm sorry, I'm sorry. I didn't mean it, you know I didn't.'

'I know you're boiled as red as a prawn this living minute.'
Nan picked up a brass jug and began filling it under the cold tap.
The pupils of her eyes were like black pin heads.

'Stand up there, now,' she spoke jeeringly, 'till we cool you
off.'

'Nan, no, Nan, no. Not cold water. It hurts me, it does
things to me . . .'

'Stop your screeching, now. Stop it, do you hear me.'

Nan stood magnificently above the cowering white body
crouching up the shallow end of the bath, her beautiful grey hair
had not a curl out of place, her apron was as crisp as virgin snow,
her perfect teeth showed in a curious smile. She trickled an icy
dribble of water out of the spout of her can in front of Miss
Pigeon, and Miss Pigeon gripped the grandly shaped arm that
held the can and whimpered in a frenzy of fear.

Nan emptied the can out into the bath and burst out
laughing.

'Aren't you very easily frightened, Miss Pigeon? Don't you
know I was only teasing you? All the same it was a very bold
and dangerous act to go turning on the hot tap. I once heard a
true story of a lady who got boiled in her bath for doing that
very thing indeed. Couldn't turn the tap off, fell back in a faint,
how are you, and hit the back of her head, imagine, stunned
herself, think of it, and boiled herself to death, fancy!'

She helped Aunt Pidgie out as she talked and wrapped her in a
towel and dried her as carefully and gently as if she was a baby,
even a Fox baby.

Poor Aunt Pidgie. She was trembling still and at the same
time whimpering with relief. Nan was so kind, so strong, so
good, one shouldn't be so silly as to mind her little jokes with
cans of cold water. She would show she was sorry by hurrying
into her clothes. Aunt Pidgie wore quantities of underclothes.
She had combinations and knickers and white split drawers on

368

top of the knickers, that drew in at the knees with embroidery, and three different spencers with long, medium and short sleeves. Her legs, about as thick as a heron's and white and hairless as a chalk stone, were eaten up in thick black stockings. The legs of the combinations were folded down below the knife-sharp promontories of her knees, and held up by tapes that went across her shoulders and down the back, cross-pieced by tape in front and behind. It was a very good device and she had worn it since her last pair of corsets gave out about two years ago. Some day Mrs. Fox was going to buy her a very special new kind of corset, but she had so much to think about it was hard for her to remember everything. That was all the clothes you put on in the bathroom, the rest went on when you go back to your own room.

XIII

Aunt Pidgie's room had once been the nursery and it still kept that curiously forlorn look which nurseries have when their children are gone. The linoleum clings to the floor. The high iron fireguard with its brass rail has never been divorced from the fires it once guarded. The paper on the wall may be different, but who is going to take the bars off the windows, or patch up the mouse hole in the wainscot that so many oddments were put down for the mice, or put back the two missing handles on the white-painted chest of drawers, much less repaint it? People who don't matter to anybody are put to sleep in old nurseries. This is odd when one thinks of the time when the nursery was the most considered room in the house. Now there is about it the sad unnecessary air of a deserted beehive. The rocking-horse in the window ramps eternally idle on his rockers, no nor always idle, for sometimes when Miss Pigeon knew herself to be alone for hours she would mount him very slowly and carefully and rock herself gently while she gazed out of the window, from which she could see the river water and hear the river water flow, sliding past her and beyond her, as now everything went by her, people and happenings all unrelated to her life, all but Nan.

Now she was back in her room and the rest of her clothes were lying there ready to put on. First her sporran had to be adjusted, which was always a business as Nan objected to the lump it made under her skirt when it was full of precious things, so she would tie its top by the very ends round her waist and sling the paunch down between her legs. Then came her black and white checked petticoat, and to-day was the day for her purple skirt. She liked her purple skirt though she always wished she had a blouse to match it as then the violet colour might reflect in her eyes. But a navy blue blouse was the best she could do, with a cream lace guimpe upstanding, a little boned palisade, round her neck. She wore a couple of cardigans, the inner one a marled black and white weave, the outer a very long navy blue model with a tasselled belt blousing it slightly at the waist.

She sat in a chair while Nan put a towel round her shoulders and did up her hair. Her hair, once so yellow, and now the indeterminate colour of water in which many teacups have been washed. She still wore the yellow combs in it that had matched it so well. They felt just the same in her hair now as they had done in that person's hair who had been herself, herself before she got ill. She did not think of herself as particularly old, only as ill and cold and always rather tired.

Nan put her boots on too and she sighed as she did every morning about that sharp lump inside the left boot, or was it the right boot? which ran into her foot like a dagger before the end of the day. But in the morning she could never remember distinctly which foot it was, as she did not feel the lump until she had walked a bit, and Nan would bamboozle and mislead her, saying, 'Are you sure it's not the right foot you mean, Miss Pigeon? Make certain now, and I'll take them back to the man in the boot department. But I'd want to know which for certain,' all the time lacing up the boots like wildfire so that Miss Pigeon got confused and would not say for certain which foot it was.

Grania would often call in to see her at breakfast time, Grania

371

in a ragged blue kimono with a stork on the back, on her way to her bath. Grania had a fancy for the nursery bathroom and often came there for her bath and if she was not in too great a hurry she would look in on Aunt Pidgie.

Somehow these visits gave Aunt Pidgie exactly the same feeling of being apart and alone as the sight and sound of the passing river water under her window gave her. Grania's fat little behind would waggle cosily inside the tightly clasped kimono, and her fat white elbows would come through the long split sleeves, her hair would be screwed up in curlers and she would sit down or lean across the rocking-horse in the window, and make conversation to Aunt Pidgie for a few minutes.

'Lovely morning, Aunt Pidgie.'

'Yes, dear, I think it's an east wind though.'

'Oh, Aunt Pidgie, how can you tell? You haven't been out.'

'Feel it all over me.'

'What are you having for breakfast?'

'Just a cup of tea and a little bread and butter.'

'You ought to eat more, Aunt Pidgie.'

'Oh, I couldn't touch another thing, not possibly. People eat far too much, that's what I always say. Just a slice of bread and butter for me, and a little piece over for my Diblins, that's all I want. What are you having for breakfast downstairs, I wonder?'

'Kedgeree perhaps. It was salmon last night for dinner.'

'Oh, a lovely pink heap of kedgeree with chopped eggs in it and some parsley on top, I expect.'

'Shall I save some for your Diblins?'

'Oh, nasty indigestible stuff. You'll give every Diblin on the place the height of indigestion,' Nan might put in.

'Nasty indigestible stuff,' Miss Pidgie repeated sadly after her.

Grania laughed. 'Oh, well, perhaps it's not kedgeree at all.'

'Perhaps it's bacon and eggs?'

'Perhaps.'

372

'What are you doing to-day, Grania?' And whatever Grania was doing, riding or playing tennis or going down to see the salmon net drawn it was so apart from Miss Pigeon that when it was told it seemed to drop Miss Pigeon further and deeper into the cold shaft of loneliness where her life was lived. . . . Still she liked to see Grania in the mornings. Grania was still a little like the baby and the child Grania that Aunt Pidgie had spoilt and patronised and fascinated with stories of her Diblins. She was not like that stuck-up little Sylvia who had never really believed in Diblins, Aunt Pidgie knew, nor in T. Runk, the God of travelling either. Sylvia had always been cool and calm and collected, and it was always her dog, that nasty neat, smooth fox terrier that Aunt Pidgie found nosing round the secret places where the Diblins' food was left for them. Aunt Pidgie hated Titsy. She would never look when Titsy was going through her repertoire of tricks, she could do them all so well and neatly and with such dispatch and obedience, but Aunt Pidgie preferred Grania's Soo and would get her to beg-up, jump-up, and die for Ireland in endless opposition to Titsy's accomplishments. And if Soo was not there when Titsy was showing off Aunt Pidgie would shut her eyes and groan loudly at the applause. Another faintly annoying thing about Titsy was that she never, never got in the family way. Not even when Sylvia intended that she should. She was indefeatably spinsterish. She bit her lovers and sat down firmly and snarled at all advances; while Soo, poor passionate little gipsy, could hardly be restrained from the most indiscreet affairs, she had been desperately in love with a mastiff, and many other gentlemen had fancied her too.

That was one of the games Aunt Pidgie and Grania played with most enjoyment, talking about Soo's life and asking Soo questions about it. They would think up questions to ask Soo in front of Sylvia, about what Soo thought of Titsy, and make up Soo's answers, but Sylvia was so abominably quick-witted that

373

she often thought up on the spur of the moment the most devastating cracks back for Titsy, and Grania and Aunt Pidgie, who were neither of them very quick—though they were painstaking—would be reduced to broadsides, such as: 'What a pity Titsy's such a fool.' 'What a pity Titsy lost her figure.'

It was only through such childish games as these that Aunt Pidgie climbed out of her loneliness and felt gloriousy equal to the glorious young. To-day after her fright in the bath she felt more thrust into herself than ever, and she was still rather shaky when she sat down to her tea and bread and butter.

'Where's Miss Grania to-day, I wonder,' she ventured presently.

'Fishing for minnows.' Nan always prided herself on knowing the exact whereabouts and occupation of all the Fox's at all hours of the day or night. You could not catch her out.

'She'll catch cold, out so early.'

'People don't catch cold as easy as you think.'

'No.'

'No, they don't, and I think it's high time we took away one of your winter blankets.'

'Oh, Nan, I'm so cold at night. I want them all.'

'Well, want must be your master (that was a favourite saying of Nan's), I can't have you getting yourself into a perspiration at night just for a fancy. No, Miss Pigeon, that wouldn't do at all. Who's responsible for your health? Who has the job of nursing you when you're sick? Who? Tell me that now, who?'

'You, Nan.'

'And you don't want to give me any more trouble than you can help, do you?'

'Oh, no, Nan.' Miss Pigeon gazed at the loaf of bread longing for another slice but much too frightened of giving extra trouble to ask for it. Nan was very busy dusting now, she hooshed and flapped with her duster making a great to-do

374

among the photographs and ornaments on the mantelpiece, her duster flew out like a kite, and folded up as absorbent as a sponge, and went into all corners after the most invisible specks of dust or untidiness. She rattled an empty match box and Miss Pigeon screamed out:

'Oh, my eggs! my eggs!'

'How should I know your eggs were in there. Are they for your Diblins.'

'Yes, Nan, yes.'

Nan opened the box, 'But these are blown.'

'Yes, I blew them last night.'

Nan looked at her curiously, and Miss Pidgie began to think of excuses for having blown her eggs, but after a pause Nan said, 'Well, why shouldn't you?' and shut the box laughing. Miss Pigeon was very relieved that no further questions had been asked. But that danger past, as always happens, another difficulty blew up in her mind to do away with the joy from relief that she had briefly known. Now she was in quite a fidget to get out because if she did not get out soon it would be too late. . . . Aunt Pidgie's life was just a vortex and a tangle of plans and adventures that nobody knew about.

XIV

Frazer, the butler, knew his place all right, and he knew a lot of other interesting things too, but knowing his place came first. He was not English, though he sounded very English, he came from the North of Ireland, and had a sour, abiding dislike of these Southerners, and no one could have been more unpopular with the natives of Aragon than he was. He always managed to know who stole what, and who idled most. Oddly enough he and Nan disliked each other intensely. There was not room for two such powers at Aragon, and Nan's way of dispensing her power was far more imaginative and grand than Frazer's. She was royal in the disposition of favour or rebuke. He was meticulous and petty and could overlook nothing that he saw wrong in the house, or the garden, the river or even the stables, for he would poke his nose into every department of the estate, and appraise its conduct to a nicety.

He was very partial to the soldiery who visited Aragon. They seemed right and civilised to his mind, with their clipped moustaches, clean flannels, well-made shoes and good manners. They represented the things he respected most, and he hoped he would see Miss Sylvia married to one of them. He had a real liking for her. Yes, she was a lady. Her little cold ways and clever fingers, her skill with horses or her skill on the river were very nice to him. He admired her tidiness and punctuality. There was

376

something low to his mind in Miss Grania's dirty childish ways and in Mrs. Fox's airy flexible irresponsibility, and her indulgence towards delinquencies on the place, and her familiarity with Nan. He had often timed those long cosy talks at bedtime or the day-time murmurs in the morning-room. Their length filled him with disproportionate jealousy, although he would never have permitted the freedom to himself. He knew his mistress's place better. A 'Yes, Madam,' or 'No, Madam,' from him could always put her in it. There was an inverted pleasure in keeping the family in its place. Then he knew better than Nan did their comings and goings and exactly which of the young officers was paying most marked attention to the young ladies. He read all postcards religiously, and could remember every telegram that came to Aragon in the course of a year.

Although it was far from his place to do so he often prepared platefuls of chicken and cress sandwiches with which he would waylay Miss Pigeon in some out of the way spot saying with tremendous ceremony, 'For the Diblins, Miss, and if you would kindly leave the plate beneath this laurel bush I will collect it in due course.' Then he would bow and leave her among the gloomy leaves of the rhododendrons. He would not have dreamed of watching her as she darted in among the dry twisty branches, rooted and layered to the ground.

Frazer hated Nan, that was the truth. And Nan loved to torment him. To seek him out in his own pantry and torment him, show her power and boast to him till she had him in a frenzy of annoyance. On some morning when he was feeling particularly sour and conscious of his ills she might come crisply in, and the conversation go something like this:

'Good-morning, Mr. Frazer.'

A pause while he swept three crumbs ceremoniously off a table. Then 'Good-morning, Mrs. O'Neill.'

'Would you kindly leave out a bottle of light port wine for Miss Pigeon's lunch biscuit, Mr. Frazer.'

377

'I thought you had a bottle of that last week, Mrs. O'Neill.'

'*And* how many glasses go to a bottle, will you tell me? Am I dreaming or is it seven?'

'I'd say Miss Pigeon did most of the dreaming where that port was concerned, Mrs. O'Neill.'

That was how it would go on between them, or it might be:

'May I glance at the *Irish Times*, Mr. Frazer? I'd like to see the results of the Clonmel Horse Show.'

Again the scene would be in his pantry, just after the post came in.

'I have it folded for the drawing-room, Mrs. O'Neill.'

'I'll fold it again. I just want to see if my son's horse won a prize?' She knew very well he had. So did Frazer. And he was not going to wait to be boasted to either. He would not give her that much satisfaction. Certainly not. He made for the door, a tray of letters in his hand. But he found he could not get out, not get out of his own pantry. Mrs. O'Neill was between him and the door and deaf to all, 'Excuse me's' 'Kindly allow me to pass.'

'Am I stopping you, Mr. Frazer. Excuse me! Oh, look——' flapping wide the paper and folding down a page of photographs——'Mr. F. O'Neill on "Mountain Brig," winner of the class for hunters up to 14 stone.' Well, isn't that nice. Foley will be pleased. And such a gorgeous picture of him, isn't it? Don't you think so, Mr. Frazer?'

'I scarcely noticed it, Mrs. O'Neill.'

'A lot of horses in his class and a Baronet and an Honourable and a Lord showing in it too, fancy!'

'Pardon me, Mrs. O'Neill, but I have my morning's work to do, if all you want is to read the papers. Kindly let me out of my own pantry.'

'Oh, Mr. Frazer, excuse me every time. What was I thinking of? Only such a triumph would make any mother thoughtless, wouldn't it?'

Long and long ago Frazer had looked on Nan with admiring eyes. Nan had known it and with every light malicious twist in her had shown how she despised him then. That was very long ago, but the seeds of hatred it had sown between them had thriven well. Frazer knew many things about Nan to her detriment, but not enough, never quite enough for her undoing, but he had waited years and he could wait longer for that hour. It might not be so long now either for he sensed something that was afoot between Miss Grania and Foley O'Neill. It might be nothing. It was too soon to say. But there were signs about, things that needed watching. For instance; the day Miss Grania was so late for dinner, a ferret of Foley's breed had joined the horrid hutchful in the stables. Everyone knew these ferrets with the spot. Of course it might have come through Nan. He was preparing a test for her to find this out. And where had Miss Grania gone this morning? He had seen her, through the pantry window, bicycling down the mist-ridden avenue going at high speed past the fogged sleepy groups of black cattle and pale towers of the lime trees. It was early hours for one who liked her bed so well as Miss Grania did. He put on one of his tests at breakfast time.

'Shall I leave the lamp under the coffee for Miss Grania, Madam?' he asked Mrs. Fox as she was distractedly sorting her letters from bills and catalogues before she flew down, rather late, to see the cook.

'Always late. Yes, I suppose so, yes Frazer, please.'

'I thought perhaps she would be out for breakfast, ma'am.'

'Out? She's not up yet.'

'Ah, I must have been mistaken, madam.'

'Oh, "mistaken," Frazer?'

'I imagined I saw Miss Grania cycling down the avenue at 7 o'clock this morning, madam.'

'Oh, no, Frazer, you must have been mistaken.'

'Obviously my mistake, Madam.'

So, she was off on the quiet was she, and why? For what?
There was something more in this to nose into. And she
wouldn't be back to breakfast this morning, not likely. Whatever business had Miss Grania out of bed at six would be
important enough to occupy her well into the morning. Perhaps
he had been foolish to say anything to Mrs. Fox, but at least
he now knew there was something queer about this morning's
business. His mind went back to the glimpse of her pedalling
madly down the avenue. What was it that had struck him as
peculiar about it? Why, of course, she was in riding clothes. . .
Frazer pulled the little spirit lamps out from under coffee and
silver dishes and extinguished them each with a sour smile. No,
Miss Grania certainly would not be back to breakfast.

As he cleared the table he saw Miss Pidgie scurrying along the
path between the house and the terraces. He saw her against the
shining water. The sun glistened and the wind blew in some
black cock's feathers in her hat, turning them to ice green. Everyone seemed on business bent this morning. He opened the window to intercept her, in his hand a plate of scrambled eggs, fried
toast and bacon. 'Excuse me, Miss,' he leant out towards the
black feathered hat with tremendous ceremony, 'for the Diblins,
Miss, and if you would kindly leave the plate beneath that laurel
bush I will collect it in due course.'

'Oh, thank you, Frazer, thank you. It's a hungry morning for
them, isn't it?'

He saw her change her course and disappear down a dark little
side walk towards the river. 'Now I wonder what *she* had for her
breakfast,' he pondered, 'If I could fix that on the old bitch I'd be
content. Starved that's what she is, starved to death, and no one
gives a damn. These cursed Irish they're all the same, rich and
bloody poor, they're all alike,' for in his own extreme self Frazer
had a loose way of talking that would have shocked deeply the self
he had made.

380

XV

The Wren's Nest. Foley did not mean to stop at Roche's public house that morning, but he saw the sign the boys used when they were there at the door. The wooden crosspiece of a plough leaning against the wall. The boys knew his car well enough and someone would be on the lookout to report they had seen him go by when the sign was out. It was the sign of the Irish Republican army and he dared not pass by.

He stopped his car in the sunny road. A black-faced mountainy sheep skipped back across the low stone wall to the heather and gorse stretching high and wide and away up to the sharp blue cloud shadows that travelled the mountain distances. The gorse and low spring heather were dry as cages, he knew because he had lain on the mountain this morning with Grania in the sun and light wind, teasing her and making love in the morning sun until she was wild for love.

She had all the unshamed and natural dignity of her wild blood. For so young a creature she was superb and at her ease. Afterwards she lay in the dark heather laughing at her lover and talking in a deep low voice. Presently she said, picking at a tight curl of bracken that pressed itself like a blue question mark out of the ground.

'We're all right, aren't we, Foley? Not that I'd mind whatever happened, would you?'

'Mind what?' He was wondering how soon he could leave her and go on to get the nurse for Doatie.

'Mind if we started a baby.'

'Good God—you don't think?'

His voice disturbed Grania. There was nothing in it of what she had supposed would be there for her if she told him this. There was no tenderness, only rough alarm.

'You're not trying to tell me anything, are you?'

Grania laughed and moved away from him. A dizzy little panic that would not be quite forbidden came over her. I won't say any more. Not till I know. Not till I'm certain. I won't speak of it. Not to this stranger.

He was a stranger, they were not together. This was the first time it had occurred to Grania that they could be apart without a rush of understanding and sympathy. Always she had followed his mind in doglike devotion, in apt anticipation. It was not such a business really. His mind was not so complicated. But that hers should go with it was one of the miracles of this loving. Now, in a moment, from a tone in his voice, she guessed and would not guess how different things might be between them, how short a way his love and mind might go with hers.

'You're very silent,' he said.

She was looking away from him and he turned her chin back towards him with one finger.

'Sulks?' he said. His eyes laughed at her, caressing and reassuring. He adored any resistance. Fostered it by teasing. 'You look like sister Sylvia now,' he said. 'Why don't you talk to me about the price of oats?'

'Oh, how dare you?' Grania never could resist a giggle at Sylvia. She let her head fall back in the arm crooked ready for it. First and last he knew how to make you comfortable. Cosy was the word for it. Her seeing moment retreated. She only knew she would not tell. Not yet. Soon. Not to-day.

382

'Do you think she talks about oats much?' Only for something to say. It was nice talking in a dreaming voice with the sky above you and an arm under your head and the sun on the bank behind.

'I wouldn't know. I wouldn't want to know.'

'Does she have kisses, do you think?'

'Not much I shouldn't think.'

'That's why she's such a sour puss, do you think?'

'Who would she have them with?'

'Michael Purvis.'

'He's nice. He's easily the best of the fellows in the barracks.'

'I don't think he would be very good for kisses.'

'You haven't tried. He might be lots better than me. I think he'll buy the horse that flattened little Doatie this morning.'

'Do you? Would he be able for him?'

'Yes, he would. He's got sense about things. I like him. Is he really courting Sylvia?'

'Oh, they're so cool. Love is like a frost with them. She keeps away. He keeps away. I don't know why I say it's an affair, but I'm sure it is.'

'That's right. That's what you'd expect.'

His tone of approval startled Grania.

'Do you think everyone should keep away or only the Sylvias and Michaels?'

'Only the Sylvias and Michaels,' he laughed and pulled her close. 'Don't you begin it.'

'I'm rather late to, aren't I?' Grania said. She did not know that her lip trembled.

'Well don't. Promise. Promise?'

She nodded. Her hair flew about in a breeze and shone in the sun. He gave her a cigarette and lit it and his own. Grania did not really like smoking. But, of course, one must not be childish. She was not old enough for that.

383

'And poor Doatie,' he said after a minute. 'You should be ashamed of yourself keeping me here when I should have the nurse back to her by this.'

'I'm not keeping you.'

'Yes, you are. I can't help myself, see? I have to stay with you.'

He pulled her to her feet and they parted as he intended they should part, with Grania looking for love, waiting for her next hour of love.

Foley wanted nothing of her beyond this. She was no real mate for him. He did not understand her careless chatter born of the idleness and centuries of rich living behind her. Her absurdities and importances were like those of a child to him. He did not once in his mind cross her mind. Her very freedom in love seemed shameless to the peasant in him and his own wickedness in taking her love frightened the Catholic that was behind his character. It was a terrible thing he was doing. It was against all his beliefs and all his conscience. Nothing was engaged in it but his body, but that could not give her up, he could not let go. Every time they were together he had to make a plan for the next time. Between their secret meetings he was full of fear and disgust at himself, and a kind of coarse pity for Grania. For she was doing everything he most despised in women, there was nothing he could at all respect about her. When they met publicly they had no common ground. She was ignorant about horses and talked a great deal of nonsense to him about them. She had no racing technique. She was not like Doatie, whom you could entrust any time to get £25 on a horse at the best price and with lightning speed. No, Grania could never back a horse. She couldn't put two shillings on without telling everyone she knew that it was a certainty and why and who had told her and who had told them. She was a silly in everything that mattered to him except one thing, and he could not give that up.

This morning when he left her near Aragon and turned his car round to drive to the town for Doatie's nurse his mind was far more with Doatie in her injured and useless state than it was with Grania. He blamed himself disgustedly for all that dallying and love-making in the heather and now at the Wren's Nest on the crosses, he was held up again for the Boys' Sign was out.

The Wren's Nest was a yellow-washed house built long and low and thatched deeply against the mountain weather. It stood at the meeting of five roads and was the only public house for miles around. A cripple man and his mother kept it, and between the Boys on the Run who sheltered with them at night and the British soldiers who searched the place for them by day, their lives were kept on a perpetual rack.

Foley greeted Popsy the Weasel, this was the cripple's name, who was sitting behind the high counter bar where the light darkly met the dark bottles, all set within the reach of his long arms. His arms stretched and reached like a spider's dark limbs as he served the drinks and washed glasses without moving from his stool because his legs were withered, no bigger than those of a child of five. His little feet were twisted round the legs of his stool while his big body and pale face leaned about in the darkness, and he talked with nervous affability to everyone, and pinched the quantity of drink he served whenever he thought he could.

'Good-morning, Popsy.'

'Oh, what a beautiful morning, isn't it, Mr. O'Neill? What will you drink, Mr. O'Neill? Or is it too early for you, Mr. O'Neill?'

'A Guinness, Popsy.' Foley chucked his head towards the door that led from the public house to a little dark private room. 'I'll bring it in there, boy.' They would be waiting for him in there, he knew, though what they wanted from him to-day he did not know. Transport for someone in his car, he supposed . . . it was always that, when it wasn't money or a bed for the night. Indeed they might not want him at all, but the sign was out for someone.

He walked into the room with the friendly kind of swagger he

385

affected towards the boys because he knew they mistrusted him. Not that they had any cause to do so, his trade in horses was reason real enough for his association with the English soldiery and their like in the country. He had to live. He had never refused bed, food or shelter to a lad on the run, though God knew how he hated the whole business. All he wanted was to be left in peace to make a bit of money out of his horses. But on all sides he was beset, lying to one, lying to the other, held fast by old oaths to Ireland and the boys; by inclination, association and livelihood easy with their enemies.

Three tired grave young men were sitting in the little dark hole of a room behind the public bar. They sat round, two of them on the stiff little couch and one on a straight-backed chair rather as if they were at a tea party, they hardly looked as though they had been out in the mountains all nights, but their eyes were tired and sly and fierce as ill-used dogs. They were all three wearing their belted mackintosh coats, because they were hunted men, at any moment ready to run, always on the watch for their lives. Three or four or five of them up here in the mountains and a regiment of soldiers in the garrison town below, yet they have no cunning to put against these three or four or five.

'Hallo, Tim. Hallo, Matty. Hallo,——' he stopped at the third name. Bold, dark, and tough, he was slouching across the end of the table and looking up towards Foley though his head was bent.

'Captain Cussens—Mr. O'Neill.' One of the other boys effected an introduction with the formality of a rectory garden party.

Foley shook hands with Denny the Killer, so this was him, the brains and the daring behind many an ambush. When Denny was around there was trouble, dirty trouble for all. He was not sent from headquarters for nothing. Where he was

things moved along. He could frighten the guts out of the lonely
country people, and at the same time light anew in them the
burning flame for Ireland. He used men and women and sent
them to their deaths, and slept all night and the night after
it too. His own bravery and cunning and ruthlessness were so
great that he required and got a higher measure of the three from
others.

'Take a drink, boys?' Foley invited them all politely, and they
all shook their heads. Foley sat down with a great show of ease.
His mind was cursing and fumbling, wondering what the gunman was doing down here. What he and the boys wanted of
him, for they were not surprised to see him come in. They had
known he was around all right. It was for him the sign had been
out. Still they did not speak to him. Foley got angry.

'Anything I can do for you? I was on my way to get a nurse.
Someone met with an accident at my place this morning.'

'We'll not keep you long,' Killer Denny spoke. 'All we want
from you, now see, is a little information. You're the man that
can tell us what we want to know, now see, you're the only
bloody man.'

Foley sat dark and silent on his chair. He seemed strangely of
the other side, too much and too little a gentleman in his smart
clothes, the breath and the smell of Grania close about him still,
in this dark old cold little room with these three quiet toughs.

'What do you want to know?'

'Oh, you mightn't have the information to-day, or to-
morrow even, or the next day, but we'll depend on you getting
it, now see, before the end of next week shall we say?'

'What's this you want to know? Maybe it's not the right
Bureau of Information you're at, at all.'

'Well, if I had any doubts, Boy, they were settled after the
kissing and fondling I seen this morning on the mountain side.'

Foley stood up.

'Mind your own bloody business,' he said. He stood over the other.

'Easy, now, easy.' They were all smiling. 'We've all got guns now see, and what have you but your nice gentlemanly feelings? And you wouldn't expect chaps the like of us to understand them, would you, eh, would you, Boy? Now take it easy. Sit down. Sit down.'

Foley sat down. What else could he do. Guns or no guns they were three to one. They could beat him up here and now and lead him off to a lonely little execution in the mountains any time they liked. He knew enough and too much about all three of them and their whereabouts and secret hiding places for them to chance letting him go free as their enemy. Only as their comrade and agent would he go free of them. He sat down, their hostile faces closed in on him in the stuffy room, dangerous, hunted young faces. Killer Denny's was insolent and darkly vain. His hat sloughed jauntily over his eyes, his jaw was shaved navy blue, even in the mountains he managed a shave. His neck was strong as a young bull above his collar. The other two were weaker, commoner types. Matty had bright intelligent eyes, a long ugly nose, thin ascetic mouth and a sharp chin. Tim was pale and delicate looking, he had a restless cough and a poisoned finger, and a martyr's obstinate fatality looked out of his eyes. He had left a good job in the Post Office for this hell for Ireland game, the agony and discomforts of it came cruelly hard on him, and he would have been the first of the lot of them to put a shot into Foley, for he was a nervous, tortured, rabid little patriot.

'Well, let's get the thing straight now,' Killer Denny spoke at the heavy end of a pause. His pause, of his making, and his voice was changed to that of an officer giving his orders. 'We need information as to the comings and goings of certain British officers who visit regularly at Aragon house, and from your familiarity with the Fox family, O'Neill, you should be able to

388

tell us all we want to know about their movements.'

So that was it. He was to do the spy for their work. This was to be his cursed punishment for all he had done with Grania. He had always known that such wickedness (and with a Protestant, too) would only bring its own punishment. Here he was now, trapped and tied and circled by his own ill-doing. 'Your familiarity with the Fox family,' the threat and sneer had been patent in this politer phrase. They must know he could get what they wanted. Foley's heart knocked disgustedly against his ribs, sick for his powerlessness.

The little room that saw no sun was sticky with their breath and the smell of tired unwashed bodies. The fight for Ireland was planned and won in many such sordid sad corners of the country. Tired men afraid of one another laid plans against overwhelming odds; dirty ambushes and cowardly assassinations they were called by the British officers who persistently refused to conduct themselves as though they were at war and in an enemy's country. They must have their game of tennis, their day's shooting, their hunting too, though at every turn of the road death might be waiting. It made cruelly hard situations for those natives of the countryside who were in any position to give information of their comings and goings between barracks and country houses. In those extraordinary days there was every chance of bloodshed after tea and tennis with strawberries and cream. Gramophone dances started at four o'clock in the afternoon and lasted, grim tests of endurance, until the next day, for to travel the roads at night, where bridges might be blown to bits and stars look upwards from the black water below, or barricaded roads gave masked adventurers their opportunity, seemed (even to a young and hot-blooded British soldier) a slightly foolish undertaking.

Foley knew all this, knew to a nicety his probable use to Killer Denny. He could not dramatise whatever murder was to be done here and to the doing of which he was to be instrumental, into an act of war for Ireland. It was no more than a job, a mean dirty job, and the Killer would see it got done too. He came to a place for one reason and one reason only, for a killing.

'I see all right. I understand what you want.' Foley spoke with heavy indecision. Keep them guessing was his idea, keep their faith in him somehow and he might scramble through yet. 'I can't promise I'll be all that use to you though I might be able.'

'Oh, you're able right enough, the only manjack of us that is able.' Again the jocose sneer from the Killer and sour smiles of disapproval from the other two sick ascetic boys. Yes, they had all seen too much. He had no defence on that side.

'Who do you want news of particularly?'

A dark look ran between the three. He saw from it that they trusted him so little that they would not give him the names of the wanted. It was not to be in his power to give any warning. The meanest class of spy work, that was all he was good for and his own side could not even trust him the full length in that. God curse him they were right, rat and louse and ill-living fool that he was. A wave of revulsion towards himself was followed by a fury of sudden anger against the three of them. A voice that delighted and set free some hot and glorious thing in Foley was speaking for him. He did not know, cute and tough and calculating as he was, where it found the guts to betray him.

'God blast you and your dirty work,' it was saying. 'Take me out in the heather now and shoot me as you're well able. I'll not play the bloody spy for you. I've given help and shelter and put myself in danger time and again for you boys when you came to me quenched with fear and cold, and I'll do it again any night. But I'll be no go-between to bring chaps to their bloody deaths, chaps that come to my house and buy my horses, decent poor fools of boys whichever side they fight on. Get on with it

390

yourselves for blast the word you'll get from me.'

'Shut that.' The Killer had his gun on him. Foley put his hands on the table, leaning forward, white-faced, helpless in their hands, three men with guns who sat and sneered at him. It was then that they heard the cripple Popsy the Weasel's shrill voice rising high in the other room.

'No, sir, Mr. O'Neill's not here, sir. Yes, it's his car all right, indeed, but he's gone up the mountain now not ten minutes ago, up to the little farm above to see a poor man's sick ram.'

And the voice that answered was the clipped educated voice of one of the soldiers Foley knew— Captain Purvis.

'Oh, well, he'll be back soon I suppose. We'll wait. What about a bottle of beer, Tony?'

'Bit early for one, old chap. Got such a thing as a drop of milk for this little dog? Little devil, she's been underground for two days. We had her up here badger digging on Sunday morning . . .'

Patsy went softly to the door, opened it a narrow slit and peered through. He turned round from it with blazing eyes.

'He's there,' he whispered.

'Bit of luck O'Neill should be about,' the voice outside went on, 'We'll get the doctor to look at that bite, Judy-girl. Here's her milk. Thank you. Doesn't want it. Never were one for milk, were you.'

They were squatting on the ground like two little boys trying to persuade the tired terrier to lap milk when Denny and his boys walked in on them. They had their backs to the boys as they coaxed their dog in a patch of sunlight that came through the open door from the hot sweet May morning outside.

Foley heard the scuffle of their capture. The two boys had sprung on them from behind while Denny covered them with his revolver from the doorway. Someone had kicked or trodden on the terrier, a piercing yelp of pain and then a moment's silence before the cripple's high agonised voice screamed out, 'Don't do it here, boys! Don't do it here! God blast it, I'll never get the place clean. For God's sake spare the cripple and take them outside!'

In the dreadful little anti-chamber to death Foley sat staring through the open door. He could not see the group, the bar was the other end of the room, the door on to the road beside it. Fools, he was thinking, poor bloody fools, up in these mountains, unarmed probably, to look for a dog they lost badger digging. Yet looking for the dog was the only part of it he could understand, if it was a good dog. Ah, she must have been good to stay down with a badger two days. He had heard Michael Purvis had a good terrier, how had he heard it. He knew now, his accurate unwavering memory set a finger on the knowledge, Grania had told him when she told him about Purvis and Sylvia. That was why they had chosen him to spy on the comings and goings to Aragon. It was Purvis they wanted, and now they had got him without any help from Foley. They had got him, and some other poor chap would have to die with him. It was too dangerous to let a live man go. It was their lives or his life. That was fair. That was only fair. Oh, God help them, Foley was thinking, but he knew they were past helping now.

Denny the Killer came back into the room and closed the door.

'O'Neill,' he said, 'we've got the chap we want and without any help from you. Now see, you'll drive us up to Mooncoin caves. We want to get a bit of information from them and that's a quiet place.'

'I'd as soon they didn't recognise me,' Foley said. He was thinking how he had planned to sell the Knight of Aragon horse to Michael Purvis, and of the roan cob he had bought from him and of that afternoon he had come over to try him at Mountain Brig. He knew well enough there lay no danger for him in their

392

escape. There was no escape for them. Denny understood this. He had grown very quiet since his easily won capture. The tough bullying side was subdued. He seemed only gentle and intent.

'Right, boy. They're blindfold,' he said. 'Take us up to the caves and that's all we want from you for the present, now see.' All the time he was talking so quietly, he had Foley covered with his gun. He signed him to come out through the door and Foley obeyed. He could do nothing for the two soldiers. What part of a chance had they, and what part of a chance had he if he informed? It might not be to-morrow, it might not be next week or next month, but the boys would come for him and get him all right.

The two young prisoners were standing up against the dark fireplace. Their eyes were bandaged and they held their hands behind them. This attitude gave them a curious nonchalant look as if they were just waiting about for their drinks. Their pale tweed coats and flannel trousers, their soft well-cut shirt collars, the scent of their hair oil, all these things were so widely at variance from their immediate killing, it was not possible to grasp that they would in such a little space of time be dead.

'Outside, boys,' Denny spoke and the other two guided the prisoners towards the door which they had shut and locked. As they went down the room the little terrier jumped up on Purvis. He turned his head in the direction of nobody, because he could not see, and said, as he supposed, to the cripple:

'Would you be a good fellow, look after the little dog for me, and if you let Miss Fox of Aragon know that you found her straying up here, she'll give you a reward.' He turned his head again, 'If that would be all right by you,' he spoke politely to his captors.

Before Denny could answer the cripple was shrilling from his chair:

393

'Let yous take the bitch. Take her with yous and stone her and give her the lough. You'll have the damn' soldiers on me, God help me, with your fashionable bred dogs.'

A look of awful despair broke across Purvis's bandaged face. 'I see,' he said, quite patiently. 'Well, perhaps she could come with us? I'd be very grateful if one of you chaps could shoot her for me. I hate drowning dogs, don't you?'

'Oh, I wouldn't drown a dog,' said one.

'I couldn't shoot a dog,' said another.

'I wouldn't harm a little dog for any money,' said Denny the Killer.

'Take her away, take her out of this!' screamed the cripple.

It was quite a situation. Foley forgot they were not to hear his voice.

'I'll take her,' he said. 'I'll see she's all right. I will really. She's a lovely little thing.'

'She's as brave as a lion,' the other boy said. He was trembling. 'Could we have a drink?' he said, 'How many of us are there? I'll stand a round.' He put a pound note on the counter. 'Keep the change,' he said to the cripple, 'that's all right.'

The cripple took the note and stuffed it away. He served six exact double Irish whiskys. One of the boys put the glasses into the prisoners' hands. Not one of them touched the drinks on the counter. Popsy the Weasel eyed them, greedily planning to bottle them again—four double whiskys—as soon as the party here left for the execution.

'Well, outside, boys,' Denny said again. Matty unlocked the door and the sun flooded in hot and yellow, smelling of gorse. The prisoners held out their empty glasses, and the cripple reached out his long arms for them eagerly, afraid that they might be dropped and broken, and he hated to lose a glass.

Denny looked up the road and down. It was empty and full of sunshine. He signed the rest to come out. Denny said loudly to the cripple, 'When Mr. O'Neill comes back tell him he'll have to walk it home.'

Foley felt grateful for this misleading piece of nonsense as he started the car. Tim sat beside him with his gun across his knee. The other two guarded the prisoners who were squeezed up like children on the floor in the back, the little terrier between them.

'Drive on,' the Killer said.

XVI

Sylvia was ready for her tennis party. She was beautifully dressed in a white pleated crêpe de chine skirt, and long white alpaca wool jersey with a tasselled belt at the waist and a neat V neck, out of which her round throat rose as pretty as a bird's and circled by her row of river pearls. Her fair hair was neatly waved and tucked into a small gleaming bun at the back, not one hair ever got out of place in the most strenuous games, unlike Grania's yellow feathers that flew more wildly at every ball she missed. She wore white silk stockings and white buckskin shoes, whiter and softer and sounder looking than new tennis balls even. Her well-made little body swelled and retreated at precisely the right places inside her clothes. Strong, and poised and determined she looked and as rooted and suited to the life she led as young flag leaves are to a river bank. She looked truly set and exactly meant for marriage with the most eligible young soldier possible (just such a one as Michael Purvis), one who in due course would fall heir to a nice estate, most probably in Norfolk, and even his mother would be able to find no fault in Sylvia Fox of Aragon.

Aragon was at the supreme height of its beauty this late April afternoon. The house was like an elegant woman sitting quietly in front of her mirror, restful and still in her perfection, for Aragon was a very female house both within and without and wore the more exquisite moments of the year with a wonderful grandeur and quietness. About her cherry trees there was nothing girlish or fluffy. Their groups were frozen out against the dark of other trees, on the hill behind the house, and down the fall to the river below. Flowers and shrubs and flowering trees were all a little apart from the house. They did not flounce and jostle against the austere walls. Shallow gracious heights and wide sunny spaces of grass were empty between the sheltered groups of azaleas and camellias, magnolias, rhododendrons, and thickets of slight bamboo enclosing a light blue fog in their narrow straight pillars. Camellias, white and red, flowered freely, their foreign expensive faces looked as if they had been cut out of leather and painted and put smartly together and placed in position in the healthy gleam of their leaves. But the magnolias narrowing purple and white cups held all the secret dignity and resolve of flowers that come to perfection on hard twisted wood. Never in all their history had magnolia flowers been placed in a posy with lace paper and ribbon round. They are too wildly uncomplacent. Funeral wreaths have not seen magnolia either, for its death is too quick for deaths delayings. Great lilac bushes were softer than cats and the cut sallow leaves of golden oaks sharper than paper crowns. Red rhododendrons reared their ways, striving like horses up the hill. Azaleas, low as sheep in comparison, went in honey-blond flocks downwards to the back of the house. In the strong sunlight the garden gave nothing of what it was. It only waited, falsely gay, protecting itself, holding back its strength till the evening time, its flowing hours.

It was three o'clock, the brightest most nothing-like hour of afternoon. Sylvia was in the hall taking new tennis balls out of their box, and their separate dressings of tissue paper. The bright purple writing looked very smart on their whiteness. They smelt of rubber and clean unplayed games. The hall was so gloomy cool that the great jars of lilac smelt only of lilac in the rain, all richness frozen and quelled from its scent. The leaves of the lilac drooped a little exhausted, although the branches had only just been gathered and put in water, because in these days people were not so knowing and sophisticated about their flower decorations as they are now. They liked lots of nice greenery and thought gypsophila and asparagus fern went very prettily with sweet peas, and maidenhair fern with carnations and everything looked its best in a silver vase or, failing that, a tall thin green glass which, like a long green throat, swallowed the length of stems and posed the flower heads neatly where they should be.

Sylvia was happily of her age and time. Competent, not wild. Pretty in the right and accepted way. Nothing embarrassingly clever about her. Everything she had was buttoned up and put away in little boxes. She was strong. Two of her girl friends arrived. They came on bicycles and leant their bicycles against the pillars of the portico and came into the cool hall with their rackets in their hands.

'Hallo, Sylvia.'

'Hallo, Cecily, Hallo, Violet.'

'Hallo, Sylvia.'

'Lovely new balls.'

'Who's coming?'

'Tony, Michael, Major Radley, John Wade, I think.'

'How nice.'

'What fun.'

'I like your new blouse, Violet.'

'I did all that faggot stitch myself.'

'I hope there's coffee cake for tea.'

'Yes, there is, greedy pig.'

'Are they going to stay late?'

'Shall we dance?'

'We might. There's lots of cold food for supper.'

'I want to play "Whispering." '

'The gramophone's outside.'

' "Whispering while you cuddle near me', oh, it's so lovely." '

' 'Whispering so no one near can hear me." ' They sang, wandering out of the house in their white shoes and stockings, carrying rackets and tennis balls to the smooth sunny grass where white painted seats were set in the wide fern-like shade of a cedar tree. There they waited for their men to arrive, pulling at their clothes and preening their hair like hen birds picking down the lengths of a breast-feather, answering each other absently, their minds put forward to the gay challenge of the hours to come.

Presently Grania came out and joined them. She was not fond of Sylvia's two girl friends. They played tennis too well and spoke to her almost kindly, but now she felt so grand and whole compared to them, half-living on kisses and glances and little no's that she was able to compete with them.

'How late your men are,' she said, beginning with a wholesome broadside. She threw herself down on a rug, feeling the short grass with her hands.

'Just as well, dear,' Sylvia said. 'It will give you time to tuck your shirt inside your skirt, and even put on a pair of stockings without a hole in them. If you hurry.'

'Oh, I can't really go to all that bother for a few men.' Grania lay closer to the ground. 'Though I admire you girls a lot for the trouble you take about yourselves.'

'How are your other backhand shots getting on?' one of the friends asked.

'Oh, not bad at all.'

'Don't underrate yourself, dear, you broke the drawing-room window so cleverly yesterday—one of your best strokes.'

Grania giggled. Sylvia couldn't upset her. Generally she felt
hot and ashamed when they tormented her about her tennis.
Really she felt quite earnest and embarrassed at her shocking
inaptitude for the game but to-day she didn't mind how many
smart young soldiers treated her with silent contempt and
indulgence as she panted and flew about the courts, trying and
failing, a bundle of nervous stupidity, so different from the
serious capable serenity of Sylvia and her friends upon the courts.
Laziness was behind Grania's failure to play tennis. The same
laziness that left her clothes in holes and her hair unbrushed and
her mind in a wild chaos with only the most immediate question
uppermost. She could never sort herself out. She would never
know herself to a turn. She would grow older confusedly and
accomplishing little. But all through her life there would be
spread flat places of unbelievable calm where her idle mind could
laze unreproached by any better self and her body could indulge
itself without cruel recrimination from a soured and defeated
sense of the supposed right. She had the exact reverse of her
sister's nature in working or playing. There was no nicety about
her or skill, only eagerness and strange aptitudes which she
hardly or never followed through to any conclusion. And for
that very reason her aptitudes would keep their charm and
novelty for her. They would never be worn smooth by too
much attainment. Always, as now, she would feel elated if she
answered back to Sylvia, because she would never own so quick
a wit that its speed or flexibility could fail to surprise herself.

Now they might say what they liked to her, Sylvia and the
girls. Her shot was spent, but it had got home, she could ignore
them contented. She parted Soo's black hair for fleas, but found
not one. The hairs closed over again into a dog's coat with the
sunlight on it like a polished shell. Soo was lying in her mouse
shape, humped behind and head low between her forelegs.

The girls played the gramophone. It was totally wrong out

400

there with its silly little drift of music. But they fastened their girlish emotions to the tune. Ten minutes more passed by. Twenty minutes.

Grania raised her head from her arms to say:

'Why don't you have a girlish rally, dears. Your boys seem to have forgotten you, don't they.' She had given herself time to prepare this one.

The girls laughed nervously. The idea of being the forgotten ones is so lessening. So cruelly depriving of confidence. They could not even answer back to Baby Grania. Sylvia said, 'Well, perhaps you're right. We'll each give you a lesson. That ought to take our minds off anything else, oughtn't it.'

Grania said, 'No, I'm far too tired to be scolded and made run about.'

'Tired? What have you been doing. What do you ever do?'

'Well, I rode a school this morning, that's more than any of you can say.'

'How very interesting. What horse did you ride. And whose? And where?'

Grania knew she had been a fool to say so much. It was pure boasting. An effort to put these tennis players in their places. But if she had been foolish she was not going to be silly enough to lie about it now.

'A young horse of Foley O'Neill's,' she said grandly. It always sounded better to say 'a young horse' or 'a four-year-old' at the oldest.

'Really. Since when have you been getting out of your cosy bed to ride Foley's horses.'

'Since to-day, actually.'

'Fancy, and is he a jolly companion in the early morning? "Steady yourself, Miss Grania." "Hit her a good one now." '

Sylvia's imitation of Foley's voice was mercilessly right. It placed him accurately where, till so short a time ago, he had

belonged in Grania's estimation too. But now it filled her with a
flame of pure defensive rage that swept all sense of proportion
out of reach in her loving angry heart. She sat up, her cheeks
crimson, tears almost in her eyes.

'Oh, yes, it's all very well for you to laugh at any one in that
beastly way. The laugh's the other way when he rides rings
round any of your soldier-boys. He makes them look a pretty
silly lot of row-the-boats coming up the straight, doesn't he?
Well, doesn't he?'

Sylvia looked at her with live curiosity. What was this?
There was something here to look into.

'Yes, he's a very beautiful jockey,' she said, 'and a wonderful
man to show a horse. Better than any one I know.'

Grania's eyes subdued themselves. The crimson in her cheeks
died. But she still trembled a little. This admission from Sylvia
showed her that she had let Sylvia guess too much. Sylvia was
such a one for keeping things quiet. She would have to cover
Grania before the girls. But afterwards. . . .

'Well, what about it? Shall we have a ladies' four?'

Till tea-time they played their uninterrupted ladies' four.
Their white legs flying about the bright court. The new balls
thudding high and with lovely precision in the sunshine. Lonely
girls voices called the scores and commended each other's play.
'Too good.' 'O, Sylvia!' 'Can you?' 'O, good *shot*.' 'Played,
partner.' They gave as religious atttention to their game as
though their men were present to admire them. Even Grania,
excited and upset and hitting only one ball in five that came her
way, could not turn their holy practice of lawn tennis into an
irreligious game.

402

XVII

Tea-time. Dozens of little iced coffee cakes and cucumber sandwiches with gentlemen's relish. Hot cakes and a confection rich
with fruit and wine and age, china tea and many many blue cups
that had been set out early for the lost party. This tea was served
in the green spaces of the drawing-room. The tide in the river
was full, and a boat with sails came up on it. This boat provided
a nice subject for comment and speculation. They had to keep
talking, each to show the other that she cared nothing for
the society of men. Only Mrs. Fox wondered, alone and shame-
lessly, why her party had been forgotten.

'It's very odd, isn't it, Sylvia? Tony and Michael are so keen
on a game of tennis.'

'And Major Radley adores playing bridge with you, Mum.'

'I wonder what's happened?'

'Oh, we'd have heard if anything had happened, really.'

'Yes, of course we would.'

'Bound to.' One of the girls bit an iced cake in half. The
other asked for more tea. Everyone was bent on showing everyone else that things were just as they should be.

The tide flooded smoothly up the river, milk green as honeysuckle leaves. But the young leaves in the afternoon spring light
turned the old water to grey. It was a grey light reflected back
and up into the windows of the drawing-room and made the

girls' faces look paler than water-weeds, alas for all their jolly disregard of sad possibility.

Frazer came in. He was only faintly disordered and moved when he said:

'Captain Michael Purvis and Mr. Tony Craye are reported missing since this morning, madam. The soldiers are out in parties searching in the mountains for them.'

Sylvia was very white. She said:

'What did you hear exactly, Frazer?'

'I heard they went up after a dog they lost badger digging on Sunday, Miss, and the Fenians got them up there, poor young gentlemen.'

'Oh, the poor children,' Mrs. Fox cried out softly. She would soon be in tears, consoling herself. Sylvia and Frazer's eyes met and her voice came to him in a wintry whisper:

'Anything else, Frazer?'

'I heard no more at the Post Office, Miss, but I was thinking of cycling into town to find out if there was any news.'

'Yes, please go, Frazer, please go.'

He was back in an hour's time. There was a look of such triumph about him that their hearts leaped in anticipation of his news.

'They haven't got the poor young gentlemen,' he said, 'but they have arrested Mister Foley O'Neill.'

XVIII

Nan was sitting sewing in her kingdom, the nursery, that bright afternoon. She had sent her poor baby, Miss Pidgie, out for a walk. The sun poured in on the grey behind of the rocking-horse. From this big window there was no watery intimacy with the river, as there was from the drawing-room windows. The nursery windows were not formed to curve voluptuously towards the swelling or retreating tides, they did not drink in the river light and breath, but flatly sprucely curtained they looked demurely out upon the river below, and some hedged fields, and hills, and airy blue of mountains beyond.

Nan had a pile of linen to mend beside her, fine soft linen that was a pride and delight to her mind and to her hands; Fox linen, Aragon linen, linen that had been in the house, some of it, for generations, cool and gentle with age and darned and patched with an exquisite patience and skill worthy of its luxurious frailty. Nan revelled in the smooth coldness of the sheets, their less than knife-thick hems, the pillow-cases as fine as handker-chiefs, and the old face towels woven soft and with little fringes to finish their ends. The new house linen, of which she had Mrs. Fox buy a supply every year, was always of the finest to be got and Nan would mark and number it in tiny clear sampler let-tering sewn in special red thread that would never run in the washing or fade from its colour. She was very careful of this thread and had a supply of the spools put by, for, like so many other things, she maintained you could not get it now. A friend used to send it to her from Paris and the friend was dead or the shop was shut, or something had happened to add immeasurably to the value of the red thread which marked the linen at Aragon.

Nan felt very calm and powerful as her needle went in and out making a tiny ticking sound in the darn as small as sixpence which she was putting into a towel. On her finger was a large gold thimble which Sylvia and Grania had given her once, it looked older and paler than it was from constant use. Nothing had such an easy look as a well-used thimble on a clever hand. Nan's beautiful grey hair curled crisp and healthy on her strong brown neck bent over the sewing. Her white collar went round it as crisp as a petal and narrow white cuffs were sewn to the wrists of her grey dress. Her apron was so white your eyes blinked once before they found rest in the contrasts of its curvings and shadows.

The top sash of one high window was open and Miss Pigeon's tea was laid neatly at one end of the square centre table. The air that was more of summer than the present spring flowed gently into the room and Nan's thoughts were running and rippling pleasantly about her as she worked. . . .

These towels have worn well; yes, glancing at the date she had worked in the corner, of course, that was the year she had been in Dublin at Horseshow time, the year Foley had won the Championship of the Show. How elated and easy she had felt. Nothing but the best was good enough to buy for Aragon, the better than best. The hours she had spent, thumb to the corners of choice samples of linen, and at last the shopman, appreciative of and indulgent to a connoisseur, had agreed with her on a special weaving. Yes, this linen marked the sort of ecstasy of success she had reached that year, with Foley winning the Championship and Sylvia's first grown-up Horse Show too.

And such a success the child had. Nan had not expected it. Miss Sylvia looked a Fox and a lady. That was the best she had ever thought of the child, but something had been added to the Fox and the lady. The little body carried clothes with a distinction that you could not miss. The girlish white dance frock took on a *chic* false simplicity as if worn by a successful beauty of thirty. And why? Nan smiled secretly, knowing why. The small whys. The neat posy unpicked from its meaningless perch on the shoulder of the white taffeta gown and pinned decisively between the breasts. Nan had a great appreciation for such small gestures to the male. 'Bold and cold and pity help the boys.' Nan with a white apron over her navy blue skirt and elaborate blouse thought with satisfaction of Sylvia as she bustled about the hotel bedroom tidying up such few things as Sylvia had left out of their proper places when she went out to dine and dance. The blue habit to be brushed and pressed for the next day, and the child would look a little queen when she rode Foley's horse in the ladies' class. Nan gloried to think of it. She held the small firmness of a pair of rolled stockings tight in her hand and paused to think of it; of herself leaning on the rail by the ringside, silent, missing no detail, drinking every detail of the scene with strong effortless perception of the moment. So certain of her cast-iron memory that she used not consciously to memorise anything. Afterwards she would know without a thought which of the ladies had a hair astray. A tie badly tied, a spur unpolished, she wasted not a thought on the horses. They were not her province. Not even Foley's horse, except that Foley owned him and Sylvia rode him. But the riders would not escape her tongue unscathed. Hers was the present mind that sees and acts and grasps the moment, ever conscious, unknowing the power and the glory of its strength. . . .

The cunning way a stranger from the Heythrop country did her hair. 'A couple of clips in front of the ears, Miss Sylvia and the bun a roll, not a plaster.' Poor old Lady Alice Montgomery had a new patch on the seat of her breeches this year. A coloured tie looks very common no matter who wears it, but a veil with a small spot is always nice. Oh, but such a look as she gave the judge, oh, the *look* if ever I saw it, watch for trouble there. She's a light little piece and her family were all the same. And she would watch Sylvia passionately as the horses galloped round her, leaning forward to be more with her, revelling in the set of the small straight shoulders, the skill that went with so little strength. Nan's own eyes were to her as the eyes of many, and as she watched she fed on the praise that must be given, given to Sylvia and to Foley and to Aragon—all to the glory of Aragon.

Now she was sewing quietly and intently and her mind had gone back to that evening in a Dublin hotel when she had folded away Sylvia's clothes and thought about the to-morrow which was long since past but as clear to her as her own plans for this evening and the next day. All her life was as clear to her as if she opened an atlas and looked at a map. It would be a map of Aragon with the blood of her life and the strength of her mind and her body marked on it in strong visible ways.

The bright rich surfaces of the furniture. How many slave girls had she driven to the polishing? The exquisite store of linen, the children's straight backs, Miss Pigeon's subjection, the nut walk, the late peaches, the breed of fighting Bantam cocks, the wide and easy curve of turf steps up the pleasure ground—the slightest glance towards the time past showed these few of the many marks that Nan had left on Aragon. But none, only Nan, would ever know the secrets that Aragon had left with her. The marks and wounds of grief and rapture and of bitter failure. The calm of patience that can build over again.

The dark storm of her youth; now she could look back to it as a whole thing, a separate piece of her life, not the only stuff of life itself. Because of the grief and rapture of her failing her power over Aragon and her love for it had grown. Power must grow with secrecy. Power is force controlled, and there is no control like silence. To have kept silence half a life-time is to be strong.

XIX

Since Nan was a child Aragon had been the dream in her life. The house was spoken of by Nan's mother hushedly, secretly. Tales of Aragon were never told before Nan's father, but when the child and her mother were alone they would pour between them. Nan's mother had been in service at Aragon before she married and it was hard to tell whether it was as hell or as heaven that she looked towards the house. Her life had been somewhere between hell and heaven, a glorious and dramatic purgatory, before she had married one of the keepers and settled in the lonely house where Nan was born, where the river got small, and the woodlands scarce, and the mountain heather began.

Nan's mother was a stupid loquacious slattern with blackberry coloured eyes and honey-coloured hair. There she would sit and talk by the hour, her stories always changing a bit more towards the remarkable. Looking out of the door towards the mountains, tears would start in her purple eyes as a new torture inflicted on her in the past by Ann Daly, the head housemaid, was composed and related. With the torture went the splendour of such a life. Compliments and presents from lovely ladies of title. Accounts of their ravishing ball gowns, their tiny feet, their propped white breasts, where diamond pendants hung in mists of tulle and roses.

'Ah, I was a whack hand to lay them out on the beds. Ah, not every young girl would have the taste for such a thing. The way I'd lay the dress on the white counterpane, a pinch in at the waist, and spread wide the skirt, you'd say a ghost lady was being dressed, for I had a knack of enticement with them, indeed, under a red silk canopy, perhaps, and all the branch wax candles burning on the dressing-table, and a coal fire up the chimney, and curtains drawn full against the river fog.'

The full-drawn curtains, the crimson carpets and canopies, the many, many oil lamps and wax candles (it was one servant's entire work to tend them, one of the untold number that served the great house). Nan's mother would tell about them all, and their work for the upper servants, everyone of whom seemed to have a couple of satellites, and Nan's mother had been slave to the upper housemaid.

'Because I was so neat, see now, and pretty and fit to be about the ladies. "Where's Goldilocks?" Mrs. Fox would say, imagine. Old Ann Daly would take the strap to me if I pulled a curl out under my cap, ah, she knew right enough. I'm telling you, Dymphnia, hide your looks, child, hide your beauty from the gentry. It's a snap-trap on your own leg, now look, pet, for it's more than the mistress will see it.'

There were noddings and whisperings and tales of childbeds in far corners of the big house, and pale heavy-breasted girls dragging themselves again about their work. Ah, Ann Daly was a whack-hand at any business like that, and the river is handy for any little things that you wouldn't want to be keeping. 'Dead, dear, she'd say, and aren't you lucky? Another cat for the river, she'd say, and she'd laugh, she'd glory in it,'twas like a medicine to her. . . . The young gentlemen were very great with Ann. She had a bedpost filled with pieces of gold they gave her, and one way and another she served them well. She was a great one for boiling roots and seeds at the right turn of the moon and a terrible effect they took if a girl went to her in time with her trouble. . . .

411

'Master Hubert was her pet, Master Hubert was a bold unruly boy. God help me, he was . . . Oh, child, mind yourself now on a November evening when the lamps be scarce on the long passages. No delay, Dymphnia, but to get about your work and down to the company in the servants' hall, and a good plate of beef and the men roaring songs and the cook cursing and the tallow candles and the lamps burning. Light, child, light's the thing. You wouldn't know where you'd be in the dark indeed. You wouldn't rightly know what you'd be doing, God forgive you. . . . "Child" Master Hubert called me always for he never could remember my name. . . .

'Ah, Dymphnia, what a man he was, so proud and so kind, Ah, child, never do what I did. Never get yourself caught like that. You'll never know peace after. Your father is a kind man and a good man, but I knew too much before I married him, twice too much to be happy after. You're the only child I have, Dymphnia, and I'm proud you are, and proud you should be of your breeding, and ever good to your poor mother for you cost her a lot. Ah, well, my sports was finished when I came to live up here on the heather with the lonely grouse. Ah, but Master Hubert did it all for the best when he made the match for me with your Dada. He thought too much of me to give me over to Ann Daly, a sight too much indeed.'

Such thinly-veiled tales of her aristocratic parenthood were the bedtime stories of Nan's girlhood, for her mother was an unquenchable gossip and neither the grouse on the mountain nor Nan's stepfather were specially good audiences for the passions and tumults of her past in the grand house. She had not seen it for years, because John Briscoe the keeper, although not too proud to put shoes once on a gentleman's pleasure (and indeed it had been made worth his while), was strict to a degree with that whining weak-minded beauty to whose daughter he had given his name. In the fourteen years of her married life she

412

had never been down to the village four miles distant. When she died of a belated stillborn child he knew for a certainty that it was his own.

Strange enough he loved Nan, and the gentry side of her made her take to him for he had the lonely free aristocracy of outlook that comes from living hard on mountains and rivers, with dogs for company and fish and birds to care. He loved his wife too, for she was a beautiful creature and in spite of all she might say to Nan of the poverty of married life after the splendours of her short love life, she was an amorous creature as well as beautiful and was more than contented with him.

It was her stepfather who insisted that Nan was to train as a nurse, he had the lowest opinion of domestic service with the gentry, and when her mother died, he sent the girl away as soon as might be to a hospital.

She worked hard and did excellently, discussed her ambitions with no one at all and at the age of thirty gave up a good position in a Dublin hospital, and went to Aragon as nurse to Sylvia Fox.

XX

In 1900 Nan had got to Aragon. Even now she could remember her first day breathing its air, the feel of door handles as she opened Aragon doors, the consciousness of dead Fox's stirring in her blood. She was not yet aware how Aragon would drown itself in her power and love. She was for the first year like a person on the edge of a great and only love affair. She made strong her links with the beloved, she set her feet firmly on the path she wished to follow. Nan was going to stay at Aragon. She invented little difficulties and delicacies for Sylvia, a wiry and hardy child really, discussed them with Mrs. Fox who was wildly anxious about her first baby, tried little regimens and diets and brought the child on in a remarkable way, while maintaining the theory that her constitution was far from robust.

Nan's control of Mrs. Fox had its roots in that first year too. Nothing was too much for Nan to do to help her, she nursed her carefully towards dependence. She magnified the importance of little rests and glasses of milk, she petted and flattered and never, never obtruded herself. She sewed for the child with skill and pains. All the time she stitched at the little dresses, stiff with embroidery, and awful white pelisses, her mind was gone ahead to the day when her hands would be among the Aragon linen, mending and marking and sorting and putting aside.

414

Mrs. Fox had a miscarriage that year which put her more completely into Nan's hands. Nan had brilliant technique in encouraging people to love being ill. Delicious trays of invalid food, fresh carnations daily, temperature takings and head shakings, ever so little of a serious look and then a professionally cheerful voice, washings and powderings and scentings in bed, a bow to tie the hair, blinds drawn and rests at the same moment daily, Sylvia with her hair brushed round Nan's finger brought in for long enough to amuse, not long enough to tire.

Nan was so good looking then. She had a fineness with her strength that came through her breeding. She was tall and wide in the shoulders, with narrow hips and long strong legs. Her gold brown hair showed in crisp waves under her cap. It was good coarse hair and the commonest thing about her. Everything else showed her father's quality and mother's beauty; the long eyes and rather thin mouth; the line of the jaw cutting in against the long neck; all the look of slightness and small bones in so big a woman came from Aragon. Nan knew this and gloried in it.

When Sylvia was asleep on a summer night she would sometimes leave the nursery maid in charge, saying briskly that she would take a 'breath of air' or a 'little trot.' Then on with her long blue coat with its short shoulder cape and the bonnet and veil that nurses wore then. Going from the nursery she would pass the top of the wide double staircase and standing there desire would be in her feet to run down its shallow steps past all the pictures of her ancestors and out through the hall where the scent of lilies in their pots came strained through cold space and muted light. But no, the respect for Aragon was beyond such trifling. The nurses of Aragon did not use these stairs; they were for the family. So she would go through the swing door of red baize and down the narrow wooden stairs, where so many old prints in maple frames were hung, and a black plaster nigger in a blue starred petticoat that everyone thought so hideous, stood on the landing half-way down. She would go out through a side door, where a dark sticky escalonia filled the air with its delicious gummy scent, and a shadowy white jasmine breathed of sex and swoons against such cleanly briskness. She might stand at the corner of the house and look down its length of windows and urns and balustrading. She might breathe sharply, knowing her share in a serene magnificence that was as precious as flesh to her. Because this share was not owned nor admitted, and could not be, it was stronger in her than any good thing in her life. It was danger, romance, the very stuff and part of dreams. For how could her love for Aragon ever be admitted, or her share in the Fox family ever be allowed—the vanity and reverence for her own blood were the first to deny its admission. The long arms in their blue sleeves would move outwards in a small flowing gesture. Presently her feet would move quickly away from the house. Through the park she might go, where black cattle breathed heavily, moving about in heavy groups through the lime avenue where the scent came down like a great bell upon you, a light, pale, wide bell of sensation, and back then to the house, the summer air warm as milk about it, the night darker, the river sounds nearly audible.

XXI

The year Grania was born Nan put Mrs. Fox to bed for about six months. She was not going to have a mistake about this baby. It was to be a son for Aragon. Nan knew it, told it in signs and portents, things she said and did not say, mysterious calculations and assumptions all arriving at that, the only conclusion.

Hugh Fox was anxious enough for a son to be born too. He had had a pitiful time of it in the last couple of years with his wife's delicacy and miscarrying, and further delicacy and temperaments and tears, all consequent, they told him, on her loss of the babies. He was sorry for her, but sorry with the intolerance of the strong for the sick. There is nothing to undo love like the disaster of bad health. That is perhaps what lends to some women the strength for its defeat. But Mrs. Fox enjoyed her bad health. In and out of pregnancies she had Nan to stand between her and trouble. Nan to keep strong in her a faith in her own importance, Nan's will and power and care forcing her to keep this baby.

This was the winter of Nan's great trial, the trial between Aragon, her secret life and pride, and this other glorious calamity that was upon her.

She fell in love with Hugh Fox, her master and her half-cousin, and he with her. When the river mists were thick against the window panes in November, and the curtains drawn full and nice as her mother had told, she would lock herself into the nursery with the child Sylvia, enduring such contest of flesh and spirit as leave marks past hiding—the gay rocking-horse, the scattered toys, the sleeping child, her sewing, the white gas-light, what were these to the unbearable calling between them? Sitting there, the simple shape of nursery shadows round her, everything around her clean and simple and good, she was waiting, only living, for the moment when she would go in to Mrs. Fox's room to give her her medicine and settle her for the night. He would be there perhaps or maybe not. Oh, the doubt, the torture, and the knowing that because of her strength she would always say no to him.

He was the consummation and the end of all that Aragon stood for to Nan. Pale, fine, long-handed, narrow-eyed, like all their common ancestry. A soft thick mouth, and soft thick hair, weak and demanding and enchanting, the very counterpart for her strength and generosity.

Then Nan knew how all Mrs. Fox's gentle whimpering no's put him beside himself. She ached with pain past belief to comfort and give love.

Self-respect, vanity, obstinacy—whatever it is called, there is a quality in some people that they cannot be parted from but to their great loss. Nan had this. If she had yielded to her love she would have lost her very self, and for the rest of her life have had no reason for being.

Nan would go quickly down the passages from the nursery to the room where Mrs. Fox lay in a little piece of the big double bed. It was before the time when beds got low, and this bed was like a great pale country for sickness bounded top and bottom by dark mahogany. Pink duvets lay light as clouds. Yards of rose-wreathed chintz were gathered round in a valance to hide the legs of the bed. Drifts of white pillows were heaped behind the weak little back. A fair and faintly sticky plait of hair hung down

418

over one shoulder, half-hidden in a smother of lace and ribbons, the prettiest bed-jacket of all. Everywhere in slender vases of silver and glass, pink carnations were sprayed about the room, their colour melted into the roses in the chintz. The wallpaper was white with silver stripes. The carpet *vieux rose*, and satin cushions to pick up its colour. A wood fire burnt lavishly. Scents of fresh and old lavender water and eau de cologne drifted here and there. A pekinese snuffled and slumbered in the embrace of its basket. Mrs. Fox was petulant. She had not been able to get a word out of her husband for the last half-hour. He sat in his armchair under the green-shaded table-lamp reading the same paper that he had taken up after dinner. Even the same page of the same paper. Sulking, defensive, secret, very much on his dignity if she spoke to him. His face pale and those full eyelids and black lashes low, his mouth set and not amiable. Very still, very dark in his black evening clothes, full of nervous restraint, answering, 'Yes, my dear,' 'No, my dear,' if she spoke, as though his mouth would never form her name, or not willingly. She was delighted to see Nan when she came in. It woke the room up, made a break, charged the air with life in some way. He got up and came over to the bed when Nan was shaking the pillows.

'Good-night, I suppose,' he said. There was life in his voice. He bent over her and kissed the top of her head.

'Won't you come back.'

'I've got some letters to write. You'd better go to sleep. Hadn't she, Nan?'

'Just as she likes,' Nan said, she would not help him to keep away. 'You had a sleep this afternoon, didn't you, madam?'

He straightened himself and held her little bed-warmed hand and smiled across at Nan.

'All right, come and tell me when you're finished with her. I'll be in the study.' He was laughing at her. He knew she would not go to him in the study. There was something very natural and funny about the way he could sometimes for a moment laugh at all the weights of love that held him and tease her with her strictness. A light stick to sting her with. Everything about this love was light and impatient. Except Nan's reply to it, which had so much sorrow and dignity and value.

Nan put Mrs. Fox to bed, curling the feathery hair, folding away the ribboned coat, carefully, unhasty, forgetful of nothing, attentive to the disconnected chatter about this and about that. Sylvia. The flowers. The new housemaid. What the doctor said. What she felt about the baby, and how her feeling differed from what she had felt before the last disaster. It was all so little. It was still all there was of first importance, and Nan gave it the attention which was its due. She was fond of Mrs. Fox and saw nothing to despise in her because her husband's love had wandered. Under the circumstances it was not so very surprising. Nan knew it took a super-woman to hold a Fox true to her, that was Nan's outlook really. There were Fox's in the world and other people. There was Aragon in the world and other places.

Now she listened attentive and interested to the chatter of a Fox mother, though all her being was thrust away from her towards the room where Hugh Fox was sitting alone.

'Oh, Nan, look, do you think I've knitted enough to cast off yet?'

'Ah, it's going to be a bigger boy than that.'

'It is going to be a boy, I'm certain. Nan, there's how long now? One, two, three, four months. To the twenty-third, I should say.'

'It will be the twenty-seventh.'

'I feel so much better than I did with the others. Isn't that a good sign?'

'Not too good, you must keep yourself quiet.'

'I wish they would send the blue ribbon from Dublin. They

are so slow. I want to see what sized holes to make for it.'

'The size you have done will be all right.'

'I think that vase of carnations might go.'

'Yes, indeed. I saw some red ones in the greenhouse to-day, but they aren't so nice for a bedroom, are they?'

'No, I like pale pink in a bedroom or violets are nice. Mr. Fox likes violets. He said he shot a jack-snipe to-day. Tell the cook to send it up for my lunch to-morrow.'

'It's no more than a mouthful, madam. No bigger than a moth you might say.'

'I've got everything now, I think. My glass of water, my biscuit. I'll take my medicine, Nan, shall I?'

'And your hot milk.'

'You know I think that glass of milk gives me indigestion.'

'Well, we'll leave it off to-morrow night.'

'You've said that for the last three months.'

'No, it's good for him; it builds the bones.'

'Well, all right. . . . Nan, go down to the study and tell Mr. Fox I want to see him.'

'Couldn't you go to sleep, Madam?'

'I've been asleep half the day. Go down yourself, Nan, don't send any one, and say I really want to see him. I really do.'

'Don't fuss yourself, now, Madam. I'll see to it.'

'Go yourself, Nan. Promise.'

Poor little silly, she could recognise Nan's power, but not the implications of such power. There is felicity in such silliness.

Nan put the last un-needed touches to the complete order of the room before she went downstairs. She went down the wide staircase, her hand touching lightly along the smooth bannister. She took this way to lend herself a kind of strength, to borrow resistance from all the pale Fox's. The intensive vanity, the highest end of snobbery made possible the connection between Nan and these pallid brown portraits, hung and settled on the walls of the house. They did indeed influence her to a denial that was then close to martyrdom.

'Well, so you did come down to me?' He was standing in front of the fire, smoking a cigarette. The restraint, the teasing of his upstairs-manner were gone.

Nan held the door open at her back.

'Mrs. Fox would particularly like to see you, Sir.'

'Nan, come here to me. Please.'

'I must go back to the nursery.'

'Don't I matter at all?' He crossed the room in a moment and closed the door behind her. 'Don't you mind about me, Nan?' His arms were round her. 'Nan.' For a moment all the power that was in her was changed into a strength of love, beyond thought, beyond resistance. There was a force in this terrible loving that would never be lost by giving.

She put him from her. Her eyes were dark with pain. She would murder love. Her hands were strong and cold with despair, and when she spoke her voice was strong. She said:

'I don't want to trouble Mrs. Fox as things are, but I should let you know, Sir, that I must leave when the child is born. I am going to be married to Owen O'Neill.'

He stood apart from her. 'I'm so sorry, Nan,' he said.

It was then that she longed most to comfort him. What was she that she denied him anything? Her love, her little boy, her dearest and only cause and reason for living.

He had gone back to the fire before she opened the door to go, and just before she went he said, softly and gently:

'Good-night, Cousin Nan.'

It was a wonderful acceptance of her refusal. It gave back into her keeping entire the world of Aragon, for which she had just given her all, and to give your all is so dangerous even for the strong. The object for which so much is sacrificed must at the time be exaggerated far out of the true, and when such lovely illusion goes, only the sour emptiness of loss is left to the giver.

Now, in two words, her dream and her secret had been made a reality. Hugh Fox paid her for a lifetime of service with those two words, 'Cousin Nan,' spoken so sweetly and gravely at that moment. He was of his time in that faintly dramatic respect of a woman who could withstand him, and of his time too in knowing the strength and depth of value to Nan this brief recognition of their cousinship would be. But he was real and gentle in that he took the gravest means in his power to console her for what he knew now she would always put away from her. He knew she loved him far more deeply than he looked for. He was afraid and grateful for her strength in denying a force that might be beyond them both. He was to have no easy joy of her.

Nan went down the passage slowly from the study door to the hall. What he had said brought her no comfort yet. She felt weak and suffocated by a kind of nausea for which there was no relief. It was very cold in the passage and the high hall where the gaslight was turned down to a pale worm of light. Nan's arms were folded across her white apron, her hands grasping either arm above the elbow. Her tall body was bent to a hollow weariness. She was empty of all resolve. If he had been there now that she knew what her refusal meant. . . . But he did not follow her. She was alone with despair. Despair takes so long about its business. It has a sort of mild finality, even in its first moments. It is an empty, dirty house with old foggy windows.

Nan's only reason for going into the drawing-room that night was her wish to hide for a little while. She could not face the bright nursery and the curious eyes of the nursery-maid left there in charge of Sylvia.

She opened the high thin mahogany door quietly, and shutting it she went slowly, still stooping, across the room to one of the windows that looked over the river. The sharp stars were squared again and again in the small panes of the windows. She was kneeling on the floor. Her dress flowed free from her narrow waist, it was a delicate, dark, sweeping line to the floor. She was not crying. She was alone in her house, alone in body and spirit. Her despair and her desire were too close and high about her for any comfort to come near. It was not then but long afterwards that the dead Fox's came near her. That night she was comfortless, and that night her pity for pain in others died. She would live to hurt somebody for this terrible wrong she had done herself. She would twist a revenge out of life yet.

She knelt a long time in the cold room above the cold river, and when at last she got up from her knees she felt as cold as death. It was a help to have any sensation that she could assuage, any feeling that said to the supremely sensible woman in her, 'Have sense. Help yourself.' She went out of the drawing-room and through the hall and up the back stairs to the nursery, where she dismissed the maid, and brewed herself a cup of tea.

That cup of tea in moments of crisis, whether disastrous or happy, is to the peasant Irish what his opium is to the Chinaman. Habit and her mother's blood were strong enough in Nan to make it her tonic and her opiate. Its strong comfort was ready for her to-night and gave her back some reliance on herself. She shuddered as she drank the first mouthful, but then, catching herself together half-angrily, she drank for her good concentrating in the pleasure it gave her. Then she wrote a letter to Gipsy O'Neill saying she would come to tea with her on her next free afternoon. The letter contained an arch reference to her brother, Owen O'Neill. When Nan stuck up the envelope there was a look about her mouth, a wry, hard look, that Aunt Pidgie was to see often in later years.

XXII

Nan left Aragon before Grania was born. She could not trust herself to stay near Hugh Fox any longer. She arranged her marriage with Owen O'Neill and went to live at Clonamore. When her son was born she was very happy. He was a lovely child, although there was much more of the O'Neill than the Fox about him. His father died of pneumonia when he was three years' old and when he was six, Nan left him in charge of her sister-in-law and went back to Aragon. Hugh Fox had hurt his back so terribly in a hunting accident that the doctors said he could not live six months. Nan kept him alive for twelve, and then she was glad to see him die. After that she could never leave Aragon.

It was when he was dying that she first knew the ghosts in the house. The ghosts at Aragon were only seen and heard by the Fox's, and the Fox's were usually afraid of them and denied their presence. When one of the family was near death they would keep all together and lights burning and drinking, and fires roaring up the chimneys, and no lonely venturing round the house after nightfall.

But for Nan it was another thing, and a glorious thing. She went towards the hauntings, the shadows, the fullness in empty rooms, with a great embracement of spirit.

To her this proof of her Fox blood was a wonder and a

satisfaction beyond price. She accepted and gloried in their presence. If a door opened a little, Nan would get up from her chair,
leave down her sewing, and open it wide, wide to her dead. She
would set off like a happy ship down the dark passages to fetch
trays from the kitchen at night, trays which the servants were
frightened to bring though they saw nothing, heard nothing,
but their vulgar minds were full of the house's old stories.

It was on one of these excursions that Nan first knew the
height of the one she called 'the Child' trotting beside her, and
knew when she stretched down her hand where its hand would
meet hers. There was happiness in the air when it was there. But
there were other ghosts at Aragon not quite so happy. Were the
girls such as Ann Daly had dealt with (and many a one before her)
coming back with their wrongs, a crazed haunting of the beautiful house where they had been coaxed or forced to wickedness
and where babies' bones were little and green scattered skeletons
on the river bottom? Nan passed off her knowing of these with a
shrug—such things were. Take it or leave it, such things have
been. She could turn over and go to sleep when she had been
woken by the clash of duelling swords on the path below her
window. The path that ran between the house and the shallow
terrace and the drop to the river.

Aragon's living and dying and dead all turned to Nan in that
wonderful year of her return, so filled with sadness and satisfaction. Afterwards she would turn the events of that year over in
her mind, its happenings were like objects, she could put them
away in a bag and take them out one by one, almost in her hands
and turn over and dwell upon them.

Nan had a wonderful enjoyment in using words. No matter
how often she might discuss or dissect an incident with Mrs. Fox
she always had new words in which to state its outline and
embroider its detail. Away from the glorious details of illness
and death, funeral wreaths or a difficult birth, what might she

picture? Grouse—a brace of grouse, and how shall we eat them?

'They are young birds, Madam. No spurs, see, imagine, and their feet as soft as a baby's. Would you have them roast? Not too much done, see, on a piece of soft toast, a good thick slice that will hold their goodness, and a rich brown sauce, and a spoonful of crumbs, and a nice bread sauce, and we'll start in on the late line of peas, and a few mushrooms, and a sharp salad, and a half-bottle of the old Burgundy—the birds deserve it. And a grill of the legs for breakfast with scrambled eggs and sliced tomato and chippy bacon. How would that be, Madam? How would you eat that? Wouldn't it be good?'

Food is wonderful and consoling when it is spoken of by a clean enthusiastic woman, especially when it is not her business or province. But life was Nan's province, every aspect of life on which she could lay a finger, some octopus like quality in her seemed able to reach out its sensitive strength and grasp the essential of what she heard or saw, and hold it tenaciously within herself until the moment for its use should come.

Little by little Nan had achieved the ruling of Aragon. There was no coarseness or violence shown in the methods by which her opponents were weeded out. Slowly, and one by one they went, and with their going, her power over the rest tightened its grip. Everyone on the place was afraid of Nan and Nan's influence on Mrs. Fox, who was the perfect doll to be manipulated by Nan.

Perhaps, for all her power Nan's only enemy was Frazer, and Frazer knew her too well to come out into the open in his defiance. Besides what had he to hold against her except his hatred, and his shadowy knowledge that Miss Pidgie often went hungry for Nan's pleasure.

Frazer hated pleasure, and life, and himself, and other people, and Ireland. He was bitter and efficient and savagely honest. He hated Catholics. His chilblains gave him a lot of trouble in winter-time, and his digestion all the year round. He used to write his grudges and his discoveries about other people's wrong-doings down on dirty little pieces of ruled paper torn from his notebook, and lock them away in a drawer in the pantry, against the time they might come in useful. He was a horrid little man, but an excellent and honourable butler. Even Nan's and her own dislike of him had not been enough to make Mrs. Fox dismiss him, and for years, as long as Nan's, he had remained at Aragon. Sylvia he liked, and Miss Pidgie he pitied, the more hotly because his pity was linked with his hatred of Nan and her easy powerful ways in every province of the house . . . and for her son, for that thing abhorent to all bitter old servants, one who is not so far above themselves but who, because of an ability and knowledge they will never attain, is accepted and questioned and respected by the gentry they serve in their different measures. For her son, Gentleman Bloody Foley, as he called him from between the teeth of his mind, Frazer had a dislike equal to and beyond that which he felt for the mother. He hated horses and never for a moment dissociated a racecourse from evil and dishonest practice of every description, and Foley was the prophet of all these matters. The young soldiers who came to Aragon would rather talk to him than to each other if he chanced to be there. He had sometimes come to a meal, and Frazer regretted that he hardly ever drank, because it deprived him of the satisfaction of stinting the drink he poured into his glass. Never were there such fairy slices of game placed on any plate as on Foley's. Almost, if the butler's marrow in his bones had not prevented him, he snatched the vegetables from him as he handed the silver dish. He could not possibly recognise the natural tough simplicity of Foley's character which made him take the elaborate service of meals in the big house as easily as he would take the boiling of eggs for his own tea, and service from the stately Frazer as indifferently as service from Doatie or Aunt Gipsy.

428

XXIII

What a moment of supreme and blissful triumph for Frazer, what an exquisite hour of fulfilment was here on that spring evening as he closed the drawing-room door on the ring of pale faces, faces paled and shocked by his story, faces consternated in the still air of the room, when he left them to go, before any could forestall him, and carry the tale to Nan's kingdom, the nursery. He did not hurry, he paused and rolled the taste of each moment on his tongue as he went steadily up the staircase to the nursery. It was a strange way to him, for, though Nan might sail into the pantry with dreadful unabashed freedom when the notion took her, Frazer never, never went near the nursery. So to-day when he knocked at the door it was like knocking at the door of a strange house—his enemy's house.

'Come in,' Nan called. If she was startled when she looked up from her stitching and saw him there instead of a maid with the tea, she did not show it, but bit the end of her thread and snapped a new piece from the spool before she said:

'It's a pleasure to see you here, fancy, Mr. Frazer.'

'It's not for my pleasure but for my duty I come into this room, Mrs. O'Neill.'

'Duty, really, fancy again, Mr. Frazer! And when did your duty go beyond cleaning silver with your thumb?'

'Ah, Nan O'Neill, my thumb and my duty alike are my

business, and I know my place. I know my place and I keep my place, and I never seek to puff myself up with power, like some I know, not so far away.'

'Oh, it's great sport to hear you give out a sermon, all the same, Mr. Frazer.'

'Like some I know.'

'Not so far away, didn't you say, Mr. Frazer?'

'Like some I know that will get the cap of conceit torn off them in a way they *don't* expect.'

'You and I have lived here a good few years now, and the only cap I have left off is my nurse's cap, at Mrs. Fox's special request.' Nan passed her fingers through her strong grey curls with an expression on her face of overbearing and maddening self-content. She was Queen of Aragon, and maybe this was her last contest with one who had been for so long a spy and a dark opponent. Her eyes danced for the battle, and her quick brain went flashing down the possible methods of his attack and her own counter thrusts and out-manoeuvring to come. She was a little discountenanced when he sat down without invitation and laughed—a rude and certain laugh.

Nan got up and folded away her sewing, an angry colour in her cheeks now.

'If it's all the same to you, Mr. Frazer, would you remember that Miss Pigeon will be in to her tea at any moment, and that happens to be her chair you are settled in.'

'Poor Miss Pigeon, indeed. A chair is about all she does get for a meal, tea or any other meal, a chair and little more than a crust, don't I know it? Don't I know where my good grouse goes, or my nice ham, or my bit of sole and melted butter I send up on a hot plate, so tasty from the dining-room? Don't I know who starves and bullies Miss Pigeon for their own wickedness?'

'Would Mrs. Fox and myself and the doctor be the best judges of Miss Pigeon's diet, or would we get you in to advise us, now tell me?' Nan's face was livid. 'What medicine do you think she should take, now tell me? What time should she go to bed, since you know so much?'

'It's little medicine she'd want if she got a square meal once in a way, God help her.'

'The same as He'll twist you for interference.'

'It's the twist of hunger in a harmless old creature you'll have to answer for, see, and good food in plenty all around her. Oh, I've kept the life in her, she'd be dead long ago, like a light old bird in winter, only for me. I know when she's hungry, though she never asked me for a bite yet. I know when I see that old disgrace of a hat you keep on her go nodding along past the dining-room window or the pantry window maybe, and the cold wind whistling out through the cock's feathers in it. I know she's hungry though she's too proud to look in the window, just by way of—only by chance, she'll go by. Ah, Nan, for all your cruel tricks, many a good plate of cold game or mushrooms and bacon on toast I've kept there for her from the breakfast, sizzling on the hot plate, "Just a morsel for your Diblins, Miss," I say, to save her pride.'

'You'll kindly repeat every word of that before Mrs. Fox. Yes, and Miss Pigeon shall be there, and see then will she uphold one word of it.'

'And, long ago, I'd have said it to Mrs. Fox, Nan, only I knew who would get the dirty end of that stick, and that's the old lady.'

'And what ails you now to drag your lies and your dirty grudges into the daylight?'

'Ah, things are changed now, Nan. Things are changed.' He almost sang the words at her. He was trembling to deal her his blow. But there were other matters to be dealt with first, and bitter satisfactions that could not be foregone.

'For thirty years I've watched you in this place.'

431

'And have you known me do a thing that wasn't for this place and the good of the family?'

'Ah, the bastard's pride in you!'

'John Frazer, you low, tinker bred scum! Out now. Out, or I'll put you out? You little rat——'

'Easy, Nan, easy a minute. It's the pride that held you out against the poor Master, I wouldn't blame it——'

'Don't speak to me, don't dare.'

'I can, girl, I saw it. Ah, I watched you then with the eyes of love, but you changed my love to hate, and every year with more reason I hate what you are. You got all you wanted from life, didn't you, Nan? Full power over the house of your blood and the Fox's within it? But you charged yourself with the bitter loss of love in all your life of content, that torment is threaded in you, in and out, in and out.'

'Hold your tongue. Hold your tongue. Have you gone mad?'

'The one good act you did, you did it for a bad reason, and the bad grudge it left in you is vented on the only Fox you are able to torment. The want of goodness through you and through you wouldn't let time pacify your lust, but had to twist it out of you in cruel goings on to one more helpless than a baby in your wicked hands.'

'And what have I done? Speak up and say can you lay a finger on one of your wicked accusations?'

Frazer took a dirty little notebook out of his pocket, and opened its pages silently. Nan would have given much to snatch it from his hands and watch it fall far fluttering downwards to the river below, the river that had hidden so much in time past.

'April 3rd, 1917,' Frazer read out, 'Miss P. very lame. Have you a sore foot, Miss P? I have a blistered heel, Frazer, she replied, there is a nail in my boot. Give me the boot, Miss P., I replied, and took it from her. There was a brad up into the side

432

of her foot and a welt out in the leather in the heel. I adjusted the boot with a hammer. Is it long like that, Miss P., I inquired. Oh, a long time, Frazer, she replied, but Nan says the soldiers in France have more to put up with,' And that's only one little thing.' He put an elastic band twice round the little book and put it away in his pocket. 'Only one little thing in the ten years you're minding Miss Pigeon, and I'm watching you minding Miss Pigeon.'

'And do you think any one is more likely to believe your lies, because you write them down, you fool?'

'They look better so. 1917 is a long way back. But I have day and date and time for many a thing.'

'And what brings you up here to-day with your insults and your nonsense?'

'What brings me up here to-day, is it? Oh, didn't I nearly forget. Fancy, Nan, that I could forget such an important young chap—so gentlemanly, such a friend of all the officers! Well, Nan, tch, tch, where's my head? Indeed it's time I gave up my job.'

'What are you talking about now? Get out of here. I'll see you again with Mrs. Fox.'

'Well, now, I'm going, I'm just going. But before I go I'd like to be the first to tell you that your son, *Mr.* Bloody Foley, is arrested and in the barracks for aiding and abetting in the murder of Captain Purvis and Mr. Craye in the mountains this morning! Ah, ha, the Fox blood, the Aragon touch ran a bit thin in the laddo, eh?'

Nan was white. She looked white all the way through to her bones and past them. Through and through her the blood of her strength had failed.

'I don't believe you.'

'You do believe me,' he said.

'Tell me more.'

433

'You'll hear time enough.' He shook his head and got up to go. He was a hard old man, righteous and hard as flint. 'Run with the hare and hunt with the hounds,' he said, 'but it won't last for ever, will it, Nan?' He was sniggering with pleasure as he went softly out of the nursery.

XXIV

Nan stood facing the window. The linen she had been marking lay in a pile on the floor, it looked like a great ruin of snow melting in wreaths and circles back to water and dark earth. An hour ago this linen had been rich and crisply dignified, an emblem of Nan's sound position at Aragon, exquisite and dearly bought. Nan looked out across the full river. What had Foley done? What foolish mistake had he made that could put such words into her enemy's mouth, that could empower him to taunt and torment and insult her? Frazer was the sort who would not hit until he knew undoubtedly his foe was down. He would have waited his lifetime, he would have died before he struck a meaningless blow.

Nan had never thought of admitting to herself that her treatment of Miss Pigeon amounted to cruelty. Of course not. The moments of tense satisfaction when she knew Miss Pigeon's fear of her was a fluttering living thing, the moments when satisfied power made her indulgent, as one might be with a tiresome petted dog, not because the dog is less tiresome, but because some gland of generosity, suddenly freed, for the moment requires an outlet; these moments she neither noticed nor understood, but thought of herself as a tower of patience towards Miss Pigeon's cracked childish ways, and as a healthy deterrent and guard against many nasty and rather dirty ways. She kept her

435

clean. She fed her. She kept her away from visitors. She frightened her into good behaviour. She gave her pills when she was
constipated, and saw to it that she did not cost Mrs. Fox a penny
more than could be helped in clothes. She had done her duty by
Miss Pigeon, of course she had, more than her duty. Yet a dark
wind of fear was blowing through Nan. She could not possibly
understand the reasons for some of the feelings she had towards
Miss Pigeon, for some of the things she had done to her, she
could not even remember them. What was written down in
that little book? What had Miss Pigeon told him? How much
and how often had they talked? Some of Frazer's words came
back to Nan:

'The bitter loss of love in all your life. . . . A bad grudge left
in you and vented on the only Fox you can torment . . .'

Nan could reject his wild charges, of course she could reject
them all, but with such charges went a loss of her dignity, of her
great connection with Aragon. She might be watched. She
might be questioned—the Queenship halted or lost, and what
indeed was this about Foley? She must go over to Mountain
Brig after Miss Pidgie's tea. (Life, death or imprisonment cannot
interfere with a good nannie's idea of a tea-hour.) Mrs. Fox
would send her in the car. The anxiety for Foley was imple-
mented in the anxiety for herself and for Aragon. She was far
more proud than fond of him. She was not a fond person. She
only had her passions—the one passion—Aragon. So far in life
Foley, the handsome little boy, the prodigy of childish
horsemanship—Foley, the clever big boy who passed all exami-
nations so easily—Foley, the successful owner of horses, had
been a credit and a pride and a bolster to her importance. The
kind of son she felt it right that she should have. The kind of son
other women did not achieve, other women without a trickle of
Fox blood in their veins. Now, what had he done, what sort of
trouble was he in, how would it effect and disgrace her? Could

she carry him over it? Whom should she approach in his favour? What next, what next?

How late Miss Pigeon was for her tea. She was usually in early and sat waiting for her bread and butter and her slice of cake in a state of great expectancy. The maid tapped at the door and came in with the tray. Nan looked out of the window furiously and saw a little figure, far below, foreshortened as flat as a beetle, hurrying and bundling along the flagged path beneath the windows.

Miss Pigeon was panting when she came in, the speed of her coming still stirred the feathers in her hat.

'I'm a little late, Nan,' she said anxiously. 'My watch stopped at 4.15, and when I looked again it was still 4.15.'

'And what does it say now?'

'Oh, I set it by the clock in the hall as I came through.'

'Well, Miss Pigeon, you must have been very quick to get round by the hall, and it not three minutes since I saw you come in by the side door.'

'Oh, I was very quick, Nan. I ran, Nan.'

'You're sure you didn't fly, Miss Pigeon?' Nan's temper was mounting as it always did in these contests with Miss Pigeon. It made the excuse greater for punishment. To-night it had reached the 'No cake' level in a flash when something halted her, made her look at the creature she had cared for so long. It was fear, fear unalloyed that stayed her mind for that second's looking. What a small creature she saw, small, unattractive and frightened. Miss Pigeon's face was pale under the big feathered hat. The blue ribbon bow on her breast jumped and quivered as if there was a wire spring behind it.

'Take off your hat, now, and sit down to your tea.' Nan took the ginger cake out of its box and cut a large slice from it, the largest Miss Pigeon had seen for a long time. 'And no more fibs to Nan mind, or it's early bed and no supper.' She poured out

Miss Pigeon's tea and went into the bedroom to dress in her blue coat and skirt, for she must get to Mountain Brig as soon as possible. Nan had a most trustworthy belief in her own power to compete with any situation better than anybody else if she could be on the spot where it was taking place, if she could gather its threads into her grasp. She could snap them and roll them up and tidy the tangle.

She was putting on her hat when she heard a voice, an excited strong stormy voice speaking to Miss Pigeon in the nursery. It was Aunt Gipsy, Aunt Gipsy to whom Aragon was an Elysium of forbidden ground and unencountered aristocracy. Nan swung open the door before Aunt Gipsy could embark on the reasons for her visit to the tiny piece of faded gentlewoman who was begging her to sit down and offering her a solitary slice of ginger cake.

'Gipsy!' Nan said from the door, her voice an icy frame for reproof, 'you've had your tea, I suppose.'

'Tea, dear? No, indeed, nor dinner, scarcely what you'd see. Oh, Nan, what a day! Oh, Nan, wait now till I tell you all I know. Be brave now, Nan, to take a knock, but God is good and he will see you over it, and if we have a nice cup of tea wouldn't it hearten us? Well, don't trouble for me, of course, but it's a terrible business to take it out of you to buy a new hat. Do you like me in it? Well, when I was in Dungarvan I thought I'd be the right fool to pass it by, though it's not the one I intended buying.'

'I think it's a show,' Nan said sourly. She came forward into the room and put up a hand that was to put the room in two halves and divide the spate of words from Miss Pigeon.

'Would you care to go out, Miss,' she said, 'and take your cake, too. Perhaps another slice for those Diblins.'

Miss Pigeon put on her hat again and hurried out. She was used to being shooed away when Nan had visitors.

438

Gipsy followed Nan into the bedroom. While she talked she kept diving between the two looking glasses. A close view in the dressing-table glass, a distant impression in the long one on the wardrobe door. Her pre-occupation with her hat made curiously light of all she had to say.

'How did you get here?' Nan asked.

'Oh, my dear, the car that brought out Nurse Dwyer for Doatie took me back.'

'Nurse Dwyer for Doatie?'

'Oh, Nan, did you not see Miss Grania all day?'

'No.' Nan paused. 'She was out all day.' What was in store, what lay in that blank? Gipsy must not recognise her ignorance of any point. Gipsy, that vulgar lesser creature, Foley's servant, her servant—and what an indifferent one. What then? What now?

'You didn't hear herself and Foley nearly came home with my poor child corpsed this morning to breakfast?'

'I haven't seen Miss Grania. She had been away all day.'

'Well, I never will forget it. What a morning I put over me. I hardly had my cup of tea in the kitchen when I lit on this little hat in the paper. No, but it wasn't this one, only the girl in Beirney's persuaded me this one was the one for me, and only the three shillings between them, so I said, I'll chance it. Well, my mind, dear, was very taken with my little hat after they went off. Though, indeed, I went out to the yard several times to see would Foley's black hen lay a brown egg for his breakfast, and made a cake of white bread on the pan with my own two hands, mind, and slapped up a bit of fresh butter and took the money out of the good teapot, and had all set out as nice as you like ready for them to come back with Miss Grania.'

'How did you know Miss Grania was coming back with them?' The blank must be filled though she hated to question Gipsy.

439

'Ah, dear, Foley doesn't keep back much from Aunt Gipsy.'
Gipsy knew in a flash that Nan was ignorant of any familiarity
between Foley and Grania. She wondered whether to build or to
lessen that side of the day's picture. Build, perhaps, since Nan
knew so little. 'She's coming out with us to ride a school,
Auntie, he said, so get a nice breakfast, mind, and I think it was
then he said I ought to buy a new hat for myself. Ah, child, I
said, it's little indeed my hats troubles me, if I can keep any old
thing on me a bit decent for the chapel is all I need. Well, Aunt
Gipsy, he said, you must go to Beirneys in Dungarvan and . . .'

'Gipsy, will you kindly forget your hat for a moment and tell
me what has happened to-day.'

'Hats, Nan, hats, I never give them a thought, only to keep a
little bit of respectability going between Mountain Brig and the
chapel.'

'Well, what happened Doatie?'

'Do you think one of them would trouble to tell me what
that lion of a horse did to her? Only to bring her home and lay
her cold at my feet is what he did. Aunt Gipsy, he said, it's a
black hat you nearly had a right to buy yourself this day. Oh, I
could see myself—all in black and a black hat, standing by that
little grave.'

'And how is the corpse now?' Nan shot out the question
before the picture grew so gloomy that Gipsy must refuse to
admit any possibility of recovery to her child. You could only
guess at the truth behind Gipsy's accounts and the guesses even
had to be daggered out by thrusting words.

'Oh, she's conscious all right, now. ''Where am I mother
darling?'' Those were the first words she spoke, and, oh, Mrs.
Bohane, nurse said to me, what a mother's love can do!'

'Are you sure it was nurse said it, Gipsy? I thought you left
her in charge and went off to Dungarvan to buy a hat.'

'Well if it wasn't nurse, it was little Josie.'

'Well, so Doatie's in bed with a hospital nurse in charge. You're driving round the country buying hats. And where, do you know, is Foley and when did you see him last?'

'The last I saw of Foley was driving Miss Grania back to her bicycle this morning after her breakfast, and when I came back from Dungarvan with my hat who met me in the yard with a white face on him and the eyes jumping from his head but Micky Brown. Micky, I said, is Miss Doatie . . ? and I couldn't say the word. But it passed through my mind would they change the hat for a black hat. Keep the car Missus, Micky said, you might want it yet. There was a party of Military here and you out. What, Micky, I said, did I miss the military? Did they get a cup of tea? It wasn't tea, they took, he said, but searched the place out till they found a little dog Mr. Foley brought home with him to-day, and with that they put Mr. Foley in the lorry and took him off. Oh, Nan, the disgrace! For all to see him driving through the country, a common prisoner to the bare light of day.'

'A common prisoner to the bare light of day,' that was the phrase that struck Nan to the heart. What he had done, what he might not have done, whatever bad case of danger he was in, this was what stood out from it for her first. Her son, proud Nan O'Neill's son, a common prisoner to the bare light of day.

Nan looked round her wildly. She was shaking. She moistened her lips. She put her hands up, pressing the backs of them against her eyes for a second, pulling them out against her temples, she leaned towards Gipsy, she had to be at one with this fool for the moment, to find out what she could from her.

'There was no word left why he was taken?'

'Not a word.'

'What do you know, Gipsy? Do you know any more? What did Micky say? That's a sensible boy.'

'Micky said, "Excuse me remarking it, Mrs. Bohane, but that's a lovely hat."'

'Gipsy, could you tell me straight, did he give you any reason why the soldiers came to Mountain Brig to-day. Was it to see your new hat?'

Gipsy whirled on her shrill and furious.

'Ah, your airs and grandeurs will take a toss now. Yes, Nan, it's little a hat is to you or any little thing like that that keeps life in the woman of a lonely place like myself. How many years am I there, Nan, working for your boy, and I love the boy, he's not his mother's boy but my poor brother's, ah, the maker's name is on the blade, indeed. But for all the gentry ways you may strive to give him he's in a British jail, now, God help him, for aiding his own against the enemy I wouldn't wonder, and you laughing on the Q.T. at my new hat, the way you always made yourself out a high cry above the O'Neills. What finished me was how you came to marry my poor brother. God make good to him the four years' anguish he had with you.'

'Gipsy, are you gone mad? You that I kept at Mountain Brig . . .'

'At Clonamore as it should be called. . . .'

'And your little daughter all these years. . . .'

'Doatie worked for Foley since she was eight years of age. How many children's ponies did that child make and sell for him?'

'How much did I pay the good Nuns for the schooling she and you were too savage and ignorant to appreciate, tell me.'

'And I minding Foley for you through every child's sickness and you engrossed in your high life and your gentry ways.'

'Take care I'd leave you in it a day longer to mind him.'

'Ah, that's good, indeed, and the jailers tending him now with a tin plate, who knows.'

'Did you come out here in a hired car to rain down abuse on me or what did you come for?'

'I came to tell you anything I knew about Foley, and all I get from you is rude remarks passed on my new hat, and who are you in any case to pass remarks? You never could buy a hat that it didn't look a holy show on you and your mind never rose above navy blue. And anything you ever did put on your head has the forbidding look of one who drove a pram before her for many years.'

'Are we all gone mad, I wonder?' Nan's strength came down to earth in a supreme gesture of sanity. 'Would a cup of tea ease our minds?'

'Well, I wonder now, would it?'

Quite suddenly they both fell from the heights of real antipathy which they felt for each other to the state of placid giving and taking which for so long their lives had required of them.

'Gipsy, take your hat off. And I will say it's not a bad little hat at all.'

Gipsy took it off and twirled it slowly round.

'Well, it looks nice on the hand,' she said, 'but it had a big buck of a hairpin driven into my head till I could faint from the pain.'

'God help you girl.'

'And did I tell you that Micky said, 'twas a little dog they found shut in the loft fixed poor Foley for them?'

'A dog, Gipsy?'

'Micky said 'was belonging one of the officers who was captured.'

'Oh, my God on High.' Nan accepted the implication very quietly.

They went into the nursery where Nan's slave had left a fresh pot of tea and sat down, the neutrality of years settling again between them.

Two women drinking tea and the shadow of death between them.

443

XXV

Death and new hats, tea and fear and pain—Aunt Gipsy's remembrance of Doatie's pain. Grave clothes and lilies and mourning, grandeur and power, old grudges and mistrusts, the tremblings and small gaieties of Aunt Pidgie's life, all these things were so thick they were almost within the touch of hands on the old nursery air that evening. What was there then in the air of houses that is not now? Was it more stirred by the emotions of the past than now when the life of the present is gay and firm in the ether with the radio ministering to the loneliest. Radio has stirred away the hauntings and stillnesses in old rooms. There is not the same heaviness and langour in the air of afternoon, air that can at any moment be broken by the good, the vulgar, the wholesome, the beautiful, the terrifying, the useful things of the present. The waves of the past cannot lap and lap quietly encroaching on the solid sands of now. Houses and memories have less power to injure, less power to assuage. But this afternoon was April, 1920, an afternoon in the time of long memories and quietness and dull ageless stretches of time. A time when a bitter little war went untidily on, and news of its progresses went from mouth to mouth in whispers. Many old and beautiful houses that year had their last hours of life. They were stilled for death that summer. They waited in beauty and quiet for fire and the end. Did they have a foreknowing of their deaths? Was that air of desolate distance, of exquisite sadness, that lesser fainter appearance which Irish houses have in comparison to the stability of their kind in England, was it foretold in their stars, grown sadly in their very stones? An awareness and an acceptance of violence and desertion, desertion far more tragic than any sudden ending.

This tea-time pause in Nan's terrible day had the quality of waiting; it was right and calm and polite. Bad news and cruel words had been flowing about the room, anxious thoughts and furious plans. Now stillness. It was as if nothing had happened before tea and nothing would happen after it. Small ships would sail up and down the river between the grey willow trees on the banks and senna coloured stumps, bare at low water, but covered when the ships passed by, riding on bosomy tides of olive water under olive skies. Her life at Aragon would flow on. Its good and its bad ghosts massing quietly along the generations, some ghosts so old that they were quieting gradually in their graves and seldom stirred. Some happy spirits like the child who must come back, it had been so happy here, and sometimes a strong and violent influence from bad lives and hard deaths of the past would plunge into the present of the house and use its air for cruelty and unnamed sports.

XXVI

Sylvia said good-bye to her friends. She was so coolly, perfectly modulated all through that even now she could control any weakness towards hysteria, any relief that might come to her from an admission of her love that asked for pity. And within the tidy shell that held it banded fast, her heart was in such constriction of pain as she had never thought could be.

She said good-bye among the cool shadows and lilac scents in the hall. She stood under the great porch to see the girls mount their bicycles and ride off. On either side of the porch at Aragon there is a surprise. On either side there is an alcove for a statue and in each alcove is a life-size nymph, an exquisite lime-white plaster girl, and the alcoves are painted cold grey which looks like light blue against the warm sallow walls of the house. Sylvia standing between them with the door into the hall open behind her made the third. She looked as set and as unknowable as the two white girls in their blue alcoves.

She was thinking with a persistence more intense than any pain she had known, of his dead body. She saw his body clothed and dead and everything in her hard trim little body and soul was in agony. A pain that had no outlet in any remembrance of real love, its failure or its satisfaction, is an all pervading pain, holding the creature who suffers it in a torture beyond any consoling. Sylvia might have said, 'My heart aches. I am cold,' and these little

446

words would have spoken their cruel truth taken from the trivial circumstances in which they are used and spoken. 'My heart aches, my heart aches, and I am cold.' She was quite stiff with cold. She trembled in the chill of the hall and sickened at the scent of the branches of lilac. She could do nothing. She would ask nothing. She was quite powerless for anything but waiting. She thought she would wait here in the hall, then she would hear the first of any news that was brought. Even at such a time Sylvia's orderly nature exerted itself to console her. If she waited in the hall she must have her needlework. She went into the drawing-room to collect it. Frazer was there clearing away the tea.

'Miss Sylvia,' he said, 'if you'll excuse me saying so they might get the young gentlemen safe yet.'

'Frazer?'

'Yes, Miss. And I'll take a further liberty in suggesting you might ask Miss Grania what she could tell you of Mr. Foley O'Neill's movements this morning. As little as she might know it could dot an "i" or cross a "t" for those who are looking for the two officers now.'

'Frazer, what could Miss Grania know?'

'Miss Sylvia, there's things going on and I am sorry for them but maybe Miss Grania could explain to yourself what she would be doing with a ferret of O'Neill's and why she set out on one of the boys' cycles in her riding clothes at crack of day this morning, yes, and in her best new jodhpurs too, and left a lie with the Mistress to say she was going fishing. Oh, there's wheels going nicely within wheels, Miss Sylvia, could have the axle of truth through them, mind you, though I don't forget my place in saying this.'

Frazer hunched his shoulders like a sick crow, and stooped again to dirty tea-cups and crumby plates.

Sylvia said, 'Thank you, Frazer.' She stood a moment frozen in quietness and then shot out of the room like a poisoned arrow.

447

XXVII

Poor Grania, poor little lump of passion and grief, tears and despair and exhaustion. What to do? How to save? Who to tell? She was so far removed from Sylvia's dignified frozen acceptance of sorrow. There was no affinity between Grania and those plaster girls. She lay on her bed now sobbing with despair and excitement. What did they think he had done, her love, her dear? What might happen to him before the truth could be proven that he was innocent. Grania was caught between two beliefs. Her belief in Foley and her belief in everything that the British Army stood for. Half of Foley's glamour for her lay in his superficial likeness to the young soldiers who were his friends. He was a super imitation in all but voice, and in the fact that he did, fundamentally from the very roots of himself, and excelled in doing, the things that they more or less accomplished as a skilled pastime. Horses were his living and their life. Then beneath the surface he was tough, reasonable and tough. Not one of the young men Grania and Sylvia knew would have thought of being their lovers. Foley not only thought of this but put his thoughts into practice, and did this in spite of a Catholic upbringing. So he was really tough.

Although she could not know it, it was all this hard rough stuff that appealed to Grania. She was utterly ravished and fascinated by her first experience of love, and had the most exaggerated view in the world of her lover's perfections. It is only when girls grow older that they can tolerate the idea of their lovers being imperfect, or in fact admit the idea at all. Grania, sobbing on her bed, great easy tears pouring through her fingers into her pillow, sobbed in a sort of hushed torment of heart that allowed every fear possible to assail her. Her fat arms even were wet with great salty drops. Her hair stuck like wet feathers to her temples. She squeezed her mouth against her pillow because even in her desperation she knew what an awful noise she made when she cried. It was not so long really since the days when she had roared for what she wanted, for this poor fat creature who sobbed with so much abandon was no more than eighteen on this shocking evening.

Grania's bedroom was a dreadful example of girlish taste of the date. There were blue birds swinging in pink rings on the wallpaper. The cretonne curtains were a mass of rich pink roses and frilled white muslin hanging inside them. A great many of the larger, richer blossoms on the curtains had been carefully snipped out and stitched on to the net and lace bedspread, which was laid across a piece of pink sateen on the bed, very pretty indeed. The china on the marble-topped washstand was equally be-rosed and be-ribboned, and the carpet had wreaths of darker roses on its paler ground shade. Here the girlish note might be said to have been struck for what it was worth, and the motif le sport added in emphatic superstructure. One fox mask hung down in ghostly realism, tongue out, lolling low between bright teeth. The relic was hung on a piece of leather, not stuck outwards from a shield of wood, and its place was the centre of the mantelshelf. Underneath the mask was a photograph of Grania (though Grania would have told anybody that it was a photograph of Grania's horse). Grania had been photographed at a meet and just a thought drunk on a glass of sloe gin. She was sitting beautifully and at her ease with her horse standing just right. Rather long coat, rather long leathers, rather large hat. All very 1920, and most enviable and right. She often gazed in wonder at that picture, and asked herself, 'Can this be I?' She loved people to look at it, and then she would tell them about the horse and how he was bred, and where he was bought, and how good he was. This was not the only picture on the mantelpiece. It was covered with framed photographs, with other little unframed snapshots stuck into their frames. There was no picture of Foley except in groups, but Grania had a sheaf of his photographs locked away in her writing case, which she smoothed and yearned over a great deal. All this gallery was composed of sporting groups taken either at race meetings, point-to-points, or ready to pursue the chase of the fox. And there were quite a few pictures of Soo looking like a monkey or a cat or a black satin shoe, but not in the least like a dog. Not the same person that Grania parceled down in her rug inside her basket at night. Down she would settle like a bird in her nest and never stir till morning. No toe-nailish wanderings through the night with imaginary desires for a drink of water or an outing. No, Soo kept her basket until Grania was called in the morning and then came out of her cosiness like a little black snail out of a brown shell. No photograph resembled her. She was too rare. She could not be caught and hung on the walls like those girl friends framed in black *passe-partout* round vast white mounts. None of them were friends that Grania cared much about but at that time photographs were such a habit that she even had one of Sylvia (Sylvia translated winningly by Lenare) standing on her chest of drawers. You had photographs. You did not necessarily look at them. Then there was a small gramophone, from which the record 'Whispering' had hardly been removed this summer. Heavily and bluntly embossed silver lay about on the dressing-table. Actually, as it was kept shiningly clean it looked rather rich and nice on the white spot muslin over pink calico shrouded dressing-table.

450

All this girlish tricking out of the rather bleak height and tall spare windows of the room gave it the look of a sad twenty-five year old girl who has never had a moment's success but is forever compelled to attend parties in debutantish tulle and taffeta, and Grania sobbing on the bed had joined now the sadness of the room behind all the flutter of muslin and bustle of chintz.

She had quietened a little when Sylvia came in, and the nasty surprise of her coming made her gasp back her sobs, and take her rather dirty shoes off the net and roses of her bedspread.

Sylvia locked the door and put the key in the pocket of her jersey before she sat down in a little basket work arm-chair. She sat neatly and prettily because that was the way she would have sat even if she was being electrocuted. It was not in her to sit in any other way. A bird cannot look anything but tidy on its nest, no matter what deathly fears are shattering its heart.

'Grania,' she said, 'you were out riding with Foley O'Neill this morning, weren't you?'

'Mind your own business.'

'Exactly what I'm doing.'

'Actually I haven't seen him for days.'

'Oh, why bother to tell lies. You told us you were riding a school with him.'

'Shut up, and get out.'

'I'll do both as soon as you tell me anything you know about Foley's movements this morning.'

'Why should I? Why should I be cross-questioned by you? What has it got to do with you what I do?'

'My dear child it's got everything to do with me. Grania, I'm a fool to say it, but do you know what Michael means to me. And even if he meant nothing, don't you realise he'll be killed, he'll be murdered, if he's not dead now. Grania, you've got to

451

say anything you know. The littlest thing might be the very link they need, don't you see that?'

Grania flung herself on her pillow again.

'You always want to torment me. You're only trying to make me frightened. How dare you think Foley had anything to do with it? How dare you? You don't know a thing about him, and if you dare to think such a thing about him, you shouldn't say such a thing about him, so there! Do you think I'll tell you a thing?'

'Oh, don't be so gabbling and hysterical. Obviously you know more than you'll say. Don't you?'

'I'm a spy and a rebel, I suppose.'

'Is Foley? That's the question, is Foley?'

'I know you'd like to think so, wouldn't you? You'd like to get me to say so, wouldn't you?'

'Is he?'

'Wouldn't you?'

'What are you hiding? What are you lying about?'

'I haven't got a thing to hide.'

'Then why did you tell mother you were going fishing this morning when you were going out schooling with Foley?'

'I didn't intend to go till the last minute.'

'Oh, nonsense. Don't be silly. You must have known there'd be a horse for you to ride.'

'We're not all as bright as you are.'

'Oh, Grania, don't be such an obstinate baby.'

'Leave me alone, get out of my room, who asked you in here?'

'You can't answer a question, not the simplest question, can you?'

'I'll kill you.'

'Why did you tell lies about schooling with Foley, and now that I know you were with him why won't you say where you went?'

452

'Because I won't.'

'I'm arguing with you as if you were a child while Michael and Tony are nearer death every minute, if they aren't dead now. Don't you realise what you're doing? Can't you take it in, or what is it? Grania, does Foley mean anything to you more than one of our own friends?'

'They are your friends, not my friends.'

'They're surely more your friends than Foley O'Neill. My dear Grania, you can't call him a friend of yours, can you? Nice as he is and all that, but he doesn't quite come up to that standard does he?'

'He's my friend, and if you're such a cad as to talk like that about him, shut up about him. Do you hear me? Shut up about him.'

'Now you're going on like a poor class housemaid. He's your boy, I suppose. Do you meet him on your Sunday afternoon's off? It must be a terrible strain getting in by eight o'clock with such a fascinator. What do you talk about when horses are finished? The Irish Republic, I suppose, and who's going to get shot from behind a ditch next. And which of the brave boys will do the job. Don't you see what you're stepping into, mixing yourself up with people like Foley?'

Grania had grown rather white while Sylvia was talking. Her eyes looked strained and the tears were lying in faint white rivers on her cheeks. Little pieces of her hair were crisp with salt like seaweed dried in the sun. She sat up on the edge of the bed. Soo sat up beside her looking horrified and worried. Her tiny black sphinx face regarding chaos with emotion for once. Sadly enough there was a sort of desperate calm setting itself through Grania. A maturity was coming quickly through her tearful obstinacy and childish pigheadedness. A child was drowning in strange waters—a child was passing. Poor Grania! She was not missish and well-grounded in the fine joys of girlishness. She was dirty and passionate and generous. She was greedy and had only begun to live. She had not grown steady, learnt to fear danger, or settled to any soberness in life. She wanted danger from horses, and hardship any way she could get it. There was something between her and river water, and the blood of rabbits she shot, and the feel of wind in her bleached untidy hair, and the feel of running, and the new-found sight of something wild—an otter blowing out its cheeks on a little shaley river beach, dark beneath alders—there was something between her and these things which made her strong. She knew she could never have enough of the salty earth. Her strong fat body could stand up to its pains and hardships, to cold hours of waiting, and hours of working, and long speechless times of idle silence. She had gathered her strength in these ways, and Sylvia's decorous probing and gibing did no more than pick the surface of her determination.

Now she said:

'I haven't got anything to tell and I'm not going to tell it.'

'It will be very pleasant if they send up here from the Barracks to question you.'

'They can't connect me with something I'm not connected with.'

'They can and will if they know you were out with Foley this morning.'

'All right. I don't mind.'

'Are you going to say what you know?'

'I don't know anything.'

Sylvia got up and went out.

Grania went to her window and looked out of it. Up to the flowing slope of the pleasure grounds. It was seven o'clock and the light was still strong and full on the new yellow ribbon-green of leaves, the cherry blossoms glared like· snow in Switzerland, the birds sang like awful choirs of children. There was no proper melancholy in the evening. To-night Grania forgot that peace had ever belonged to a spring evening. She was torn and torn again with anxious uncertain previsions, and outside the world was brightly and harshly divided from all her fears.

XXVIII

Mrs. Fox came fluttering into her room. A tap, so soft it was like the brush of a frightened bird's wing on a glass pane, and she came in on top of it in her gentle headlong way, before there was a possibility of denial.

The vague serene face was crumpled and quartered in anxiety and disturbance. The grey little feathers of hair were raised and disturbed like those of a shocked hen. She affected deliberation to give herself a moment's pause, shutting the door softly and securely, her hand dwelling on the china knob as if to assure herself that they were alone.

'Grania, my child, my darling child, what do I hear?'

'Some lying twaddle of Sylvia's, I suppose.'

'Oh, my little girl, I am so glad you can assure your mother it's all a mistake. It is, darling, I know it is, just a ghastly mistake. Oh, poor Sylvia, poor pet, she's in such a state! One understands. One has to forgive her, poor sweet, hasn't one, doesn't one?'

'What did she tell you, mother?'

'Oh, darling, I didn't believe her until I asked you, but she told me you were going about with Foley, Nan's son, Foley. She said you'd rather Michael and Tony were shot than say where Foley was this morning. Now, can that be possible, Sylvia, I said. Be careful what you say about the poor child, the poor lamb, my poor baby. It's not true, is it darling? Of course not.'

'It is true, mother. I did ride with Foley, why not? Why shouldn't I? I wanted to try the pony.'

'Oh, darling, is that all? From what Sylvia said mother didn't know what to think. But if that's all, it's all right. You've only got to say where you were, dear, it's too simple, and every one will understand. You just went to try the pony. Nothing could be simpler. Though, another time, Grania, let mother know before you do a thing like that. You are a big girl now, you know, and people start talking so dreadfully quickly if a girl gets too—too—well, you know. However, darling, I didn't mind this time, as it's rather lucky really, you can come down to the Barracks with me and tell the Colonel just where Foley was when you saw him last—anything that might give him a hint that would be helpful. Sometimes just a word, you know, will prove something, and I'll tell Colonel James it's quite confidential.'

The gulf between love and death and danger, and this patter of drawing-room values, left Grania somewhere in mid-air, stranded in a coldness of reality which frightened her. Her mother's free gabble of relief when her suspicion of Grania's intimacy with Foley lulled itself, was much greater than her anxiety over the other part of the situation. And her assumption that Grania would be too ready to betray anything she might know about his movements was hinged to the relief in her mind that his fate would have no importance to Grania. Vaguely, Grania realised that soon she would find herself in much more cruel difficulties. She sat on the edge of her bed, staring out of the window, chin up and swallowing tears desperately.

'I'm not going to say anything to any one about Foley. Why should I?'

'But, Grania, my poor child, even if he's innocent you are

457

associating yourself with him by this silence. Think what you are doing—a Fox siding with a rebel! You've got to say something. It looks better.'

'Mother!'

'Well, it's the truth,' Mrs. Fox said a little sulkily; she had not quite meant that phrase, 'it looks better,' to get beyond her mind's keeping. But it had slipped from her unawares now, and even Mrs. Fox could see what a buttressed platform it would give to Grania's obstinacy. What childish mind could fail to grasp such an opportunity for heroism. Such phrases are spoken by their elders only to seal past all undoing the lips of their young. 'It looks better.' Could any words be framed that might put the matter on a lower footing? They are dreadful little words taken in the slightest context, but here with life and death to weigh against them they were fatal—they put something like a flaming sword into Grania's hand—an awkward weapon, and dangerous at an age when one thinks only in extremes.

'You want me to make a statement about Foley's movements as far as I know them this morning? So that if possible he is accused of Michael and Tony's deaths. Mother, do you know what you mean? I'm to do this so that no one thinks Foley and I are in—are anything to each other. That's what you mean. Isn't it, mother?'

'I should not dream of going so far as to suggest, or let anybody dare to think that you could have any interest in poor Foley, my dear.' Oh, the dry, cold retirement in the voice of an embarrassed elder. The power to harm, the dangerous power to estrange for the rest of human time together, and done so entirely for the best of motives. Power used unkindly only to save, to keep a child from disaster. Power used with brain, blindly, clumsily, from motives of terrible excellence. There is no pity in heaven and none in earth for the tragic holders of such power. They are condemned to lose so soon what they

458

love and chasten, and chasten only from their too much loving.

'Wouldn't you dream of it? Why not? Wouldn't you dream of it? I'm going to tell you I love Foley. I love him, and I'll never love any one else, so now. So there. So now, it's true, it's true.' She fell on her pillow sobbing again. Tearing childish howls that seemed to come from her extreme centre of emotion, deep ugly crying.

Mrs. Fox was frightened, there was nothing in her to meet such a situation, such an outburst, from reality. Suddenly in an hour her happy fluttering sighing way of life had been disrupted. Importances beyond the success of her flowers and her games of bridge and gossips with Nan at bed-time and new kinds of biscuits were suddenly thrust on her and she had no way to meet them. No familiar procedure to trust in and follow. She knew no course to take. She was lost indeed.

'My child, my poor little Grania, has he been making love to you? Oh, dear, what would Nan think? Nan's own son to do such a thing. Oh, Grania, and what have you been thinking of? A, a person like that, what can anybody nice think of you if this gets known? Oh, you don't know what you've done, you're young, but it's a deeply terrible shocking thing, my child, to let a man like that touch you, and of course if anybody gets to know you have let him then it's too dreadful, it's too dreadful then. Oh, Grania, for all our sakes, if not for your own sake, you must do the right thing now.'

'Well, I won't,' Grania broke off her crying to say this, and went on to it again with more lusty agony than before.

'Grania, you'll disgrace yourself. You'll disgrace us all.'

Such little words. Little wooden words, tapping like weak hammers against a wall of impenetrable passion and unreason.

Mrs. Fox waited. She could not yet believe in this rebellion or take in all the confession implied. There would come a break and Grania would yield.

'Well, my child?' she said at last.

'Well, what?'

'Are you coming with me. It's very painful for me too, you must remember.'

'You? What do you care? You don't know a thing, or you wouldn't torment me like this.'

'I wonder if Nan would be able to make you see sense.'

'You're not going to tell Nan? You're not going to be so cruel?'

'After all, she must hear sometime.'

'Why need she? No one need if you'll let me alone.'

Mrs. Fox rose resolutely to her feet and went to the door. Grania flounced up off her bed and rushed across the room. Confusion and despair were in her. She was in a place of nowhere and all were her enemies. At least she would get Nan on her side before she was set and poisoned against her.

'I'll tell Nan myself.' She passed her mother and ran down the passage. A ship, a fatal ship, flying before the storm, she ran down the corridor, above the well of the staircase, past the tall doorways and the frigid plaques and mouldings and garlands between them. She bowed her poor head, she squeezed her fat young hands together. She had no helper. Soo, a black little wild pig, pursued, forgotten, desolate but attentive, till the stars should change and her moment of love come again.

XXIX

When she got to the nursery Aunt Gipsy was settling her hat at the glass over the mantelpiece, preparatory for departure.

'——, well,' she said to me, Nan. 'No, of course it's not every one could wear that colour, Mrs. Bohane, but——Oh, Miss Grania, child, what is it?' Nan came forward like a tower, like a cave of refuge from the other room.

'I know Miss Grania's upset for my sake.' She surrounded her in an invaluable protection, she built a wall about her in a moment's time. 'Gipsy, dear, I think maybe I'll follow you a bit later to Mountain Brig. You start away now, and I'm sure Mrs. Fox will send me in the car. Good-bye now, Gipsy, I'll be after you. You know your way down to the side door? Good-bye.' Gipsy was pushed out of the room. The door was closed behind her.

'Now, child, now lamb, here's Nannie's poor baby. I know you're upset child. Tell us all about it now, and you and I will find a way out. Never fear but you and I will scheme out something. God help you it's a drink you want to pull you together. A glass of Miss Pigeon's port wine and Nan will have one too for company.'

What is there about a cupboard, a high cupboard leaning backwards a little into its corner? It seems as though privacies have wings that smell of jam and apples and flutter out a little

461

way when the smoothed key turns and the door opens. For a
fleeting second Grania was back in littleness again as Nan stood,
Queen before her cupboard, reaching up strongly to take the bottle
from its high shelf. Once it had been sugar biscuits on that shelf,
now it was port. Nan produced the needful on all occasions, it was
there beneath her hand and without effort, she was the truest and
strongest person ever known. She was the core of life itself.

The two wine glasses were set down on the cloth and filled
ceremoniously, unhurriedly, as if there was all time for a drink and a
discussion. The effect was calming and widening to the mind. It
made stranded objects float again as though a tide lifted them. This
busyness with bottle and cupboard was far more effective than the
drink itself. Nan took off her blue hat too and ran her fingers
through her stiff grey waves and sat back in a low chair near
Grania's.

'Now, Miss Grania, drink that up and have another. That's
right dear, now don't you feel different? I do myself, it's been a
shock to me too, yes, of course, to hear that my poor Foley had got
himself into any kind of trouble. It's a mistake of course and everything will be cleared up before to-morrow I don't doubt, but it's a
nasty mistake and it gives you a nasty turn as a nasty thing will, my
goodness, but we'll get over it and it will get forgotten, child, and
you mustn't fret yourself. Though poor Nan is terribly touched,
imagine, that you should worry for her, and Foley will be so upset
when he hears he had one of the Miss Fox's in tears, child, hush,
now, hush birdie, hush.'

'Nan, Nan——'

'Yes, dear, yes, tell Nan what it is.'

'Oh, Nan, mother says I'm to go to the barracks and tell them
where Foley was this morning.'

'And how would you know that?'

'Because I was with him, Nan.'

'You were with him, Miss Grania?'

462

'Didn't Mrs. Bohane tell you we went schooling?'

'Well, as it happens, I knew it, dear.'

'Well, why shouldn't I?'

'Why not, indeed? Foley would be only delighted to be of any use or help to you or Miss Sylvia.'

'Oh, Nan, don't talk like that, don't talk as if he was a servant. Don't you understand I love Foley, Nan. I love him terribly.'

'In love with my Foley, child? Love is a big word, Miss Grania, from you to him. It's a big rock of a word.'

'You aren't going to join against us too, Nan?'

'No, no, God forbid, but tell me everything now, Miss Grania, don't keep anything back or how can I help you, child?'

'You will help me, Nan, won't you?'

'Oh, you can trust Nan, can't you?'

'Oh, Nan, I need somebody to trust, I need somebody.'

'Why, dear? Why?'

'Nan, don't be angry with Foley, it's just as much my fault. It's more my fault.'

'What, Grania, tell me all the trouble dear.'

'I'm so frightened I've started a baby, Nan, and what am I to do? Is there anything we can do Nan?'

'You—Oh, God above!'

A look of such desperation broke across Nan's face as was near madness. Was this the end of her sacrifice to the God of Aragon? Was the high giving of her life to be twisted to nothingness in an hour? A Fox daughter in vulgar trouble with a servant's child. In just such trouble as the poor country girls who worked in the house had been in with the bad Fox's of all times, and they had been despised and aborted, their babies, dead or dying thrown to the river, unless they were lucky like Nan's own mother and found some man to put shoes on a Fox's pleasure. All these things have happened, all these things were true and strong in the past. They have happened again and again. Cruelty and pain and tears and death had been common mates to childbirth at Aragon. The family and the house had kept their horrid ministers for such times, women like old Anne. There had always been somebody like that old Anne, tolerant, understanding, skilled and merciless.

Nan sat back in her chair biting her lip and considering.

'Oh, Nan, they wouldn't do anything to Foley no matter what he's done if they knew about me would they?'

'No one must know about this. No one at all. My God to disgrace the house and the family. What are you thinking of? Is it nothing to you that you are a Miss Fox of Aragon?'

Grania felt suddenly intensely more frightened than she had been. The passion in Nan's voice, the fact that she herself had put into words and made real, and a matter to be dealt with, what up to now had been only a fear made a dark frightening grove of the present, a close little wood of fears.

Nan asked her some questions in a coarse brisk way, and though she answered them truthfully Grania suddenly felt guarded and sulky, a way she had never felt with Nan before. She was in a very dark country, she was swayed by fear. She was uncertain and weak. She could not hold on to the only real importance, to Foley's danger, she tried again.

'Nan, it doesn't matter about me, I'm not frightened. It's Foley, Nan, are they going to do anything to Foley? Oh, can't we make a plan? It may be good, it may help if I'm like this, they can't do anything to Foley if they know. You must see he's the only thing that matters.'

'No, you're the only thing that matters, Miss Grania.'

'You don't mean what you are saying, Nan. Foley your own son. Don't you mind what happens to him? Oh, do help me, do help me. No one will help me.'

'God will help us all child.'

'What's the use of that?'

'Now, Miss Grania, crying won't help.' In the midst of all this terror the phrase from childhood came as clear and unhelpful as it had ever sounded. Crying won't help, nor words, nor wishes, nor passionate rebellion won't help. Tears and cruel despairs are beyond the scope of sensible dealing. Besides, crying does help, and there are happenings which are beyond any sensible dealings, and demand a wild acceptance and extravagance in their treatment.

Grania knew that this was such an hour. She knew that the time for sane consideration was not now. She must race ahead and beat the full tide of disaster that was swelling behind her. She must reach a strange shore and find her feet there and run before the coming waves. Clear childish terror filled her and a true instinct to tell no more. Not a word to any one.

Nan was sitting very still in her chair, thinking and calculating. The glass of port she had poured out for herself stood untouched, deeply smooth and red on the table beside her. She was breathing quickly and Grania was not sure whether she was praying. She did not like the look of Nan at all. All the dear spoiling easiness of contact with her was gone. Nan had become in a moment a coarse strong person who would fight you and defeat you on all counts unless you cheated her, unless perhaps you gave in and agreed. Nan to whom she had gone for help in her despair was against her. Nan was going to do things to her. She was thinking far more about this poor baby than she was thinking about Foley or what was likely to happen to Foley. Grania felt sluttish and ashamed about the baby now. Before she had thought of it as a calamity not as a furtive shaming little happening, to be dealt with in furtive and cruel ways. The world had been clouded by fear, but it had been a big and terrifying thunder cloud, a dramatic and shattering fear, and in an hour she had seen how she could turn it to Foley's account. Yes, and keep him through it too, for that idea had not been forgotten in her heroics. Ah, what a word to give to the intense and moving passion of so young and unknowing a creature. Every thought Grania had was real and genuine, real down to her silly young bones, untainted by the cynical mistrust with which age and experience and a better wit might have tortured itself.

Nan was still thinking, she sat quietly pulling down her upper lip, and then letting it go again, and catching severely at her lower lip with her teeth, or pulling in her cheeks and biting at their insides as she reviewed the problems of the hour and the possibilities of their solving. At last she got up saying briskly, with rather an affected matter of factness:

'Well, I must get to the chemist before he shuts and then I'll fix you up all right, dear. Oh, it's quite simple, you just leave it to Nan. Thank goodness you came to me at the very right moment. Your troubles will soon be over, dear, and no more bother to any one. But wait till I see Foley, just let Foley wait till he sees me. I'll go to Mountain Brig and hear what I can hear from Micky before I go near the barracks. Mickey's a good boy and a sensible boy, yes, I'll go and see Mickey. I might not get back till later, now so don't go and do anything foolish till I get back, and then we'll see.'

'What shall we see, Nan? Foley dead and me having an abortion?'

'Miss Grania, what a word for a lady to use.'

'You'd do it, Nan, but you wouldn't say it. It's true. That's what you want to do to me, but I'm not going to let you, do you understand Nan? I won't touch any of your medicine. I won't let you touch me. Do you think I'm a child that I don't know what you want to do to me? You're not going to do it to me, you don't know about anything that matters.'

'You're not yourself, dear. How could you be, poor child.' Nan's tone was professionally soothing and equally infuriating to Grania.

466

'I am myself. I know what I've done, and I know what I'm going to do. I'm——'

The door opened and Miss Pigeon came gently in.

'I'm in good time for bed aren't I, Nan?' she asked anxiously.

'Yes, indeed, Miss Pigeon.' Nan went over and shut the door quietly behind her.

'Yes, indeed. I'll just go in and turn your bed down. Perhaps you would manage to get yourself to bed to-night, Miss, and I'll excuse your hair brushing and prayers.' She went into the other room without any hurry and quietly slipped the bolt over into it's socket as she closed the door between her old nurseries, dividing the day from the night.

'Well, Grania,' Aunt Pidgie said, 'you've been crying, you shouldn't cry you know, it's no use. I found that out a long time ago. Nobody knows and nobody minds, not a bit.'

Grania got up and kissed Aunt Pidgie a little patronisingly as one did. Her troubles were so little and unreal.

'Good night, Aunt Pidgie, dear. I must go. You'll have supper soon, won't you?'

'Perhaps I shall, perhaps I shan't.'

'Oh, of course you will.' Grania turned the door handle.

'It's locked,' Aunt Pidgie said.

'I saw her lock it.'

Grania did not answer. She flew across to the dividing door.

'It's bolted,' Aunt Pidgie said, 'I heard her bolt it.'

'But we're locked in,' Grania said stupidly, and then in a risen voice again, 'we're locked in.'

'Oh, that's nothing,' Aunt Pidgie sat down and began to take her boots off. 'Wait till you've been locked in on a dark night in December, and no supper, and no hot bottle and no fire and then you'll know it.'

'Aunt Pidgie, you oughtn't to say such things.'

'Well now, she's got you too, so you may as well know
what's in store, my dear. Aunt Pidgie can tell you a thing or
two.' Aunt Pidgie peered into one of the boots she had taken off
in a very knowing way before she set it down beside its fellow.
'And a nice pair you are,' she said, looking at them vindictively.
She raised her head and shook it at Grania. 'Ah, it's no good
struggling with that door. It's no good calling out. No one can
hear you in the nursery. Believe me, no one can hear what goes
on in the nursery.'

Grania suddenly felt herself to be in a very strange and awful
little world, a complete and finished world of small fears and
great loneliness, Aunt Pidgie's world. Aunt Pidgie's accepted
world. Suddenly, through all her own storm of trouble, it came
to her that the fears might not be so very small, that the terror
was perhaps as great as the loneliness.

What happens when crying stops? A sort of dreadful clarity,
a seeing power is born for a minute's life. A life as brief as the
ease that follows tears and the anaesthesia of tears. Grania looked
at Aunt Pidgie and saw how thin and pale Aunt Pidgie was and
wondered if there was any reason for it. Could it be connected
with the coarseness and hardness which she had never seen in
Nan before this evening? She looked at Aunt Pidgie's boots and
at Aunt Pidgie's tiny flat feet set side by side in their thin black
cotton stockings, they were as thin and dark as little fins and an
extraordinary feeling came to her that she would like to sit down
and pick up Aunt Pidgie's poor little narrow feet and hold them
in her hands as if they were Soo's feet or a baby's feet.

'Come away from the door, dear.' Aunt Pidgie spoke like
one old lag to another, telling the ins and outs of a prison
familiar to her. 'Come away from the door,' she beckoned.
'Come here, come, dear.'

Grania went over, 'Nearer, where's your ear, child?' In a
whisper Aunt Pidgie shouted, so that her breath was red-hot in

468

Grania's ear, '*Don't say anything yet, she's sure to be listening. She'd like to catch us out and punish us. Don't give her the chance.*'

Grania whispered back, 'All right, I won't.'

Then she had an idea. She went to the cupboard and reached high for Nan's bottle of port. Nan had not touched the glass she had poured out for herself. It still stood on the table—egg-shaped, ruby, smooth and intoxicating.

'Have some,' Grania whispered, holding it out towards Aunt Pidgie. Aunt Pidgie had. She raised her glass and looked through wine to the window and freedom.

'May she die,' she said suddenly. Grania's expression must have shown some silly christian demur, because Aunt Pidgie raised her glass again, 'Yes, and rot,' she amended. She tossed back the wine and licked her old warm lips. It seemed to Grania that she saw an undreamed of Aunt Pidgie. An Aunt Pidgie who had been young and devilish and known such weakness of passion as Grania knew, such helplessness, ah, but never known the joy of yielding. And all her daring now was to match a blue bow with eyes no longer blue at all.

Grania refilled Aunt Pidgie's glass and then her own. Between tears and port she was already rather intoxicated.

'I'll drink to my love,' she spoke grandly. Then, feeling rather silly, she caught Soo up and said, 'Then we'll drink to Soo. Won't we drink to the Sweetie then?'

What an evening! Foley in danger of death. Sylvia's man dead by now most likely. Lying on his back in the dark young heather. Nan gone like an evil old power to wheedle aborting drugs from some good little Catholic chemist, and herself locked in the nursery and getting drunk with Aunt Pidgie, where the evening sun missed the windows, and the rocking-horse, emblem of childhood's jolly hours, wore a bored and vindictive air, a long coffin-headed look, a curling grin, as he pranced timelessly on his rockers.

After the third glass of port went down, Grania slid to the floor beside Aunt Pidgie and picked up one of the mole-like little feet.

'Oo,' said Aunt Pidgie, 'Oo, oo, that's my bad foot.'

'What's the matter with it, Aunt Pidgie?'

'She says it is nonsense. But I say it's a nail in my boot.'

'Is there a nail in your boot?'

'There's always a nail in my boot. There's been a nail in my boot for as long as I can remember.'

Grania picked up the boots, the kind a boy of ten might wear to go to the national school. She slid her narrow, fat, spoiled hand down and along, exploring with cushioned fingers.

'Oh, Aunt Pidgie, it's a dagger.' She took her hand out slowly. 'Do you know what we'll do, Aunt Pidgie?'

Aunt Pidgie took a sip of port. 'No, what?'

'We'll burn these boots.'

'And while you're at it you may as well pop my last winter's combinations on the fire, too, dear. They're like sitting in a gorse bush. Really they are.'

'Where are they?'

'Second long drawer.'

Grania made her blaze, and they giggled together and put on some wood to make the boots burn better. Grania's cheeks were glowing and her head singing. Matters seemed less desperate than they had done an hour ago. Still, she could not lose sight of their urgency.

'Do you think we'd better shout for somebody to come and let us out? She must have gone by now.'

'Don't shout for anybody.' Aunt Pidgie began fumbling and rumbling about in her pocket hole. 'Don't shout for anybody at all. Wait and see what I've got in my sporran. Now, what do you think of that?' She produced a key and pointed it triumphantly towards the door. 'I've kept this key for two years,' she said, 'and she never knew I had it. Fancy that.'

'Does it fit the lock, Aunt Pidgie?' You have to remember that a key was a key to Aunt Pidgie, and any key might serve as an emblem for opening locks that she would never dare to put it in.

'Does it fit? Of course it does. Why, what do you think I'd do the times I have to get out to meet my Diblins? What about the nights there's leprosy in my bed, and I have to make a nest up the stairs? What about the nights when I'm a Birdie? What do you think I'd do then if I can't let myself out for a fly when she's locked the door and gone away?'

'What *do* you do, Aunt Pidgie?'

'Oh, dear, I stay in my bed,' Aunt Pidgie's eyes filled with tears—'but I *could* get out, I could get out.' It was like a child beating its fists.

Grania stretched up an arm and took one of Aunt Pidgie's hands.

'What would she do to you if you did get out, Aunt Pidgie? What would happen if she found out?'

'Oh, nothing, nothing, nothing. She's always so kind to me, my dear, so thoughtful, so careful.' The desperate twittering words came as a little dam to block the truth that Aunt Pidgie had let flow. Again a dismayed child's hands against a loosed force of water.

Grania said, 'Well, I won't tell her anything you've told me, if you won't tell anything about me.'

'Oh, I won't tell. I'm a cagey birdie, I'm mum.'

'What do you hate most, Aunt Pidgie?'

'Cold water on my back. Castor oil. My boots. No supper days. No hot bottle nights.'

Grania stared at her. She had seen enough to open up a perfectly horrid little vista of neglects and tortures.

'But what do you like best?'

471

'My Diblins. Hot bacon. Frazer. My warm bed. My sporran. Wednesday.'

'Wednesday?'

'I see the Sunday papers on Wednesday, when they've finished with them in the servant's hall.'

'Oh, Aunt Pidgie!'

'It's very nice. There's a very good serial running in the *Graphic* just now—a real good crimer. Frazer reads it too. Then there are the beauty notes. Very good too, very helpful, I find. My face would have been lined long ago but for them. You should read them, dear. And the delicious recipes for food. If you are ever thinking of getting married, Grania, be sure you have a cook who can do a nice steak and mushrooms. That and a bottle of red wine, and then a little bit of Camembert. Yes, and a good bacon and eggs is as nice as anything else.'

'I will, Aunt Pidgie, I will, and you can come and live with us and have it every day for lunch,' Grania promised with generous abandon.

'Ah, no, dear,' Aunt Pidgie sighed, 'she'd never let me. I couldn't expect it. And then I wouldn't have the right clothes. And how could I leave my Diblins, I ask you?'

'You could leave messages for your Diblins in all their places, and they could follow after you.'

'Then there's T. Runk.'

'T. who?'

'T. Runk, the God of Travel who lives in the attics with the empty suit cases.'

'But he'd come too. A journey is just his affair, Aunt Pidgie. You couldn't start without him.'

'I'd like to go to a little house by the sea, and grow big juicy pink dahlias in the garden, and have fried fish for my supper.'

'Would you like a pebble pattern on the gate posts, Aunt Pidgie?'

'Yes, I would, and two glass balls, two great big balls.'

'And you could always wear sandshoes.'

'And I would feed the seagulls?'

'Of course.'

'Oh, Grania, I'd promise truly never, never to rob a birdie's nest again. Oh, I do hate to do it. But I have to, you know. Sometimes it's got to be done.'

'Why, Aunt Pidgie?'

'Oh, my dear, I do get such a pain sometimes. She says it's only wind, but when I get a little more to eat, it goes away and I can get to sleep.'

'Are you hungry now?'

'No, I had a big slice of cake for my tea.'

'Well, we might have some more.' Grania went to the cupboard.

'Well, why not, we've burned our boots, haven't we?' Aunt Pidgie hazarded this as a joke. She said it in a 'Have you heard this one' sort of voice, and planted her little stockinged feet firmly before her on the hearth-rug. 'Hurrah,' she said suddenly, 'Hip Hip, Hurrah!'

'You and I are mates, Aunt Pidgie. Have another glass with your cake.'

'I certainly will,' Aunt Pidgie sipped and put back her head and shut up her eyes after each mouthful.

'Why are you doing that, Aunt Pidgie?' Grania asked.

'I'm a Birdie. I'm a real Birdie.'

Then Grania realised that she had made Aunt Pidgie exceedingly drunk.

'You're not really a Birdie, you're Aunt Pidgie. Aren't you, Aunt Pidgie?'

'Twee, Twee-Twee-Twee-Twee,' Aunt Pidgie answered.

'And I'm none too sober myself,' Grania reflected hazily. She ate a large slice of cake and watched Aunt Pidgie dipping her beak in the wineglass and throwing back her head to drink. What was she to do with her? Intoxicated and alone among the burned boots and combinations and empty bottles and sacked cupboards, retribution might fall heavily on Aunt Pidgie when Nan returned and Grania would not be there to stave it off. Full of wine and courage now, she was determined to be far away from Aragon before Nan came back to her kingdom.

XXX

'It was the little dog, Mrs. O'Neill, they were on the look out for, and it was that made a fixture of Mr. Foley's arrest. I believe, whatever connection they had between all.' Micky Brown and Nan were talking in the saddle-room at Mountain Brig. Micky was doing up his tack as if nothing had happened during the day, and as he talked to Nan he worked up and down the length of an unbuckled rein with a piece of soapy sponge.

Nan seemed as much at home with Micky in the saddle-room as she was in her own nursery. She had a way of going to the core of things that made her easy anywhere and in any circumstances. She was sitting on a backless wooden chair with the window behind her, and as she talked to Micky it ran through her mind how much she and Foley had spent doing up this saddle-room—the nice panelling, the stove, the big window, the rows of fixtures for saddles and bridles, all good, and plenty of room for everything. The whole room was an expression of Nan's fundamental concern with real things. Although she had no knowledge of horses she had an understanding of work concerning them, and she knew the value to the eye of a well-appointed, well-kept saddle room. She would have none of those dark, cramped damp little holes, with ill-kept tack hanging on nails and broken pegs, and never sufficient space to put anything away, nor light enough to see if leather was clean or dirty. Nan and Foley spared and skimped nothing on the stabling at Mountain Brig. And she had been right—how right she had been. The good ample air of the yard, the light roomy boxes had a psychological effect on many a buyer. They paid more than they meant to for bad horses as well as good in that atmosphere of space and plenty and cleanliness. Even the roses on the walls outside had a trimmed up, clipped-out sort of look about them. And Nan had made all this from a dirty mountain farm, a yard where, when she first came there, they laid chopped furze from the kitchen door all across the yard in winter time, so that you could walk over the slush and carts could travel their loads without going deep into the ground. And here Nan had bred a son like Foley, handsome and hardy, from her union with a consumptive mountain farmer with little education or ability. It was all Nan's work, and done as it were with one hand while her heart beat and her whole being lived for Aragon alone.

'A dog, Micky,' she said. 'What dog?'

Micky went on with his account.

'Well, I should say, a bitch, Mrs. O'Neill. A little smoothly white terrier with one tan ear and a lot of old foxbites on her. Oh, a proper little article and as wicked as a bee.'

'One tan ear, you said, Micky?'

'Yes, missus.'

'Did you ever see her before to remember her?'

'Well, I wouldn't say it to one only yourself, but I did.'

'Where, Micky?'

'With Captain Purvis.'

'Did you know she was here to-day?'

'I did not. Mr. Foley had her snuggled down in the little potato house. It was when she heard the other gentlemen talking that she gave tongue, you bet.'

'Ah.' When Nan said 'Ah,' she breathed deeply outwards, and it was as if she expelled all that was bad and untrue from her

476

and left room for facts, and power to work on them. Room for her strength to grasp and turn things to her liking. She was like a tree; you knew that her unseen roots had more than the spread and strength of branches.

'That's enough,' she said at last. 'He knows more than he should know. He's deeper into this business than I like, deeper far. Micky, I'm afraid the young boss is in an ugly spot.'

'The young boss'—they had not called Foley that since he was twelve years old. It seemed as though because he was in trouble Nan thought of him in a past tense of youth and helplessness. She was both angry and deeply concerned.

'Micky,' she said, 'do you know any more? For God's sake if you do, boy, let me in on it now. To-morrow might be too late for all concerned.'

Micky said, 'I went through the car after they took the boss off.'

'What did you find?'

'Under the seat in the back there was an old envelope with Captain Purvis' name on it and Askemore Caves scraped on it with the nail of a person's hand-like.'

'They were in the car so?'

'They were in the car so.'

'My God above, he had a bigger hand in this than I thought.'

'Or I, Missus.'

Nan thought for a time. 'Micky, child,' she said gently at last, 'would I chance going out to the caves myself and see what I'd see.'

'Merciful heaven, Mrs. O'Neill, what good would you do?'

'I wouldn't say that till I'd get there.'

'You're late to help them.'

'It's early to say that till I get there.'

'Then what do you think they did with them all day?'

'They might wait till evening when no one would be around.'

477

Neither Nan nor Micky would say the words shoot or execute. Nan said: 'If anything happens them, it might go badly with Foley.'

Micky said, 'Do you think the boys would give a curse what happened Mr. Foley? When their job is done, they're off, and that's the holy all about it. Don't meddle with them, Missus, you'll do no good.'

'Ah,' Nan said again, breathing and thinking, 'maybe so. Maybe not. I'll see you again, Micky,' she said, getting up. 'I must go and have a look at the poor child within. She got a terrible knocking about. Is the horse anything the worse of it?'

'He hit himself a bit of a belt, but it is a thing of nothing. He's hardly lame on it.'

'That's good, I'm glad to hear that.' She spoke with much satisfaction as if there was nothing else left to trouble about. So she could detach matters and consider them separately. Now it was Doatie's turn. She got up and shook out her skirt before walking over the yard towards the house, her eye alert for any change or disorder and her tongue ready to comment tartly or to praise. Nan did not live in the present minute so much as in the present second.

Gipsy met her in the kitchen. She would not have thought of going across the yard to speak to Nan. The yard was not her province and she was a one for the conventions no matter what happened. The conventions and a nice new hat and you were all right. Now she had a cup of tea ready. A cup of tea was always right, it was always the thing. And a nice bit of sliced bread and fresh butter. It was not as much as two hours since they had had tea at Aragon. But then it had been a very upsetting sort of day and you couldn't go far wrong with a cup of tea.

'How nice, Gipsy,' Nan said while her eye swept the kitchen. A warm heavy smell came from a pot of potatoes boiling for the chickens. Nan appreciated it at its good worth. She stood for a

478

moment as Grania had stood in the morning light, but in no
such transparent stillness of speculation and hope. And the evening light was deeper and heavier against the white walls, sinking sullenly into their thickness, melting towards darkness in the
breadth of the open fireplace, waiting for the day's end. Grania
had stood and trembled for the future, to-night the struggle of
past years surged to Nan's memory, years past with all the old
harshness unforgotten. There was nothing pretty to remember
about these years she had spent here and away from Aragon. In
these years she had pulled the place little by little and one thing
after another from its unkept ragged status of mountain farm,
from its chill and snivelling and unnecessary state of weakness
and dirtiness, disorder and seeming poverty, to the tidy sound
affair it was now. One thing after another she had managed and
arranged and kept going—the chickens out of the kitchen, that
had been her first battle when she came here from the state and
luxury of Aragon. After that the stream which, in winter time,
spread over the yard, a boggy and desolate lake where there was
a hollow to hold water, and an endless sluice of dirty water-
courses where steep channels could carry it away. Nan's mind
went back to age-long tiresome arguments with her delicate
thriftless husband. He had never said 'no' to any scheme of hers,
but he had never put forward hand or foot to help in its accomplishment. Next week, it had always been, or, when the turnips
are thinned, or, when the corn is carried, the dung spread. Nan
had found this uncertain obstructionism exhausting and hateful,
but she met and defeated it with unfailing cheerful will and
strength. She would look at the delicate man and tell herself to
a nicety how soon he would be dead. She was very good to him
because she saw an end to it . . . then there had been the
complacent satisfaction of the years when Foley grew up, herself
over again for strength and good tidy living, they could put their
heads together, they could work out schemes and see things in a

479

definite orderly outline as they would be next year or next week. Foley had been in every way the son she had wanted, bred to her own mind and liking, inheriting her own breadth and virility of mind and body, her own looks and strong ability and charm of manner. Foley had had all she could give him, and made very good use of it until now.

Nan had not stood half a minute in the kitchen, yet the whole consciousness of the situation past and present had flowed through her mind. The sense of things past is never so serenely, cruelly sure as when one returns to a place once more familiar than old sheets at a week's end, returns with a changed mind, with trouble at heart and no clear plan for the near future. Nan stood in the sad remembered evening light and wondered suddenly how it was that she had lived through the first long light springtime of her marriage.

'Well,' she said, turning from the doorway, with a firm nurse's smile fixed on her face, 'may I go up and see poor Doatie?'

'Oh, certainly, Nan, certainly, and oh, when I think, you could be looking at her in the Habit (and I was looking at such a nice one for a young girl to-day, Nan, imagine) and the candles lit, and all white flowers, of course, wouldn't it look lovely? Oh, but I mean things are never so bad but they could be worse, are they?'

'Gipsy, there are people in this world, and things are *never* bad enough to please them.'

Nan walked unhurriedly out of the kitchen with this shot, leaving Gipsy uncertain whether or not to take it as a personal insult, constituting a new breach in the amity so lately re-established. On the whole she was pretty sure she had been insulted again.

Upstairs Nan found Doatie flushed and in pain, vague and sick from concussion one moment, and the next in floods of tears.

'Well, dear, well,' she took a hard hot little hand in hers and sat down beside the bed, nodding affably across the world of sickness to the young nurse.

It was characteristic of Foley that he should have succeeded in procuring her presence here despite the changes and chances of his day.

'Well, poor little Doatie-girl. Don't be worrying your head about anything. The horse is all right, the dirty brute, and so will you be soon, love.'

'Oh, Aunt Dymphnia, what's happened to Foley?'

'He had to go and see a horse in Kilkenny, dear.'

'Oh, no, Aunt Dymphnia. It's something else. Mother won't say but she has the head nodded off herself with mystery and secrets about Foley all day.'

'Ah, child, don't trouble yourself, Foley's all right. I do assure you. It's the crack you gave your poor head has you bothered.'

'Aunt Dymphnia, I'd like to speak to you, please, if nurse wouldn't mind.'

The nurses, old and young, exchanged nods and glances and the young one slipped out of the room.

'What's on your mind, child? Just tell me and don't be talking any more then.'

'Is Foley gone off with Miss Grania, Aunt Dymphnia?'

'Is Foley—fiddlesticks! Now, what in God's wide earthly world put such an idea in your head?'

'Are you sure, Aunt Dymphnia? Are you certain?'

'Doatie,' said Dymphnia with awful certitude, 'Foley will never while he lives go off with Miss Grania. Now do you believe me? I promise it, child.'

'Yes, Aunt Dymphnia.' Doatie rolled her head deeper into her pillow. The outline of her little body went slack under the blankets, her eyes closed. This dreadful day of fear and grief and pain was yielding towards evening. She believed Aunt Dymphnia. Aunt Dymphnia was never wrong. She was strong and frightening and hard but she was not afraid to tell you the truth. Foley would not go off with Miss Grania. He would come back to her and she would tell him she was afraid. Tell him everything. There would be understanding for her and forgiveness. Doatie worn out with pain dropped into sleep, happy in her belief that life could not change, content as the sick can be looking to that strange future when they shall be well. Then the most ordinary things shall be shining and glamorous and bridges fling themselves between possible and impossible. To-night in the nowhere of sickness Doatie was at peace.

XXXI

Nan had no definite plan in her mind when Micky dropped her on the lonely road with dark mountain rising above it and dark mountain falling below. She knew the way well from here to the Askemore Caves. How many children's picnic parties had she not conducted there in years past. And Nan never forgot the road to any place.

'Thank you for bringing me this far, Micky,' she said in her easy voice. She stood in the road looking at Micky's strained frightened face with understanding and respect for his trouble. She was sensible of his danger, although she might not believe it to be so great as he did himself.

'Remember, Micky, if you're asked any questions, it was on my information you brought me here. You don't know anything, mind. Home now as quick as you can. And thank you, child, you're a real good boy, and I'll not forget it to you.'

'Mrs. O'Neill, you're doing a terrible foolish thing,' Micky said it for the last time, and Nan smiled at him, she was still smiling her nurse's smile when he had turned the car round and driven away.

But when the car had gone out of sight she rested her face from smiling. She stood looking round her with her face in dark unsmiling repose. She looked to left and right of her, to the mountain rising on her right hand to the mouse-soft evening

483

sky, and dropping on her left hand to the depth of a little river before it started its upward slope again.

'A long, lonely road,' Nan said to herself. 'A long, lonely road and no gate on it. That would give you an idea how lonely it is.' Nan's road was the green ghost of an old coach road through the mountains. Part of the stone-built stable where they had changed coach horses still stood up darkly against the stones and heather, its usefulness and importance dead and long forgotten, its reality slowly sucked back into the wildness that it had once broken and disturbed with so much transient bustle.

Perhaps it was part of Nan's inheritance from the Fox's that she should have an instinct for wild places, an eye for a road and a memory for a turning not frequent in women who lead indoor lives; such a feeling comes either through natural necessity or through generations when the occupations of idle years have bred gentlemanly familiarity with wild places; shooting grouse in these mountains, hunting in the valleys, and home at night for indoor sports in the bad old house below.

As Nan walked stoutly forward along the faint road, the sound of water was loud below her in the evening. She was not thinking of what she might find or what she might do in a little while. The idea of danger for herself in this unplanned undertaking did not present itself to her at all, and indeed it did not seem as though danger could overtake the bold strong woman in her good navy blue suit and thick pearly silk blouse. Her neat dark blue hat had a little pad of pheasants' feathers tucked inside its ribbon band, and turned up at the back off her coiled neat hair and strong neck. She wore gloves too, yellow chamois gloves with one button, washed soft as velvet by herself. She was no imitation lady, Nan. She was a person to whom, in her own right, order and beauty and an earned and duly valued luxury belonged. Her cruelty belonged to this same streak of luxury. A curious and ugly freak in her soundness and strength. Her ability to dwell on Aragon's beauty was a part of the same. She could feed a strange part of herself as she stood before some portrait of a forebear, some young man with dreamy eyes, lace at his woman's hands, jewels on his fingers, something in her agreed with any excess they had known in their time, agreed with and commended the unknown pleasure.

As Nan walked stoutly along the mountain road her thoughts were all below at Aragon. When she was away her mind would go back there and pass through stone-pillared gates and walk the avenues or explore the groves. Her mind was often in the groves, beech woods and the blowing air between their stems, and the round bare ground beneath them. Ash groves: women's long round limbs in form of trees, pale images, powerless and rooted in their soft decaying selves, clothed and held in the close dark stink of nettles and briars, chalk-white in such darkness. Fir woods with their close little paths gay and provoking at first to lead you into their own quietness, threatening, unhappy, and still as a tank of water. Her mind was familiar in these places.

Nan knew her way well along this road—picnics at the caves had been one of the regular summer treats of the young at Aragon. Although the last of such picnics was years ago now she could have told which hazel tree in the little thicket round the caves bore the best nuts, where the richest blackberries ripened, and, given a torch to guide herself by, there was not an inch of those rather awful caves through which she would not have remembered the way with bold accuracy. As she walked on towards that place where last she had sat in sun and shelter spreading bramble jelly on buttered scones and colouring the sugared milk in pink mugs with tea (tea for outings and holidays) the mountainy air blew a little colder on Nan's warm healthy cheek. It was always cold, she remembered, round this corner of the mountain. The wind came in cutting draughts down the heather, through the sheep's bent horns, whistle

485

round and sharp. Here she had always said, 'Put your coats on,' to her children. It was the best part of another mile to the upstanding rocks and the caves beneath from here. Now the roadway bent downhill. Near below five poplars grew in a group planted in a watery hollow. Pencil tall, valley green, they looked as exotic as palms in a Scotch garden. You could see the plains of two counties below. This evening they seemed as shining and as soft as if a green oil was poured between the distances, softening honey-coloured distances and puce under a sky of orchid green. The lands below had no connection with the austerity of the mountain places where Nan walked. She passed the gap by the road where water always lay and the children had dabbled and rattled sticks. A little stream had been led about and about by queer devices. Up here men's hands alone were used for all engineering. Awkward ideas were followed out with pious care, walls built with earnest meticulous method, stones fitted in as carefully as bones in a fish, and the method of wall building varied every mile or so with the inherited ideas of the builder. Mountain sheep bounced on and off impossible obstacles and made away into the heather with a rattle of little hoofs. Black cattle ran along the fence tops as actively and cunningly as dogs. Short grass came up to meet the heather and dark gorse with hardly a flower on it grew in patches through the grass fields beyond, but the nearest farmhouse was a mile away at least as Nan rounded a shoulder of the hill and turned off the road on to a less used path that went close round the mountain foot. Before her now were tall rocks like pillars, and deep in their faces, five stone steps leading down to it, was the little iron gate set before the narrow cave mouth and locked against adventurous children.

It was only when Nan set foot on the top step that she knew clearly what she was going to do. She went down the steps in a gay brisk manner, her between nursery and bathroom walk,

486

quick and preoccupied, and she shook the little iron gate in a determined rattle with her gloved hands.

'Hullo there!' she called.

'Hullo there! Just a minute. Just a word with you. It's important. I'm from friends.'

She knew in the hush that followed she had been heard. She knew it before she heard the tread of boots on broken steps below. She knew how a whisper would echo down there, magnified by some trickery of echo, how often on the picnic afternoons had they played at that game, and now she waited for an answer.

'Put your hands up,' a voice came. She saw the white glimmer of a face in the dark below, streaked by the iron bars of the little gate, and up went her hands, the palm flesh coming in comfortable little hills through the buttoned glove opening. She looked faintly absurd standing there facing death with her neat gloved hands flung up against the mountain side. She looked so unlike violent death, that indeed the possibility of such a happening was compelled to retreat before so strong and well-dressed a woman.

'Come along,' Nan called as she might have coaxed one of her children, 'I'm quite alone and I've got a message for you.'

'Who is it?'

'Who is it?'

'Foley O'Neill's mother it is.'

The bottom of the gate grated on the stone beneath it and a pale young man, masked and with a gun in his hand, stood a moment in the opening before he advanced towards Nan, motioning her back up the steps until they stood on the level together. There she appeared immeasurably greater than he who was young, tired and sick with dread at the thought of that hour of execution when night should fall on the heather.

'You'll find the message in my coat pocket, child,' Nan said gently, her hands still above her head. 'No, the right-hand pocket,' and in the moment when they stood so near she raised her powerful knee and dealt him a low blow like the kick of a horse.

'I learnt that trick off a medical student.' Nan stooped down and picked up his gun that had rattled on to the stones as he doubled up in pain. 'Take your time, my boy,' she said kindly. 'I know how this works too, imagine. Sure, you hadn't it cocked it all.' She stood there covering him while his pain lessened.

'Now, then,' she put the gun to the back of his neck, 'I don't care how many of you is down below, you'll be the first to get an ugly dirty death.'

'I mightn't be the last, you bloody old chancer,' the boy was crying with pain and exhaustion and rage.

'No rude talk now. Take me in to where you have the prisoners and if we aren't there in five minutes' time, mind, you get the contents of this,' she gave him a dreadful poke with the gun, 'and I'll find them myself. Believe it or not I know these caves backwards, and you wouldn't spend five minutes getting any place in them. Better now. On please.'

She followed him down the crooked flight of stairs that plunged towards darkness. Strong and brisk on her feet. His torch flashed out, a thin fan of light. Nan had only one hand to help herself to lean against the sweaty rock walls. Sometimes she had to step from rock to rock with a black depth under her feet. 'Go slow, boy,' she warned him pleasantly, 'or the gun might go off on me and we don't want a nasty accident, do we, imagine!'

Round them the rocks mouthed and gaped their strange formations like growths; half-known half-guessed stalactites reached down and more awful stalactites reached up. Yellow greasy rocks below mounting bluntly towards rocks that dripped like candle-grease of a thousand years above. Narrow, dark throats of rock opened into huge bellies where echoes played and rattled about together.

These caves had been a favourite resort of picnickers from the time of their discovery in Victorian days when the passages and rock formations had been named with heavy appropriateness. The voices of many guides had uttered those names, leaving that place-tamed feeling in the sombre air, domesticating the ugliness, as though it had been painted on a souvenir mug, or a German waterfall, complete with pine trees, dashing its way across a painted china plate. Such is the influence of guides' voices naming for years a pendulous mass: 'The Golden Fleece.' An upthrust of smooth stone: 'The Ladies' Saddle.' Or again: 'The Monkey's Head,' 'The Horses' Teeth,' 'The Elephant's Foot,' and, rather a show-piece, 'The Organ.'

Nan could name them each as she passed. Her accurate mind going strongly back to the picnic days when the children had stood enthralled by the rock shapes so remarkably true to their names, when they had hopped and floundered on uncertain feet from chamber to chamber, from the House of Commons to the still nastier House of Lords, walking upright where Nan had to bend low under the toothed ceilings, slopping delightfully through puddles fed constantly by the drip from the roof.

Nan called the names out now as she passed the objects by, her voice as easy as though, when this exploration was over, she would sit on a rug in the sun and spread again the butter and bramble jelly on brown scones.

Everything Nan undertook she achieved with the ease of a full river between its banks, even in the course of achievement she moved freely and uncramped, her flowing style in life unimpeded, unlet, unhindered by any circumstance whatsoever. Now Nan scarcely even felt elation when she heard the muted hollow sound of voices in front of them.

489

'Stop,' she whispered to her guide, 'and shout out for every man to put his hands up.'

'The boys is gone,' he answered, 'They're out settling a grave. There's only the prisoners and myself here.'

'Shut up, and shout out,' she ordered sharply. In the dark he felt her poking at him with the gun, an alarming fumble. 'I have it now,' she grunted easily. 'Shout out, child, shout out, or—'

'Hands up, boys, we're surrounded,' he screamed into the dark and the echo bounded off the 'Ladies' Saddle' and 'Seal's Head' and went crashing into the unseen domes of the House of Lords.

A faint cheer (which would not have disgraced one of R. M. Ballantyne's own heroes) answered this announcement.

'Ah,' said Nan. 'In the Chamber of Horrors, are they? Isn't that very good? Now I might as well get you out of my way, mightn't I? But I won't, child. Be good now and you'll be all right.'

The two boys were sitting quietly on two stalactites, rather like picnickers of old, except that their hands and feet were tied. They were not gagged, as their captors were undramatic and rather sympathetic men, who had no wish to make this short imprisonment more tiresome and incommodious than necessary. They would gladly have played cards with their prisoners or done any little thing to while away time before nightfall and execution, but they had to get the graves dug.

'Good-evening, Captain Purvis. Good-evening, Mr. Craye.' Nan said pleasantly. 'Isn't this an unfortunate business, imagine! Do you remember me, of course you don't. It's Nan from Aragon, Foley O'Neill's mother.' Even now she took time for an introduction, and saw nothing strange in their polite How do you do's from the darkness.

'Unfasten the Captain,' she said to her guide, much in the same voice in which she might have set a nursery maid some bit of business.

'I have no knife,' he answered surlily.

490

'I thought of that,' she said. 'Take my nail scissors and hurry.'

It was all rather like a picnic. A get—your—socks—on, don't—delay, now—then—where's—our—jersey, sort of rhythm about it.

The two soldiers stood up unsteadily, twisting their hands gently round their numb wrists. They tied their guard up without any rancour or bad feeling, asking him if he was quite comfy, and saying 'good-bye' before they turned to follow Nan back through the labyrinth where she found her way as easily as if she followed a thread.

Nan kept warning them as if they were children of this or that obstacle as they went along. Where the roof sagged low, where the path dropped steeply. The air was bad and no one wanted to speak for the effort was heavy and the necessity for haste was great.

Among the hazel bushes, grey as cats at evening, Nan handed over the revolver as if it had been a jammed scone.

'Take the awful thing,' she said. 'I couldn't shoot it off if you paid me, and hook it for the barracks like blazes. You'll get through if you're lucky, and mind when you get there and see no harm comes to my Foley. Give nobody away, remember that, please. I've taken a bit of a chance for you, and that's what I ask you. Keep quiet. Foley has to get his living in this country and so do I. Go separate ways down the mountain, and go, excuse me, like hell.'

'We can't leave you up here alone, Mrs. O'Neill,' they protested.

'Now, whatever chance I have alone I have none with you two near me.' She clapped hands as though she was starting them in a race, and they went off without any kind of farewells or thanks, simply doing as they were told.

Nan saw them go and waved one of her gloved hands as they

491

disappeared from her sight. Then she went down the steps to the iron gate again as she had a sudden idea that matters might be still further delayed if she locked it and threw away the key. This she did with neatness and dispatch. She was coming up the steps dusting her gloves together when Killer Denny and his mate came round the corner of the hazels. They carried a spade with which they had been digging a shallow grave at a peat cutting a mile away. The mountain people who had seen them had kept away knowing that death and trouble were near.

'Oh, good-evening,' Nan said pleasantly, 'Can you tell me, I wonder, is there any one could show me over the caves? I hear they're very interesting and I'd love to see them, imagine.'

'The caves are not on show,' Killer Denny answered, 'Who are you, and what's your name?'

Nan thought a moment. If she told a lie she might get a start down the road, but they could catch up with her without any trouble. They could overtake her before she had gone a mile.

'My name is O'Neill,' she told them. 'I'm Foley O'Neill's mother, and I'm here to ask you to let those two officers go free for the military are holding my boy as hostage for them.'

'He yapped, I suppose, or you wouldn't be here. I'm sorry, Missus, but I can do nothing for you. It's hard on your son, for God knows it was little he did to assist us.' Denny spoke in the harsh voice of a person repelling a professional beggar, but Nan ignored the rudeness as if it was unheard and kept pleasantly on.

'Isn't it a wonder to you then that he hadn't the soldiers here hours ago? Maybe he can hold his tongue if he can do nothing else, eh? Wouldn't you agree?'

She was burning to know how large a part Foley had played in the capture. She had so strong and natural a curiosity that she would have chanced anything now, to satisfy herself exactly.

'Oh, a very heroic silence,' Denny jeered, 'and he cock-certain they were dead in the heather since twelve o'clock this

492

morning. Why would he put himself wrong with the I.R.A. for two cold corpses, eh? He is selling horses long enough, now see, to cod the military over any two little things like that and no trouble to him.'

'And they're not dead?' Nan rapped it out with swift certainty. 'They're not dead, aren't they?'

'Who told you so?'

'Oh, child, it's plain in what you say.'

'Well, see now, listen, Missus. You can do no good here and you might do a lot of harm. So off you go and keep quiet or it'll come harder on your gentleman son. When his English friends are done with him the I.R.A. might be knocking at his door, now see, and while we're at it, how did you know to come here to-night, for all he couldn't split?'

Nan put her hand in her pocket and took out the scrap of paper with Askemore scrawled on it.

'As good jailers as you are, boys, one of your prisoners left that after him in Foley's car; it takes a nosey old Nannie to stick her nose into the like o' that, eh? To turn up the floor mats, and lift out the cushions, what? She nosed out something, imagine! So take advice, let yous be quits.'

In excitement Nan's speech plunged towards the idiom of her youth, her beautiful voice rang now against the hollow hill behind her, it sounded roundly in the birdless mountain evening.

Killer Denny was a really hard and wicked little man. Of the three he only had no dread of this hour of execution. He had spent years in America, he had never known a lucky day there, and he was tough with a toughness from the underworld of big and cruel towns. There was a greater hatred in him for these things that Nan stood for and Aragon stood for than there was love for Ireland or hatred for the English enemy.

The other two boys knew fear and prayer and were sustained

through ordeal by a terrible martyr's spirit of patriotism, but to Denny the Irish war was only a business, a dangerous, exciting and highly remunerative business. He was the mercenary soldier of all time, the same tough guy who did the job on the princes in the tower. That and something more, something worse, for he had a little education and a bitter grudge against the world for the great hardships he had known, the hunger, and the coldness of charity.

The boy with him had not spoken. Now he said, nervously, 'We should hurry, captain, we should hurry.'

'What hurry are you in?' Denny stooped to light a cigarette with provoking deliberation. He liked playing on any one's nerves. 'Didn't you hear Mrs. O'Neill say her heroic son would never split to the British that he drove ourselves and two of his late customers as far as the seven crosses this morning. Ah, boy, he mightn't die for Ireland in the style you or I would, but he knows bloody well he should keep his mouth shut. It's waiting for him on all sides, now see, if he don't sing dumb.'

'We should hurry, Captain, we should hurry,' the boy repeated, his face was desperately pinched and nervous, framed in the upturned collar of his trench coat.

'What a hurry you're in for your first execution, aren't you?'

'Oh, Jesu!'

'Jesu!'

Nan and the boy breathed it out together.

Killer Denny showed his small regular teeth in a smile. 'All the talk that goes on about Ireland and her holy wars,' he said, 'but someone has to do her dirty work, now see, for all the prayers and priests never got her very far. Well, come on now, I'll not delay the little matter any longer.'

The boy turned round with a green face. He was suddenly sick, retching and heaving, his hands to his head.

'Let me off it, Captain, for Christ's sake,' he gasped. 'A fight is O.K., yes, but a bloody murder on a nice evening spare us. O Lord, oh holy Jesu have mercy on the poor beggars. Oh, Jesu, did you hear one give me a winner for Thursday? And I'm to turn round and pump lead through him. God knows I'm a poor shot, I wouldn't know where I'd hit him.' His voice rose to a scream. 'You wouldn't know how long a chap would be dying, he mightn't be rightly dead and we throwing the sods in on his poor bloody eyes.'

Nan too turned on the killer.

'How long, I wonder, before yourself's corpsed in a wicked ending and your toes cocked in the grave and not a word more about you, God damn you, that had no pity for another.'

'What's your interesting proposition?' The Killer was delighted by their hysteria. 'That we should let these two prisoners go so that they can identify any one of the three of us at leisure?' He spat. 'You and your talk about fair fighting,' he spat again. 'How many of us are there in this country and how do you think we're to take on the whole British Army, can you give me an idea?' He sank his head and spoke low to Nan. 'You and yours on any side of the blankets—Oh, I know your noble ancestry, Missus—is backing the British against your own. Mind you, your connection with the Fox family was well looked into before gentleman O'Neill was ordered to do a bit for Ireland beyond a drink or a bed for a boy that might need it.'

'What was he to do?' Nan fired out the question.

'Oh, a little liaison work, will we call it, between the big house where he's so popular with his lady cousins, and their friends at the barracks. But, as it happens, we didn't need his help this time. The two fools we were after as good as asked us to take care of them, without any assistance from Aragon or its bastards.'

Nan swung back her hand and arm and hit him a savage blow across the face.

495

'You rat,' she said. 'You Yankee rat, keep the name of Aragon out of your dirty mouth. Even to name it, oh.' Her face was white and her eyes blazing. 'Bastard I am, and thankful for the blood and breed that sets me the world away from scum like your wicked little self.'

They were a strange group on the side of the hill. Nan, immeasurably beautiful in her rage and pride, facing like a tigress the little gunman who cleared his eyes of the stinging tears her blow had brought to them, and the boy who knelt among the stones now, gabbling prayers and shivering in the sheltered still air. Round them the leaf-like pallor of the evening light sank in faint levels towards night. Then, shattering the hush that followed on Nan's blow, coming before the pause of surprise could break or lessen, a voice was shouting through the echoing dark below.

'Captain Denny, Captain Denny,' it cried. 'They're gone. They're gone, Captain, they're gone,' the voice grew nearer, changed from echo to voice. Soon there was the sound of stumbling hurrying feet, uncertain in the dark with the echo fumbling after them, a rush of feet up the last broken stair, and a white face behind the iron gate, and incoherent speech while hands gripped the bars and shook at them, and the two men outside listened stunned to the broken story. Nan helpless to fly, stood silently, a figure of immense triumph between them. The last of the evening sun flung her shadow, compact and orderly, up against the rock face.

'They couldn't even tie me up,' the boy inside the gate was panting, 'I got myself free.'

'As bad as they were they were able for you,' Denny snarled.

'Only for her and her trickery we had them yet. Oh, she beats all for devilment.'

Nan laughed a splendid joyful laugh.

'There's no great difference between Ireland's soldiers and

496

boys in the nursery when it comes to managing either,' she said. 'And now if I was you chaps I'd hop it quick for your prisoners are tidy runners, and they have a nice start of you, and they might be back with a reinforcement, imagine, to turn the tables, who knows?'

The Killer caught Nan by the arm.

'And you, Missus,' he put his face near hers, 'do you think you'll get out of this hole alive, do you? Do you? You won't strike me three times, I'm telling you.'

The praying boy said again, 'We should hurry, Captain, we should hurry,' but his voice was glad now, not anguished.

'I'd count my life well given,' Nan said, though the first shadow of fear crossed her face and for the first moment she looked lost in their power.

'You would, would you?' The Killer said quietly, 'I believe you, Missus. Well, I'll do better than shoot you. I'll do better for you than an easy death in the heather. March now to the house you're so proud of, and see what I have in store for you.'

'Hey, hey,' shouted the boy who was behind the bars, 'let a fella out, will you, am I to stop here like a chained dog, eh?'

'Let yourself out.'

'I have no key.'

'And where would we get a key. Break the lock at your leisure.'

'Tis the lock of a tower, 'tis the lock of a tower,' the boy cried, 'Jesus, Mary and Joseph save. Jesus, Mary and Joseph have mercy. . . .'

His voice pierced the silent mountain air as his hands rattled at the gate.

Nan said reasonably:

'We wouldn't spoil five minutes letting him out. See there where I threw the key in the young brackens.'

Her level sense held them. The three bent their eyes to the

ground searching among the little bits of gorse and the springing heather and bracken. It was like a game of hunt the thimble, or looking for a chocolate Easter egg hidden in the daffodil leaves. The praying boy crossed himself and sent up a little petition to Saint Anthony.

'Saint Anthony is very good,' Nan said with satisfaction when the key was found. The boy nodded complacently. 'I'm always praying to him.' He spoke in the voice of one who says, 'He ought to be used to me.'

They opened the gate in the rock face, locked it again and threw the key farther away. Then they hurried Nan off down the road on the way to her execution.

XXXII

Foley was being put through his third examination since he had been brought a prisoner to the military barracks that afternoon.

The first conversation had been a tell-us-old-chap affair with one of the young officers whom he knew well. That is to say, he had sold him one very good horse and talked him into buying two moderate horses, and afterwards assisted him to pass them on. So, though they might be said to know each other pretty well, yet here they could find no common ground at all. It was a futile and embarrassing business.

'Look here, O'Neill, I know you'd want to help us get our chaps out of trouble. They're your friends too, dammit old boy, and you're far too stout a chap to lie up with the shinners.'

Foley replied, 'If I knew anything any good to you or them I'd have said it hours ago. I don't. Your chaps are finished, I'm sorry to say, and I'm not going to inform on the other crowd.'

'But look here, O'Neill, you can't admit you know as much as that and lie low about the fellows who've murdered Michael and Tony. There are limits.'

'There's no limit to the difficulties you soldiers can put the likes of myself in this country into.'

'All we want is a straight answer to a straight question, and every minute lost getting it is a chance lost for Michael and

Tony. After all, O'Neill, you've ridden hunts with them, you've sold bad horses to them.'

'And good.'

'And good certainly. We've always treated you as one of ourselves here, and now we're in a jam you're going to turn it all up and act, you'll forgive me, pretty yellow. Poor show, you know.'

'See here,' Foley frowned in an effort to get through all the good fellowship implied in the earnest stilted speech, 'I've got to live in this country and earn my living in it and work hard for my living. You chaps are only fighting in it.'

'And if we could count on a decent bit of co-operation from you people living here, there'd be damn' little fighting left for us to do.'

'Ah,' Foley said. 'Well, make the country safe for co-operation then. See to it that those who give you information aren't taken out of their own lonely beds and shot a week after.'

'That's what you're afraid of, is it?'

'Yes,' Foley said, 'I am afraid of it.'

'Well, for a chap who can ride a hunt or a race like yourself it's a poor show.'

'Ah, talk sense, man.'

'Sense? When Michael and Tony may be getting it any minute. For the last time, O'Neill, will you tell me what you know about this business, or will you not?'

'I will not.'

'I see. I'll have to tell the Colonel I was wrong about you. I really thought you'd the guts to lie up for a gallop of this sort with the right chaps. I'm not a great judge but, by God, O'Neill, I'm disappointed in the form you've shown. It's a rotten show.'

'Well, there's the position,' Foley said hopelessly.

'I'm afraid you aren't quite at the end of this business, you know, old chap. You may find it healthier to talk to me now of your own free will.'

'I'll talk to no one.'

'You may find you'll have to.'

'I may find this, and I may find that. I'll deal with what I find when I find it. If you and your Majors and your Colonels have no more common sense in fighting the war in this country than the lot of you have in making, breaking or buying horses in this country, God help England and her army.'

Now this was an insult, and Foley was very mistaken to have made it. To connive at the shooting of one's pals and at the escape of their murderers was one thing, but to follow that up by insulting the horsey side of The Regiment was another. It was worse than a sneer at their women kind, or at least quite as bad. It got under the skin of vanity and simple pride. Coming from Foley who had always made it his business to ask opinions of horses from the soldiers, and rarely, if ever, to give his own, the bitter truthful jeer was the more venomously barbed.

The boy said, 'Thanks for your opinion of us,' and got up. His face was white with temper. He would not try another yard in the matter. Foley could hardly have taken a more conclusive way of putting every officer in the barracks against himself.

XXXIII

When the boy had left him, Foley sat thinking and measuring things out in his mind. To himself his position was clear enough.

This morning he had been more than unwillingly involved in the death of two officers, two men who by their personal carelessness, in a country with which they were supposedly at war, could put himself and others like him in a stick as cleft and awkward as could be found. It was entirely out of his power to save them, and to the best of his belief they were dead men an hour from the time he had left them on the mountain road with their captors. To him there had been no reason for, and every reason against, his going to the barracks and informing as to where and with whom they had last been seen. Foley had perceived no chance at all for them and so had set his mind on the next problem of his day, finding a nurse for Doatie.

He had chosen the best looking of the two girls available at the County Hospital, and flirted with her on the way out to Mountain Brig. He could not help himself. Everything in him and about him was a challenge to the female. He could not look without a caress in his eyes, he could not touch a girl's elbow without impelling her to know his interest, he could not speak except on a tender bantering note, as if his voice would play with her stranger's hand, or pinch a neck, frigid still to him.

502

Foley was the 'Oh—you—are—awful' boy of all time and all class. The Fox licence in his blood was coarsened and made more natural by the peasant side of his breeding. At the same time this peasant side of his nature had a revolted primness, a chill recoil from his own acts and ventures in love. It was bred in him as strong as his good looks and came through as many generations of austere mountain ancestry as Nan's Fox strain came through generations of mannered bad living.

It was the O'Neill side of Foley that went out to Doatie and the pure (because untouched by him) quality of her childish passion and obedience towards him. In the back of the car now there were paper bags of fruit and sweets he had taken pains to choose for her. Beside him the nurse he had found for her eyed him roguishly. Through her alert talk of racing, she was a bookmaker's handsome daughter, and with every response she made to his challenge he thought the less of her (that was his way), and drove faster to get her to Doatie, his wounded child.

There was an exalted cruel streak in Foley which was fully conscious of Doatie's present fear of horses and rejoiced that she should subdue and hide it from him . . . rejoiced that for him she had known terror and been hurt. . . .

In Aragon's basements there was a passage that ran its length to reach one room only, a room distant from any other, a room whose lonely window looked straight out over the river, deaf sailing ships might pass below it but no other traffic. This room was unused for many years. There had been an effort made once to turn it into a butler's bedroom, but butlers less austere than Frazer could not enjoy a night's quiet sleep in airs so shaken and petrified by long past doings. The walls of this room had been papered over in blue and white, but where the paper had peeled in the damp air from the near river, you could see underneath one of old chinese design, a most peculiar design, perhaps rightly hidden and in parts purposely defaced. About this room there

503

remained still an air of past luxuries. White and gold pelmets over the windows, an Italian decoration on the ceiling, a thin marble mantel and steel basket grate—a strange room to find in the basements of Aragon where the hordes of servants had slept in dirt and confusion. Once the room had been hung with mirrors. Other curious contrivances were set in the walls. There was still an old ottoman covered in faded *petit-point*, white rose wreaths on a shadowy blue background. And it was locked. It was fifty years now since any one had opened it and closed it, sick and shuddering at a half-understanding of delicate ivory-headed cutting whips and other fine and very curious instruments.

'It must be burnt,' Mrs. Fox had exclaimed. 'It must be burnt immediately.' She had hurried wildly away from it, nor ever solved the problem of who to entrust with its destruction, or how, most delicately, she could convey to Mr. Fox her horrid knowledge of such a wicked boxful. Somehow she could never speak of it, for it was his grandfather who had used such dreadful tools, who had built this far-off room for his pleasures. She would tremble. *It was Mr. Fox's own grandfather . . .* and Foley's great-great-grandfather. No wonder a little cruelty made his blood quicken, made the idea of sacrifice and pain pleasant to him, and Grania's youthful uninstructed passion a little less than necessary, a little more than he wanted. Had it been given him without the implied difficulty of her different birth he would have most likely passed her safely by, but the challenge of the whole thing had been irresistible.

He thought, with some relief, as he sat in the bleak guard-room, that this affair at least would put an end to all that. If he had been an unlikely suitor before to-day, he was an impossible one to-night. Foley was so without imagination that his mind could fling a bridge across any hell and see Grania in an unimaginable placid older life, in which he would be forgotten

504

as though their encounter had never been. He saw the truth. But he was unseeing of the pain that must go before such a terrible forgetfulness—a pain so beyond any help but his, that the placid future was hardly reason enough for its endurance.

But Foley lived in the present and in some untouched future, he did not live in that nervous place just beyond the present, he had no ecstatic to-morrows or sad fainting yesterdays, his life was in Now and in Then, and to-night in his Now, Grania was only by the way. His concern was for himself alone. He knew he was in a certain degree of danger, but he would rather stand in a grave degree of danger from the British enemy than in an uncertain disfavour with Ireland's soldiers. So he was implacable in his resolve for silence.

A Major came next to interrogate him. There was nothing friendly about this interview. The Major had entertained no great fancy for Foley at any time in his popular career. The Major was a keen hard soldier, and a hard and brilliant man to hounds, and knowledgeable enough about horses to have avoided buying any from or through Foley. He did not share in the younger soldiers' respect and enthusiasm for Foley's horsemanship, or liking for him as a person. He was a jealous man to hounds and very serious in his pursuit of the chase. It troubled him unduly that Foley should so often have the best of a hunt, and should achieve it with such seeming ease. Where the Major set his teeth and sweated blood, and put himself and his horse quite frequently in hideous and spectacular danger, Foley would slip over the country with an effortless appearance of ease, a boldness so quick and artful that it hardly seemed bold. The Major had never got the better of Foley in a hunt or a race although they had had some contests of wits and endurance in both. He valued his only superiority to Foley in any way that was important to him, and as he was a very simple social snob, he was careful to foster the gap that so divided them. He found

505

Foley's widespread popularity most distasteful, in fact it was hateful to him.

He looked on Foley's present position without understanding of any kind, indeed with some satisfaction. Bitterly and deeply as he felt about the almost certain deaths (murders rather, all English soldiers killed in the Irish war were murdered) of his two most able young officers, it was with a deep sense of bringing many things he hated to justice and to light that he confronted Foley this evening.

'Good-evening,' he said coldly, doubtful rather whether he should recognise Foley as anything except a traitor and murderer. But this was not a formal military inquiry, nor was guilt actually proved satisfactorily, except to the Major himself. However.

'Good-evening,' he had said it, and Foley had nodded and murmured a polite abstracted reply. Not the attitude for any man in so grave a situation as that in which Foley was placed. Not the right attitude at all.

The Major put a pad on which he had pencilled notes in front of him on the table.

'I gather from Mr. Young that you prefer to keep any information as to the probable murders of Captain Purvis and Mr. Craye to yourself, Mister O'Neill.' There was a great deal of emphasis on the Captains and the Misters. 'Is this the case?'

'Yes, Major.'

'You admit you have some knowledge of their whereabouts?'

'I don't admit anything.'

'Yet you say you prefer to keep what you know to yourself?'

'I explained my position to Mr. Young, Major. I have not got anything more to say.'

'I think, Mr. O'Neill, that we must try to persuade you to say just a little more. Just a short explanation perhaps, of your morning's activities. And please remember I can check up on most of them. Do you, for instance, know a public-house called the Wren's Nest?'

'Yes, I think every one knows the Wren's Nest.'

'It's a cosy little bar, isn't it? And very popular with some of the gentlemen on the run in this country.'

'It's not a spot I'm often in, Major.'

'You don't go to Bungaron much, then?'

'Oh, you mean the Wren's Nest on the Quay?'

'Ah, and why should you think I meant any other Wren's Nest? Why, Sir? Why do you immediately think of another pub called the Wren's Nest?'

'There is a Wren's Nest on the mountain road behind our house, Major, I often pass it. I don't think I know the Bungaron one as well as you do, Sir. But I've heard it is a nice place.'

There was a quite insolence in Foley's speech that enraged the Major. Foley had fallen into and out of his elaborately arranged pitfall, and then cheeked him quite as if he was not on suspicion of a horrible charge of murder.

'Perhaps, Mr. O'Neill, you can tell me why you visited your favoured Nest at 10.30 this morning?'

'I called in to get a glass of beer.'

'You were on your way—where?'

'I was on my way to Bungaron to get hold of a nurse.'

'And do you generally go to Bungaron by that road?'

'Not generally. It's out of the way.'

'Then why did you choose it this morning?'

'I had a reason.'

'Why did you choose it this morning?'

Foley thought sulkily for a moment. It was not from any motive of chivalry that he kept quiet about Grania. It simply seemed easier not to drag her into it too.

'That's my business,' he said. Then he smiled. 'It's part of what I won't tell.' Nothing could have been worse for him than this piece of ill-timed levity. But he could not help having a mild dig at so much round about pomposity.

'I see. So you have reasons which you will not state for going twenty miles instead of ten to get a nurse this morning. I imagine someone in your house must be rather ill, Mr. O'Neill, if you have to get the services of a nurse?'

'Yes, my cousin had a bad fall this morning.'

'Ah, ah. Then you must have had a very excellent reason for your delay in fetching the nurse?'

'It's a perfectly simple reason, Sir, but it's my own business.'

'Quite. Quite. Well, perhaps later on you will explain that part of your business to us. There's a good deal about your business, Mr. O'Neill—let's leave your horse business out of it, shall we?' (His tone dragged the horse business to the forefront of the matter.) 'That is a bit shaky, a bit mean, a bit difficult to understand by simple chaps like us soldiers, Mr. O'Neill. It seems to me that it is not only in the way of your business that you know how to put your friends through it.'

There was a refinement of passionate dislike in his voice. He paused a minute and bent his head, writing on the paper in front of him. The dreary room was growing darker with the slow stretching dusk of the spring evening. The sound of a car stopping outside in the barrack square came through the slightly opened window. The Major raised his head and looked long and thoughtfully at Foley.

'Where did you find Captain Purviss' dog?' he asked quietly.

'I didn't find any dog,' Foley answered slowly.

'You deny that Captain Purvis' dog was in your possession, do you? You deny any knowledge of Captain Purvis' dog?'

'Yes, I deny any knowledge of Captain Purvis' dog.' Foley suspended his voice—he had more to say. The Major waited now he had him. He had him now. 'But perhaps you mean

508

Captain Purvis' little bitch, Judy? Would you know a little dog from a little bitch, Major? Maybe you know more about dogs than you do about horses, only it sounds funny calling Captain Purvis' bitch, Judy, a dog—I thought everybody knew Judy.' Foley lit a cigarette with an air of amused disquiet. Fancy any one being so silly, in every line of his easiness.

The Major's eyes snapped. His temper snapped too.

'Insolence isn't going to help you much, Mr. O'Neill, I'm afraid, although it may be a certain relief to your feelings, and if you have got any, they may need relief, or I imagine they would, under the circumstances.'

Foley murmured.

'I've got very tender feelings.'

'Look here.' The Major stood up. If he had not been so aware of being an officer and a gentleman he would have screamed at Foley. 'That's enough. We know you were involved in the murders of Captain Purvis and Mr. Craye this morning. We know you were in the pub with their murderers. We know you drove them to their deaths. We know that you gave us no information which might have prevented their deaths. And we know that you refuse any information that may lead to the capture of their murderers.'

Foley said, 'You could frighten any story you wanted out of the cripple, you know.'

'Not a story that hangs together quite so convincingly as this one, I'm afraid. Perhaps you don't realise that a fellow who plays traitor, as you have done, can put himself in a very danger-ous position, in a very dirty position. Do you realise, or do you not, that you may have to answer for this with your life? Even the British Government is getting a bit fed up with chaps like you, and justice can be done quickly under martial law, you know.'

Foley was not looking at the Major, he was staring across the

room over the Major's trim shoulder to the open doorway
where Grania stood, and there was a look both stricken and
exalted about her. It gave age to her fat youth, it hollowed
awkward shadows in her sweet and silly face. Somewhere all
exuberance had been shed, she had gone from young girl back
to bluntly determined child, or, perhaps, to savage extreme,
womanhood.

Behind her in the doorway her mother fussed and whispered
to the Colonel. The Colonel fussed and whispered back, unsol-
dierly, embarrassed. He was a nice man.

Foley stood up, but did not come forward. Grania smiled at
him quickly, but he did not smile back.

Mrs. Fox put her arm through Grania's and said:

'How do you do, Major Radley. My daughter has some
information she is anxious to give you about, er, O'Neill's
movements this morning.'

Foley looked at Grania across a width of amazed dislike.
What was she going to say? What could she say? What now?
What next?

Addressing herself to the Major, Grania said, in a weak clear
voice, the voice of youth that can only say the thing it means, to
whom the truth is of violent disproportionate importance.

'I heard you. But you can't do anything to Foley. None of
you can. You are our friends, and you can't, because the thing
is——' She stopped and looked from the Major to the Colonel,
and then, with as much defiance as though it was her mother's
doing, at Mrs. Fox, 'the thing I've got to say is, that Foley and
I are going to have a baby.'

There was a shocking silence. Mrs. Fox did not look more
appalled than Foley. The Colonel, alarmed now, as well as
embarrassed, turned his back on the party and gazed out of the
windows. The Major looked down at his notes and fiddled with
a pencil.

510

Grania stood, shaking and swaying a little, gazing with deep alarmed eyes at Foley, she was gazing over a coldness as of water, a coldness that slowly became real and deep to her, more real even than his danger.

'Oh, Foley,' she went across to him. 'I had to say it, Foley. It's true and true, and what would I do if they killed you? What would I do then? I ask you, I ask everybody.'

Mrs. Fox followed her across the room and stood between her and Foley, a fierce if rather a belated chaperon. Every feeling she had, of pride, of restraint, of decency, of rectitude, was outraged beyond a raw and quivering limit, and beyond this again a passion of maternal protectiveness, quickened to an awful strength within her.

'Darling,' she said, and love and bitter chastisement were mingled in the word. 'Come away with me, come away at once.'

She was the other world of Foley, her neat profile with its expensive veil, twisted into a little ball under her firm, plump chin, and tied in a neat bow at the back of an expensive toque, a brown fur stole round her neck, a bunch of scentless purple auriculas pinned in it. He saw her hands in neat expensive gloves, and her feet in neat expensive shoes. The rest of her he did not see. But he passionately approved her, and as passionately revolted from Grania's generous lawlessness. The Fox man in him found in Grania what Fox's approved only in their mistresses and detested in their wives.

'Shut up,' Foley said to Grania. 'Shut your mouth, will you, will you, you dirty little tart.'

Grania did not spring back from him, nor cower away. She was not defeated by this angry coarseness. Something in her was well matched to it. While the others in the room drew in a breath of shocked indecision, she turned from him to them, saying:

511

'You hear what he says about me? You see it's true what I told you. Now will you save him for me?'

Mrs. Fox was in tears.

'Colonel, I apologise,' she said again and again. 'I apologise. I had no idea the crazy child. . . . Oh, she just told me she would tell you, would tell you where the man had been this morning. It's all too shameful, too terrible. . . . I apologise. I'm sorry.'

The Colonel was murmuring and helping her into one of the shiny leather seated chairs with wooden arms. Mrs. Fox was so little, her neat shoes swung off the floor as she sat, and she buried her neatly toqued head in her scented white handkerchief—Parma violet. In emotion and excitement she exhaled the scent of Rimmel's Toilet Vinegar and Parma Violets, rather delicious.

So far, the Colonel had not addressed his prisoner. He had only played with the blind tassel, and consoled Mrs. Fox as gently as he could. He turned to Foley now, and it was not to say, 'You are a cad, Sir,' but to say:

'O'Neill, I think you find yourself in a very cruel position.'

Foley said:

'I do, Sir.'

Grania clasped her hands towards Foley. Major Radley rattled among his notes, and Mrs. Fox did her very utmost to subdue her crying.

The Colonel then said:

'I know you were implicated in the capture of our two boys this morning. I should guess against your will. I'm sure of it, in fact. However, it's not impossible for you to make amends for that terrible business if you will give us all the information in your power that will lead to the capture of their murderers. Will you do this? In asking you I am not unaware of the grievous danger I ask you to put yourself in, because I know you are far from a cowardly fellow.'

'Oh, Foley, do tell him, please, tell him,' Grania pleaded, and Foley could have struck her. He said:

'If I tell you anything of any help to you I'm bloody well finished in this country. I've kept out of doing I.R.A. work, beyond a meal and a bed for a boy on the run.'

'Harbouring gunmen,' the Major interrupted, 'we thought you did a bit of that too.'

Foley paused. Then he said with the simple ignorant bitterness of a peasant:

'The ruin of Ireland, Major, is chaps like you and Cromwell.'

The major, whose ancestors had fought with Charles, sniggered silently, and put the remark away in his mind to use as an Irish story. For years after the British Army had left Ireland he carried his own punishment about with him in the shape of Irish stories, stories that caused any whose interest he sought to shun and fly from him.

'I suppose Cromwell has got to come into it somewhere,' he said now, 'but I don't think we can blame him altogether for this situation.' Something in the way in which he avoided looking at Grania made her even more the situation than the murdered and their murderers.

Foley got up and stepped forward:

'If I chose to take what's coming to me, and keep my mouth shut, it's none of your damn' nosey business.'

'Keep yourself quiet, boy,' the Colonel said easily. 'We don't want any rough stuff. You know that yourself. No help to anything.'

Mrs. Fox said:

'I think we'd better be going. We cannot do any more. Come Grania.'

Grania said:

'You go. I'm staying till I know what happens to Foley.'

The Colonel said:

'Nothing will happen to any of us to-night, child.'

'For God's sake, Grania, go home.' Foley was white and tired. 'Go home like a good little one.'

513

Blind with tears, Grania stood up. By so much as she had given, by just so much was she apart from Foley now. It was not her poor body, that had taken far more than she gave or knew how to give, but worship and faith were broken and slighted in this her fight for his life. The young do expect to get as good as they give to those they love, and the first disillusionment is ashes and bitter water to drink.

It was then that the two boys, Michael Purvis and Tony Craye, came in, quietly and without drama.

'Well, you two have given us a nice bit of bother to-day haven't you?' the Colonel said with gentle sourness. They grinned uneasily.

'Now you'll be able to spare Mr. O'Neill the ordeal of informing on the soldiers of his country,' the Major said. There was disappointment in his voice. 'And you'll also be able to tell us how he assisted in your little affair to-day.'

'Foley? Never saw Foley all day,' Purvis said. 'But he's for it all right, I'm afraid. You know who got us out?'

'Foley's mother, Nan, Mrs. O'Neill.' The other boy hurried out the names that would explain her to all.

'What?' Foley was profoundly upset. What had she been doing?

'Made fools of the lot of them. Put our jailer in his place, and talked to us as if we were back in the nursery.'

'What are you talking about?' The Colonel leaned across the table towards them, 'Let's get it straight.'

'Well, it was like this, Sir, she just walked in, disarmed the guard and let us out.'

'Walked in where?'

'That's just what we can't say, Sir.'

'We promised we'd keep quiet about it, or every one would be in trouble.'

'More people keeping quiet?' The Major's voice was chill.

'If it's not putting it too strongly, Sir——'

'It sounds silly, I know——'

'But she absolutely saved our lives, Sir.'

'And asked us to lay off making any bother for the other side. Said they'd have it in for Foley, you see, if we did.'

'So we can't talk. Really we can't, can we? You know, she was damn' wonderful.'

'Most marvellous woman I've ever seen. It was a hell of a show.'

'Oh, awfully good show. We were for it, you know.'

'Absolutely for it.'

The babble of excited relief showed plainly enough the nervous tension they had been through.

'Nan could do anything,' Mrs. Fox said with desperate quiet conviction, 'anything in the world I think. But where is she now?'

'Putting Miss Pigeon to bed, I should think. She shooed us off—said she'd be better off alone.'

The Colonel said, 'She seems to have managed a good deal, while we chaps sat twiddling our thumbs.'

'There wasn't a thing you could do, Sir.'

'And all we could get out of Foley was Judy.'

Foley said, 'I made sure you two would be cooling on the hill-side before twelve o'clock this morning.'

'So did we.'

'It was terribly decent of you to keep Judy.'

The Major looked at his watch. 'As this has turned from an inquiry into a party of mutual congratulation, I think, if I may, Sir, I'll go and have my bath.'

'Sorry to spoil your crack at the Shinners, Sir.'

'Very sorry, Sir.'

The Major said, 'I'll overlook it for once. But next time you

515

are nearly murdered, go through with it, won't you? Don't disappoint your superior officers.'

When he had gone, the Colonel said:

'Now then, what about Foley? This isn't official. But I think he'd be better out of Ireland. What do you think yourself?'

Foley thought. 'Yes,' he said, 'the boys won't forget it to my mother. They'll have it in for her all right over this day's work. They're bound to example her.'

'And you are their obvious victim, unless we make a political prisoner of you.'

'That's right.'

'You'd do better to take a chance out of this country for a couple of years. Till things get forgotten.'

A couple of years—the words were cold stones dropping through cold water to Grania's heart.

Foley said, slowly, 'I've got every penny I own in the horses and the little place.' His voice made it sound very pat and cosy, comfortable and profitable.

The boy who came from Norfolk spoke:

'It would be rather an investment for us, Foley,' he said, 'to help you set up an establishment on the other side—the same sort of thing.'

'I will help, too.' Mrs. Fox said eagerly, 'for Nan's sake.'

Grania squeezed her fat cold hands together in her lap. What about my sake? What about Grania's sake? The words racked her but she did not speak. No. She looked down sulkily at one hand squeezing agonisingly at the other.

The boys took it up:

'We could buy young horses over here and send them across for you to finish and sell.'

'It's easy money.'

Foley thought, 'Easy money for the people who sell you the horses.' He was puzzled and furious, angry with his mother for

516

this uncalled for heroism which had so undone his silence. Angry from the centre of his vanity with Grania who had so shamed him and herself. Angry and hurt that outside circumstances should uproot his life, the hard but pleasant life that he had made, the life that suited him so well. His horses, his trade, his hunting, his girls. He felt desperately lonely at the thought of starting again in a strange world of men and horses, none of his own used ways about him. Hardy as he was, Foley had a sort of passion for the things he knew. His own things. The familiar ways of Mountain Brig, Aunt Gipsy knew how long he liked his egg boiled, the saddle-room he and Micky had made, where he could put a hand without thought on any piece of tack he wanted. The stove that boiled the linseed, a cross little affair, but he and Micky knew how to humour it exactly. He was proud of his dining-room, with his cups and the photographs of himself and his horses, and the pictures of the Pope. He had all his mother's strong liking for things and her ability to take care of what she had, to hold things fast and keep them in good order. His bantams too, those game little cocks, no one had a breed of bantams to touch Foley's. Sometimes Aunt Gipsy would roast one for his supper, a better bird than a partridge. Somehow the bantams were uppermost in Foley's mind as he said:

'Ah, I'll chance things here, I think. I don't think I'll run. Thank you very much all the same.'

Mrs. Fox said with blue-lipped calm, 'If what Grania has just told us all is unfortunately true, don't you owe it to her not to take any risk with your life which you can help?'

The Colonel said, and for the first time he spoke coldly, 'I more than agree with Mrs. Fox—the sooner you get out of this country the better.'

Grania looked across at him, dumb and stupefied. All she was she would have given for a secret kept, for a body freed by any drastic drug of Nan's. She would not speak again.

'You should go to-night,' one of the boys said. 'Have you got the ready? We can lend it to you.'

Foley muttered, 'I couldn't get a boat to-night.'

'The timber ship,' Grania said, 'she went down the river at tea time, you'd catch her in Bungaron. I'll drive you down. If you won't let me—' she turned at her mother's immediate protest, 'I'll do something awful, I really will.'

Mrs. Fox wavered and abandoned her principles, the look of Grania frightened her.

XXXIV

The road to Bungaron followed the river, ran beside the river through the wooded valley. It passed Aragon on the opposite bank of the river, its walls dropping to the drop beneath them, rising from the trees and river below to the trees and hill above. The river light was bottle-green in the windows, the little stone foxes, their bushes straight out behind, flew motionlessly through the swimming dusk. The river tide was still high as they drove along, Grania and Foley. It carried the lower branches of the willows, dragging blue leaves in its green bosomy floods.

Grania drove the big car very badly. It was a mark of her severance from Foley that she should drive at all, not leave all that to him while she leaned and chattered by his side. Now she reached for her clutch and rammed in the awkward gears that caught and tore their teeth, one in the other. Sometimes tears fled down her cheeks and sometimes not. So close to each other in the near dark, they were each minute of silence farther away, the distance lengthening inevitably between them.

Only seven miles now, Grania thought, as they passed the different places that marked distances for her in a road she had always known. The road to the sea and Christmas trees; to the dancing class, and to tennis parties and balls. Now the road to cold without end, to ceaseless desire, the road into this new pain

519

of loss which was too great to be borne. Grania's love had been much beyond any strength of pride or spirit, and now that she had lost these things, nothing was left her, no place of cool strength that was her own. No room for the vanity that the young should have. All had been lost in her great silly act of love. Not for years was Grania to feel anything but the hot shock of shame in thinking of her confession that evening. Not till she was established in a life of love and success, which the same round generosity and abandon of her nature brought her equally with this disaster, was she able to look back with understanding and pride, not with shame and pity, to the child she had been then; the shamed and crying child driving along the familiar road, driving her love out of her life, in six miles, five miles now, while the soft airs of the spring evening stirred and crept round them; the indifferent primroses spread themselves like light growing in a room, pale wedges and pools up and down the dark rocky banks of the road, and the river water flowed past, the same cold, milky green as the willow branches it dragged down hopelessly to its breast; the luminous strong-smelling pads of the elder flowers; grew along the road, and white hemlock in the ditches was only less mooney and solid. The water birds were uttering lonely independent cries, and soon the foxes would be barking through the night woods, and Foley, like any other travelling fox, would be gone. But only in her very death, Grania thought, could her longing and hope for him be quieted.

Ah, if hope could die more quickly! Many brave and affecting little speeches got as far as Grania's lips that evening, speeches to which he could not but respond as he ought with protestations of faithful and enduring love; with plans and promises of gold rings and little houses. But the words died before they were spoken, so remote he looked, so tough, so far removed from love's pity or the touching reach of words.

Now they had left the darkness of demesne woods behind,

520

and the river grew wider and more still as it reached towards sea water. The fields beside it grew smaller and their high flowering banks taller, as the sea was closer; and far beyond the thought of the little striving fields of men, the river turns lay under the mountains. The intervening land was hidden. The mountains spread their quartered spaces bare against the sky. In the evening they were white and grey and deeper grey, no pretty blue shadows, only height and depth and the quietness of the sky, great height and distance falling to the water and splitting the sky into deep V's of evening light. Little white houses glimmered in the dusk, a light burning in some and others dark. Red brown fishing nets were hung on poles outside the houses to dry; heavy swags and garlands against the pale water, water so full and still that a gull flying slowly over seemed to be dipping the points of its wings in its own shadows, it kept so low across the river.

It was Foley who spoke at last, and said:

'Was that true, what you said at the barracks, or did you say it because you thought it would get me off?'

It was not the words but the light, unkind tone of his voice that found in Grania some still unwounded place, some last small place, and so hurt it that pride and anger were born of it together, and she turned on him and cried:

'No, it wasn't true. Thank God it wasn't true. I'm all right, and even if I wasn't I never want to see you again. I'm glad you have got to go. You're bad. You're like Nan. You're cruel.'

'Oh, don't start that stuff,' he spoke with that savage sourness through which men seek to avoid a scene, and through which they precipitate the disaster of untold grievance upon themselves for ever. 'If you're all right, you're all right, aren't you? Be glad you're not mixed up in my life any more. It wouldn't suit you, believe me. We've had lots of fun, hadn't we? You'll remember that part and forget about me in no time.'

521

Nothing could have been more light and cruel than his care-less, vulgar reassurance. His assumption that the affair between them had been as slight to her as to him. It was as if her heart was a little old basket he held in his hand and squeezed its dry frail sides together and threw away the carefully made thing for the dusty winds to play with and rattle through its ribs.

Now they were near to the sea. The land-locked sea welled inwards up the river across the narrow Bay of Bungaron, the fields on the opposite headland maintaining their pattern as far as you could see in the dusk. A small town was built low under the headland, pink houses and white cottages and queer stiff Geor-gian shops and houses. There was a high stone-built quay where the sailing ship waited, its masts and rigging wild as a dream against the low-built town and ribbed mountains above. Now, in the evening it was as easy to look at the bright sea as it is to look up a church.

'You don't mind about any one, do you?' She stopped the car by the sea wall and turned to him. 'What about your mother? Not even a question. What about the two boys? You knew all about them, but you wouldn't take a chance, would you? Not a chance to save them.'

'And I wasn't any too grateful for your own heroic act to-night, was I?' He could tease her still.

'I did that,' Grania said, 'for a reason you'll never know anything about.'

'What reason, child?'

'For love,' she said, in an ordinary voice, because it was so true. 'And here we are at Bungaron, so get out.'

'Are you taking me to the boat?'

'No, I don't want to be seen with you very much, you can walk. It's no distance.'

'You're very cross, aren't you?'

'Not cross, really,' she put the back of her hand to her eyes, and up against her silvery hair in a complete gesture of sadness, 'only frightened that people can be so different from what you think.'

'Well,' he got out of the car, 'don't let us part bad friends. Ah, Grania, don't let's.' He bent towards her, any resistance calling to him, as always, to be defeated and subdued to himself.

'You wouldn't know when I'd come back to you, and then you'd be sorry you'd been so mean, wouldn't you?'

The voice that had shaken her and enchanted her, the strong sweet common voice speaking half-words of love, implying anything, promising nothing, charmed Grania once again. And when he saw he had won, Foley turned light again.

'Of course, you're right,' he said, 'forget me as quick as ever you can.' He kissed her cheek, not her mouth, and leaned away from her again. He stood beside the car for a moment, patted her hand through the open window, lit a cigarette, and went off down the road, the sea on the left, the mountains on his right. Foley had not got the niggling short-stepped walk of so many horsy men, he strode out like his mother, carrying his strong beautiful figure along with unaffected swagger and endless challenge.

Grania watched the sway of his shoulders and head. He was a sailor in a foreign seaport town who left her. It was a man as strange and unpitying as that. That moment passed too, and a wild panic for herself, herself only, took its place.

'Listen! Wait, wait,' she called in a passion of lonely fear, 'where shall I find you?'

But he walked on to the turn. He had not heard her.

Grania sat on in the car after he had gone out of her sight. She could not take in that this was an end. He would come back along the road. He would say, come with me, Grania, and they would be on the ship together, going down the last of the river to the night and the sea. How unspeakable the joy of it would

523

be. She put her hand in her teeth and bit on it to hold herself quiet. Then sorrow, going to her stomach, as it will, she leaned out of the car, pale, and vomiting dryly and hopelessly, hands clasped against a sweating forehead. She felt very cold. She could not make herself leave the chill sea wall where little never-breaking waves sucked and lipped at the stones—there was a star out now, she could see it high over the ship's lonely rigging, high above the mountains and the town. It must be nine o'clock and more. The headlands were faded out, ruled no more one behind another, the mountains were theatrical, violet cardboard now, and the town, which had been so grey and white and quiet in the dusk, became garish and too much of a thing with clusters of lights, and light's long shiverings in the water. Again the desperate thought of being deserted in a gay foreign town was with Grania. But she did not know what it was to feel quite alone until she saw the sailing ship leave the quay and go down the river on the turn of the night's tide.

There are no words to describe the anguish which may possess the young in such straits of emotion, in such utter loss as this—there are no words for a finality of height or depth, and there is a region of sadness which it is a little death to know, a gap, and blank of terror. But in this place mercifully there is no real abiding. It cannot hold the very young. They escape and recover. But at that time nothing except a strong and natural fear of death kept Grania from wading through the surging weeds into the tide of the sea and the river current, and swimming with them after Foley's ship until she should be drowned.

XXXV

She was not really so near doing this as she thought. She was too young and fat and frightened for the moment of insanity to have grip enough on her despair for such an ending. She could only turn the big car round and drive her breaking heart home to bed. She did not even drive as recklessly as the occasion demanded. Indeed she could not see well enough for reckless driving because of her tears. So she went slowly and waveringly along, and the sea road and its little fields gave place again to the river road, with its dark trees and pale primroses and demesne gates with high stone pillars and gravelled sweeps. This was the gentry's valley. The river was lower now. Its mud banks wet, dark, pearly, the water and the willows parted till to-morrow, the green pallor of the spring night growing narrower every five minutes in the emptying river until it was only long and smooth as an old candle. All the faint spring yellow of the woods was olive dark now, and tall houses showed through their trees as white as geese, with here and there a light among the lines of dark windows to show there was life and business still to do. These houses were built too high above the river for their lights to reach the water. Great clumps and masses of rhododendron and laurel and oak trees, bare of leaves still, grew down the steep banks between the houses and the river.

Grania drove past these houses that she knew, feeling as if

525

each held her enemies: hostile mothers, cool daughters, sons to ignore her politely, arrogantly avoiding the embarrassement of her company. She knew the formality of the society in which she lived, knew and respected it enough to fear its ostracism. Even to-night in all the great despair of her loss she could imagine the little slights and little politenesses by which these faint houses would put and keep her in her outcast place. After all, this was Grania's only world, and a world she would have met with glad defiance if Foley's love had been behind her, but robbed of any love or help from him she cringed at its strictures and feared its displeasure. All the cold august Georgian houses down the length of the river valley seemed to turn their long goose faces from her as she passed.

Shall I have to go away, I wonder, Grania thought desperately, for she loved Aragon. Abroad, no Soo to comfort? Will Nan be able to . . .? Nan had been right. Merciless and quick. But to end it, that was the thing. Be free of him. Be free of this warm strong pain in the breasts, of this fear that was certainty, and certainty that was not sure, but dreaded and longed and feared most of all. It had not been fear when she had thought she could use her pregnancy for him. Then she had been glad. Not even ashamed. A little rapturous in fact, to own it. Now she flinched from the vain fool she had been an hour ago, crazed and blinded by the thought that he loved her.

Another two miles and she would be home again. She would have to face her mother and Nan and Sylvia. Ah, Sylvia. If she had thought of Sylvia when she was down by the sea she might really have climbed the wall and felt the cold water flowing bigger and higher until she could not save herself. But it was only now that the thought of Sylvia, cool and polished, and odious, overcame her to distraction. In the thought of Sylvia her despair quickened. It was like a hot wire in her wound, a bee sting on her lip, a nettle in her armpits, the thought of Sylvia, calm, vile inquisitress!

526

From the peak of her grief Grania slipped suddenly into a kind exhaustion, and exhaustion founded on a pain in her back that called only for bed, for bed and a hot water bottle in knitted bag, for the kind of pause that is extinction. She thought with passion of her bed, of Nan magnificently caring for her because now she would be obeyed. Ah, the comfort of being ill with Nan. Nan did not fuss and pet you. She upheld you with her strength and skill, her good taste in food and flowers. The finest bed linen in her cupboards was brought out of its scented dark for the invalid. Sickness was dramatised and cossetted with an artist's instinct so long as Nan was all powerful with the patient, the giver or withholder of all good things—oh, she could have her way with Grania now, she could do what she liked, so long only as she would be kind—the memory of all her resolves for Aunt Pidgie, resolves taken when she was drunk, faded from Grania's mind. Probably, almost certainly, Aunt Pidgie had exaggerated; certainly she had been blind drunk when Grania had left the nursery, full of wine herself, and had turned the key in the door to lock Aunt Pidgie in, so that she might go blameless and unpunished on Nan's return. Aunt Pidgie did tell such awful stories. The black men who tried to get in at her windows. The Diblins who gave her shells in the woods. T-runk, the god of travel in the attic. The leprosy which infested her sheets at the full moon. . . . No, you could not pay serious attention to anything Aunt Pidgie said about Nan. Grania blamed herself uncomfortably for having listened and encouraged, and wondered with dismay how she was to explain away the burning of the boots and the winter combinations. She could not let Aunt Pidgie take the blame, not all the blame, although it was absurd to suppose that Nan could really punish her. The nearer she came to Aragon and to Nan, her only supporter, her strength still, her help to come, the more Grania wavered towards Aunt Pidgie's cause. The strength of the truth she had

527

known this evening in the nursery became fantasy, love and pity for Aunt Pidgie were succeeded by the exasperated indulgence which she usually inspired. Now, against Grania's own overpowering sea of trouble Aunt Pidgie's case seemed a slight matter, not the horrifying tragedy it had been when Grania promised her the house by the sea with pebbles on the gateposts, and beefsteaks for her dinner, and fine leather shoes, and lambswool of the softest to wear next her skin. Now she found herself planning to buy Aunt Pidgie a handsome present of soft shoes and fine wool combinations and so settle the question. She would forget this wild talk they had had together soon enough. Perhaps the combinations only, not the shoes. She would speak to her mother about shoes, in fact she could not quite see why her mother should not buy both shoes and combinations, Grania could choose them . . . if Nan would not be too much offended by such interference. . . .

Grania was nearly opposite to Aragon now on the other side of the river, the lovely house would soon dawn upon her sight, spread above the sunken wax river, the mountains low beyond its high standing, and the sky hollow over house and lands. Grania was always sensible of the dramatic, vision like quality to this aspect of Aragon. Even to-night she waited the moment when the pale walls would rear up against the sky and she would see the muffs and capes of cherry blossom lace dark trees to the river edge with the faint accustomed stir in her mind.

When she rounded the high wooded corner she saw Aragon on fire. Its height and beauty dwarfed and crippled by the height of flames, flames that burst out from the windows and wound their tongues like awful roses through the stone balustrade along the roof and leapt about against the faint sky and sank from it again, the soft, unpitying sky. Under the house the little foxes and the formal stone urns were terribly lit, ghastly disinterest surrounding their remote stoney formality. The foxes would be

528

there and the urns would hold their scorched flowers to-
morrow. White magnolias and cherry blossom stood out like
paper between the firelight and the dark of trees and hill. The
roaring of a mountain side of gorse on fire rose and crashed
louder on the air carrying the peculiar deathly smell of fire. Such
wind as there was bellied the fire outwards towards the river
below and the strip of deep water would redden and grow dark
again as the fire blew or straightened like ribbon to the sky. The
wet mud banks glowed and gleamed hideously and sucked up
the true and the reflected showers of flame and spark that fell to
them.

The shock of fire, a shock beyond any other struck at Grania.
She screamed and stopped herself angrily and then she screamed
again and all feeling of her sorrow fell from her, for she remembered Aunt Pidgie was locked in the nursery and none but she
and Nan knew this, Aunt Pidgie and Soo. The key of the door
was in Grania's room. Aunt Pidgie's secret key, hidden so that
Nan might not guess how Grania had escaped and perhaps blame
Aunt Pidgie for her going. The house was so changed in its
consuming fire and smoke that Grania could not tell whether or
not the nursery windows showed flame too. Surely someone had
got Aunt Pidgie and Soo out in time. Surely they had got the
door open. Grania's heart sank terribly as she thought of those
heavy mahogany doors, smooth and beautifully fitting, and who
was to know that the key was hidden in the shell box on
Grania's dressing-table? Despairing and terrified Grania set the
car going as fast as she could, faster than she had ever driven or
dared to think of driving. She dashed up to the corners, and this
road had as many turns as a snail shell, and trod on the brakes as
she reached them, skating round and on again. The powerful
awkward old car charged along like a heavy, angry bull. Grania
found a new kind of nerve, born of terror and uncaring despair,
and it gave her a desperate grand pleasure to drive in this way,

529

wielding a power that frightened her, tearing through the evening with crashing brakes and screaming horn (when she found a hand to blow it) but the steering took most of her time and all her strength. It was three miles and more to get round and over the bridge, across the river to Aragon, and Grania went, bundling madly along, for more than two of them with success, punctuated by hairbreadth escape and wicked venturing. A dog was her undoing. She could not kill a dog no matter what was happening to Aunt Pidgie, and the greyhound puppy that ran out of a farm gate on her left and the slight bend which the road took to her right, combined to send the car skidding and hurtling and diving into a deep ditch where she stood quivering on her radiator for a moment before sinking backwards, like the outraged gentlewoman she was, instead of pitching over into the field beyond, as she might well have done.

Grania got out and ran to the cottage from which the greyhound had come. She hammered at the door and shouted, but no one answered her. Her hopes of a borrowed bicyle faded. As the mountain people had kept to their houses to-day, so did these people who had seen the great burning of Aragon.

Grania left the house after a minute and went running down the road, running and sobbing for breath, pausing and running on again. The evening was like one of those dreams of vast stations, trains that will not be caught, foggy disaster and endless forgetting. Yet as she reached the high pillars of Aragon's gates and ran between the two cut stone foxes and entered the grove of lime trees that bordered this avenue, part of Grania's dream changed to the exquisite relief of waking, for now she knew that she was not going to have any baby, had she guessed, never been going to have any baby at all.

XXXVI

They gagged Nan on the mountain that evening, pulling the scarf from her neck to bandage the gag into her mouth; they tied her hands together and marched her along between them, the killer and the boy she had outwitted.

Nan was a strong walker, but now her heart was beating and choking her and she could not breathe properly with the gag in her mouth. Soon she was dragging and stumbling between them along the rough mountain track, frightened and breathless now, all her bravery dead, and only a terrible fluttering failing sensation of fear possessing her. If she could breathe she could bear anything, she felt, and her eyes moved in a pitiful distorted way in her head as she tried to express without hands or voice how much she longed to be freed from her gag. She staggered and barged into her captors, trying to make them understand that she could go no further. But they only laughed at her and barged back in return, and the Killer showed her a pin he would prick her with if she did not hurry herself. A piece of heather as sharp as a thorn got into Nan's shoe and tortured each step she made. She walked lame but they only laughed at her tricks and jogged her on again. Oddly enough, the thought of Miss Pigeon and the nail in her shoe did not cross Nan's memory then. Not so strange is reality perhaps because if Nan's imagination had ever touched Miss Pigeon she could never have used her so

531

unkindly for so many years. Nan had not seen herself as cruel. Frazer's indictment of her this evening had come as a shock, an enraging shock to her, but now all past feeling was lost in her present pain and fear.

The endless soft evening melted round them as they walked over the mountainy highland. Below the country lay, particular as an old map, as artificial and unreal. The loops of its deep river were unwound and laid out flat and silver, its woods and mansions dwarfed blobs, its fields meaningless tatty little patterns. Nan saw that they were making towards Aragon, dwarfed on its river height below, and she grew more frightened and breathless with every painful step she took. Her heavy heart beat against her side and leaped towards her stuffed mouth. Everything she passed added to her pain. The shrill lettuce gleam of moss growing in a wet spot among the heather, birds' wings in the evening, the dodging of the horned blackfaced sheep, the yellow of the gorse, the rain-whitened lichen on the stones of a wall, they bundled her over it, hurting her knees and grazing her hands. All these ordinary mountain sights assailed her spirit with the awful importance assumed by objects which may never be seen again. It does not make the object valuable, this vision through fear, but it squares it out and fixes its place in the tortured mind. Here are things which can never suffer, contrasting with an hour of waiting and fear.

They reached the shelter of the woods of hazel and little native oaks that grew between the heathery upper country and the carefully planted woodlands nearer Aragon. Rides and cross paths had been cut for the woodcock shooting, the stems of the oaks and hazels were crooked and pale, and darkness itself was enveloped in the mosses and old leaves and distances under and between them. Now and again heights of wet-faced rose among the trees paler than the stems of birches, blotted with the lime green of lichen. Hazel trees and alders, dark as plums, grew in

532

thickets, meeting each the others branches across the deep narrow glen river that ran down towards Aragon. It was a place intended for any dark and nasty deed, and Nan pulled back in terrified strength as she entered its shelter.

'What ails you now? they laughed at her. 'Tired? You were not too tired to walk the mountains and loose our prisoners, no? Well, you can go a bit further now and see what traitors get.'

'Who opened the hen-house door, eh?'

'Oh, it's a dose, I tell you it's a dose.'

'Oh, not a nice dose at all, that traitors get.'

They dragged at her arms, but she was a big woman, and she sank like a bag of meal, her head, in its smart hat, dropping forward, her chin, in the crisp white V of her shirt front, her knees gave way and she knelt between them on the rutted path through the wood.

'Ah,' said the boy who had prayed, 'you were too rough on her, Captain. Jesus, she couldn't stick it. This is too much of a dose she got. Give her a chance now. Take out the gag. We'll get no good of her this way.'

They took the gag out of her mouth. 'Let ye sing dumb now,' they warned her. 'One yelp and back it goes.'

Nan gasped with relief, stretching her stiff jaw, wetting her dry blistered lips with her tongue, taking a terrible moment of ease while she could, whispering her thanks in humbleness and despair. Her grandeur was gone, melted from her bones like style off a sick bloodhound. She would have done anything for mercy now.

'I'll not speak,' she whispered. 'Look boys, away with ye now, and I'll send fifty golden sovereigns from my savings to any safe address you'll give me.'

They laughed at her. 'Oh, that's an easy one, Missus. Try another way.'

'I swear before God,' she said.

'Do you remember, Missus,' the Killer said in a dreamy voice—they were smoking, and the smoke from their cigarettes went up faint and easy among the little trees. 'Do you remember the dirty little boy you caught in the brush room, and he doubled in two and vomiting with an inward pain, poor little sod, and you with a nurse's veil on your head and a starched apron, hunting him out to clean the boots, do you remember? Ah, these were the days!'

Nan remembered. She remembered her easy conviction that the pantry boy, like all pantry boys, was deceiving her, playing sick and shirking work. But there had been a sequel that had given her a twinge of conscience then and a pang of fear now.

'Ah,' Denny said, his eyes boring into her, 'two months after he got the sack for drinking cream from the dining-room jug, and a week after that again the Nuns were knocking hell out of him, his poor little belly stuck full oozing tubes in Bungaron Hospital. He pulled out of it, he pulled out of it, though. They kept the life in him—wasn't it a great pity, see now, Missus, they to keep the life in him for this evening's wicked work?'

She put her face down in her strong hands, and tears came running down through the fingers.

'What do you want with me?' she said in a low voice. 'Whatever it is do it quickly.'

'After that the poor little beggar got another nice job in a gentleman's house.' Denny the Killer went smoothly on with his story. 'Ah, if he had got in there he might be a bully butler to-day, see, and never troubling Ireland's cause, but what happened the job? Some party made it her sacred bloody business to warn the lady engaging him, to watch the dining-room cream jug, yes, and count the dried fruit in their boxes, yes, and the candy, coffee and sugar, how are you, so in the wind up he never got the job, only a hungry, weary, knockabout life kept him small and a bad stomach kept him cross, and at eighteen years he

534

was a starving dirty little rat South of the Slot in Chicago, him that might have been bowing behind his buttons in gentry service, a stout, well-grown, harmless fool, only for you, now see.'

Nan flung out her arms in the dark woods of her dear Aragon, the dark and unfriendly woods, the cold frivolous birches, little sour oaks and pale ash trees; the groves she loved leaned from her, apart in their own cold way of living. Their light airs and mists would accept her dead and rotted body in wavering unconcern.

'I did you wrong,' she said. 'I did you wrong. Forgive me.'

He rose to his feet, and his mates rose uncertainly too. They seemed to make awkward copies of his every gesture. They looked around them, peering through the trees.

'These trees are very small,' said one.

'She's a big woman,' said the other.

'It will soon be dark now,' the Captain said. He looked down at his hands and rubbed them together.

XXXVII

Aunt Pidgie woke out of her drunken stupor at ten minutes past nine. She came of a family that had always been able to hold its liquor like Fox's and gentlemen. Now, although a little dim and dazed, she felt perfectly well, and rather strengthened than otherwise by her unaccustomed outbreak. She peered at the clock on the mantelshelf for some moments before she took in that the time was advanced so far beyond her usual supper hour. What a silly little doze, she scolded herself severely, denying to herself that she had been asleep since seven o'clock, what a naughty little doze. Her eye travelled from the clock to the table where the sight of the port bottle and the half-eaten cake filled her with foreboding. I'm afraid I have been rather a naughty thing. She moistened her lips and swallowed some spittle in anticipation of possible punishments. Would it be a cold bath? No hotty? No supper? Or no cake for a week? The memory of the burnt boots suddenly assailed her. She feared very much it might be all of them, and all for a week.

So far there had been no supper, and although it was past bed-time, no Nan. Perhaps this was some new kind of punishment. Aunt Pigeon went over to the window, discovering as she moved a slight pain in her head and dizziness. She leant her hot forehead to the pane and gazed up the river and down the river between the iron nursery bars. She felt vague and lonely.

536

Almost she would have welcomed Nan's angry footsteps outside the nursery door. Then she found herself trying to remember what Grania had told her to say in explanation of her own disappearance; anyhow, she decided, I'll say she drank up the port. She breathed into her hands trying to cup and sniff her breath. No, perhaps I'd better not say that. Just a little drop, Nannie, half a glass to warm my tummy. After that I felt so queer I dropped my boots in the fire. She shook her head rather hopelessly. I know I'll make a mess of it somehow. I know I will.

Aunt Pidgie felt more and more depressed and agitated as she gazed down on the slowly sinking river, on the cherry blossom pluming the steep banks, white as owls' feathers in the evening, at the dark foxes running their endless chase at proper intervals on the stone balustrade where it parted for shallow descending steps. On many, many brimming summer nights Aunt Pidgie had gazed out on this prospect, on stone and falling distance, trees meeting water and water that had its ending in the sky, so deeply were the mountains clefted down to the river bed.

Aunt Pidgie hated the beauty and isolation of the prospect with all her heart. She would look out on the wildness and beauty she had always known, with her heart mourning for that dream cottage with its trim garden path and gate posts stuck with pebbles and sea shells and blue sea-smoothed pieces of glass bottles—the cottage where she could be her own mistress and lie half the morning in a hot bath if it pleased her. She would set places for her Diblins at the table, the table that would groan under its burden of beefsteak and macaroons, fried eggs and bacon and mushrooms, home-made lemonade, strong tea and crème-de-menthe, boiled brown eggs and butter and toast. The wildest fancies pleased her as to life in the little house while she gazed, as she was gazing now, at the green sky and the evening star. In the summer months she felt the smack of little waves on pebbly shore, and saw the clearest mark in the world—bird's feet on sand. She thought of the chains of rock pools that held whopping monster shrimps, the colour of sand and water; lustrous rough-bearded and prong-eyed shrimps. She could see the blue plate that would hold them at tea-time, their once transparent bodies blushing now a succulent pink. She imagined visits that would be paid her by the children and their mother—not long visits, rarely or ever would she have a guest to sleep in the spare bedroom. She would like to keep that nice. A white quilt on the bed, and red velvet with a bobbled fringe tacked to the mantelpiece, and all along it would stand her shell boxes. She looked forward to collecting cowrie shells in the summer and sticking them neatly on to little boxes during the long winter evenings, evenings when she would sit at ease by her fire, piling it up with coal and pieces of driftwood that burnt with blue and salty flames. The mornings she would spend gathering wood along the shore, after a nice hot breakfast, with a good hot lunch in prospect.

Aunt Pidgie saw herself hard at work or hard at play, eating a lot and sleeping deeply. In her dream she was strong enough to undertake anything. Her dream had no relation with an old lady, but with a strong-bodied, strong-minded individual. Now, these tea-times when the girls and their mother paid her a visit, it would be: You sit here, my dear, and you sit here. No sugar? Really! The doctors say it is most strengthening, they have ordered me three lumps in every cup. And how long do you like your egg boiled? Brown bread and butter with your shrimps? Try some of Mary's chocolate cake—quite one of her best, and I have a lark's nest to show you in the field after tea. Perhaps you would like a lobster to take back to Aragon. . . . Nan, she never allowed herself to see in the house, not even for the pleasure of putting her bang in her place. No, that shadow was kept without the gate. That dreadful strength never dwarfed the cottage. That terrible common sense never got near enough to block a fancy. And now she leaned her tired mad head against the window and sighed all alone to her fancies and to the single star. Presently she wondered dreamily if she should not go to bed, wondered if another slice out of the ginger cake would add much to the total of her punishments, but in a sad fuss and reaction from her earlier daring, decided against its consumption.

She left off staring at the cake and went across to the door into her bedroom. Locked still! She was locked up—locked up and forgotten. It had happened before and would befall her again, but always a terrifying sense of being a prisoner, and a hungry prisoner too, assailed her with this punishment. It nearly always came on her unexpectedly. She would not know the exact minute when Nan locked the door and left her. But she would find out, running from one door to the other. Sitting down and resolving to be calm. Getting up again to make sure she had not been a silly and failed to turn the handle properly. Hop, hop, from place to place, like a newly-caged bird. Tap on the window in case it might arrest some person's attention below. Not that she would have dreamed of asking anybody to come up and let her out. She only wanted the feeling that someone knew where she was, it was a link with outer things, this waving and pretending, it postponed the time that certainly came during these punishments when she sat by herself softly screaming— but softly, very softly, that Nan might not hear if she was outside the door; a rasping sigh and a bat-like squeak, her face covered by her hands to shut out the all-aloneness, and a voice as papery and thin as the old moon that might be white as a bone in the sky. The thin voice and the thin moon. But the moon sailed free and cold, and Aunt Pidgie was caught and kept till death should be her rescuer.

Usually if these corrections were enforced in the evening

hours she could at least go to bed—supperless, hot bottleless, but still curled, head and toes under the blankets, you could at any rate fancy yourself to be a birdie in its nest on four eggs. To-night, even this pretence was denied her. She sat in her low chair, drawn up to where the fire had burned, her black-stockinged feet out before her, and waited. It did not strike her that Nan had been ignorant of any of her crimes when the doors were locked. She only supposed that Nan knew. Nan always knew.

Outside the evening grew deeper, the river darker, and as the tide lessened, more full of the sounds of its flowing. There was too much beauty round Aragon, and too much beauty is danger-ous. A complete thing is near its ending. The white brooms in the garden, even such slight mountainy things, had grown to a false fat stature, sleek as white, overfed cats in their ordered groupings. Behind the brooms rose the trimmed plumes of lilacs, grossly unbearably sweet at night. A magnolia's horned and flowerless bones were crucified against a shallow alcove in a wall alcoved for no reason but to complete an alcove at the house's farther extreme.

Rising above the river bank and the stone flights of fox-watched steps, the house with its balustraded height and out-flung walls, had the attitude of a bird on its wings over water. It had the lonely quality of bird flight—only stone and water-fowl have this isolation from lush surroundings. As a wild duck might rise uncaring, from a pool of lily flowers, so Aragon was detached from the gardens and the evenings; there was no meeting place where the house yielded at all to their awful sweetness. Not on this night did Aragon yield, nor on those other nights to come when the breath of lilacs and azaleas was to billow in at glassless windows and blow through again to the farther side of the house; not when birds, growing used to desolation, were to fly through the roofless hall, from the river side to the red castles of rhododendrons on the hill behind would Aragon yield familiarly to desolation.

There was a time to come when seeded ash saplings would crack the cut stone steps apart, and elders flourish horridly in the round embrace of the drawing-room wall, out-curved above the river, high windows dark in it as holes burnt in a blanket. Stone by parted stone, Aragon would fight her way against desolation and holding to her life be rescued.

Some houses become ruins with meek despair, fallen masonry and rubbish is rounded over by the sod, quiet and solid as a grave. Cattle wander in and out from deserted pleasure grounds, seeking shade on hot summer days, and shelter on stormy nights—then the walls of a ruined house are useful and at rest again, no longer the racked ghosts of a dwelling-house. It is well, too, when white grass and brambles choke the exotic shrubs and wreathe and crush their bones, ending a sordid and indifferent struggle to survive.

But Aragon had been so long lived in and the gardens so well cared, that the lilacs passed only slowly from double to single, flowering more meanly each succeeding spring, pale suckers struggling from their roots. The sleek brooms withered sooner into rusty cages. Only the magnolias, breaking free from their crucifixion, propped crooked elbows to the ground and flowered with extravagant perversity. And the rhododendrons, towering magnificent above the desolation, thrust down roots into their own rotting leaves and grew from themselves. Azaleas that flowered here once, exquisite and artificial, were to fade from flame and scarlet to honey and paler honey, and succumb at last to nettles and brambles, like so many meek hungry gentle-women, to the strong obliteration of charity. But the house, with its five cracked plaster nymphs and little stone foxes, was to endure, purged by fire and rain and sun and frosts, of its evil and

541

its ghosts, good and bad, until the day came for Aragon to be
built again by young Fox's.

Pale and hungry was Aunt Pidgie on that last night, as she sat on
and waited. She was so far removed from the busyness of the
house that she could not even hear the sounds of night-time
maids, drawing blinds and bringing cans of hot water to the
bedrooms, where they would turn down the beds swiftly and
neatly and pop delicious hot-water bottles in bags of wool or
quilted satin between the chill linen sheets. Aunt Pidgie could
hear nothing, and this evening no one came out of the house to
sit on the low wall and look dangerously down into the river.
Careful, careful, Aunt Pidgie often longed to call to the girls and
their beaux when she saw them do this. But she never liked to,
for fear they might think she was spying on them from her
window. Though after all, if they leant back even *that*
much. . . . Everyone forgot the poor Aragon bride who had
once gone crashing and hurtling down through the tree tops to
her death. It was her widower who had built the little wall
before he had married again. It was not quite high enough to be
much use, but why hide so lovely a prospect because of one
stupid little bride? Taught her a good lesson, I expect, Aunt
Pidgie would say in her fiercer moments. Or again as she looked
out and down by herself, she would shrink and tremble to think
of the poor bride breaking through the branches, bouncing off
the ground and ending with a great splash in the river. Her
Brussels lace veil caught in the top of a tree, and two garden boys
(clumsy fellows) broke a leg and an arm apiece in their efforts to
fetch down an object which must so grieve the master. But he
had grieved for her deeply in spite of this sad reminder being
detached. He gave two black swans to the river, planted a double
white cherry on the bank, and married again within the year, for
he could not bear to live alone with such a memory.

542

Aunt Pidgie knew any number of little stories like this, both sad and gay, connected with Aragon and the Fox's who had lived there. She often ran over the dramas in her own mind standing on the spot, or as near to the spot as she judged safe, or could guess where they had been enacted. To-night when she was very weary of her chair she crossed again to the window and looked out across the empty terrace and down to where the Bride's Tree glimmered like old snow in the dark. I wish someone would come. I wish someone would come, she said. Her voice was like one mosquito in the summer dark. As she gazed, a curious procession came into her view—a procession that filed down the shallow terrace flight and halted at the river wall, halting with their backs to the river below and their hands held high over their heads. It was the servants, Frazer, the cook and kitchen maid (always changing, Aunt Pidgie could never know her rightly) and Kathleen and Rosie, the two housemaids. Behind them came Sylvia in her smoke-pale evening dress, with a paler ribbon tied high above her little waist, and her arms up too, pretty graceful little beast, and that horrid dog of hers after her as usual. Last there came a man in a belted coat, a dark hat pulled down over his eyes, and something wrong with his face; it was bandaged, and he had something in his hand. Aunt Pidgie looked out as at a little play, peering from her bad seat in the gallery, and saw that it was a gun he had in his hand. The group stood quite silent and still on the gravel. Frazer's shirt was a milky gleaming petal between his dark coat fronts; the maids' aprons frothed and swirled about them in the light evening air—what were they all doing. Suddenly it came clearly to Aunt Pidgie's slight, slow brain—this was a hold-up. The man in the overcoat was a masked gunman, and what, it flashed through her mind, would he do to Sylvia before all was over? Aunt Pidgie was glad of her locked doors now—no nasty men would get into her room, whatever they did to Sylvia. She and Soo had

543

only to keep quiet to come through the ordeal unnoticed and unmolested. Whatever happened, keep quiet, keep quiet till Nan came back.

Peering round the edge of her curtain, Aunt Pidgie saw every lifted hand pointing towards her window. Like a chorus on a stage, the line took a forward step and pointed violently at her windows. Oh dear, dear, the mean cowardly things to give her away like that. Even Frazer had pointed. Was she to join that group who would no doubt be shot one by one and their bodies hurled backwards like the Aragon brides down through the trees to the river. Ah, Aunt Pidgie shivered. She would not join that doomed party if she could help it. She looked wildly about her, wondering where she could hide. Suppose they broke the lock to drag her out! As the thought struck her she heard heavy steps running up the stairs, and a strange voice shouting, 'Any one there? Any one there?' and fists smashed on doors and rattled at handles.

A violent trembling took Aunt Pidgie. She sat down in her little chair. Signed to Soo to jump on to her knee, pulled her skirt over her head so that they were both in a private cage within this house of terror, and stopping her ears violently with her fingers— I'm a Birdie, I'm a Birdie, I'm a Birdie, she said to herself over and over again. So she did not hear her door rattled and shaken, or the voice that called, 'Speak up now. Speak up if you're in there. We're firing the house. Fire! Fire! Fire!'

The voices went shouting past her unheard. I'm a Birdie, a Birdie, a Birdie, she repeated, hearing only the blood in her stoppered ears, and the clatter made by the 'D' in Birdie against the roof of her mouth. She did not hear Killer Denny shouting to hurry and get on with the work, the old B. was safe enough or she'd have squealed out long ago. Blind and deaf, she sat on, busily being a Birdie until Soo, suddenly restless and frightened, struggled out of her dark nest and went, whining and sniffling, to the door.

Then Aunt Pidgie threw back her skirt and raised her head and sniffed a curious smell, a smell of burning, and heard a crackling rustling noise, the sort of noise, she thought, a big bonfire might make. She stole over to the window and peeped out. Smoke was pouring out of the windows below her, blowing up against the glass of her own so that she could hardly see, but it puffed between the close white iron bars and blurred the glass.

She gazed out stupidly, smelling the queer, dangerous, hungry smell of fire, hearing its hidden roar and crackle. At last, seeing a little curl of flame in the smoke far below, she knew what had happened.

She sprang about and rushed to the door, shaking its handle and piping out in that lone mosquito voice: 'Fire! Fire! Fire! Help. Help. Fire! Fire!' But only silence poured back to her. Not even the roar of flames could be heard from this side of the room. Back to the window again; she pushed up the heavy sash and pressed her head between the upright bars, calling: 'Frazer, Frazer, Frazer.'

She heard Frazer shouting in answer, and through the clouds of smoke she saw the white-aproned maids sinking to their knees in prayer, sinking down in the stones with their eyes hidden in their hands. She saw Frazer and Sylvia and their guard running towards the house—they shouted:

'All right, Aunt Pidgie.'

'We'll get you, Miss——'

Then she turned round and saw Soo beside her, licking her lips uneasily, licking her thin black lips and coughing a little. Poor Soo, little French tart in sore trouble, though her exquisite waist looked an inch smaller from anxiety and her dark brown eyes popped out of her head a little as the best French girls' do at times. Aunt Pidgie picked her up. As she held her strong anxious little body between her hands, that basket of strong ribs,

that round and thrusting head, she felt like a young person in her
determination that Soo should not burn. Her brain, for once concentrated and alert, worked at lightning speed. She sat down and
took off her black stockings. She tied them round Soo, making a
harness of stockings. Then she went to the drawer where the ball
of string was kept, and knotted and double-knotted the end of the
string in the harness. Soo mimbled and curtseyed and licked her
lips. 'Now,' said Aunt Pidgie, and lifted her up on the window-
sill.

'Hallo, hallo,' she coughed and coughed again, for she was
speaking into a cloud of smoke. The figures at prayer still on the
terrace below looked far away, tears poured down Aunt Pidgie's
face, and Soo's eyes looked watery enough as she shrank and
cringed in her harness on the sill.

'Cook,' Aunt Pidgie screamed. 'Damn you, come here,
Cook!'

They heard her and advanced, overcoming with difficulty that
horror of the doomed which so often besets the living. They
advanced, crying, towards her window.

'It's Soo,' Aunt Pidgie shouted. 'Do you hear me? Come
nearer, you fools, it's Soo.'

'Yes, Miss; yes, Miss,' they said, standing exactly where they
were.

'Come near.'

'Yes, Miss.'

'It's Soo,' she screamed out again through the smoke. Without looking at Soo, or she could never have done it, she pushed her
over the edge of the window-sill, and started to unwind the ball of
string, tautened to snapping point by the struggling nine pounds
of weight dependent on it.

It was the kitchen maid, the youngest and least intelligent in
household matters, who grasped what was to be done and rushed
into the smoke. 'I have her, Miss, I have her,' she shrieked.

Aunt Pidgie felt the string slacken in her hands. Alone now, she threw the ball out of the window, and stood still trembling with fear, 'Frazer, Frazer,' she whimpered. 'Nan, oh Nan, come back.' She stood still, rubbing her thin withered fingers where Soo's weight on the string had bruised into their slight flesh. Her back was turned stupidly to the open window where the smoke gushed in. Her eyes were fixed on the locked door.

XXXVIII

It never occurred to Sylvia not to dress for dinner that evening when she feared her love lay newly murdered up in the heather. At 7.30 she took her bath with its accustomed drops of rose-geranium and washed herself with as much meticulous concentration as usual. She had felt cold as lead when she lay down in the hot water. When she got out and dried herself she was still cold and shivered as she walked across the passage, past all the tall mahogany doors, to her bedroom—her bedroom that had no more colour in it than the whites and greys and near-greens of river weeds, with all the distinction of such water flowers. Sylvia sat in front of her clear glass with its old nibbled frame of worn gilt and its pale golden bird posing in a leaf circle. In the glass she saw tears pouring down her clean chill cheeks, she saw a girl weeping in despair and hardly knew it was herself. She could know her love dead; her glass-cold little heart be shivered in pieces, but the pieces were still glass. Shock acts strangely. With Sylvia it delayed her yielding to despair although it left her without a movement towards hope. She was shut in a neat square box of despair and being Sylvia she moved with her usual grace and precision in this small dark place. She blew her nose and stuffed back the awful tears, but they flew up through her head again. She despised her own crying. I'll be good, I'll be good, she strained against the cruel evening air. Is it over? Yes.

Yes. The tears went back. Four or six defeated her will and raced down her face and fell on her bare knees that were laced together, twisted up for strength to resist this crying. This was sorrow. Not to think of him. She didn't think of him. She thought backwards very quickly about a woman's face in church. What was she wearing? Make a list, don't lose hold. Hat, blouse, coat, skirt, shoes . . . don't lose hold. . . . She brushed her hair back and back from the little peaks in which it grew down her forehead and above her ears. She would not look in the glass at her shaking mouth. She turned her back on the glass and put on her clean fine underclothes, her grey dress with its faint high-tied ribbon, her short string of river pearls. She picked up her work-bag and went down to the drawing-room to wait alone for dinner. As she waited she stitched at the flowers in her tapestry. It was as if she made a neat little wreath for a grave.

Frazer came in at five minutes to eight, he shut the door quietly and crossed over to where she was sitting.

'Will you have dinner at eight, Miss, or will you wait for Mrs. Fox and Miss Grania?' He always spoke with the soft distinctness of a good servant, but this evening he breathed the words gently, as if he would rebuke his own voice for speaking at all, and if speak he must, the air should hardly be stirred by him.

'I won't wait beyond 8.15.'

Sylvia's voice sounded improperly natural, 'They may be very late.'

'Very good, Miss.'

She was left alone again, the perfect figure in such a room, as right as any of the marble reliefs that stooped with their garlands of pointed leaves in the plaques on the mantelpiece. Her strong small neck was bowed, her hands busy and steady as on the day before, when she had finished her swan's wing, and eaten her dinner with so much pleasure and good appetite.

To-night, as yesterday, the river and the April light were joined and took the indoor air together, sharpening the red in the coats of dead dull Fox soldiers and hunting men, dwelling and drowning in the pale round carpet, turning the white glaze on china milk-soft and luxurious to the eye, swelling light romantic and untruthful through the room. The air was burdened with ragged water scents. Broken river smells lifted the lilac on their strength as scent is built, so that lilac, doubly, terribly sweet filled the room too, and the rich heart-breaking songs of birds.

Sylvia sat on, her hands moving busily at her work. She thought with passionate liking of the silent grave herons, glad that she could not even see that lonely flight from their nest in a flat-topped cedar to the river below, they had no connection with sweet scents or rapturous songs. She could think of them.

The gong sounded and Frazer opened the drawing-room door and stood inside it with a murmur, dinner was served.

Dinner was eaten, soup, fish, cold lamb, a tiny savoury. Sylvia would show no silly signs of heartbreak through plates of untouched food. She ate steadily and went back to the drawing-room for her coffee, then the paper. After dinner she always read the paper. To-night, beyond any other night, there must be no change. The *Morning Post* of the day before was lying folded on the table by the sofa where it was always put. The fire, ten minutes lighted, gave out no heat. The curtains were not drawn and only one lamp near the fire was burning. Sylvia picked up the paper and sat down beside the light. She began to read the leading article, a furious indictment of England's weakness in the conduct of this Irish war. She read on in bitter agreement with all the *Morning Post* proposed to do to Rebels and Gunmen, read on until the door opened and she looked up to take her coffee from Frazer.

It was Killer Denny who stood there with his two boys, one on either side of him, and all three had guns in their hands.

'Good-evening,' Sylvia leaned out of her chair towards the fireplace.

'Don't touch that bell.'

'What do you want?' Sylvia asked as steadily as possible, for there is something unutterably alarming about three masked men with guns in their hands standing suddenly in your drawing-room on a spring evening. None the less so because you have just been reading that their country is at war with the government under which you live. None the less surprising because to-day they had killed your lover that to-night they should stand in your house with guns in their hands.

Sylvia was frightened, and because she was frightened she spoke boldly and rudely.

'Get out,' she said. 'Get out of this house at once.' How silly, how shrill.

Killer Denny laughed quite naturally.

'It's you who'll do the getting out, now see,' he said going up to her, 'and quick mind you, unless you want to burn along with your ancestral bloody home, now see.' He went to the fireplace. 'Not much heat out of that,' he said. 'We'll soon have a better blaze.'

He stood over Sylvia. He did not touch her. He did not put out a hand towards her. He looked at her out of his bold little dark eyes, bright as a rat's through his mask, and he turned his head on his strong neck and spat on the carpet.

'I've wanted to do that,' he said, 'for a long time.' When he had done it he was ashamed. It looked awful. It is one thing to burn a beautiful house, it is another thing to spit on its floor.

Sylvia was recovering some of her horrid poise.

'A childish thing to do,' she said, pulling her skirt closer to herself, 'childish and dirty, don't you think so, hardly what one expects from an officer of the I.R.A.'

He turned to his two men, 'Go and get the servants out, boys,' he said, 'and quick. Bring the lot in here.'

'There's a very old lady upstairs,' Sylvia said, 'may I go up and explain this little party to her? She may be rather alarmed, you know.'

'One of the servants can get her out. You stay where you are. We don't want any help from you.'

Sylvia sat back in her chair—was it any good arguing? was it any good doing anything? What did one save when houses were burnt? Silver? Jewellery? Papers?

'Could I collect a few personal belongings,' she said, frigidly, pompously.

'No.'

Suddenly she stood up, thin and straight in her grey dress as smoke in a frost.

'It's outrageous, it's awful, what good will you do to anybody by burning Aragon?' She looked wildly around the room. At the mantelpiece. At the dark glass. At the honey-coloured shells curling in the inlay of dark thin tables. At the china she had always seen, the gay-flowered coats of groups of Worcester and Chelsea. Suddenly she felt again the ache to touch that bright china gives to children, she cried out in their defence:

'You can't do it. Why are you doing this?'

Killer Denny followed her eyes to the Chelsea group.

'I had a great admiration for that ornament when I was a little fellow,' he said softly. 'Mrs. O'Neill got me one day with it in my hand, she took it from me and she beat hell out of me.'

He picked it up again, a boy in a mulberry coat with a hen in a basket under his arm. He looked at the pretty silly thing and then dropped it on the flat stone before the fireplace, it broke, but not much, because it was tough and light.

'You'll have to try again,' Sylvia said.

He picked it up and held it in his hands, fitting the broken bits together.

'Nothing I do,' he said oddly, 'would divide me from that little boy.'

'I don't remember you.'

'One dirty pantry boy is very like another.' He put the broken figure back on the mantelpiece as the boys came in driving the whispering, terrified servants before them. Even in such a pass they felt very uncomfortable in the drawing-room. The housemaid thought the cook would take offence because she was pushed in before her, and the tweenie was miserably conscious that even such a disaster as this promised to be could not save her from a row because she had no cap on her head. Frazer was quite undone, pale and shaking and terrified for his northern blood.

'Out there, now.' Denny pointed through the window to the wall above the river, 'and if there's a word or a stir out of one of them, fire, boys.' It sounded very alarming.

'Can't we save anything,' Sylvia asked.

'Christ, God,' he swore, 'how much more time are we to waste? Till the soldiers are here, I suppose? Quick now, out with them.'

'But Aunt Pidgie,' Sylvia cried wildly, 'she is not here, let me get her.'

'Get out. I'll see to her, we don't want to burn old ladies, but we will if we're short of time. Out now the lot of you and keep quiet.'

Sylvia wanted to get a coat from the hall, but the boy in charge, the boy who had been captured by Nan, was too uncertain of himself to allow any leniency. Sylvia recognised early that he was far more likely to shoot one of them for disobedience than was his tough superior. He had the shaky manner in bullying that turns quickly to extremities for its support. It was

553

better to hurry out into the garden, out into the chill evening and stand against a wall to watch the house burn.

Every few minutes she would say to the boy, 'What about the old lady? Why don't they bring her out?' And he would answer in the voice of an official in the customs:

'Captain Cussens will deal with that matter.'

She broke out of the line once crying desperately that she must find Aunt Pidgie, but she was halted, ordered back with such temper that she knew the foolishness of persistence. The wind that blew under the maids' aprons nipped her bare arms and roughed her neat hair. 'Mayn't we put our hands down?' Sylvia asked then, 'we haven't any arms and it is so tiring.'

'Captain Cussens orders,' he answered, so they continued to stand like people in a game painted on a box lid, backs to the river, palms up towards the house.

Sylvia began to cry when she saw no sign of Aunt Pidgie being brought out. It was so terrifying not to know about her. By accident she might burn. No one's evil intention, but fluster and hurry and excitement would leave her helpless and unaccessible with Aragon burning round her. The burning house cutting off the way to the nursery, there would be no way of getting her out through the barred windows. Sylvia clapped her hands, and shouted, 'Aunt Pidgie!' 'Aunt Pidgie!' the cook shouted. The other servants were too timid. Afraid a little of their own voices or far more of their guard. Frazer grew pale and looked like a little frightened man, all butlerhood cast aside. 'Miss Sylvia, Miss Sylvia,' he whispered, 'do you want to get us all butchered?'

'If there's another word out of any of you,' the guard said, 'I'll fire.'

Sylvia was silenced. Indeed it was as well, for Miss Pidgie was sitting now with her ears stopped, so that she could not have heard a sound from the garden far below. She did not even hear the boys when they knocked at the door, calling and shaking the handle. She did not hear the steps going away or the shouts. It was Soo and the smoke that brought her to the window twenty minutes later.

'She's there, she's in there still,' Sylvia cried.

'Oh, my God, she's done for,' Frazer said. 'There's flames from the landing window, there's flames from the linen-room.'

'Ah, the poor little old dickens,' the boy said, horror in the light curious words.

It was then that Aunt Pidgie saw the three break from the line, Sylvia, Frazer and the boy with the gun. They ran towards the house calling confused reassuring words while the maids left behind sank down on their knees on the stones.

XXXIX

Burning curtains are madly beautiful, but there is something terrible about the sight of a flaming bed, as shocking as though a good comfortable hen was on fire. It is an unbearable sight, one would as soon look at a fat cosy bishop on his pyre.

It was through the open doors of the bedroom (left open to fan draughts) that Sylvia saw the fat beds blazing. Smoke poured out on to the stairs blinding and choking her. On the stairway going up to the nursery linen and blankets and pink eiderdowns had been pulled out and blazed in heaps and wreaths.

Frazer stood appalled. 'We'll never get her,' he said; it was like someone in a hunt saying: You can't go there. You can't get through there, wire, it's wired.

Sylvia said, 'It's only the linen burning, get some water, get the minimax.' Fraser and the boy stood coughing and doing nothing.

The two who had done the burning came running up the stairs. They had the savage desperate look of boys who had committed some outrage beyond their own believing, an outrage that has got beyond them and taken on a strength of its own.

'Outside,' they shouted, 'what the hell are you doing here?' The boy said, 'The old lady is above yet.'

'Come away, come away,' Frazer said. 'Do you want to be listening to her in her death?'

556

'There's no one in the house,' Denny said. 'God damn, didn't we try every door.'

'She's there, she was at the window.' Sylvia tore past him to the corner at the end of the corridor where a fire extinguisher was hung. As in all large houses there were perhaps three at extreme distance throughout the house, refilled last not less than ten years past.

'Get water, show them where to get water,' she shouted to Frazer. He put his hands over his eyes and ran coughing down the stairs and out of the house.

'Well, the old rat,' Denny looked down into the hall below, 'would you believe that, eh? Would you trust the sight of your sacred eyes?'

The boys had run down the corridor after Sylvia. They came back with cans of water in their hands like housemaids at their ordinary evening business.

'Yes, do, boys, and then fire down a spit and make a job of it.' He took the minimax from Sylvia. 'Go and put a coat on you,' he said. 'One spark and you're up in a blaze, now see. Give that here, and you chaps lift a carpet out of that room at the end, it's not burning.'

He cracked the knob of the extinguisher and sprayed the burning blankets on the stairs. They threw the carpet down and stamped out the curling flames. He shut the door of the burning linen-room and ran shouting up towards the nurseries.

'Keep the fire off the stairs, boys,' he called down behind him.

Sylvia came flying up from the hall, coated obedient to his order, she ran past the two on the stairs, past the awful roaring sound of the burning linen-room. He stood above her in the dark passage, white-faced, coughing, he had pulled off his mask and his hat, he was stooping down trying to get his breath.

'Aunt Pidgie, are you there?' Sylvia called at the nursery

557

door. She twisted the handle. 'Open the door, Aunt Pidgie, quickly. It's all right. It's Sylvia. It's Sylvia, do you hear me?'

'Nan locked me up,' Aunt Pidgie spoke in a clear, trembling voice. 'All the doors are locked, Sylvia. I can't get out. There's no way out, Sylvia.'

'What does she say?' Killer Denny was whispering at Sylvia's shoulder, they were alone together with the terror and horror of Aunt Pidgie's certain death around them.

'Captain, Captain, this stair won't last,' the boys' voices came calling.

'She's locked in.'

The Killer pulled Sylvia gently away from the door and crashed his shoulder against it trying to burst it open. Then he said, 'Tell her to go back from it. I'll try to shoot the lock off.'

'Aunt Pidgie, do you hear me? Go into the night nursery.'

'The door's bolted,' came Aunt Pidgie's clear hopeless little voice again.

'Get away from this door, go over to the window. Get into the cupboard, Aunt Pidgie. We've got to shoot off the lock.'

He was profiled against the door, arm out, head sunk. Sylvia was close as a plaque to the wall behind him. He fired, once, twice. The shot crashed and echoed in the narrow place. The smell bit its way through the other smoke. He tried the door again. The wood was bruised and splintered but the beautifully made lock held firm. In the succeeding silence Aunt Pidgie's gnat's voice spoke.

'It's all right, Sylvia. Frazer says the soldiers are coming, he sees the lorries on the road across the river.'

'Do you hear that?' Sylvia whispered to the Killer, he was squeezing a splinter out of the ball of his thumb. He nodded and ran to the stairs.

Tears poured down Sylvia's face as she wrenched at the handle and flung herself on the door, she would have broken every bone in her body to get in. She was alone now. She knew that it was madness to stay here. She was doing no good. In a few minutes she herself would be more hopelessly trapped than Aunt Pidgie.

Sylvia was not in the least fond of Aunt Pidgie. She would have done this for her own dog as readily. With the same vain protectiveness of the strong towards the weak. All that was tough and cold and fair in her, all indeed that was least pleasant went to the sacrifice.

'Would Nan's big scissors help?' came Aunt Pidgie's voice again in most sensible suggestion.

'Yes, yes, shove it under the door.'

Sweat and tears running down her cheeks, Sylvia was struggling to drive the scissors through the splintered wood and somehow catch the lock when a hand was put on her arm and she looked up through her fallen hair and saw Denny.

'You came back. But you'll be caught.'

He gave her a direct look. A look that crossed fire and death and their opposite ways of living. A look straight from a tough guy to a tough girl. There was a streak of divine humour in the soft way he said:

'Ah, no. You'll get me off, now see, won't you?'

'I will,' Sylvia said, and the promise was given. She would do as much for his safety now as for Aunt Pidgie or for her dog's safety.

Then it was again, 'Stand back, Aunt Pidgie, say when you're in the cupboard.'

'One, two three. Fire.'

Aunt Pidgie's voice came brave and oddly strong before the crash and echo of the gun. It was like a child playing soldiers afraid to be afraid of the bang.

This time more of the wood was shattered away. Denny picked cleverly and slowly at the bared lock. It was as if he had an afternoon before him to do a neat carpenter's job. His hands were as leisurely and as sure. Sylvia found herself forgetting the fire that was raging under them. He said to her, 'Go and keep water on the stairs where the boys were, if you can, and look out for yourself. The wall of that linen-room will go any minute.'

The hot crackle of fire was coming between the door he had shut and the jambs, the wall was like a plate out of the oven. Sylvia picked up the jugs the boys had left down when they had gone and ran down the passage to the bathroom, they had shut the bedroom doors, smoke came out flat underneath them and rose up in puffs. It poured up from the hall, the heat was terrifying, and what had she heard about putting wet cloths on your mouth in a fire? She had no cloths. She came heavily back with her jugs of water, sobbing out her coughs. She flung the water weakly, and it seemed to her pitiably, at the sizzling blistered door of the linen-room. She could hardly see as she set back down the wide end landing again towards the bathroom.

When she got back the door had fallen inwards. She looked into a hellish bowl of flame, of insupportable, impossible, raging flame. It was blown outwards to the stairs, through the door, like rain flat before a storm of wind. Sylvia put up her hands to save her face from the intense awful heat. She screamed upwards to the man she could not see:

'Come down, come down. It's too late, do you hear, come down.' There was no answer. She made an effort she did not know she had in her. She staggered up the six steps to where the fire would come through on to the stairs, and she poured her two cans of water on the steps, and screamed out again.

Then she saw him. He came down the dark corridor, and he carried in his arms a bundle as small as a six-year-old child, covered in a blanket. Aunt Pidgie's head against his shoulder showed out round through the blanket, like the drawing of some holy child underneath the mother's shawl. He stood for a moment at the head of that flight of stairs with the fire he had lighted belching towards it, then he tightened his grip on Aunt Pidgie and ran down into the smoke and flames.

Who can measure how intense the shock of burning is? He was trembling and crying and holding the wrist of his burnt hand while Sylvia squeezed the flame and scorch out of his clothes. Aunt Pidgie, out from under her blanket, was shaking but unsinged and obedient to orders.

They ran all three hand in hand down the wide staircase. 'Can we get through the kitchen way?' Sylvia asked. He nodded, coughing. They pushed through the heavy swing door that divided the hall from the back passages and suddenly the quiet was like that of a cold still well. The quiet of a dripping tunnel with a burning hot road at either end. The musty smell of back passages, plate powder and damp and firelessness, the smell of old pocket linings and empty wine cases was soothing to their throats. They felt real again. He said suddenly, and all the time they were running, 'I could do with a drink.'

'Yes,' Sylvia said, 'so could I.' In Frazer's pantry they found a bottle of whisky, the rows of clean tumblers in the cupboard looked sane and peaceful. It was worth waiting to get this, they needed this.

Sylvia said, 'We must keep Aunt Pidgie with us and they'll think we're all trapped up there. They'll be getting ladders.'

He said, 'But no one knows I'm with you.'

'Listen, I'm not bargaining.' Sylvia turned the cold tap into their whisky. 'But what have you done with Captain Purvis and Mr. Craye?'

'My God,' he said, 'and I'd forgotten her, too.'

'Who?'

They drank, gulping in haste and looking at each other, a new distrust growing between them.

'I'd like a drop too,' said Aunt Pidgie.

561

'Yes, perhaps you do need it.' Sylvia measured it out like medicine.

'Ah, for God's sake, give her a drink,' he laughed.

'Who have you forgotten?'

'Listen, child, when I'm gone, away with you down the mountain avenue, and you'll find what I've forgotten.'

He would not say any more. She realised it was because he was afraid she would not help him. Sylvia grew a little afraid too. What would she find.

'What about the two officers?' she whispered.

'Safe back in barracks, when they should be cooling in the heather.'

They were growing apart, the bond of death and fear loosened.

'Thank God!'

'What about me now?' He looked at her closely, he did not trust her as he had done when she said, 'I will' in the darkness and the smoke.

Sylvia said, 'I'll get you out,' she looked at Aunt Pidgie who had shrunk in importance now, shrunk back into the poor little old nuisance she really was. What a situation Aunt Pidgie had put her in.

'You'd want to hurry yourself,' he said roughly.

Sylvia said, 'Out through the stable yard would be the best.'

They were running again, Aunt Pidgie bundled along between them. In the yard she grew suddenly very weighty on their arms, her legs did not seem able to keep up with them. Once they pulled her back on to her feet which trailed behind like a dead duck's.

'Aunt Pidgie, are you all right?'

Aunt Pidgie shook her head peacefully. 'Put me on my nest,' she said, 'I'm a clocker. I'm broodie.'

'What are you talking about?'

'I'm a broodie birdie.'

Denny looked across her at Sylvia, there was laughter in his eyes, 'Blind,' he said.

Sylvia said, 'We'll shut her in a loose box. She'll be all right.' They opened one of the painted wooden stable doors and put her in. There was a heap of straw in one corner. There Aunt Pidgie nested contentedly.

'Don't move till I get back, Aunt Pidgie.'

'It takes twenty-one days,' Aunt Pidgie murmured, closing her eyes.

As she settled down they saw that her feet were bare. They had hurried her down the flagged passages and across the gravel on her bare feet and she had not said a word in complaint.

Sylvia felt a sudden pride in Aunt Pidgie. Again to-night those tortured little feet had their strange effect on cruel youth.

'Oh, Aunt Pidgie, your poor feet.'

Aunt Pidgie curled them away beneath her, 'Chook, chook,' she murmured drowsily. 'Chook, chook, chook.'

Sylvia saw the soldiers first. They came through the back door. They had rifles in their hands and they looked as foreign as men in uniforms always do.

'Get back, quick,' she said, 'get back with Aunt Pidgie,' she spoke without turning her head, and as she spoke a flood of determination to save him rose in her, the hunted creature must be saved. Danger is sacred; she was glad that her word bound her.

The soldiers, five of them, came running across the yard towards her.

'Any shinners 'ere, Miss?'

'They've cleared off.' How unsteady a lie makes the coldest voice.

'We've got orders to search the stables and out-offices.'

'For heaven's sake go up to the yard and get the long ladder, there's an old lady trapped upstairs.'

563

'Sorry, Miss, the poor old lady's done for. Terrible thing.'

'Butler says, floor went five minutes ago.'

'Quite a tragedy, Miss.'

'Yes, shocking, and the other old girl gone west on the drive. We were upset.'

'Who do you mean, not Nan?'

'That's it. That's what the young lady called her.'

Sylvia leaned against the high door of the loose box where Killer Denny crouched against the wall, his empty gun in his hand, and Aunt Pidgie stirred in her nest.

'Right,' she said, raising her head, 'get on with it, boys. Don't mind me. Careful of the chestnut mare at the end, she's a bit free with her heels. And leave this box alone, my young horse is here, he's half-cracked with the smoke and the smell.'

'Better get the 'orses out, I'd say.'

'The wind's all the other way. Send the stable boys down like good chaps when you're through. The horses will go handier with them.'

'Right, Miss, we'll carry on.'

They went down the line of boxes.

Sylvia went in to Denny.

'Woa, boy, steady, little man.' She spoke idiotic words of horse comfort and love, while Denny watched her with fierce bright eyes, the look of the cornered wolf was on him.

'Right, Miss,' they called, coming back.

'O.K.'

'Thank you.'

'The beggars weren't going to 'ang around, were they? Do the dirty and run, that's them——'

'Quiet, old chap; quiet, little fellow,' Sylvia soothed the air.

Their voices faded across the yard. 'Quick,' she beckoned Denny. She went up the pigeon hole ladder to the lofts before him, her long dress catching and tearing as she climbed. They were up in the green, powdery dark of the lofts together. Sylvia went running ahead between the heaps of hay and straw, the carefully turned piles of oats, dark and blond. She knew the lofts in the particular way remembered from childhood. Knew the holes in the boards and the windows where the stable lads always undid the wire so that they could drop down on to the dung-heap below and short cut it into the village.

Yes, it was open. She knew it would be open. These things are unchanging.

'I'll be all right, now,' he said.

Suddenly she put out her hand.

'Thank you,' she said, 'and good luck.'

He held her hand in the smooth, dry grip of unnervous people.

'I didn't do Nan in,' he said, 'I don't know what's happened to her.'

'Hurry! Hurry!' Sylvia felt that even Nan's death was less important than his escape.

But when he went, dropping off the window-sill and disappearing into the night, she felt the hour empty, she was drained of all purpose. She was left with a sense of horror at what she had done and a sense of triumph in having done it. She had let a dangerous man go free, because he had chanced his life to save a cracked little old woman. He had nearly murdered her lover to-day and to-night she had his life in his hands and she had held it safe for him. Who would understand, no one, no one, least of all her lover. She sat in the dark, forgetting Aragon, forgetting Nan, crying over her secret she must never tell. Crying because her heart had shrunk so that there was not even room in it for relief and joy that her lover was safe. Because of what she had done, she had lessened her love to herself. Because of this past hour of peril with a tough stranger her importances were changed. She had played traitor to them and in their betrayal she

565

had known an hour of truth. For that hour she had been closer, more obedient to one from whom by every law of her nature she was divided, than she had ever been to any man or woman in her life. And now the hour and the man were lost to her. Before she became once more the Sylvia of tennis parties and white hunting ties and blue habits, the Sylvia meet and right for her Norfolk lover (heir to a respectable old baronetcy) she must know tears for all that was lost to her. A bitter unreasoning grief that left her exhausted and unstrung.

XL

The evening light was still steady under the level bottom branches of the pale limes where the three boys hurried now out of the woods and across the field to the long and empty avenue. Nan could expect nothing from them now, the desperation of hurry was on them. Whatever they were going to do to her their minds were beyond it, and on their next business. Her feet felt the smooth avenue under them, the avenue she had walked up and down so often with the beautiful blue pram, and God help the nursery maid who did not keep it as Nan required. Ah, the blue pram with its goffered white pillows and its soft wool rug and its lusty baby. Lovely example of Nan's sacred pride in health, example for all to see of her professional skill. Those golden busy days, she thought of them this evening as clearly as if they were last week's memories, far more clearly; but then her feet never walked the full nice round of the avenue's surface without her mind carrying back to those years, so why not to-night?

Where the limes ended and the rhododendron and laurel at the outskirts of the pleasure grounds arched their branches out over the avenue, the house could be seen. Not all of it, but a stretch of stone, pale as a face, broken across by trees and the spread of mown grass. There the boys stopped and one of them jumped up the low wall to the level where the dark laurels grew, he bent down a strong limb of laurels towards the avenue below; the rank sweet smell of its dusty white flowers was bruised and shaken out. A pigeon clattered away into the still evening. The moderate white iron gate between Nan and Aragon looked easy and domestic as it had done when she took the pram back through it at tea-times. When the bough was bent down to the avenue, Killer Denny took a little rope out of his pocket and the boys crossed themselves.

Nan knelt on the gravel. Then she sat, awkwardly as a child, flat on the smooth avenue, and held the ground and the grass at the side of the avenue with her fingers gripping, her nails sunk into the very body of Aragon. She watched as the Killer tried the noose in the rope to see how did it run. It ran smoothly and freely, as tidy as could be. The other boy caught the strong laurel and held it down. His face was whiter than its dusty flowers. The smooth pointed leaves smelt of almonds, sharp and cleanly different from the flower smell.

They stood Nan up under the bough and slipped the rope over her gay hat and pulled it round her neck. It was too dark to see her desperate eyes among the laurel leaves. Suddenly she lurched and leaned against their hands, and rocked heavily to the ground unconscious.

'Quick, man,' said Denny, 'we have the guts frightened out of her, she'll do.' He fastened the rope so that it could slip no tighter, and knotted the free end to the bent bough. 'She may rattle and choke like a fish on a string, but she won't hang,' he said.

'I think we should make a job of it, Denny,' said the more frightened of the two boys, the one who had prayed for her release from death on the mountain, 'if we get caught she'll be a terrible witness.'

Denny spat, a big spit down on the avenue. 'There's enough to recognise you now, boy, without calling on her testimony. So mind yourself and don't get caught.'

They left Nan half-hanging, half-sprawling in the avenue and went on up to the house.

When Nan got back her consciousness she was in such extremity as cannot be found either in life or death. She was exhausted, so exhausted that her mind was almost free from the heavy business of her body. But her mind was, for the time, wrecked by the mental fear and torture it had been through. She was like a person waking after an operation. She felt her way back to the business of pain, the life under ether retreated from her. Again she would not know whether she had suffered or been glad. Now, as ideas came back to her brokenly she hardly knew if she was hanged till she had died before Aragon, or if she was still alive. Her hands were still fastened, stiff and numb behind her back, the gag was in her mouth, if she turned the rope chucked in her neck. She could not say a prayer. Only she fixed her terrible eyes on the house and drank some consolation from its walls and windows, she thought of the beds inside. She would be laid in one of them if she did not die. She trembled to think of their kindness and beauty. She thought of her staircase, of its wide shallow steps, ease in their climbing. 'If I am alive,' she thought, 'they will carry me up the front staircase, it will be the easiest, and put me in my good bed. I shall need care if I am alive.'

Now she knew she lived. She was fully aware of the pain and the hideous discomfort that wrenched at her till there was not a nerve in her body that did not scream out for a second's ease. Only a second, free from this torture. Her eyes and her nose were running with the dusty powdery strength of the laurel flowers, pulled down like a wreath round her face. Nothing could deepen this hour's pain.

As she felt this, a terrible knowledge bounded up in her, sent her heart soaring and knocking again in her body, sent sweat in

569

rivers down between her breasts, and every hair on her body itching with terror. For she saw that Aragon was burning. They had tied her here to watch the burning. Tied her so that she might watch her own soul burning. For Aragon was her soul. For Aragon she had given her life long years before when she had denied her love. And, dying to herself, she had taken the house and its ghosts into the comfort of her strong lonely life.

Now she saw the smoke and the rosy flames from her linen-room window. My linen, my pillow cases, my sheets. Like all the furnishings of Aragon, they were hers, she had always experience a sound satisfaction in so calling things 'mine.' My good brocade curtains, my fine new towels. Hers to keep from sun and moth and careless hands—most truly hers who could so cherish them, playing the careful steward to their excellence.

She saw fires lighting, one after the other, down the length of bedroom windows. Flames springing up behind the dark small panes of the windows, making the rooms behind the unblinded windows suddenly visible in the growing darkness. It was a stripping aside of that hushed and curtained privacy preserved so long and carefully.

She moaned against her gag and swayed, her hands in torture to rush towards the flames and drag out such treasures as she could, to beat down the flames with the great strength and power of her mind and her body. And then beyond the thought of her consuming treasures, there came to her with horror the remembrance of Miss Grania and Miss Pidgie locked in the nurseries. She could not reassure herself. She could not even hope that they would be freed and saved. She could hold no thought beyond despair. She leaned towards the house, and in her nurse's mind she saw clearly what their burning would be like. Sobs thickened in her throat and broke against the gag. Aragon was burning. All that she had piled on all was consumed before her eyes. And with Aragon, Miss Pidgie, her charge, and

Miss Grania, her last baby, would die by burning.

Nan sawed with her chin at the rope round her neck, tucking down her chin, trying to get inside the loop that held her. It was no use. She stood quiet at last, bound fast to her laurel. Her hat had gone now and her beautiful round head was flung back in its curious wreath of leaves, her eyes had in them the horror and the madness of one who has looked at the execution of a loved person.

Now, when she came, as she thought, to the end of despair, a quietness drew closer and closer around her, a calm of different things, and at her side she felt the height of the one she called 'the Child,' close at her side, but she had no hand to put down to the level of its hand, no voice to whisper a word towards it. Others were with her too, Fox's who had loved Aragon with the same madness as Nan. Dull, good Fox's, and bad amusing Fox's, they came from the woods and from the soft kept places in the pleasure grounds where they walked among the trees and flowering shrubs they had planted in their time at Aragon. The dashing lady who had brought the first magnolia from Spain was here, and the pale, decorous Mr. Fox who had returned from an appalling honeymoon in Italy about the year 1870 with the seed of that stone pine where the herons nested now, so much more happily than he had done with his young bride.

These present shades were calm, they were so long dead that this burning of Aragon was only a chapter to them in Aragon's story. They looked at the consuming flames as they had looked at the fireworks and the bonfires which had celebrated their coming of age, their marriages and the births of their heirs. All time with them, they knew the house would rise again. A house would be built here for happy Grania's children. Grania looking back to the lusty foolish child she had been, and a little proud of the brave child she had been, would live here with her children, and the garden of Aragon flower after its desolation, and Fox's

571

go fishing and courting and hunting from Aragon.

This calm knowledge flowing from them was like a bed under Nan's weary broken body. It was hands in her hair. It was solace to her guilty heart, the Fox's were her holy ghosts and comforters. They were standing close about her when she heard the sound of a car far down the straight avenue, the sound of a big engine gathering speed as it came towards her. She tried to turn her head, but she could not see through the thick glossy leaves of her laurel. But as the sound drew nearer she knew it was the soldiers come to save her house. A great surge of thankfulness and relief was lifting her heart as on a splendid wave when the lorry struck her down and killed her, on the smooth well-kept avenue.

XLI

'Instantaneous,' the Sergeant said to Grania, 'that's some consolation, isn't it, lady? Well, I mean you must look for the bright
side, mustn't you? But it's a tragedy and no mistake. Can't
blame the driver, Miss. We all saw some parties standing round,
looking at the burning like, but they cleared off as our lorry
approached. A chap couldn't be expected to know a lady was
tied to the bush, could he? I mean, fair's fair, isn't it . . .? Yes,
we *was* driving fast, and fast we must drive. Can't 'ang about
and give the Shinners time to crack us off, can we? Very sorry,
lady, but fair's fair, as I said, and we're not in any too 'ealthy a
spot right here this minute. We're isolated. Straight on for the
mansion, I suppose . . .?'

They drove through the gate, hitting a post as they went and
cutting across a corner of mown grass, old rich turf, abruptly
torn and scarred after its years of repose.

A terror of Nan's dead and battered body seized Grania. She
would not stay alone with her. She ran away crying, like a child
that is lost in a bad dream, down a dark side path towards the
stables, away from the burning house and the dreadful Nan she
had left.

Sylvia was coming up the path from the stables. They met
between the great box bushes cut into castles and peacocks and
arches, the bushes that always smelt of cats, a smell they had not

minded once, this had been their favourite playing place as children, before their strange hate divided them. Here they met and caught each other's hands for comfort and sobbed in the dark.

'Aunt Pidgie is safe, Soo is safe.'

'Michael and Tony are safe.'

'Nan?'

'Nan is dead.'

They sobbed on, still holding hands. Neither told the other what lost love she mourned.

THE END